Praise for *Nightkeepers*

"Raw passion, dark romance, and seat-of-your-pants suspense all set in an astounding paranormal world—I swear ancient Mayan gods and demons walk the modern earth!"

—*New York Times* bestselling author
J. R. Ward

"A fun mix of humor, suspense, mythology, and fantasy, *Nightkeepers* kicks off a series that's sure to be an instant reader favorite, and will put Andersen's books on keeper shelves around the world. She's made it onto mine."

—*New York Times* bestselling author
Suzanne Brockmann on WritersareReaders.com

"I deeply enjoyed the story. It really hooked me!"
—*New York Times* bestselling author
Angela Knight

"Part romance, mystery, and fairy tale . . . a captivating book with wide appeal."   —*Booklist*

"A compelling read . . . scorching chemistry, vivid descriptions . . . a keeper."   —*Ro___ __ Times*

DAWN KEEPERS

✳

A NOVEL OF THE FINAL PROPHECY

JESSICA ANDERSEN

A SIGNET ECLIPSE BOOK

SIGNET ECLIPSE
Published by New American Library, a division of
Penguin Group (USA) Inc., 375 Hudson Street,
New York, New York 10014, USA
Penguin Group (Canada), 90 Eglinton Avenue East, Suite 700, Toronto,
Ontario M4P 2Y3, Canada (a division of Pearson Penguin Canada Inc.)
Penguin Books Ltd., 80 Strand, London WC2R 0RL, England
Penguin Ireland, 25 St. Stephen's Green, Dublin 2,
Ireland (a division of Penguin Books Ltd.)
Penguin Group (Australia), 250 Camberwell Road, Camberwell, Victoria 3124,
Australia (a division of Pearson Australia Group Pty. Ltd.)
Penguin Books India Pvt. Ltd., 11 Community Centre, Panchsheel Park,
New Delhi - 110 017, India
Penguin Group (NZ), 67 Apollo Drive, Rosedale, North Shore 0632,
New Zealand (a division of Pearson New Zealand Ltd.)
Penguin Books (South Africa) (Pty.) Ltd., 24 Sturdee Avenue,
Rosebank, Johannesburg 2196, South Africa

Penguin Books Ltd., Registered Offices:
80 Strand, London WC2R 0RL, England

First published by Signet Eclipse, an imprint of New American Library,
a division of Penguin Group (USA) Inc.

First Printing, January 2009
10 9 8 7 6 5 4 3 2 1

*This book is dedicated to the readers
who have made these books their own.
Thank you so much for joining me on the
roller-coaster ride to 2012!*

AUTHOR'S NOTE

The Nightkeepers' world is well hidden within our own; bringing it to light isn't always an easy process. My heartfelt thanks go to Deidre Knight, Kara Cesare, Claire Zion, Kara Welsh, and Kerry Donovan for helping me take these books from a dream to a reality; to J. R. Ward for critiques and help each step of the way; to Suz Brockmann for being a mentor and an inspiration; to Angela Knight for her friendship and encouragement; to Marley Gibson, Charlene Glatkowski, and my many friends in the New England Chapter of Romance Writers of America for being there for me every day without fail; to Sally Hinkle Russell for keeping me sane; and to Brian Hogan for too many things to name in this small space.

Just as the few surviving Nightkeepers live among us today, their ancestors lived with the ancient Egyptians, Olmec, Maya, and Hopi during the course of their twenty-six-thousand-year history; they left their imprint on each of these cultures, and were influenced in turn. Thus, while their culture is best reflected in the myths and beliefs of the Maya, the parallel is not absolute. For a full list of references and recommended reading on the ancient Maya and the 2012 doomsday prophecy, and to explore the Nightkeepers' online community, please visit www.JessicaAndersen.com.

GLOSSARY

Like much of the Nightkeepers' culture, their spell words come from the people they have lived with throughout their history. Or if we want to chicken-and-egg things, it's more likely that the other cultures took the words from the Nightkeepers and incorporated them into their developing languages. As such, some of the words have slightly different meanings and/or spellings in the old tongue of the Nightkeepers compared to their acknowledged meanings in the languages of ancient Egypt, the Mayan Empire, the modern Quiche Maya, and elsewhere.

Entities (people, gods, demons, and other creatures)

Banol Kax—The lords of the underworld, Xibalba. Driven from the earth and locked behind the barrier after the last Great Conjunction in 24,000 B.C. by the many-times great-ancestors of the modern Nightkeepers, the *Banol Kax* seek to pierce the barrier and wrest control of the earth from mankind.

boluntiku—The underworld minions of the *Banol Kax*, the *boluntiku* are lava creatures that draw their energy from the molten mantle of the earth. They can come to earth only when the barrier is very thin (during a solstice or eclipse), and then only at the expense of great magic. The creatures are killing machines that can sense magic and royalty; they travel in an insubstantial vapor form, turning solid in the moment they attack, using six-clawed hands and wicked teeth.

Camazotz—A member of the *Banol Kax* also known as Sudden Bloodletter, Camazotz is the ruler of night, death, and sacrifice. His sons are the seven death bats responsible for ensuring the completion of the demon prophecies.

Daykeeper—A Mayan shaman-priest responsible for keeping track of the calendar and using divining rituals to make horoscope-like predictions.

First Father—The only adult survivor of the Nightkeepers' exodus from Egypt, this mage bound the slaves into *winikin*, and codified the Nightkeepers' beliefs into the writs and the thirteen prophecies, in order to guide his descendants over the next five millennia until the end-time.

Godkeeper—A female Nightkeeper who has undergone a ritual near-death experience followed by a sexual encounter with a Nightkeeper male, leading to her being bonded with one of the sky gods. Channeling the gods' powers with the help of their Nightkeeper mates, the Godkeepers are prophesied to form the core of the Nightkeepers' fighting force during the 2012 doomsday.

itza'at—A female Nightkeeper with visionary powers; a seer. The *itza'at* talent is often associated with depression, mental instability, and suicide, because the seer can envision the future but not change it. The visions will always come to pass.

Ixchel—The goddess of rainbows, loomcraft, and fertility. May also be associated with medicine and the moon. Often depicted as an aged grandmother with jaguar ears, but may also be seen as a beautiful young woman.

Kulkulkan—The winged serpent god, later known as Quetzalcoatl. An extremely powerful god, one of the creators, Kulkulkan has both light and dark halves. The light half is associated with learning, logic, medicine, and art, while the dark aspects are associated with war and rage.

makol (*ajaw-makol*)—The earthly minions of the *Banol Kax*, these demon souls are capable of reaching through the barrier to possess an evil-natured human host. Recognized by their luminous green eyes, a *makol*-bound human retains his/her own thoughts and actions in direct proportion to the amount of evil in his/her soul. An *ajaw-makol* is a *makol* created through direct spell casting by the *Banol Kax* or the human host. The *ajaw-makol* can then create lesser *makol* through blood rituals on earth.

nahwal—Humanoid spirit entities that exist in the barrier and hold within them all of the accumulated wisdom of each Nightkeeper bloodline. They can be asked for information, but cannot be trusted. In the Mayan culture, they came to be known as *nahual* (or *uay*), and were feared as shape-shifting sorcerers and devious alter egos of the Mayan ruling elite.

Nightkeeper—A member of an ancient race sworn to protect mankind from annihilation in the years leading up to December 21, 2012, when the barrier separating the earth and the underworld will fall and the *Banol Kax* will seek to precipitate the apocalypse.

Order of Xibalba—Formed by renegade Nightkeepers long ago, the order courted the powers of the underworld. Its members, called Xibalbans, drew their power from the first layer of hell. The order was wiped out by the conquistadors . . . or so the Nightkeepers believe.

winikin—Descended from the conquered Sumerian warriors who served the Nightkeepers back in ancient Egypt, the *winikin* are blood-bound to the Nightkeepers. They function as the servants, protectors, and counselors of the magi, and have been instrumental in keeping the bloodlines alive through the centuries.

Places

Actun Tunichil Muknal (ATM)—A system of subterranean waterways and caves in Belize that contains numerous ceremonial relics of the Mayan shaman-priests, as well as a series of hidden submerged tunnels and caves sacred to the Nightkeepers.

Chichén Itzá—Arguably the most famous ruin of the Yucatán Peninsula, this city was a religious center built and inhabited by the Maya in the seventh through tenth centuries A.D., and later incorporated the more bloodthirsty practices of the Toltec through the thirteenth century. Today it is a huge tourist attraction aboveground. Belowground, the Nightkeepers practice their rituals and magic in a series of subterranean caverns that run beneath the ruins.

Skywatch—Built in the 1930s and renovated when the Nightkeepers were reunited, the training compound is located in a box canyon in the Chaco Canyon region of New Mexico.

Xibalba—The nine-layer underworld of the Mayan and Nightkeeper religious systems, home to the *Banol Kax*, *boluntiku*, and *makol*. The spiritual entrance to Xibalba is found in the darkest spot at the center of the Milky Way galaxy. The religious (metaphorical) entrances are the passageways at the tops of Mayan pyramids, as well as natural caves, especially those leading to subterranean rivers.

Things (spells, glyphs, prophecies, etc.)

ajawlel—The slave-master's glyph, worn by a Nightkeeper who has formed a reciprocal blood link with a human servant.

barrier—A force field of psi energy that separates the earth, sky, and underworld, and powers the Nightkeepers' magic. The strength of the barrier fluctuates with the positions of the stars and planets; the power of the magi increases as the barrier weakens.

chac-mool—An iconographic idol dedicated to the rain god, Chaac, the *chac-mool* is formed in the shape of a seated human figure, and may be used as an altar, a throne, and/or a place of blood sacrifice.

copan—The sacred incense of the Nightkeepers. This is a variation of the Mayan incense, *copal*, and is associated with the great ruined city of Copán, located in modern-day Honduras.

demon prophecies—A cycle of seven prophecies that will be triggered in the final four years before the end date. If a prophecy is fulfilled, the barrier thins slightly. If it is thwarted, the barrier strengthens to the same degree. These prophecies, revolving around the seven death-bat sons of Camazotz, are inscribed on a series of Nightkeeper artifacts that were sold off to fund the Nightkeepers' activities in the late nineteenth and early twentieth centuries. Now those relics must be recovered if the Nightkeepers hope to thwart Camazotz and his sons.

hunab ku—A pseudoglyph associated with the 2012 end date, in modern times the *hunab ku* is not a glyph within the Mayan writing system, but rather is the mark that the Nightkeeper king wears on his biceps, denoting his proximity to the gods.

intersection—Located in the sacred tunnels beneath Chichén Itzá, this is the one point on earth where the earth, sky, and underworld come very near one another, and where the barrier is its weakest. This is where the gods can come through to create Godkeepers, and where the underworld denizens focus their attacks during each solstice and equinox.

jun tan—The "beloved" glyph that signifies a Nightkeeper's mated status.

k'alaj—The slave mark worn by a human who is blood-bound to a Nightkeeper master or mistress.

pasaj och—Roughly translating to "open door open," this, coupled with a blood sacrifice, is the basic command a Nightkeeper uses to form an uplink to the barrier's power.

starscript—Ancient writings carved into temples or artifacts in such a way that the glyphs do not reflect normal sun- or moonlight. They are visible only by starlight when the moon is dark.

thirteen prophecies—A long-term prophetic cycle describing milestone events leading up to the apocalypse. The last of these mentions the Nightkeepers' king making the ultimate sacrifice in the final four years before 2012.

tzomplanti—A ceremonial pile formed of stacked human skulls, used as a beacon or a warning sign.

writs—Written by the First Father, these delineate the duties and codes of the Nightkeepers. Not all of them translate well into modern times.

On December 21, 2012, the world will end.

At least, that is what some believe the ancient Maya intended to signal when they set their five-thousand-year backward-counting calendar to zero out on that day, at the exact moment the sun, moon, and earth will align at the center of the Milky Way in a cosmic dark spot the Maya believed was the mouth of the underworld, Xibalba.

Modern scientific support for the 2012 doomsday theory comes from astronomers and physicists, who predict that this Great Conjunction, which occurs only once every twenty-six thousand years, will trigger magnetic reversals, terrible sunspots, and potentially cataclysmic planetary events. This has caused historians and spiritualists alike to credit the Maya with a level of astronomy not seen again through history until modern times.

However, the ancient Maya's knowledge of the Great Conjunction—and the havoc it will bring—comes from a far older people: the Nightkeepers.

Descended from the only survivors of a great civilization wiped out in 24,000 B.C. during the last Great Conjunction, the Nightkeepers are mortal magic users sworn to pass down their skills from generation to generation until the 2012 conjunction, when they will be the only ones capable of defeating the Banol Kax, a group of all-powerful demons who were bound in Xibalba by the Nightkeepers' ancestors, and will be released on Decem-

ber 21, 2012. *On the day of the Great Conjunction, the demons will break through the barrier separating the earth and underworld. They will destroy mankind and rule the earth . . . unless the Nightkeepers stop them.*

Ancient prophecy says that there should be hundreds of Nightkeepers at the end of the age, and among them will be the Godkeepers, a group of incredibly powerful warrior-females, each of whom will be able to wield the powers of a god with the help of her blood-bound mate and the Nightkeepers' magic, which is based on bloodletting and sex.

Together, the legends say, the Godkeepers and their mates will be instrumental in the Nightkeepers' battle against the Banol Kax *and the 2012 doomsday. But in the final four years before the zero date, when the demons begin their assault on the barrier, the Nightkeepers number less than a dozen scattered and untrained magi. The last king, Striking-Jaguar, reunites the surviving Nightkeepers in time to block the* Banol Kax *from attacking the earth. In the process, however, he claims a god-bound human woman as his mate rather than sacrificing her, defying an ancient prophecy and triggering the final countdown to the end-time.*

Now the Nightkeepers must recover the Mayan antiquities that bear the seven lost demon prophecies, which will guide them in battle as the end-time approaches.

However, they're not the only ones on the hunt for the missing artifacts. . . .

PART I

PENUMBRAL LUNAR ECLIPSE

The earth shadows the moon, making it appear orange or bloodred. May be associated with shifts in the earth's electromagnetic fields, heightened spiritual sensitivity, and rebirth.

CHAPTER ONE

February 6
Present

The smell of death hit Nate Blackhawk the moment he pushed open the door to the seashore cottage, letting him know why Edna Hopkins hadn't answered his knock.

"Hell." Mouth breathing, Nate crouched down, fumbled with his ankle holster, and pulled out a snub-nosed nine-millimeter loaded with jade-tipped bullets.

The jade would be overkill if he met up with bad news of the human variety, but the sacred stone was one of the few things that made a dent in the underworld nasties he'd gotten to know up close and personal over the past seven months, ever since his life had swerved off Reality Road and plunged into something that bore more than a passing resemblance to the quest fantasies he wrote for a living. Or what'd used to be his living.

"Mrs. Hopkins?" he called into the cottage. "It's Nate Blackhawk; we spoke on the phone yesterday. Are you okay?"

He didn't expect an answer, didn't get one.

There was a dead Christmas wreath hanging on the door, and jingle bells tinkled as he let the door swing shut at his back. The decoration was six weeks past its prime, suggesting that the old lady hadn't been kidding when she'd said she was having trouble keeping up with her house, living alone.

The Cape Cod beachfront cottage was one level, maybe four or five rooms, tops, decorated right out of the Yankee Candle catalog, with an added dose of doilies. The place made Nate—at six-three, two hundred pounds, amber eyed, dark haired and sharp featured, wearing a black-on-black combination of Nightkeeper combat gear and *don't scare the old lady* casual wear—feel seriously out of his element.

It wasn't exactly the first place he'd look for an ancient Mayan artifact that'd been out of circulation for nearly eight decades, either, but this was where the trail had led.

"Mrs. Hopkins?" He moved across the main room to a short hallway, where the air was thicker. "Edna?"

There was a bathroom on one side, followed by a closet and a neat-as-a-pin guest room done in Early Ruffle. On the opposite side was a single door, open just enough to show a slice of pale blue carpet and the edge of a lace-topped mahogany dresser. He used his toe to nudge open the door and then stepped inside, grimacing at the sight of a sunken-cheeked woman tucked into a queen-size adjustable bed, with a lace-trimmed quilt pulled up to her chin. Her eyes were closed, her skin gray, her face oddly peaceful. There was no blood, no sign of a struggle, but next to her sat a polished keepsake box Nate recognized from her description as the one that had held the small figurine she'd inherited from her grandmother, who'd gotten it from hers.

The box was open and empty, the statuette gone.

"Shit." He felt a beat of grief for the seventy-something widow, along with a serious case of the *oh, hells* at the realization that the *Banol Kax* had known what the Nightkeepers were looking for, and had somehow gotten there first.

Or had they? he wondered, frowning at the neatly smoothed quilt, the carefully positioned body. The *Banol Kax* and their blood-bound human emissaries, the *makol*, weren't big on subtlety; he would've expected her to be hacked up pretty good if they'd been the ones to steal the statuette. But if not the demons, then who had offed the old lady and taken the artifact?

Not your problem, Nate told himself. *You're just the courier.* But still, he stared down at the dead woman.

"I'm sorry," he said to her. Less than twenty-four hours ago they'd spoken by phone about the statuette, and the things she could do with the money he'd offered for it. She'd wanted to move south, where it was warmer in winter, and go into assisted living, because her daughters had no time for her and even less inclination to get involved. Nate had figured he'd offer to help her with the move; he knew what it felt like to have nobody give a crap where you were or what you were doing. That wouldn't be necessary now, though, because whoever had taken the statuette had taken her life with it. Like that had been necessary. A low burn tightened his gut. *Bastards,* he thought. What harm would it've done to leave her alive?

He wanted to tell her that he'd get the shitheels who'd taken away the promise of a better life, but he wasn't sure the sweet-seeming lady would care for the idea of revenge on her behalf, so in the end he said nothing. He just nodded to her, touched the hawk medallion he wore around his neck, and made a private promise to see justice done. Then he headed back the way he'd come, mentally tracking what he'd touched, wiping as needed, because there was no sense in being stupid when the cops had his prints on file.

He'd done his time and straightened out in the years since, but still.

Once he was outside and the jingle bells were quiet in their brown-needled wreath, he reholstered the nine-millimeter and headed for his rental. A few miles out of town he stopped at a pay phone that actually worked—the things were few and far between these days—and called in an anonymous 911. As soon as he was back on the road, headed for the airport, he palmed his cell and speed-dialed the Nightkeeper's training compound, Sky-watch.

"Yes, sir," answered his *winikin,* Carlos, proper as always.

Nate didn't bother reminding his sort-of servant to do the first-name thing, because he knew it wouldn't work. Most of the other Nightkeeper-*winikin* pairs were pretty informal with each other, having been together for decades. Nate, on the other hand, had lost his original *winikin* early on, winding up in human-style foster care instead. He'd grown up human, not having a clue about the magic in his blood until seven months earlier, when the Nightkeepers' hereditary king, Striking-Jaguar, had shown up at Hawk Enterprises, teleported him onto the roof, and dangled him over the side in order to get his attention, then promised to tell him about his parents. That'd been shock number one. Shock number two had come when Nate showed up at Skywatch and met fellow Nightkeeper trainee Alexis Gray . . . who was a pixel-perfect image of Hera, the sex-goddess Valkyrie Nate had written into five installments of his *Viking Warrior* vid games over the past four years. His friends had a running joke that Nate couldn't keep a girlfriend because he was always comparing them to Hera, and maybe there'd been some truth to that. Meeting her in the flesh, so to speak, had blown him away. Even better, Alexis had proven to be a woman of worth; he might give her grief about being a pampered princess and a goody-goody overachiever— both of which were true—but she was also tough and resourceful, and had a core of loyalty and integrity he had to admire, even if that sort of shit had never worked for him. But just because she was sexy as sin and a hell of a woman, and they'd hooked up for a few months during the worst of the hormone storms that'd come with getting their powers, didn't mean they were foreordained to be mates. Nate didn't believe in predestiny and crap like that . . . which was tantamount to blasphemy in his new life.

The Nightkeepers' entire culture was based on fate and prophecy, but as far as Nate was concerned, destiny was just what lazy game developers pulled out of their asses when they couldn't think of a better way to connect the dots. It was bullshit, right up there with magic swords and the ever-popular "amulet to be named at a later date" that most epic fantasy writers used at one point or another to get themselves out of a jam.

Nate was willing to believe in the Nightkeepers' magic because he'd experienced it firsthand, and he was willing to buy into the December 21, 2012, end date because it was based in scientific fact: The Great Conjunction was coming, and in the absence of an ozone layer, the Earth would be vulnerable to the sun flares and magnetic fluxes the eggheads were predicting. He was even willing to accept that there was a powerful barrier of psi energy separating the earth and the underworld, and that it thinned during major stellar events. Based on his recent experiences, he'd even stretch credulity and buy into the threat that the barrier would come crashing down on the 2012 end date, and that it was the Nightkeepers' job to keep the demons on their side of the barrier when that happened.

He'd seen and done enough magic of his own to buy into those things. But there was no way in hell he was going to believe that the future was already written, that he'd known what his gods-intended mate would look like years before he'd met her in the flesh, that they were destined to fall in love because fate said they should. *No frigging thanks.* Having spent his first twenty years locked up, first in the foster system, then in juvie and the Greenville penitentiary, he was all about freedom and free will.

Carlos, on the other hand, was all about "the thirteenth Nightkeeper prophecy" this and "the seven demon prophecies" that, and practically worshiped the idea that time was cyclical, that what had happened before would happen again. According to legend, the *winikin* were the descendants of the captured Sumerian warriors who had served the Nightkeepers back in ancient Egypt. When Akhenaton went monotheistic in 1300 or so B.C. and ordered his guard to off the priests of the old religion—including the Nightkeepers— the servants had managed to escape with a handful of the Nightkeepers' children. The sole surviving adult mage, acting under the influence of the gods, had magically blood-bound the servants to their Nightkeeper lineages, creating the *winikin*. Or so the story went. The upshot was that the *winikin* were fiercely loyal to their blood-bound charges. They acted partly as the Nightkeepers' protectors, partly as their servants, and almost always as the little nagging voices on their shoulders.

Carlos, who on the king's request had transferred responsibility for his original Nightkeeper charge to his daughter and taken over as Nate's *winikin* when the Nightkeepers had been reunited seven months earlier, was an Olympic-level nagger. Worse, he had ambitions. He was jonesing for Nate to follow in the footsteps of his father, Two-Hawk, and become an adviser to the king. The *winikin* just didn't get why that wasn't going to happen . . . i.e., because Nate had no intention of getting in any deeper than he absolutely had to. Hell, he'd volunteered to go get the statuette only because he'd needed some distance from all of the destiny shit, and a chance to get away from the stress of trying to be a Nightkeeper while running Hawk Enterprises long-distance. And he'd needed to put some serious miles between him and Alexis after the way things had ended between them.

Besides, he'd figured it'd be an easy deal: Fly out, buy the statuette off the old lady, and fly home.

That'd worked well. *Not.*

Nate, who kept score in his head, like any good gamer, figured that if he called the Nightkeepers' first big fight with the *Banol Kax* level one of the battle, then they had more or less won their way through when they'd banded together during the previous fall's equinox and driven the demon Zipacna back through the barrier to Xibalba, where he belonged. Which meant they were on to level two now, and the bad guys had scored the first hit when they'd snagged the demon prophecy out from under Nate's nose.

"Edna Hopkins is dead and the statuette's gone," Nate told Carlos, his voice clipped. "Someone—or something—got here ahead of me."

Which was not good news, because it meant they'd been wrong in thinking that the lack of activity at the intersection during the winter solstice had meant the *Banol Kax* had fallen back to regroup. The demons must've sent something through the barrier after all, though gods only knew how they'd done it. The sole transit point between the earth, sky, and underworld was the sacred chamber beneath Chichén Itzá, and sure as shit nothing had come through there. The Nightkeepers had been there, waiting.

Which probably meant the demons had managed to punch through the barrier and convince an evil-souled human host to undergo the *makol* ritual, as they had done at least twice the prior fall. The *makol*, who could be identified by their luminous green eyes, retained their human intelligence and free will in direct relation to their degree of evilness and willingness to be possessed. Maybe the demons had created one or more *makol* during the winter solstice and sent them after the statuette. But why now? And why had they left the body untouched?

"Are you safe?" Carlos asked, though they both knew the question was more protocol than real concern.

"Yeah. Whoever or whatever killed her is long gone."

"Was she sacrificed?"

"She's intact." Which had Nate seriously on edge. The dark magic of Xibalba was largely powered by the blood sacrifice of unwilling victims. If *makol* had taken the statue and killed Edna Hopkins, they would've taken her head and heart, too, as those were the seats of power. Yet there hadn't been a mark on her, and she'd looked peaceful rather than terrified. Which meant . . . Hell, he didn't know what it meant, and the discrepancy had him rubbing a hand across the back of his neck, where the hairs at his nape were doing a shimmy. "Don't let anyone else leave the compound until I get back, okay? I have a bad feeling about this."

Skywatch was protected by a blood ward that had been set in the 1920s by the willing sacrifice of two senior Nightkeepers, and was reinforced by regular ceremonial autolettings by the resident magi. The ward meant the training compound was impenetrable to all but the strongest of the underworld denizens. If the Nightkeepers stayed put they'd be safe from Edna Hopkins's killer, buying them time to identify the threat and figure out how to neutralize it.

Strike and the others might be willing to follow prophecies carved in stone temples. Nate preferred legwork, strategy, and firepower.

But Carlos was silent for too long. That, combined with the tickle at the back of Nate's neck, warned him there was a problem even before the *winikin* said, "Miss Alexis left last night for an estate auction in Monterey."

Nate's gut clenched and his voice went deadly chill. "And you're only just telling me this now?"

"You've made it clear that she isn't your concern." There was an edge to the *winikin's* voice, coming from Nate's refusal to buy into the whole gods-given-mate thing.

Screw refusing to buy in; he was actively fighting it. He respected Alexis, and yeah, they'd clicked physically—hell, the sex had been scorching. But it'd been too much, too fast, at a time when his life had been doing a screeching one-eighty, swerving around a bit and then skidding off into a ditch. If it hadn't been for the magic and the Nightkeepers, he and Alexis never would've met. If they had, odds were that they would've felt the spark, acknowledged it, and moved on, because it was godsdamned obvious that while they might have chemistry, they didn't always like each other.

Hera, he understood; Alexis, not so much. But that didn't stop his gut from locking up at the knowledge that she was outside the wards and didn't have a clue there was a *makol* or something after the demon prophecies. And if the demon spawn were tracking the artifacts by piggybacking on the Nightkeepers' investigations, whether by magic or good old-fashioned e-hacking, which was the only way the timing of Edna Hopkins's death made any sense, then the odds were good that Alexis was going to have company very soon, if she didn't already.

Shit. Nate hit the brakes, yanked the rental over to the side of the road, and grated, "Get Strike here. Now."

"The king's ability to teleport isn't a convenience."

"Fuck convenience. Consider this a rescue."

* * *

In the ornate ballroom of a recently foreclosed estate on the Monterey coast, the auctioneer introduced lot two twelve, a thirteen-hundred-year-old Mayan statuette of the goddess Ixchel. Bidding started at two grand and jumped almost immediately to five. At fifty-five hundred, Alexis caught the spotter's eye and nodded to bump the bid. Then she leaned back in her folding chair, projecting the calm of a collector.

It was a lie, of course. The only things she'd ever collected were parking tickets at the Newport Marina. She looked the part, though, in a stylish navy pin-striped pantsuit that nipped in at the waist and pulled a little across the shoulders, thanks to all the hand-to-hand training she'd gotten in recent months. Her streaky blond hair was caught back in a severe ponytail, tasteful makeup accented her blue eyes and wide mouth, and she wore secondhand designer shoes that put her well over six feet. A top-end bag sat at her feet beside a matching folio, both slightly scuffed around the edges.

Understated upscale, courtesy of eBay. Her godmother, Izzy, might've pushed her into finance rather than fashion, but Alexis had put her love of fabric to good use regardless, calling on it to build an image.

In her previous life as a private investment consultant, her look had been calculated to reassure her wealthy friends and clients that she belonged among them but wouldn't compete, wouldn't upstage. She'd played the part for so long prior to the *oh, by the way, you're a Nightkeeper* revelation that it'd been second nature to dress for this gig. But as bidding on the statuette topped sixty-five hundred and Alexis nodded to bump it to a cool seven grand, she felt a hum of power that had been missing from her old life.

I have money now, the buzz in her blood said. *I deserve to be here.*

It wasn't her money, not really. But she had carte blanche with the Nightkeeper Fund, and orders not to come home empty-handed.

"Ma'am?" said a cultured, amplified voice. It was the auctioneer now, not the spotter, which meant the dabblers had dropped out and he had his two or three serious bidders on the hook. "It's seventy-five hundred dollars to you."

She glanced up at the projection screen at the front of the room. It showed a magnification of the statuette, which rested near the auctioneer's elbow, top-lit on a nest of black cloth. Described in the auction catalog as "a statuette of Ixchel, Mayan goddess of rainbows and fertility, carved from chert, circa A.D. 1100; love poem inscribed in hieroglyphs on base," the statuette was lovely. The waxy, pale green stone had been carved with deceptive simplicity into the shape of a woman with a large nose and flattened forehead, her conical skull crowned with a rainbow of hair that fell forward as she tipped her head into her hands in repose, or perhaps tears. She sat upon a stone, or maybe an overturned bowl or basket, and that was where the glyphs were carved, curved and fluid and gorgeous like all Mayan writing, which was as much art as a form of communication.

Love poem, Alexis thought with an inner snort. *Not.* Or rather, it was eau-de-Hallmark read one way, but according to Jade, the Nightkeepers' archivist, if they held the statuette at the proper angle under starlight, a second layer of glyphwork would spell out the first of the seven demon prophecies they needed to combat the *Banol Kax.* Starscript, which was less about magic and more about the refractive angles and wavelengths of starlight, was apparently one of the tricks the ancestral Nightkeepers had used to bury their spells and prophecies within the carved writings of the ancient Maya, again according to Jade. And since Jade was the one who'd gotten the message from her *nahwal* ancestor during the winter solstice ritual, warning that the demon prophecies must be found, Alexis was inclined to believe her. The *nahwal* had said that the first prophecy would be triggered during the upcoming spring equinox, just over six weeks away . . . which meant it was pretty godsdamned critical that Alexis didn't let some collector type outbid her on the Ixchel statuette.

Aware that the auctioneer was waiting for her answer, she said, "Ten thousand dollars." As she'd hoped, the advance jumped the bid past fair market value by enough to make her remaining opponent shake his head and drop out. The auctioneer pronounced it a done deal, and she felt a flare of success as she flashed her bidder number, knowing there would be no problem with the money.

The Nightkeeper Fund, which had—ironically—been seeded in the late eighteen hundreds with the proceeds from her five-times-great-grandparents' generation unwisely selling off the very Mayan artifacts the modern Nightkeepers were scrambling to recover now, had been intended to fund an army of hundreds as the 2012 end date approached. That, however, was before the current king's father had led his warrior-priests in an ill-fated battle against the demons. Only a few of the youngest Nightkeepers had survived, hidden and raised in secret by their *winikin* until seven months earlier, when the intersection connecting the earth, sky, and underworld had reactivated from its two-decade dormancy, and the old king's son, Strike, had recalled his warriors.

Yeah, that had been a shocker. *Alexis, dear, you're a magic user,* Izzy had pretty much said. *I'm not your godmother; I'm your* winikin, *and we need to leave tonight for your bloodline ceremony and training. And, oh, by the way, you and the other Nightkeepers have a little over four years to save the world.*

According to the thirteenth prophecy, Strike's refusal to sacrifice Leah, the human who had become his mate and queen, meant that the countdown to the end—time had now begun in earnest. Jade's research indicated that they'd passed into the four-year cycle ruled by the demon prophecies, which predicted that seven minions of the demon Camazotz would come through the intersection one at a time, each on a cardinal day, and attack. If they succeeded, the barrier would tear and the *Banol Kax* would be freed onto the earth . . . which had the Nightkeepers hustling to find the seven artifacts inscribed with starscript clues on how to avoid the fulfillment of the prophecies.

Make that six artifacts, Alexis thought, grinning. *Because I just bagged Ixchel.*

"Excuse me, please," she murmured, and rose, snagging her folio and bag off the floor. She stepped out into the aisle while the auction house employees whisked her statuette off the podium and set up the next lot, and the auctioneer launched into his spiel. When she reached the temporary office that'd been set up in the hallway outside the big estate's ballroom, she unzipped her folio and enjoyed how the staffer's eyes got big at the sight of the neatly stacked and banded cash. She handed over her bidder's number. "What's the total damage?"

"One moment please," he said, but his eyes were still glued to the cash.

The two items she'd bought with the Nightkeepers' money—the statuette and a death mask that had been an earlier impulse buy—wouldn't be the biggest deals of the day by far, but she'd bet they'd be among only a few handled in paper money. Granted, she could've done the remote transfer thing, too, but she quite simply loved the feel of the green stuff. And no, it wasn't because she'd been deprived or picked on as a child, as *someone* back at Skywatch had unkindly suggested. Nor was it a reaction to the idea that the world was four years away from a serious crisis of being, as that same someone had offered, or a rejection of destiny or some such garbage.

She just loved money. She loved the feel and smell of it. She loved what it could buy—not just the things, but the respect. The power. It wasn't actually until she'd been at Skywatch for a few weeks that she'd realized that the money thing was simple biology. The Nightkeepers were bigger, stronger, and more graceful than average humans, pumped with charisma and loaded with talent. At least, most of them were. Alexis had somehow gotten the bigger-and-stronger part without the other stuff, particularly the grace, which meant she tended more toward the clumsy side of life. She'd worked long and hard to camouflage the klutz factor, and most days managed to control her freakishly long limbs. That effort, however, left her seriously low on charisma, and so far she was average in the magical talent department, as well.

Ergo, the cash. She liked living as large as possible. So sue her.

"It's going to take a minute," the staffer said. "The computer's being glitchy today."

"No rush." She flipped the folio shut and turned away, figuring she'd use the brief delay to check in—which consisted of powering up her PDA, shooting off a quick text message to Izzy reporting that she had the statue and was headed back to Skywatch, and then powering off the unit without checking her backlogged messages.

She wasn't in the mood for the chatter—hadn't been for a while, which was why she'd jumped at the chance to fly from New Mex out to the California coast for the auction. The quick trip had given her a chance to breathe air she wasn't sharing with the same group of Nightkeepers and *winikin* she'd been cheek-by-jowl with for the past half year. She wasn't the only one feeling it, either. Tensions were running high, thanks to the lack of both privacy and enemy activity.

Besides, she could guarantee the messages on her cell were nothing critical, because she wasn't in line for the important stuff yet. Strike had his advisers—Leah and the royal *winikin*, Jox—and the three of them handled the heavy lifting, with the lower-impact jobs delegated to the newly inducted Nightkeepers.

For now, anyway. Alexis had her sights set higher. Her mother, Gray-Smoke, had been one of King Scarred-Jaguar's most trusted advisers, holding political power equaled only by that of her adversarial coadviser, Two-Hawk. That pretty much figured, because Two-Hawk's son was Alexis's own personal nemesis, i.e., the *someone* who'd been seriously pissing her off over the past few months, ever since he'd dumped her on her ass right after the talent ceremony, with no explanation given beyond the old standard: *It's not you, it's me.*

Damn him.

"Ma'am? You're all set." The staffer held out her paperwork. "I have a couple of messages for you too. She said it was important."

"Thanks." Alexis took the slips, glanced at them, and tucked them into her pocket. Just Izzy mother-henning her. The *winikin* would've gotten the text message by now, so they were square.

A grizzled, heavyset security guard set a metal case on the table and flipped it open so she could see the

statuette nestled inside a shockproof foam bed, alongside
the Mayan death mask she'd bought earlier. At her nod,
the guard shut the case and slid it across the table to
her, rumbling in a basso profundo voice, "Dial the numbers to what you want, and hit this button." He pointed
to an inset red dot. "That'll set your combination. If you
don't want to bother, just leave it all zeros and it'll act
like a suitcase. Got it?"

"Got it." A whim had her dialing in a date and hitting
the red button. There was something satisfying about
hearing the locks click.

Hefting the case, she gave the guard a friendly nod
and headed out, mission accomplished. When she stepped
through the front door of the estate, she found herself
under the clear blue sky of a perfect February day in
Nor Cal. The warm yellow sun and crisp, faintly salty
air made her wish she'd opted for the convertible when
she'd rented her car. But it'd been drizzling when she
landed, so she'd treated herself to a sporty silver BMW
that hugged the road like a lover. Convertible or not, the
silver roadster ought to be automotive muscle enough to
entertain her on the way back to LAX.

Sure enough, once she was on the road with the metal
case in the passenger seat beside her, the feel of engine
power and smooth leather lightened her mood, sending
a victory dance through her soul. She had the statuette,
and she wasn't technically due back at Skywatch for another day. There was a sense of freedom in the thought,
one that had her cranking the radio to something loud
and edgy with a heavy backbeat as she pulled onto the
narrow shoreline drive that led away from the lavish
private estate that was being sold off, piece by piece, to
settle the owner's debts.

Alexis had thought it a stroke of luck that the sale
had come up just as they'd started tracking down the lost
artifacts, but Izzy had reminded her that there wasn't
much in the way of actual coincidence in the world. Most
of what people thought of as happy accidents was really
the will of the gods.

As she sent the BMW whipping around a low-g curve
that dropped off to the right in a steep embankment and

a million-dollar view of the Nor Cal coast, the thought of fate and the gods brought a quiver of unease, a sense that she'd already failed.

"If it was that easy to buck destiny it wouldn't be destiny," she told herself. Which was true, but still, it was hard not to feel like she'd gotten it wrong in the relationship department. Again.

The day Izzy had revealed her true heritage, Alexis had gotten a mental flash of an image: an etching of a fierce bird of prey. Then, just under a week later, she'd seen it again—on the medallion worn by Nate Blackhawk. No way that could be a coincidence. Neither could the fact that they'd immediately clicked . . . on the physical level, anyway. They'd danced around each other for the first couple of weeks, but once they'd gone through the bloodline ceremony and gotten their first forearm marks and their initial connections to the barrier, the overwhelming hormonal fluxes and enhanced sex drive that came with the magic had overridden their reservations and they'd become lovers. They'd done very, very well together sexually . . . but not so much outside the bedroom, where they'd clashed on almost every level. He was closed and difficult to read, and seemed to spend most of his time trying to prove that the gods didn't control him, that he was free to make his own choices. In the end, she hadn't been strong enough to hold them together—hadn't been sure she'd wanted to, despite the omens that said they were meant for each other, and the knowledge that the magic of a mated Nightkeeper pair was ten times that of either mage alone.

It'd helped that Izzy didn't like him either. Since the *winikin* both guided and protected the Nightkeepers, Izzy's relief at the breakup had helped ease the sting . . . particularly since Izzy was the one who was always pushing Alexis to do her best, be her best, and live up to her mother's memory. Gray-Smoke had been a legend in her own time, a powerful mage and adviser to the king. As far as Izzy was concerned, Alexis could be nothing less.

"Unfortunately, that's proving easier said than done," Alexis muttered.

Torturing herself, she shoved her sleeve up to her

elbow, baring her right forearm, where each of the Nightkeepers and *winikin* was marked with Mayan glyphs that denoted status and power. The black marks looked like tattoos but were actually magic, appearing fully formed during special ceremonies in which a Night-keeper went from child to trainee, from trainee to mage. Alexis wore two marks: the curling anthropomorphic *b'utz* glyph representing the smoke bloodline, and the three stacked blobs of the warrior's talent mark, which had given her increased reflexes and strength, along with the ability to call up shields and fireballs, though not very effectively as yet. And that was it. Two marks, smoke and warrior. She hadn't gotten an additional talent during the second ceremony. Granted, only about a third of Nightkeepers got a talent mark, and talents could sometimes appear after the formal ceremony, but that didn't make it any easier for her to accept that so far she was a dud in the magic department.

"Damn it," she muttered, shoving down her sleeve and hitting the gas too hard going into the next curve, which was a blind turn arcing along a sheer drop leading down to Monterey Bay. Easing off and cursing herself for getting all tangled up when she was supposed to be enjoying the day away and a job well-done, she nursed the car around the corner—

And drove straight into a wall of fire.

She screamed and cranked the wheel as flames lashed at the car, slapping in through the open windows and searing the air around her. Worse was the power that crackled along her skin, feeling dark and twisted.

Ambush!

Her warrior's instincts fired up; she fought the urge to slam on the brakes and hit the gas instead, hoping to punch through the fire, but it was already too late. The car cut loose and slid sideways, losing traction when all four tires blew. Heart pounding, she wrestled with the wheel and forced herself not to inhale. Smoke burned her eyes and throat and the exposed skin at her wrists and face. Then she was through the fire and back on the open road, but it was too late to steer, too late to correct, if she even could have without rubber on her rims.

The BMW was doing nearly sixty when it hit the guardrail and flipped. Alexis went weightless for a few seconds; then the vehicle crashed down on the other side of the guardrail, cartwheeling, tumbling down a steep, rocky embankment toward a thirty-foot drop-off and the ocean below.

She cried out in pain and terror as the seat belt dug into her chest and thighs. The windshield spiderwebbed, the air bag detonated with a *whumpf*, and the OnStar did its thing, sending a distress call as the car started coming apart around her. Another flip and bang, and the driver's-side door tore off, and then the vehicle was right-side up, sliding toward the edge of the precipice.

Body moving before her brain had caught up with her magic-honed warrior's instincts, Alexis yanked off her belt, grabbed the metal case, and threw herself out the open door. She hit hard and rolled in a tangle of arms and legs, unable to protect herself without letting go of the case, which she wasn't about to do. Sharp stones scratched at her, tearing her clothes and ripping shallow gouges in her scalded skin, but she clamped her teeth on the howl of pain and dug in her heels to stop the slide.

The BMW went over the edge, and the world went silent for a few seconds. Then the car hit bottom with a splashing crash, which would've been the last thing she heard if she'd still been in the vehicle.

Relief flared alongside the fear of what might happen next. Alexis lunged up and scrambled for the scant cover offered by a small pile of boulders near the edge of the embankment. She crouched down behind the rocks, heart hammering in her chest as she pressed herself against the warm stone and breathed through her mouth, panting like a dog that was damn glad to be alive.

Where the hell had the fire magic come from? Where were her attackers now? Her brain spun while her warrior's talent buffered the fear a little, dampening the panic so she could think. The firewall had been magic, but not Nightkeeper magic. It'd scraped along her skin rather than humming, sounding discordant and wrong, and tasting faintly of salt and rot. She'd really experienced the magic of the *Banol Kax* only once before, during the equinox battle the previous fall, and she didn't think it'd felt the same. But if it wasn't demon magic, then what?

"Hope shield magic works against whatever the hell it is," she muttered under her breath, and threw up the strongest shield she could muster: a six-inch-thick invisible force field that would repel projectiles and fireballs, and hopefully whatever else her attackers could throw at her. In the process, though, she'd be using up a ton of energy. That was the problem with having puny magic: Even the simplest spells kicked her ass.

Already feeling the power drain of shield magic, she eased around her boulder screen, took a look . . . and didn't see a damn thing. The roadway was clear; the fire was gone, as if it had never been there in the first place; and there was no sign of whoever had set the trap for her. There were only her skid marks, a caved-in section of guardrail, and the unholy mess the BMW had made on its way down the slope and over the cliff.

It looked for all the world like the driver had simply lost control and gone over the edge—Alexis decided to think of it that way, as "the driver," rather than dealing with the fact that she'd been in the car that'd made those marks, that she'd nearly gone over the cliff trying to get free of a firewall that hadn't left even a smudge on the street. But it'd been real, she knew, just as she knew her attacker was out there, waiting.

Figuring it'd be stupid to drain herself further, she dropped the shield and hunkered back down behind the rock. She needed a plan.

Calling for help wasn't an option—her cell phone had gone over with the car, she wasn't a natural telepath, and she didn't have a strong enough connection with any of the other Nightkeepers to get through to Skywatch via blood magic. The OnStar signal would've called in the local law, but she wasn't betting on their being in time for whatever happened next. Which meant she was on her own. Worse, her head was seriously spinning from the drain of the barrier spell, and her fireballs were for shit.

Damn, damn, damn.

Closing her eyes, she tried to remember what she'd seen in the last few seconds before she'd whipped around the corner and driven into the flames. There'd been nothing on the right side of the road but the cliff and the bay beyond, but she was pretty sure she remembered seeing a house just before things went to hell. Could she make it there and take shelter? Would she be any safer if she did? Who the hell knew, but making a run for it had to be better than huddling behind a couple of rocks, especially when power crinkled across her skin, warning that her attacker was gearing up for stage two.

"You're not getting Ixchel," she muttered under her breath, holding the suitcase close to her chest as she tried to slow her rocketing heartbeat and call on all the training she'd done recently, the sprints and balance exercises. She took a few quick breaths, managed not to throw up, and got herself in a defensive crouch. Then, casting up the best shield spell she could manage, she scrambled out from behind the rocks and bolted for the road, aiming for the house on the other side of the blind corner.

Behind her power surged, and the rocks that had formed her hiding spot suddenly exploded beneath the force of a smoky brown fireball.

Screaming, Alexis ran for her life. Her feet skidded on rocks and bits of broken glass, and her ankle turned as one of her too-high heels broke off. Cursing, sobbing, she hurled herself up the embankment and scrambled over the guardrail, kicking off her shoes once she was on the pavement. Her heart slammed against her ribs, and adrenaline spurred her on, pushing her past the pain when she stepped on another chunk of glass and it bit deep into the ball of her foot.

Blood flowed, bringing power. She felt the barrier magic reach out and grab hold of her, bolstering her failing strength as she put her head down and hauled ass.

She was halfway there when muddy brown smoke detonated in the middle of the street. Power rattled from the midst of the explosion, and a big man materialized in her path. He was as big as any of the Nightkeeper males, with slicked-back chestnut hair, green eyes, and broad features, wearing dark combat clothes and a weapons belt that looked all too familiar, loaded with a ceremonial knife and an autopistol.

Alexis skidded to a stop, freezing in disbelief at the sight of his bare forearm, where he wore an unfamiliar quatrefoil glyph, done in bloodred rather than Nightkeeper black.

Impossible.

"What *are* you?" she whispered, fear and confusion jamming her throat and almost robbing her of speech.

"I'm what your kind wish you could be." His mouth tipped up at the corners, and he held out his hand. "Give me the statuette."

"Like hell!" She pulled away, but wasn't quick enough. She wasn't sure if he'd 'ported or just moved incredibly fast, but one second she had the suitcase, and the next she was flying three feet through the air, and he was holding on to the case.

Alexis didn't think; she reacted, scrambling up with a cry that came from the warrior within her. She lunged, grabbed the big guy's knife off his belt before he knew what was happening, and plunged the weapon into the bastard's hand. He cursed bitterly and let go of the case, and Alexis grabbed the thing and ran like hell.

The enemy mage roared a curse, pulled his machine pistol, and let loose. Gunfire chattered, though most of the bullets bounced off Alexis's shield spell. At least one got through, though. It plowed into her shoulder and hurt like hell.

She screamed as pain washed her vision red, then screamed again when the rattle of dark magic surrounded her and yanked her off her feet. Pressure vised her from all sides and bound her motionless in midair, suspended on an oily brown cloud. Energy roared through her, along with the peculiar sliding sensation of teleport magic as he prepared to take her somewhere she positively didn't want to go. She poured everything she had into her shield, hoping it'd make her too bulky to transport or something. The rattle changed in pitch, dipping slightly, and the pressure eased.

Screaming, Alexis tore free of the brown mist. She tumbled to the ground, still clutching the suitcase in fingers gone numb from the death grip she had on the thing. Rolling as she hit, she scrambled up and started backing away as fast as she could, throwing the last of her strength into the shield spell.

The enemy mage fired again, burning through his first clip and slapping a second home, then resuming fire, his face set in anger and determination. Jade-tipped bullets pelted the invisible shield, deflecting no more than a foot from Alexis's face, but she couldn't flee and hold the magic at the same time, not now. Her power was too drained, her strength too low. Holding the metal case in front of her as a pitiful defense when her magic flickered and threatened to die, she crouched down, trying to make herself as small a target as possible, trying to minimize the shield's dimensions and eke it out a few minutes longer.

Help! she shouted as loud as she could along her connection to the barrier, hoping somebody—anybody, another Nightkeeper, the gods, it didn't matter—would hear. *Please help me!*

Blood trickled down her arm, but even with that sacrifice, the shield magic flickered. A bullet smacked into the edge of the case and ricocheted away; another bounced off the asphalt road a few inches from her bare, bloodied foot. Her eyes filmed with tears of desperation, of anger that this was how it would end.

She hadn't done so many of the things she'd meant to—hadn't come into her full powers as a Nightkeeper or proved herself to her king. She hadn't shown up any of her old "friends" back in Newport, or outgrown the need to do so, and she hadn't figured out why she sometimes awoke with tears in her eyes, hearing the echoes of a voice she knew belonged to the mother she'd never met. But it wasn't any of those things she saw in her mind's eye when the shield winked out of existence and the dark mage unleashed his final salvo. It was the glint of a hawk medallion, one she'd known long before she knew who wore it or what it meant. A wash of desire raced through her, the remembered echo of something that hadn't turned out the way it should've. As she braced herself for the burn of bullet strikes, his name whispered in her heart.

Oh, Nate.

Red-gold light suddenly detonated nuclear-bright, and a shock wave of displaced air knocked her back. The incoming bullets scattered in the blast, and two familiar figures slammed to the ground in front of her.

Nate Blackhawk, with the king at his side.

Both clad in black-on-black combat gear, tall and dark, and larger than life like all full-blooded Nightkeeper males, Nate and Strike should've looked similar, but didn't.

Strike was solid and stalwart, with a close-clipped jawline beard and shoulder-length hair tied back at his nape. Cobalt blue eyes steely, square jaw set, he stepped forward and threw a shield spell around her attacker, his god-boosted powers cutting through the rattle of twisted magic and startling a cry out of the enemy mage. Fighting magic with magic, the Nightkeepers' king looked like something out of a legend, a man of another age transplanted into the twenty-first century to battle the final evil.

Nate, in contrast, was wholly a man of the day, with short-cut black hair accentuating his strange, amber-colored eyes and aquiline nose. Instead of the black T-shirt most of the others wore under the thin layer of body armor, he wore a black button-down of fine cotton, open at the throat to show the glint of his gold medallion. The combination probably should have looked odd, but on him it looked exactly right, the melding of a successful businessman and a Nightkeeper mage.

Expression thunderous, he crossed to Alexis and threw a thick shield around them both. His magic was stronger than hers, damn him, and the shield muted the sounds of fighting as the king fireballed the enemy mage, who blocked the attack.

Nate glared down at her. "Do you still have the statuette?"

It took a second for the question to penetrate the relief, another for her irritation to rise to match his. She scowled and struggled to her bare, bleeding feet and waved the suitcase at him. "It's in here. And I'm fine; thanks for asking."

"Don't start." He snagged the case from her, got her by her uninjured arm, and hustled her to the king as dark magic rattled, signaling that the enemy mage was gearing up for transpo.

The muddy brown mist gathered, enshrouding the chestnut-haired man. The last thing Alexis saw was his startlingly clear emerald eyes, locked on her. She heard the echo of his words on a thread of magic. *See you soon. . . .*

Then he was gone.

Sirens wailed in the near distance as the mist cleared, leaving the three Nightkeepers standing in the middle of the shoreline drive, near the mangled guardrail and a spray of broken glass.

Strike glanced at Alexis. "You okay?"

She nodded, suddenly unable to trust herself to speak. In the aftermath of the fight, her warrior's bravery snapped out of existence like it'd never been, and she had to lock her muscles to keep from trembling.

"We should go," Nate said. "We'll have company in a minute." He nudged her closer to the king, whose teleport talent allowed him to 'port himself, along with anyone linked to him through touch, as long as he had enough power to draw from.

Nate and Strike clasped hands. Power leaped at the contact, and the hum gained in pitch as Nate boosted the king's magic, helping power a three-way teleport.

As Strike closed his eyes to find their way home and lock onto their destination, Nate glanced at the crumpled guardrail, then down at Alexis, his expression fierce. "Let me guess—that wasn't a Hyundai, and you put it on the AmEx." He paused. "Jox is going to be pissed, you know."

That surprised a bubble of laughter out of her, one that threatened to turn into a sob. The golden light powered up and the hum changed its note as Strike found the way home. The transport magic built, crowding them closer together. She found herself standing too near Nate, their bodies touching in too many places, reminding her of what they'd had, what they'd lost. That memory, and the relief of being safe, was enough to un-lock the words she wouldn't have said otherwise: "Thanks. I owe you one."

He looked away, jaw locked, and as the teleport swept them up, the last thing she heard was his clipped re-sponse: "Don't kid yourself. I came for the statuette."

CHAPTER TWO

Located in the middle of nowhere, New Mexico, the Nightkeepers' training compound was hidden within a box canyon offshoot of Chaco Canyon, deep in Pueblo country. A scattering of outbuildings served various functions, ranging from the steel-span training hall where the Nightkeepers practiced their magic, to the handful of small cottages that had once been used by Nightkeeper families and now stood empty, save for one. A single huge tree grew near the training hall, in the rectangular ash-shadow where the Great Hall had burned twenty years earlier. The main mansion itself was a big, multiwinged monster of sandstone and shaped concrete. Since being reopened seven months earlier it'd been largely renovated; some rooms had been fully done over, while others remained little more than white-painted drywall and carpet or hardwood flooring.

Strike, Nate, and Alexis materialized in the sunken main room of the mansion, which was a wide expanse of wood, chrome, and glass furnished with fat clubfooted couches and chairs. In the center of the space the royal *winikin*, Jox, had cleared a landing pad after the third coffee table had bitten the dust following Strike's 'port magic, which typically returned him home a foot or two up in the air.

The three of them landed with a jolt, and Alexis sagged against Nate. He propped her up by looping an arm around her waist, and tried to throttle the anger that rode him hard, the sharp pissed-offedness that she'd been in the line of fire. He might not want to be mated to her, but he didn't want anything bad to happen to her, either.

"I'll take her." Izzy stepped in and practically dragged Alexis away from him, glaring daggers, like he'd been the one to put her in danger.

He held up both hands in mock surrender. "By all means."

Carlos was there too, he saw, and Jox: three *winikin* to look after the three returning Nightkeepers. Each of them wore the *aj-winikin* glyph, which roughly translated to *I am your servant*, along with small bloodline glyphs, one for each living member of the Nightkeeper bloodline they served. Jox was the only surviving *winikin* with two bloodline members to protect: Strike and his sister, Anna. Carlos wore two different glyphs: the coyote for Sven, who had been his original charge, and the hawk for Nate, who had become Carlos's problem by default.

Poor bastard.

Nate waved off his *winikin* when Carlos showed signs of hovering. "I'm fine."

"You need to eat something," Carlos countered, "or you'll fall over." Magic was a huge energy sink; in the aftermath of major spell casting, the magi needed to pack in some serious calories and rest, not necessarily in that order.

"Fine. Whatever." Nate focused on Strike. "We need to bring the others up to speed on what just happened."

"No shit, Sherlock." The king strode off, firing orders as he went. "You round them up while I get Leah. Meet me back here in five, so we can discuss what just went down."

We've got company, Nate thought. That was what'd gone down.

The Nightkeepers were no longer the only magi on the block. The new guy had mad skills and looked like he'd been practicing way longer than the seven months or so the Nightkeepers had been reunited. And what was with him wearing a red forearm mark and trying to get at the lost artifacts? All high on the not-good scale.

But on the upside, the score was even. The bad guy had Mrs. Hopkins's artifact, but the Nightkeepers had the Ixchel statuette, thanks to Alexis.

He glanced over and saw her sitting at the end of one of the big sofas in the main room while her *winikin* fussed. Alexis was pale and looked shaky around the edges. Her blue eyes were huge in her face, and her full lower lip was caught between her teeth as though she were trying not to let it tremble. Her fancy suit might've been all curves and attitude when she'd put it on that morning, but it was a writeoff now, torn and soiled, one sleeve hanging by a thread to reveal the bloodstained white shirt beneath.

Close to six feet even without her heels, Alexis was rawboned and muscular, and far smarter than she gave herself credit for most days. Except for days like today, when she'd put herself in danger with no backup, and then cut off communication. Irritation rose at the thought. He was pissed that she'd ignored her messages, pissed that she'd gone all snotty on him when he'd mentioned it.

As though she sensed the impending lecture, she pushed herself to her feet, waved Izzy off, and headed for the residential wing, where most of the Nightkeepers lived in a series of three-room suites running off a main hallway. "I'll be back in five minutes," she said in his direction. Tugging her torn blazer sleeve down, she glanced at the injury she'd gotten in the firefight. "I'll clean up and grab some calories. Izzy can collect the *winikin*. You want to get the others?"

"Sure. That'll be fine," Nate gritted, doing his damnedest to keep his tone even when all he wanted to do was grab her and shake her. Nightkeepers healed fast in general, even quicker when they were jacked into the barrier or doing magic, but he hated the sight of the bullet crease and her bare, torn feet.

He should've gotten to her faster, he thought as he watched her walk away, hating the way her normally long, aggressive strides had been cut down by the slash of a glass cut across one of her heels. He almost hadn't gotten there in time. Thing was, they'd tried to get there sooner, but Strike damn well hadn't been able to lock onto her. For the king to 'port, he needed to picture a destination in his mind, either a place or a person. They didn't fully understand the limits of his talent—like so much of the Nightkeepers' magic and prophecies, crucial information had been lost over time—but the general rule seemed to be that Strike could latch onto anyone as long as they weren't underground . . . or dead.

After responding to Nate's emergency call, the king had wrestled with the teleport magic for nearly twenty agonizing minutes. Meanwhile, Nate had called Alexis's cell, called Skywatch, called the auction house, trying to get through to her or, failing that, trying to get a damned picture of the estate that Strike could use to 'port. In the end Alexis had somehow made the connection herself, calling out for help at the last possible moment. Nate had heard her whisper in his mind, both a shock and a relief. She wasn't a 'path, but the sheer volume of magic going down around her must've powered the mental shout that'd echoed through the barrier strongly enough that he'd caught it and been able to tell Strike where to look.

Lucky, Nate thought, scowling. *Goddamned lucky.* He knew he should let it go, that it was over, she was back safely, and it wouldn't happen again. They knew what they were up against now—or if not what, precisely, they at least knew that there was an enemy mage out there, tracking them. Anticipating them. Trying to scoop them on the statuettes, probably because he was either looking to fulfill the seven-demon cycle himself, or to prevent the Nightkeepers from stopping it. And that would be a serious problem, because if the cycle ran through, bringing all seven demons across the barrier to complete the tasks assigned to them by legend, the Nightkeepers were screwed.

The sound of a sliding glass door broke into Nate's mental churning, and he looked up to see Rabbit coming in from the pool area. The teen was wearing a hoodie with the hood up and the arms cut off, paired with jeans that hung low off his ass, serving mostly to hold the business end of his iPod. Just turned eighteen, Rabbit was the youngest of the magi, the half-blood son of Red-Boar, who had been the last Nightkeeper survivor of the solstice massacre of '84, when Strike's father had led the Nightkeepers to the intersection, compelled by a vision that said he could avert the end-time by sealing the barrier. Instead, he'd led his people into genocide. Red-Boar had survived the battle at the intersection, and had later joined up with Jox, who was raising Strike and his sister, Anna. It hadn't been until the previous year that Jox had admitted there were other Nightkeepers living in secret with their *winikin*—or, in Nate's case, without them.

Rumor had it that Red-Boar had sired Rabbit while on walkabout in south-central Mexico or Guatemala or something like that. Nate had heard different versions, different explanations of who the kid's mother had been, and why the teen had some scary-strong powers that didn't always act like the legends said Nightkeeper magic should.

Seeing that Nate was staring at him, Rabbit stopped dead, shoved his hands in his pockets, and scowled. "What's your problem?"

Having learned it was safer to ignore the kid's 'tude when possible, Nate said, "You hear about the meeting yet?"

"I was out at the—" The kid broke off and shrugged. "No. So?"

In other words, he'd sneaked out to the Pueblo ruins at the back of the box canyon again. Nobody knew exactly what he did up in the sprawling collection of rooms, kivas, and burial chambers, but most of the residents of Skywatch gave Rabbit a wide berth anyway. He wasn't exactly warm and fuzzy.

"Confab in the big room, five minutes," Nate said. "You want to help me round up the others?"

For a second Rabbit looked as if he were going to tell

Nate to go to hell. But surprisingly, he nodded. "I'll check the firing range; you hit the rec area and the training hall."

He was gone before Nate could ask. Not that he was going to—he didn't really want to know what was going on in Rabbit's head. Always one to walk on the moody, broody side of life, the kid had gotten even stranger in the months since his father had died during the equinox battle. It wasn't like father and son had gotten along all that well, either—they'd struck sparks off each other like nobody's business, and as far as Nate could tell, Red-Boar'd pretty much hated the kid's guts.

Then again, who was he to criticize a father-son relationship? Nate thought as he headed for the rec room, which was located past the kitchen and down a short hall toward the forty-car garage. It wasn't like he had any experience in the area. Besides, he wasn't part of the whole Nightkeepers-as-family movement that Strike, Leah, and the *winikin*—and Alexis, to a degree—kept harping on. As far as he was concerned, the current residents of Skywatch were nothing more than twenty or so people who'd grown up separately, weren't related by blood, and had their own lives outside of the whole Nightkeeper thing. They might be a team out of necessity when it came to the end-time stuff, sure, but that didn't make them inseparable, didn't make them a family. If Rabbit wanted to march to his own backbeat, Nate wasn't going to get in his way. He understood privacy and the need for freedom.

Sticking his head through the door of the room they called entertainment central, he saw two of his teammates locked in simulated battle, courtesy of the top-of-the line gaming console Jox had installed a few months earlier. "Hey, you two," Nate said. "Meeting in the main room, two minutes."

"Give us ten," Coyote-Seven said without turning around, his attention glued to the TV, his fingers flying over a gaming console as he navigated his way through the third level of *EmoPunk II*.

Lanky and athletic, with his bloodline and so-far un-identified talent marks bared by a sleeveless black tee, and his long blond hair caught back in a stubby ponytail, Sven was their resident burnout, taking nothing and nobody seriously. As Nate watched, Sven's computer-generated character took out a pair of overinked street thugs with a series of ninja chops and a kick in the 'nads that had all three of the flesh-and-blooders in the room wincing.

The computerized image shifted as Sven sent his character inside a nearby warehouse. It was dark inside, but a busted-out window in the back let in a ray of light to shine on a guy wearing a medallion that wouldn't figure in until level five, when it'd be vital. Nate wasn't sure if the other two knew that, but he did, because he'd helped write the game.

"Gotta get me some of that." Sven sent his character in a headlong charge for the medallion, missed seeing the bad guy in the shadows, and was dead two seconds later. "Shit!"

"Sucker." Sitting beside Sven, Michael Stone worked his gaming console with the finesse of a pro. His strategizing wasn't bad, either, Nate thought. Michael had let Sven charge in blindly and distract the bad guys while he sneaked around and lifted the medallion, then boogied out the back like a good little thief.

Dark and intense and a shade too slick in Nate's opinion, Michael spoke infrequently, but when he did, his words were exactly right, as though he calculated each sentence, polished each syllable to perfection. His dark eyes held secrets, and when his phone chirped—which it did frequently—he took the calls in private, often well into the night.

The two Nightkeepers in the rec room were diametric opposites: Michael had hidden depths; Sven had no depth whatsoever. Yet somehow they'd become best buds over the past few months, seeming content to shut themselves up in Skywatch while the others tried to find a workable balance between the magi they were supposed to become and the people they'd been before the Nightkeepers' magical barrier reactivated.

"Let's go," Nate said, his voice going sharp when neither of the other guys looked away from the TV screen. "We've got a problem. You can rot your brains later."

Just because Hawk Enterprises produced the *EmoPunk* games didn't mean he thought they were any good.

Nate had kept the connection to the video games on the down-low—not because he minded them knowing about the *EP*s, but because he didn't want any of them stumbling onto his connection to the *Viking Warrior* games.

Or, more accurately, Alexis's connection to them and, through them, to him.

It was bad enough that she'd admitted to having envisioned his medallion a few times in the weeks before they'd met. The last thing he wanted was for anyone to know he'd created her spitting image more than four years ago, and that his buddies had joked that he was saving himself for Hera.

Yeah. So not going there.

"We can't stop now. He's on a roll," Sven protested. Michael didn't say anything, just kept playing.

Annoyed, Nate reached down and killed the power strip just inside the door, flatlining everything. When Sven yelped, Nate growled, "Cut the shit. What're you trying to do, oust Rabbit as the local juvenile delinquent?"

Sven sneered. "Takes one to know one. At least I haven't done time."

But Michael elbowed him hard. "Shut it." He tossed the console aside and rose, squaring off opposite Nate, his dark eyes assessing. "Thought you were going after one of the statues?"

"Found a body instead. Then it got weird."

Ignoring Michael's raised brow and Sven's "No way!" Nate turned and headed for the main room, figuring that'd get them moving.

He was right. Michael and Sven trailed after him and joined the growing group in the sunken main room of the mansion. By the time Nate had scored some leftover homemade pizza from the kitchen, which was on the other side of a breakfast bar separating it from the main room, the residents of Skywatch had gathered for the meeting.

Of the eleven Nightkeepers who'd fought together during the equinox battle, Red-Boar was dead, Brandt

and Patience White-Eagle were off dealing with the sale
of their house in Philly, and Strike's sister, Anna, had
returned home to the "real" world, refusing to fully com-
mit to a life she'd rejected years ago. That left seven
Nightkeepers at Skywatch, along with seven *winikin*,
plus the twin White-Eagle toddlers, Harry and Braden,
and Strike's mate, Leah, who was fully human, yet a
Godkeeper at the same time.

Which, as far as Nate was concerned, went to prove
that the prophecies didn't always get it right. The legends said the Godkeepers would arise at the end of the
age, when the Nightkeepers needed them to guard the
barrier. So far, though, only the one god had made it
through the barrier to possess a female, and it'd bound
with Leah, in a process that had nearly cost the ex-cop her
life and resulted in an incomplete possession. Even when
Strike and Leah had attempted to form a Nightkeeper-
Godkeeper mated blood link during the winter solstice,
they hadn't been able to call the plumed snake god, Kulkulkan, and had commanded only a fraction of the god's
powers. In addition to—or perhaps because of—that failure, no god had sought to come through the barrier,
even though the Nightkeepers had enacted the transition
ritual in the sacred chamber. They had offered up Patience as a potential Godkeeper on the theory that she
was already mated to a Nightkeeper, forming the strong
bond required to support the powers of a Godkeeper.
But that hadn't worked, leaving them scrambling to find
the demon prophecies in the hopes that the starscript
writings would give them the information and spells they
would need to keep Camazotz's minions in hell, where
they belonged.

While they waited for the king, Nate gnawed on his
pizza and looked around the room, and he felt the stir
of unease that'd become all too familiar in recent weeks.
Only a few days earlier he'd finally been able to identify
the problem: The Nightkeepers were stagnating.

They had fallen into their patterns so quickly—too
quickly. Jade—quiet and pretty, with dark hair and green
eyes, an ex-therapist who'd turned out to be their resident bookworm—spent her time in the archives, catalog-

ing the huge volume of material collected by their ancestors, only a small fraction of which was actually proving useful. Michael and Sven were clearly marking time, though Nate had no clue what either of them was waiting for. The two absent Nightkeepers, dark-haired, businesslike Brandt and his pretty blond wife, Patience, were pretending for their kids' sake that they were a normal family. Nate was running his company by remote while trying to figure out how to juggle the next four years of his life . . . and Alexis was transplanting her rarified Newport existence to the compound piece by piece, while doing her damnedest to keep a 5.0 GPA in a world that wasn't keeping score the way she wanted it to.

That was largely her *winikin*'s influence, he figured. Izzy was a formidable woman in a tiny package, and he could easily picture her pushing Alexis throughout her life. He'd seen it himself—the unsubtle mentions of the power of the smoke bloodline and the importance of royal advisers, along with a few equally unsubtle mentions of the hawk bloodline and its unsuitability, whatever that meant.

Nate hadn't asked, hadn't cared. As far as he was concerned, the past didn't matter worth shit. History didn't automatically repeat itself, and he damn well got to choose his own path. Which meant no patterns, no stagnation. It was time to shake things up a little, he thought. But just then Alexis stepped through the residential hallway door, drawing his attention whether he liked it or not. She carried the heavy-looking, battle-scarred metal suitcase with ease, moving with the grace of a fighter as she set the case on an end table near the big sofa in the center of the room.

She'd cleaned up and changed into at-home jeans and a soft blue-gray shirt almost the same color as her eyes. Her multitoned golden hair spilled to her shoulders in waves that made him remember how the strands had felt between his fingers and against his skin, and that flash of sensory memory had his body hardening. He would've cursed out loud at the involuntary reaction, but forced himself to stifle the response. He couldn't afford to let her know—to let any of them know—that he still wanted her, no matter how badly matched they might be. She'd bought into the Nightkeeper ways so deeply that he suspected that a large part of her desire for him came from the portents that they were meant for each other rather than from actual volition. Or maybe lust and fate were all mixed up inside her, some of it real, some of it created by the situation.

Regardless, he wanted nothing to do with a relationship built on destiny and bullshit, and she believed too deeply for it to be anything else. So why the hell couldn't he get her out of his head? Even now, five months after they'd stopped sleeping together, he still woke thinking of her, tasting her on his lips, and feeling vague surprise when he rolled over and she wasn't there.

Blame it on Hera, he thought, and looked away from Alexis as Strike appeared from the direction of the royal quarters.

"Everybody here?" the Nightkeepers' king asked as he scanned the bodies crowded into the sunken central room of the big mansion.

Leah was at his side. With her white-blond hair pulled back in a ponytail and covered with a ball cap, wearing jeans and a tight T-shirt, she looked like what she was: a normal, attractive woman in her early thirties. The glyphs on her inner right forearm, though, marked her as more than that. Far more. She wore the flying serpent, the royal *ju* and the *jun tan* "beloved" glyph, marking her in turn as a Godkeeper, a queen, and a mated woman. The glyphs were three of the most powerful symbols in the Nightkeepers' arsenal, and by rights they shouldn't have appeared on a human's arm.

Then again, the crimson mark on the arm of the big redheaded guy who'd gone after Alexis suggested the Nightkeepers didn't know everything there was to know about the forearm marks and their significance. The magi simply didn't have nearly enough information. *As usual,* Nate thought, frowning at Alexis, who pointedly ignored him.

When the king saw that the Nightkeepers were all there, he nodded. "Good. Okay, here's the deal. . . ."

He quickly outlined what Nate had seen in the old lady's cottage, then described the attack on Alexis, ending with, "The way I see it, we've got a bunch of different issues here. We've got to figure out who this guy is and what he's planning. Is he working alone? He doesn't have the eyes of a *makol*, but what else could he be?"

"Maybe a leftover from Survivor2012?" Leah suggested, naming the *makol*-controlled human cult that had killed her brother, and had almost killed her in the search for more power, more control over the end-time.

"Maybe," Strike said, "or maybe we're dealing with something new." He waved for Leah to continue. The ex-cop was hell on wheels both as an investigator and in terms of the cat herding required to keep the Nightkeepers more or less united as a fighting force when they hadn't been raised and trained together, as they would have been had circumstances been different.

Although Strike and Leah weren't married or even engaged in the traditional human sense, the gods had marked her as both Strike's mate and the Nightkeepers' queen. In his less charitable moments, Nate had wondered if that was the gods' way of fulfilling their own prophecies by telling the two they were mated, whether they liked it or not. Granted, Strike had gone against the prophecies themselves to save her, and the love between them was pretty damn obvious just seeing them together. Nate just didn't think the gods had the right to automatically translate that to a pair bond and an insta-queen, whether or not Leah was good at the job. It wasn't like she'd really been given a choice in the matter.

"In terms of immediate goals," Leah said, her voice cop-cool, "we need to recover the missing statue and get to the other five artifacts ahead of our competition, whatever he is." She looked over at Jade. "Any more luck tracking the remaining pieces?"

The pretty, dark-haired archivist nodded. "I've got one more nailed down, and am chasing rumors on two others. The one I'm sure about is in New Orleans. We've got a meeting set up for tomorrow, and a verbal agreement that the current owner will 'discuss' a purchase with us. I think Alexis should go, since she's our best negotiator." Jade paused, glancing at Alexis. "Be warned: The owner calls herself Mistress Truth and runs a fortune-telling-slash-occult shop in the French Quarter. She thinks she's got mad skills, and leans heavily on the woo-woo side of life."

Nate thought that was a pretty ironic statement, coming from a woman who wore the scribe's glyph that denoted her as the only one among the Nightkeepers capable of crafting new spells. Then again, Jade hadn't actually produced a spell yet. For that matter, she avoided the magic as much as possible, spending most of her time in the archives.

But he locked onto the idea of Alexis doing the negotiations in person and outside the wards. He asked, "What sort of skills does our Mistress Truth think she has?"

Jade grimaced. "She claims she bought the artifact—a ceremonial knife carved out of obsidian—because it 'called to her.' " The archivist emphasized the phrase with finger quotes. "And she thinks it's been amplifying her 'natural powers.' " Again with the finger quotes.

"What's to say it doesn't?" Nate asked.

It was Strike who answered. "Unless she's got Nightkeeper blood, the artifact shouldn't do diddly for her. Even if you buy into the existence of other types of magic, the relics and resonations of one belief system shouldn't cross over to another."

" 'Shouldn't' being the operative word there," said Nate, and this time it was his turn to use finger quotes.

"Yeah, well. I'm doing my best with what I've got." Jade sounded more resigned than anything, and he couldn't blame her. The Nightkeepers had taken a number of major knowledge hits during their history: In addition to the Egyptian massacre, the conquistadors had practically wiped out the Nightkeepers' population and had burned all but a few of their texts in the 1530s, and then the Solstice Massacre in the early eighties had decimated the magi yet again, robbing them of most of their written and oral traditions, save for the creation stories passed down by the *winikin.* That left the Nightkeepers low on numbers, low on power, and limited in their understanding of what the magic could and couldn't do. Not to mention clueless about who in the hell the guy with the red marks was or worked for.

Strike turned to Nate. "I want you to go to New Orleans with Alexis, as her backup."

"Of course." Nate ignored the sharp look she shot him at that. He couldn't tell if she was pissed that he was going, surprised that he hadn't argued, or what. If he'd learned anything from the day's near disaster, though, it was that none of the Nightkeepers should be venturing out solo until they identified and neutralized the threat. Since he wasn't about to trust Sven, Michael, or Rabbit to watch her back, and the king had bigger things to worry about, it fell to Nate to make the New Orleans trip. Simple math, nothing more.

Strike nodded. "Good, that's settled." He turned to Jade. "I want you to push hard on finding the other artifacts. You've got Carter helping you?"

Carter was a private investigator, a human Jox knew through a friend-of-a-friend sort of thing. The PI had come in handy before; he'd been the one who'd tracked down the scattered Nightkeepers, including Nate, and had aided Leah in the search for her brother's killer, who had turned out to be an *ajaw-makol*, a head *makol* working on direct orders from the *Banol Kax*. Carter did his job without asking too many questions about his employers, which made him a serious asset, given that the last thing the Nightkeepers needed was to become a segment on *60 Minutes*.

Jade nodded. "He's working on one of the two threads I'm following. We've gotten one of the artifacts as far as London in the 1940s, but it's not clear what happened to it during or after D-day."

Which meant, Nate figured, it was equally likely that the thing had been blown to bits, or the Nazis had hidden it in a yet-undiscovered cache of antiquities. *Bummer.*

"Keep on it," Strike said, "and while you're at it, pull together whatever you've got on the Order of Xibalba."

There was a beat of silence; then Jox snorted. "Please." The royal *winikin* dropped down from the breakfast bar, where he and the other *winikin* had taken their customary positions watching over their charges. Jox was a small, fit man in his late fifties with longish gray-threaded hair that was caught back in a stubby ponytail. Wearing worn jeans, rope sandals, and a long-sleeved button-down, he exuded the frustrated amusement of a bewildered parent as he crossed to the edge of the sunken area and looked down at the king. "You're kidding, right?"

Strike's lips twisted into a wry smile. "Isn't that approximately what I said to you when you handed me a list of names and told me that Anna and I weren't the last of the bloodlines after all? Just because you've been told one thing your whole life doesn't always mean it's the gospel truth."

Jox rolled his eyes. "The Xibalbans are a myth, a group of bogeymen we use to scare kids into behaving."

"Maybe, maybe not," Strike said, and something in his voice suggested he knew something the others didn't. He didn't elaborate, though, saying only, "It won't hurt to have Jade look into it."

As if sensing a fight on the horizon, Leah interrupted. "I think now would be a good time for Alexis to show us the statuette she sacrificed a Beemer to save."

That earned a sour look from Jox, who was clearly not pleased about the dead car. Knowing Alexis, Nate bet she hadn't ponied up for the extra rental insurance, either.

Alexis leaned over to the suitcase, which was resting on one of the end tables that flanked the overstuffed sofas. She dialed in a combination and popped the locks open. Out of curiosity, Nate leaned in, trying to catch a glimpse. "You use the end-time?" It was an obvious guess, the date they'd all found themselves living for overnight: December 21, 2012.

"No." She shifted aside and let him see: 6/21/84. The day of the Solstice Massacre.

"Feeling nostalgic?" he asked with a little too much edge.

"Bite me." She sent him a sharp smile and turned her back on him.

Nate snorted, but didn't regret the jibe, which had

been as much a reality check as anything. The others might be buying into the *What has happened before will happen again* motto of the Nightkeeper legends, but he figured the history should stay where it belonged—in the past. The modern-day Nightkeepers, such as they were, would out of necessity be a new breed of magi. They didn't need to learn about the past; they needed to forge their own futures. Screw the prophecies; screw destiny. As far as he was concerned, they should gather the artifacts, boost their powers as far as they could manage, and bust ass through the barrier to hit the *Banol Kax* on their home turf.

Not surprisingly, he was in the minority on that one.

"Et voilà," Alexis murmured, and lifted the top of the case, revealing not one, but two artifacts.

A murmur of surprise rippled through the assembled Nightkeepers and *winikin*, and most of them leaned in to see. The first artifact was the statuette she'd been sent after; Nate recognized it from the auction catalog. The second was a flattened clay disk maybe eight inches in diameter, shaped to resemble a man's face. The formed clay face was slack mouthed, and the man's eyes were covered with the jade pebbles he would've needed on his journey through Xibalba. Holes pierced on either side showed where rope or sinew would have been threaded through, allowing the mask to be tied in place. Nate recognized it from what little reading he'd done on the Nightkeepers and the customs they'd shared with the ancient Maya. "It's a death mask."

It wasn't just any death mask, either. The dead man had vaguely porcine features, with a flattened nose and the hint of tusks rather than teeth.

"Watch this," Alexis said, and she rotated the disk one-eighty, so the peccary features were upside down. The action revealed a second set of eyes, nose, and mouth—another face hidden in the frown lines and shapes of the first. In the second incarnation, the pig-man was smiling and looked, if not happy, then at least at peace with himself and what had happened to cause his death.

It wasn't a Mayan death mask, as the auction catalog had probably stated. It was Nightkeeper made, as proven by the mark of the boar in the lower corner, a match to the bloodline glyph on Rabbit's arm.

"Nostalgic indeed," Nate said, but this time he wasn't teasing. Instead he felt a beat of grief for a lost comrade.

Red-Boar had been a prickly bastard, and he'd sucked as a role model and father, but he'd been one of the team. He'd been killed in the tunnels beneath Chichén Itzá, when one of the lesser *makol* had turned out to be a mimic, a shape-shifter capable of taking on other forms. The mimic had impersonated Leah and used the guise to slit Red-Boar's throat.

"It spoke to me," Alexis said of the mask. Looking at Jox, who was the unofficial arbiter of all purchases and decorating decisions around Skywatch, save for their personal quarters, she said, "I thought maybe we could hang it in here, or in the training hall, as a reminder. Sort of like having him looking down on us."

Jox looked to Strike. "Cool by you?"

"It's really Rabbit's call," the king answered.

The teen looked startled for a second, then thoughtful. Finally he nodded. "Yeah." He stopped, cleared his throat. "Yeah, the old man'd get a kick out of that. Just . . . just make sure he can see the ceiba tree, okay? It was . . . it mattered to him."

The tree in question, a big sucker nearly fifty feet high and about as wide, grew where the Nightkeepers' Great Hall had stood before the massacre. In the aftermath of the attack, before he'd enacted the spell that'd banished the training compound from the face of the earth for more than two decades, Jox had piled the bodies in the Great Hall and set it ablaze as a funeral pyre. When Strike and Red-Boar had reversed the spell twenty-four years later, they'd found the ceiba tree rooted in the ashes of the fallen Nightkeepers. The tree, which the Maya and Nightkeepers had revered as the symbol of community, believing that the roots stretched to the underworld and that the branches held up the sky, was native to the Yucatán and Central America. It shouldn't have been able to grow in the arid box canyon, and it sure as hell couldn't have gotten so big in the time it had. But there it was.

And yeah, it mattered. Even to someone like Nate, who didn't believe in looking back.

"The training hall it is, then," Alexis said, looking pleased, as though she hadn't been sure how her impulse buy was going to go over. Then she reached for the statuette. "Well, I guess I should introduce you to Ixchel. I sure hope she was worth—"

The moment she touched the statuette, she stiffened, her mouth opening in a round O of surprise.

"Alexis?" Nate's gut tightened as magic danced across his skin. Before any of the others could react, he shot out a hand, intending to pull hers away from the statuette. But the moment he touched her his muscles locked.

And the world around him disappeared.

CHAPTER THREE

Power burned up Alexis's arm and gathered in her core, spinning and expanding and taking over until there was only the power. She didn't know where she was, couldn't see anything but darkness, couldn't feel anything but magic. Worse, she couldn't lock on, couldn't jack in and use what little magic she possessed to get free. She could only hang suspended in the nothingness.

Panic gripped her. She would've fought but she couldn't move; would've screamed, but she couldn't make a sound.

Help! she screamed in her head. *Help me!* But there was no answer.

Gulping for air, though it seemed she wasn't actually breathing, she fought to slow her racing brain, struggled to think it through. She'd given the death mask to Rabbit, turned to lift the statuette from the case, and then—

A flash of vibrant color, a kaleidoscope of vivid hues. Then nothing.

She'd touched the statuette, and the contact had sent her . . . where? She wasn't in the barrier; she knew that much. There was no gray-green mist, no squishy surface underfoot and gray-green sky above. There was no up or down where she'd been transported, no surface or sky. There was just blackness and power. Then, suddenly, the colors returned in shimmering ribbons of light. They caressed her, curled around her, then dissipated.

When they cleared she was in a ceremonial chamber she'd never seen before.

She stood on a slender ledge that ran along one side of the narrow room. A vaulted stone ceiling arched overhead, spanning a rectangular pool of dark water. Stalactites hung down in gorgeous stone droplets, and stalagmites thrust up from the water, causing the sluggish flow to eddy and swirl in overlapping ripple patterns. Light came from torches that were set in stone sconces on either side of the narrow room. In the flickering illumination, she saw that the room was closed at either end, creating a long, narrow arcade with water instead of a floor. There were no doors or windows, but the torch smoke, which smelled faintly of sacred incense, moved along the ceiling to a narrow crack halfway down one of the long walls.

One entire short side was taken up with an elaborate thronelike structure built out of limestone blocks and carved from the living subterranean stone itself. She wasn't sure if it was a throne or an altar; the flat space in the middle could have served as either. Arching columns rose up on either side, carved with a serpent and feather pattern that made her think of Kulkulkan, along with a sinuous motif she didn't recognize. The other three walls and the vaulted ceiling were carved with human figures, not the intricate hieroglyphs used for writing, but a single extended scene, a grand mural of Mayan men and women with the flattened, elongated foreheads that had been created early in childhood with binding boards, and the exaggerated cheekbones and noses often made from clay or jade, all of it intended to make the wearer look more like a god. Hundreds of figures were carved on either side of the black pool, some bowing or kneeling, others raising their hands in supplication. All of them faced the throne at the far end.

Overhead, the archway and the stalactites themselves were carved with rippling patterns of feathers and scales and that same wavy motif, which gave the impression of wind, or the gods, or both. Some the rippling lines were painted with brilliant reds and blues, vibrant yellows and purples, oranges and greens, the hues shining impossibly true in the amber torchlight.

Drawn by the captured motion of the carvings, Alexis walked along the narrow stone ledge that ran around the pool, moving toward the throne. As she passed, her shadow danced in the flickering torchlight, making the carvings seem to come alive, to reach for her. She thought she heard them whisper her name in the soft rippling noise coming from the water.

They didn't whisper, "Alexis," though. They said something else, something that called to her, made her feel as though she were a stranger to herself. Indeed, she was wearing a stranger's clothes—not the jeans and shirt she'd put on in place of her ruined suit back at Skywatch, but combat wear of stretchy black-on-black that molded itself to her figure and moved with her.

She had seen this before, she realized suddenly. This was what she remembered when she awoke sobbing softly, hearing her mother's voice. In the dreams, she hadn't been sure if she was her mother or herself, or someone else entirely. Only now, unlike in the dreams, her senses were heightened rather than dulled by the mists of her subconscious. The crunch of limestone gravel beneath her feet was very loud, the alkaline smell of the water very sharp, and the prickle of moisture on her skin—from the air, from her pores—left her nerve endings acutely sensitized.

And as she walked to the throne, she knew she was alone, yet not alone. *He* was here, too—the lover of her dreams, the one who was Nate yet not, the one who loved her like he had, but didn't break her heart. That was how she had always known it was a dream before. Now, though, she wasn't sure what to call it. She'd touched the statuette and been transported into a dark, formless corner of the barrier, yet now she was back on earth—she knew it from the taste of the air, and the strong sense of being underground.

When she reached the end of the arcade, the pathway curved and widened, forming a platform in front of the throne. There, in the center of the flat space, she saw shadowy footprints in the dust, human and barefooted, standing facing the throne.

Almost without conscious volition, acting as she had

done in the dream, she toed off her shoes and stepped into the footprints. They fit perfectly, as they had in her fantasies. The certainty that she had been in this chamber before, that she'd done this before, was overwhelming, as was the knowledge that the moment she blooded herself, placed her hands on the altar, and said his name, he would be there with her.

The certainty—and the nerves—had her hesitating. Then, knowing she didn't have a choice, not really, she pulled a ceremonial knife she didn't recognize from a weapons belt she didn't remember putting on, and drew the blade sharply across her palm. She hissed against the pain as blood flowed, dark crimson in the amber torchlight. Then she reversed hands and cut her other palm. Her bloodied fingers slipped on the haft of the knife as she set it aside.

"Gods," she whispered, hope and fear spiraling up within her, "help me to be worthy."

Izzy had raised her on stories of the Nightkeepers and the heroic warrior-priestess Gray-Smoke, who had been adviser to the king. As a child, Alexis had wished Gray-Smoke was real, wished the Nightkeepers were real. It hadn't been until the previous year, when the barrier came back online and Strike recalled the Nightkeepers, that Izzy had revealed that not only had Gray-Smoke been a real person, she'd been Alexis's mother. Ever since then, Alexis had felt as if she were trying to keep up, trying to live up. Now, feeling another consciousness beside her own, feeling another's life overlap with hers, and knowing deep down inside that it was Gray-Smoke, or at least the memory of her, the essence of her, Alexis could only pray she'd be worthy of the mother she'd never known.

More, she prayed for the gods to help her understand what the dream was telling her. About her mother. About herself. About the man who wore the hawk medallion.

Knowing there was no other way, she closed her eyes and pressed her bloodstained palms to the altar, and said the words that had come to her in a dream, though she was no seer: *"Tzakaw muwan."* Summon the hawk.

A detonation rocked the room. Water splashed on the

footpath, and the sound of ripples turned to thin screams coming from the people carved on the walls, who hadn't moved, yet somehow seemed to gape in awe.

She turned, knowing what she would see.

He stood opposite her, at the edge where the stone and the water met. His eyes bored into hers, hard and intense and no-nonsense. He wore combat gear, with his black shirt unbuttoned at the top to show a glint of gold. He was Nate, yet not, just as she was Alexis, yet not.

She was the smoke and he was the hawk. And that was all that really mattered as his eyes darkened and he strode toward her, his intent as clear as the need inside her.

Sex.

It was a vision, Nate knew, yet it wasn't. He was part of it, yet apart from it, distancing himself even as his heart pounded and the scent of her touched him, wrapping around his soul and digging in deep, a combination of arousal, musk, and the moist warmth of the tropics. He was vaguely aware of the carved chamber, and the fact that he should be wondering how he'd gotten there. The last thing he remembered was reaching for Alexis, intending to pull her away from the statuette of Ixchel. Then the world had gone gray-green, then black, and now he was here. He didn't have a clue where "here" was, but that didn't seem to matter so much. What mattered was the woman standing near the carved stone altar, her bloodstained hands held out to him.

She was Alexis, yet she was someone else. Her features were slightly sharper, her breasts slightly fuller, and when he took her hands he felt confidence exuding from her that was lacking in the woman he knew. *He* felt different, as well, more centered, more in tune with his body's demand that he take her here and now, that it was his right and duty.

They were, he thought in a flash of insight, the people they would have become if King Scarred-Jaguar hadn't led his people to their deaths. They were the fully trained versions of themselves, warriors who had been thoroughly indoctrinated into the magic and culture of the Nightkeepers, soldiers of the end-time war who were willing to do whatever was necessary, even if it meant pimping themselves out to the gods.

He opened his mouth to speak, to ask her what the hell this was—a piece of the barrier or something else?—but before he could formulate the question, she had raised herself up on tiptoe and pressed her lips to his. He wanted to pull away, to protest, but her kiss had the new maturity of the woman she'd become, the new confidence, and the added thrill nearly dropped him. Heat slashed through him at the feel and taste of her, familiar yet not, with deeper, darker layers than before. His hands, which he'd lifted to ease her away, wound up dragging her closer instead.

"This isn't us," he managed to say in the space between one kiss and the next. "This isn't real."

She let go of him and stepped back, but she sure as hell wasn't retreating. No, she was loosening her weapons belt and letting it fall in a blatant invitation. "It's as real as we let it be. This is a better version of us. One that doesn't go beyond these walls, beyond this dream."

Was that what it was, a dream? He'd never been much of a dreamer, had never remembered his dreams once he awoke, except for the ones about the glowing orange monsters, the ones the therapists had told him were Oedipal projections of his mother and had turned out to be actual glowing orange monsters, the *boluntiku* that had slaughtered his playmates during the Solstice Massacre.

Aside from those nightmares, he'd never dreamed. Or, at least, not that he remembered.

"If this is what dreaming is like," he murmured as her hands went to the hem of her clingy black shirt, "then I've been missing out."

Her expression changed at that, showing a flash of uncertainty, a hint of vulnerability he would've expected more from the Alexis he knew than from this brighter, shinier version. But then she shimmied out of her shirt and bra, exposing herself, her nipples puckering in the golden torchlight and soft air.

He moved without being aware of making the decision, closed in on her like a hunter, his body moving under the direction of another, one who had absolutely no reservations about the two of them being together. *This is meant,* that other him thought. *This is how it should be.*

Nate balked at that, nearly drew away, because it was exactly what he was struggling to avoid—that sense of inevitability and fate, the dogma that came with the Nightkeeper way of life. He wanted to win his woman, not have her handed to him by the gods, or destiny, or some such shit. He wanted freedom, wanted—

Before he could complete the thought, that other, baser part of him kissed her and brought his hands to her creamy flesh. In an instant everything gave way to a roar of heat and need, and the two of him melded into one man—one incredibly turned-on guy who knew exactly how she felt and tasted, yet each time discovered something new about her, about the two of them together. He'd sworn he wouldn't do this again, wouldn't be with her, because it wasn't fair if he didn't intend to fall in with the gods' plans for the two of them.

This is a dream, he told himself. *Dreams don't count.* And if that played false in the back of his brain, the knowledge was quickly lost to the heat and the needs of the man who both was and wasn't him.

He pressed into her, crowding her against the throne— altar, whatever—at her back. She braced herself against the soft curves of limestone that had been built up and worn smooth by centuries of dripping water. She grabbed onto a pair of protruding bumps carved by an ancient hand into the shapes of serpents' heads, their mouths gaping open, their fangs dropping down in menace, or maybe reverence. Nate was filled with that same reverence when he brought his hands up to cup the dip of her waist and the small of her back, then higher, to the heavy weight of her breasts, which were crowned with the tight buds of her nipples.

She moaned and arched against him, digging her blunt, manicured fingernails into his biceps, then shifting to run her fingers up his chest and get to work on his shirt, freeing the top three buttons. Boosting herself up onto the altar, she leaned into him, curling her hands around his neck to find the sensitive spot at the back, just beneath his hairline.

Heat speared through him, lust flaring as that small gesture reminded him of the past. They'd been together only two short months, but they'd packed a hell of a lot of sex into those weeks, when they'd been ridden hard by pretalent hormones and the magic that had sought to bind them together. Had almost succeeded.

Memory gentled his touch, had him cupping her, shaping her the way he'd learned she liked. Her eyes went glassy and her head fell back, baring her throat to his lips. Time stretched out, spiraled inward. In that instant there were only the two of them and the small stone room, the carved audience frozen timeless on the walls, and the moving floor of water, pierced with stone teeth and ripples of movement.

"Lexie," he said, using the name he'd used only when they'd been alone together, wrapped up in each other. "I—"

"Don't," she interrupted, pressing a finger to his lips. "It's only a dream."

He wasn't sure he believed that, but knew damn sure he didn't care anymore. He eased back to strip off his shirt, and when he did she dropped down from her perch to shimmy out of her pants. Then, with a crook of her finger, she brushed past him, naked, and headed for the edge of the platform, where the stone gave way to liquid darkness. Without a word or a moment's hesitation, she lowered herself into the water, which rose to her waist, then her shoulders.

Swimming, treading water with lazy strokes, she turned and looked at him, one eyebrow raised in challenge. "Well?"

Done with hesitating and justifying, he hastily stripped off the rest of his clothes and dove in, slicing cleanly between the pale teeth of stone that broke the surface. The water was warmer than he'd expected, cool but not cold, and the thrill of it tightened his skin and ramped his excitement. There was a quiver of power, too, the resonance of sacrificial offerings that had been thrown in the pool in ages past.

The water was deep enough that he had to tread, kicking gently as he stroked toward the place where Alexis had come to rest. She was settled between two tall stalagmites that were joined at the base and split near the waterline, forming a pocket for her to sit in, with the spires branching away above, giving her freedom to move, yet an anchor to brace herself against if she desired.

Desire. It was all he felt, all he could process as he moved toward her. Her arms were linked around the stone pillars, her legs eased slightly apart in the natural stone pocket. Water licked at her navel; her wet hair clung to her shoulders and full breasts. Amber torchlight glittered on droplets of water as they ran from her hair and tracked down her breasts and belly and ran along the graceful curves of her arms.

She was an astonishingly beautiful gut-punch that took Nate's breath away. And in that instant, as he closed with her and touched his lips to hers, he thought he understood the lure of thinking that goddesses were real.

If he'd believed in such things, he would've sworn he was looking at a goddess right now.

Alexis wasn't a weeper, but a single tear gathered and broke free, sliding down her cheek as he touched his lips to hers for the first time in so long. The kiss was sweet and soft, a moment of worship from a man who didn't believe in either sweetness or the gods. She leaned into him, wrapped herself around him, holding herself firmly in the moment because thoughts of the past and the future were equally heartrending. This wasn't real; she knew it deep down inside, with both the beings that were her and not-her. This was a dream, a vision. Their bodies were back at Skywatch; they weren't really making love; nothing was really going to change. But in that instant, in that shiny, glittering instant, she could pretend, if only for a few minutes or an hour, that the hawk was hers as he'd been before.

Before? thought a small, panicked part of her, knowing the impulse went much farther back than just the previous summer. More like a previous lifetime, and that was getting weird even for Alexis. Then he changed the angle of the kiss, took it deeper, and the past, present, and future contracted to a single point, a limitless *now* that picked her up and swept her away. Murmuring agreement, encouragement, she opened to him and let herself fall into the familiar madness, the feelings she'd tried to let go of, but had really only set aside. Being with him once again unlocked those feelings, setting them free to flood her with an ache that was edged with the sharp anger of rejection.

You ditched me, she said with her next kiss. *You didn't want me enough to work out whatever got stuck in your head.* She didn't know what had happened, or how she could've changed the outcome. And really, it didn't matter now, because *now* wasn't real. Still, she wanted to punish him for the pain, wanted to dig into him for hiding the truth, for hiding himself. But the other woman inside her, the one who'd never been clumsy, never been embarrassed, that woman turned the punishment into pleasure, skimming her hands and lips over his body, using the sensitive spots Alexis had found and taking them further, dancing her fingernails on his skin and testing them with her teeth.

Heat spiraled higher, flared hotter, as she and Nate strained together, locked in a combative sort of lovemaking. The air warmed around them and the water heated— or maybe that was their bodies, and the heat they made together as they brought each other to the place where joining became as necessary as breathing.

He entered her, sliding into her on a wash of wetness and a clench of pleasure. His hollow groan echoed deep in his chest, counterpointing her soft cry. Then they were moving together and apart, one against the other, push and pull, push and pull. Alexis braced herself against the rocky spires, feeling the slide of stone without, the slide of his hard flesh within, and around it all the soft wetness of the water and moist air, and the good press of his arms around her as they clung and shuddered.

Then he gripped her hips in his big hands, holding her in place as he began to piston, setting a pace of ruthless masculine pleasure.

"Gods," Alexis whispered, going numb to everything but the sensations that rolled through her. She'd forgotten this, somehow forgotten about the moment when the sex took him over, when he went beyond the civilized veneer to a feral, animal place beyond, where he existed only for his pleasure—and hers.

He drove into her, held her, pinned her, stripping away her defenses and contracting her universe until the only things that existed were the two of them, the points at which their bodies connected, and the thundering pace of his sex.

He held her, loved her, took her over. The orgasm slapped at her, unexpected in its ferocity, which gave her no option, bowing her back and wringing a cry from deep in her throat. Her inner muscles clamped around him, feeling stronger than before, needier. She pumped him, clenched around him, and he cut loose with a roar. The pulse of his flesh within her heightened her response, prolonging the orgasm, drawing it out until she was nothing more than a bundle of neurons coalesced together, throbbing in pleasure. She hung on to the only solid objects nearby, lest she be swept away.

Then the waves passed, fading to an echo, then a fearsome memory.

Alexis clung to him with her face turned from his, her cheek pressed into his shoulder. She didn't dare pull away and look at him, didn't want to see how much the sex had—or hadn't—meant to him. And as much as she tried to tell herself that none of it was real, it'd sure as hell felt real, and the tug at her heart was real.

"Lexie," he said, his voice cracking on the endearment. "I—"

The world lurched, interrupting. The water started to swirl, and a hard, hot wind whipped through the stone chamber, coming from everywhere and nowhere at once.

Alexis heard him shout, and screamed as they were torn apart and sucked down, as everything went to flame and then gray-green, spinning and moving and howling as though they'd insulted the gods themselves. Her heart pounded in her chest, panic slicing through her as she grabbed for something, anything she could hold on to, and found nothing but air. Wind screamed around her, howling, sounding almost like words.

All of a sudden there *were* words, a multitonal voice shouting, "The Volatile must be found!" Then, out of nowhere, a strong hand gripped Alexis's wrist and yanked.

And she was back at Skywatch.

Her consciousness dropped into her body with a jarring thud. She went limp and slid sideways, saved only when Nate jammed his hip against her shoulder and shoved her back into her chair. He was still hanging on to her wrist. Somehow he'd gotten out and dragged her with him.

"Oh, gods." Alexis sagged against him, clung to him, her fingers digging into the heavy muscles of his forearm, over the stark black of his marks. "Oh, holy hell." She looked up at him. "What did you—"

She broke off, seeing in his eyes all of his usual intensity, along with the irritation she alone seemed to bring out. But that was it. She saw nothing of what they'd just done together.

He detached himself from her and stepped away. "What did I . . . what?" he prompted.

Izzy shouldered him aside and started fussing, checking Alexis's color, her pulse, making Alexis acutely aware that they weren't alone, that the other Nightkeepers and their *winikin* were still there in the great room, gathered around her and Nate and the suitcase containing the statuette of Ixchel. There was no temple, no torchlight. No lovemaking.

She swallowed hard. "What did you see?" Which wasn't even close to what she'd been about to say before. "You were in there with me, right? You were there the whole time?"

He frowned. "What whole time?" He looked at Strike. "It was only a few seconds, right?"

The king nodded, but said, "Doesn't mean she didn't

experience something that seemed longer, though. Time acts funny in the barrier.'' He cut his eyes to Alexis. "That was where you wound up, right? In the barrier?''

Her defenses snapped up, born of the insecurities that had ruled too much of her life, and she nodded quickly. "Right. The barrier.''

Strike glanced at Nate, who'd jammed his hands in his pockets and was staring over her head, as though determined to distance himself from the convo. "You, too?''

"Maybe for a few seconds,'' Nate allowed. "Then I got kicked back here, and she followed. Nothing complicated.''

Only it was very, very complicated, Alexis thought, staring down at the statuette, sure now that the woman's face was buried in her hands because she was weeping with heartache . . . and the gut-punching frustration of dealing with magic and men. The artifact had taken her to the barrier, yes, but it'd also taken her someplace else, someplace where she'd met and made love to a man who'd looked and acted like Nate, had made love like Nate, yet somehow wasn't him.

Her hair was dry, and she was wearing the jeans and loose shirt she'd put on before the meeting, not combat gear or wet skin. Yet her body echoed with the effects of having made love. More important, it echoed with having made love with *him*. As much as she'd wanted to hate him in the aftermath of their belly flop of a relationship, she'd been unable to forget that with him sex felt different, echoed different.

Yet it'd either really, truly been a dream that belonged only to her . . . or for some reason he'd blocked it from his conscious mind. He wouldn't lie about something that important. Hell, she was pretty sure he didn't lie about anything; he was scrupulously honest, even when she hated hearing what he had to say.

Which explained absolutely nothing.

"What did you see?'' Strike pressed her. "Did you speak with a *nahwal*?''

"No," Alexis said automatically. Then she paused, remembering the multitonal voice that had shouted at the end. "At least, I don't think I did."

The *nahwals* were sexless, desiccated entities that existed only within the barrier. They embodied the collective wisdom of each bloodline, and could choose to share that wisdom or not, depending on the circumstances. They never lied, but Jade's research suggested they sometimes gave only partial answers, and that they seemed to have an agenda that even the earlier generations of Nightkeepers hadn't understood. One thing was for sure: They spoke with two or more voices combined in harmonic descant.

"You don't seem certain," Nate said, turning back to look at her intently. "What *did* you see?"

"It wasn't what I saw," she evaded, "but what I heard. Just as I was coming back here, a voice said something about finding something volatile." She turned to Jade, who as usual stood at the edge of the group. "Was Ixchel an air goddess?"

The archivist shook her head. "She was—or, rather, *is*—the goddess of rainbows, fertility, and weaving." She paused, looking troubled. "I'm sure I've seen the term *volatile* recently, though, and not in a good way. Let me check into it."

Alexis looked down at the statuette, but didn't touch it. "You think that's what's written in the starscript? Something about this volatile? Maybe we need whatever it is to hold back Camazotz."

Strike hesitated for a moment, then said, "I'll call Anna and see if she can come out a few days early, to translate."

The king's sister, a Mayan studies expert at UT Austin, was staying as far away from the Nightkeepers as possible, coming to Skywatch only during the cardinal days and major ceremonies, and then only because she'd promised to do so in exchange for Red-Boar saving the life of her grad student. Anna made no secret that she wanted nothing to do with the culture and magic she'd been born to, nothing to do with her own destiny.

Sometimes, Alexis thought on a sinking sense of disappointment, *the gods get it wrong*. Which she knew was blasphemy and illogical. But at the same time, how did it make sense to pair up a mismatch like her and Nate, or force someone like Anna to be something she didn't want to be?

CHAPTER FOUR

"A volatile?" Anna frowned at her brother's question, then took a quick look through the cracked-open doorway of her office, making sure she was alone. She didn't want anyone at the university to hear her talking about Mayan myths and demons as though they were real, even if they were. Some divisions of the art history department might encourage funkiness, but not hers. Mayan epigraphy—the study and translation of the ancient glyphs and the legends they told—was serious science. Which, for better or worse, made her the logical person for her brother to call. *Damn it.* "Well," she continued, hoping info was all he wanted for a change, "the volatiles are the thirteen symbols connected with the hours of the day and the thirteen levels of the sky. But they're just symbols, not things or spells. I don't see how they'd help if you're looking to block the death bats."

"The *what*?"

Anna winced at the knowledge gap. "Camazotz is the ruler of the death bats, which are linked, as you might suspect, with death and sacrifice. You need a better researcher. Seriously. She's missing basic stuff your average Google search is going to pull up."

"She's a therapist." There was a bite in Strike's tone now. "And she's practically killing herself trying to catalog the archive, never mind looking up the things we need her to." He didn't add, *And we have a better researcher . . . or we would if you'd get your ass back here where you belong*, but they both knew that was what he was thinking.

Anna, though, was standing firm. She had a husband and a life in the real world, and didn't intend to buy back into the universe that'd killed their parents, into the mythology that would eventually kill them all. It wasn't that she didn't believe in the end-time. It was that she didn't believe a dozen or so half-trained magi were going to make a damned bit of difference determining whether it came or not, or that she could help save the world. Better that she live the next four years the best she could, and pray to the gods for forgiveness when the end came.

Still, though, she owed Strike something. Family mattered, regardless of how dysfunctional. "I'll send Jade some Web links that should help her get up to speed on Camazotz."

"Not good enough. I need you to come out early and read the starscript for us. I need to know what's on the statuette ASAP, in case it's something we can use in the eclipse ceremony," Strike persisted, once again trying to draw Anna back to the world they'd both been born into. She wanted to tell him no, to tell him to call someone else. But like it or not—and she didn't like it one bit—she was the only translator the Nightkeepers could trust.

She touched the yellow, skull-shaped quartz effigy that she wore beneath her shirt even though her seer's powers hadn't so much as twitched since the autumnal equinox. "Fine. I'll move my flight up and try to leave early tomorrow." She hated the thought of being at Skywatch longer than absolutely necessary, but she'd already been planning on being there for the penumbral lunar eclipse, which was a time of great barrier power that the Nightkeepers would try to use for one or more of the bigger spells. A couple of extra days wouldn't kill her.

Strike sighed, the sound coming from deep within his chest. "Thank you." He paused, then said in a different, more tentative tone, "So, are you okay?"

They hadn't talked much since the equinox. She'd

flown home immediately after their return from the intersection. She hadn't even stayed for Red-Boar's funeral, hadn't been able to. Not after he'd bled out in her arms and died with his eyes locked onto hers. The experience had changed her, though, made her more aware of what mattered. She'd gone straight from the airport to her husband's on-campus office in the economics building, shut the door at her back, and had the conversation they'd both been avoiding for months, i.e., the one that started with an accusation and ended with an ultimatum: *Ditch the other woman, whoever the hell she is.*

It hadn't been as easy as that, of course, because Anna had earned her fair share of the blame for the shambles their marriage had become. She'd wanted a baby, because that was what marriage and family was about. Then, when months of not using birth control had stretched to years with no baby and even their first expensive try at in vitro had failed, she'd gotten wrapped up in the failure. As many times as she'd said she didn't blame him, she knew he didn't believe her, knew she hadn't given him reason to believe. So they'd drifted, her to her work, him to his own pursuits. At first it'd been golf and hanging out at the faculty club. After a while she'd realized those were excuses, that he was actually having an affair. And the worst part was she'd been willing to go on that way, telling herself that it was okay their relationship had changed.

Her parents had died when she was fourteen, and her fledgling powers, those of an *itza'at* seer, had forced her to live through the experience with them. She'd relived it over and over in her dreams for years thereafter, until the day she'd left Strike and Jox, moving away to college at the age of twenty, after sticking it out for as long as she'd been able. She'd known even then that she was gone for good. As far as any of them had known back then, the magical backlash of the Solstice Massacre had sealed the barrier for good, averting the 2012 doomsday. She'd thought she was free to live a normal life, and had thrown herself with abandon into doing just that, meet-

ing friends and lovers, and enjoying college, then grad
school.

Always in the back of her mind had been the knowledge that she could have lovers, but wasn't supposed to
marry or have children prior to the end-time. It was one
of the laws Jox had drilled into her head, that she and
Strike had to remain unmarried and unmated. At the
time she'd thought the *winikin* was just being a pain.
Only later, when the barrier reactivated and Jox revealed that there were other Nightkeeper survivors, did
she finally understand. He'd wanted her to stay available
for a Nightkeeper mate, should the barrier reactivate
and the need arise. Whereas she and Strike had survived
because Jox had hidden them in a blood-warded safe
room designed for the royals only, the other, younger
magi had escaped the massacre because they'd been babies, too young to have been through their first binding
ceremonies. That meant the surviving males were all a
good dozen or more years younger than she, which might
not've mattered if she'd stayed in the Nightkeeper milieu. But she hadn't.

Instead she'd gone out into the world. And at twenty-
five, she'd met Dick Catori, a wunderkind economist and
sometimes poet who designed stunt kites as a hobby,
and had taught her to fly them. Standing out in a windy
Texas field with her back pressed against his front and
his clever hands atop hers, showing her how to touch
the lines and tease motion from air, she'd fallen hard
somewhere between the stall and the five-forty flat spin.

She'd moved in with him a month later, married him
six months after that, and hadn't told Jox or Strike for
nearly another year, avoiding the topic during her bian-
nual duty calls. Jox had thrown a fit, Strike had congrat-
ulated her, and she'd spoken to them less and less as
the years passed, and her new, normal life eventually
fell into a pleasing pattern, then a less pleasing one, until
one day she woke up and realized she and Dick were
sleeping in the same house but living separate lives, and
she was too much of a wimp, too afraid of failing at her
marriage, her grand act of rebellion, to do anything about

it. Then the barrier had come back online and Strike had called the Nightkeepers home. Anna had fought the call for as long as she'd been able, but in the end had been forced to return to the life she didn't want, at least part-time. Duty compelled her—and a bargain made with a dead man. But how was she supposed to balance the two pieces of her life?

She couldn't tell Dick about her heritage, because the moment the magic intruded on her normal life it wouldn't be normal anymore. Besides, things had been so much better between them since she'd taken her stand and called him on his infidelity. They were actually talking— really talking—for the first time in a long time. They were having date nights, and working with a therapist. Things weren't perfect, but they were improving. There was no way in hell she was jeopardizing their reconciliation.

She didn't tell Strike any of that, though. She loved her brother, but she didn't really know him anymore, hadn't for a long time. So instead of telling him the truth, she glanced at her watch, intending to make up an excuse to kick him off the phone.

Which was when she realized she didn't need an excuse. She was late for a meeting. Her breath hissed between her teeth. "I've got to go. I'm due in my evil boss's office five minutes ago for Lucius's thesis defense."

"How's he doing?" The question was far from casual.

Knowing that Strike didn't really give a crap about Lucius's defense as long as her senior grad student didn't mention where he'd gotten the scar on his palm, she said, "He doesn't remember going through the transition ritual, or almost becoming a *makol*. Red-Boar's mind block did the trick."

Lucius had almost been dead meat the prior fall, and he didn't even know it, didn't know he was living on probation as far as the Nightkeepers were concerned. Hell, he didn't have a clue that the Nightkeepers really existed. He liked to think they did, liked to believe in the end-time myths most Mayanists dismissed as sensationalism, but she'd deliberately steered him away from the truth, leaving him mired in fiction.

"Good to hear he doesn't remember," Strike said, but he didn't sound convinced. Back before the equinox battle, when Lucius had unwittingly offered himself up on a platter for demon possession, Red-Boar would've sacrificed him, but Strike had made a deal with her: He'd have Red-Boar reverse the *makol* spell if Anna agreed to rejoin the Nightkeepers, at least during the ceremonial days.

Now, she knew, he regretted having made the deal, and considered Lucius a liability. The younger man had undergone the transition spell once already, and his natural inclinations had called upon the *Banol Kax* rather than the gods—which perplexed the hell out of Anna, because Lucius didn't have much in the way of a dark side, but still, it'd happened. And because it had happened once, she knew Strike was worried that it would happen again.

Basically, Lucius was living on her good graces, and the knowledge weighed, especially given the political crap going on in the art history department these days. The department head, Desiree Soo, had never been warm or fuzzy, but she'd grown increasingly critical over the past half year, particularly when it came to the Mayan studies department. Anna couldn't prove it, but she was pretty sure Desiree had chased off her last intern, Neenee, who'd taken off around Christmas, leaving only a terse e-mail of nonexplanation. Since then, Anna's lab had had reimbursement requests kicked back from admin over tiny quibbles, room assignments were constantly getting screwed up, and Anna had found herself loaded down with intro-level lectures that were usually handed straight to the TAs. And then there was Lucius's thesis defense.

Desiree had been acting professionally enough back when Lucius had asked her to chair his thesis committee. Given the way she'd been behaving lately, though, Anna could pretty much guarantee there was going to be a problem.

Sighing, feeling a hundred years old rather than her own thirty-nine, Anna said, "Seriously. I've gotta go."

"I'll see you tomorrow. Call Jox with your flight info and he'll meet you at the airport."

"Will do." She hung up and headed for the dragon's lair.

Okay, so it wasn't literally Desiree's lair—they were meeting in the conference room across the hall from the department head's office—but Anna had the distinct feeling she was headed into enemy territory as she stepped through the doors. She was the last one in, which meant the entire committee was arranged on one side of the conference table, all facing a slump-shouldered Lucius.

Desiree was seated in the center of the long side of the conference table, flanked on either side by the lower-ranking committee members. She almost always wore long-sleeved, high-collared shirts in jewel tones that enhanced the red highlights in her hair, accessorizing the outfits with a heavy silver cuff on her right wrist. The cuff was embossed with Egyptian hieroglyphs, and Anna didn't remember ever seeing her without it. Desiree was long and lean and gorgeous, with high cheekbones, almond-shaped eyes, and shoulder-length hair that fell pin-straight from an off-center widow's peak. Her eyes were an unusually pale hazel that might've looked dreamy on another woman, but somehow managed to look vaguely reptilian in her face.

Or maybe Anna was projecting on that one. As far as she was concerned, the woman was a bitch, pure and simple.

The other committee members included a stout, bearded Greek mythology expert named—ironically—Thor; a cheerful, round-cheeked classics professor named Holly; and a gaunt, aged relic of an art historian whom everyone called Dr. Young. Anna was pretty sure that wasn't his name, more of a joke that'd stuck. The committee members acknowledged Anna when she came through the door, with nods from the two men, a little wave from Holly. Desiree made a mean little moue.

Lucius, on the other hand, whipped around in his chair and gave her a *where the hell have you been?* look liberally dosed with nerves.

He was tall and skinny, and typically moved with an awkward sort of grace. Now, though, sitting folded into the conference room chair, he looked pointy and angular, like a praying mantis that someone had bent the wrong way. Or maybe that was the strangeness of seeing him in a shirt and tie rather than his usual grad student uniform of bar-logo tee and ratty jeans. He'd traded his sandals for hiking boots that made a stab at formality, and somewhere over the past twelve hours had subjected his normally shaggy brown hair to an unfortunate trim that screamed "eight-dollar walk-in."

The overall effect was one of quiet desperation.

Lucius had grown up in middle America, a dreamer misfit in a large extended family of jocks. He'd escaped to the university on a scholarship and had discovered Mayan studies when he'd taken an undergrad intro course on pre-Columbian civilization as a frosh, in a bid to avoid the foreign language requirement. In the nearly ten years since—four years as an undergrad and almost six as Anna's grad student—he'd proven to be both the best and most frustrating student she'd ever dealt with. He was an intuitive epigrapher, able to tease out the most worn inscriptions and decipher them into translations that stood up remarkably well to scrutiny from even the toughest of critics, including her. Unfortunately, that same level of intuition caused him to see patterns where there weren't any—or, as in the case with the Nightkeeper myths, in places where she'd rather he not see them. When he saw such patterns, his scientific method sometimes went out the window while he focused on the answer he'd convinced himself was right, searching for evidence that proved his theory and ignoring anything that suggested otherwise.

That was *not* a good trait in a scientist, regardless of the field. Add to it his penchant for playing fast and loose with personal-property laws—like the time he'd broken into her office and stolen the codex fragment bearing the transition spell that'd nearly turned him into a *makol*—and he was something of a loose cannon.

The thing was, he was *her* loose cannon. He was sweet and funny, and when things had been at their worst with

Dick, Lucius had been there for her to lean on. And if there had been a spark or two, neither of them had acted on the temptation. Instead they had let it deepen their working friendship until it was a strong, steady piece of her life. That, along with knowing he wouldn't have come into contact with the codex fragment if she'd been more careful about keeping it hidden, meant there had been no real choice to be made when she'd faced Strike and Red-Boar over Lucius's rigor-contorted body, while his eyes flickered from luminous green to hazel and back. She'd traded her normal life for his, and though she regretted the choice, she wouldn't undo it. Nor would she admit to Strike just how much Lucius had changed in the months since his partial possession, becoming withdrawn and secretive. Hell, she was doing her best not to admit it to herself. What she hadn't been able to ignore, however, was how Lucius had started focusing his research more on the things she'd managed to steer him away from in the past . . . like the zero date, and the few sketchy rumors of a superhuman race of warrior-magi sworn to protect mankind.

She'd made him promise not to go there during his thesis defense, knowing that Desiree would crucify him if he so much as breathed a word about things the establishment considered barely a step up from tinfoil hats and Area 51, namely the 2012 doomsday and the Nightkeepers. Which was why she sent him a warning look and mouthed, *You promised.*

He nodded, but there was something in his eyes that made her wonder whether he was accepting her warning or telling her to mind her own damn business.

"Since we're finally all here," Desiree said pointedly, "I'd like to get started. If that's okay with Anna, of course."

Bitch, Anna thought, but didn't say. Instead she took the chair beside Thor and nodded. "By all means, let's get started."

By the time Lucius was about twenty minutes into his presentation, Anna was starting to relax a little, because he was sticking to the script, thank the gods. Then Desiree held up a hand, interrupting.

Lucius broke off in the middle of explaining his translation of a panel deep within the Pyramid of Kulkulkan at Chichén Itzá. "Yes?"

Desiree pointed to a badly eroded glyph at the lower right corner of the screen. "What about that one?"

Anna stiffened and tried to catch Lucius's eye. *Don't do it,* she mouthed. *Say you don't know.*

He avoided her gaze, but answered carefully enough. "There's some debate about that particular glyph."

"We're working on it," Anna interjected. "As you can see, it's not in the best condition, which unfortunately means that we may never have a conclusive answer. Or maybe we'll find a second occurrence of the glyph in the future. Regardless, it should be considered outside the scope of this project." Which was academia-speak for *back off, bitch.*

"Your opinion is noted, Professor Catori." Desiree didn't even glance at Anna; she kept her unblinking focus on Lucius, a predator sensing weakness. "However, it's not really a question of scope; it's a question of propriety. I'm well aware of what Mr. Hunt thinks this glyph represents, and frankly I'm not convinced that the university is best represented by an academician who publicly defends the validity of the Nightkeeper myth."

Lucius's color drained, and he sent Anna an *oh, shit* look.

"With all due respect," she said quickly, "that is absolutely beyond the scope of this thesis. There's no reference to that particular myth anywhere in the text or supporting material."

"With all due respect," Desiree parroted, "it's my call what is and isn't within the scope of this committee meeting." She shuffled through a small pile of papers, pointedly pausing at what looked like a printed screen capture of a message board dialogue. Glancing at Lucius, she said, "You go by the screen name 'LuHunt' on a number of the 2012 doomsday bulletin boards, right?"

Anna would've protested again, but didn't figure it'd get her anywhere. The best she could do would be to sit back and let this play out, hoping Thor, Holly, and Dr. Young would see there was an agenda at work that had nothing to do with Lucius's skills as a Mayanist . . . and further hoping they'd say as much when she brought a formal university complaint against Desiree.

Lucius looked at her as if he expected her to say something, to defend him, but what more could she do? To an extent, he'd dug his own grave. She'd told him to stay the hell away from that crap until after his defense. If he'd been posting on message boards with the doomsdayers, there wasn't much she could do about it now.

When he saw there would be no help forthcoming, his expression darkened, something shifting in his face so he almost looked like a different person—older and less open—as he met Desiree's smirk with a glare. "I don't see how my online presence should concern this committee. I've never put myself forth as a representative of this university or a member of Professor Catori's staff while on those boards."

Desiree arched one elegant eyebrow. "Shall I take your nonanswer of my question as an answer in and of itself?"

He hesitated so long that Anna thought he was going to play it smart. Then he sat up straight and squared his shoulders, suddenly looking less like a praying mantis and more like a taller-than-average guy who'd broadened out through the shoulders and gained twenty pounds or so of muscle while she hadn't been paying attention. Before she could process that realization, he said to Desiree, "I believe in the Nightkeeper myth. So what?"

Anna winced, even though she'd warned him. Not that having an out-there opinion was a crime, but with Desiree gunning for the entire Mayan studies department and not being real picky about the actual legalities of the matter, he was effectively throwing himself on the academic sword.

Desiree tapped her manicured fingernails—which were pale mauve, rather than the more appropriate bloodred—against her lips. "You actually believe that ancient magicians from Atlantis—*Atlantis*, mind you—survived the flooding that came the last time this so-called Great Conjunction rolled through, twenty-six thousand years ago, and went on to shape, not just the Mayan Empire, but the Egyptians before them?"

"There are demonstrable parallels," Lucius said before Anna could intervene. "For example, the dating of the Maya Long Count calendar begins circa 3114 B.C., which is well before the Maya were a people, before even their predecessors, the Olmec, started thinking about being more than scattered pastoralists and hunter-gatherers. It was, however, right about the time the first ancient Egyptian hieroglyphs started popping up, which many people consider the beginning of legitimate human civilization."

Thor perked up a little. "You're talking about von Däniken?"

Anna cringed. The Dutch pseudoscientist's publication of *Chariots of the Gods?* in the sixties had been good in that it'd popularized the idea of connections and parallels amongst a number of ancient civilizations, prompting "real" researchers to investigate the possibility of transoceanic voyages long before the time of the Vikings. On the downside, it'd also popularized what Lucius often called the *Stargate* effect, i.e., the notion that most of early human civilization had been shaped by aliens.

Welcome to the tinfoil-hat zone.

"Not von Däniken per se, though he wasn't entirely wrong," Lucius told Thor. "The Nightkeepers were—maybe even are—far more than that. They were mentors, magi who lived in parallel with several of the most successful early civilizations, teaching them math and science, especially astronomy." There was a subtle shift in Lucius's face, making his features sharper, more mature as he said, "The commonalities between the Egyptians and Maya are too close to be coincidental—both religions were based on the sun and sky, and on the movement of the stars."

Thor frowned. "I thought the Egyptians worshiped a single sun god. The Maya were polytheistic."

"Exactly." Lucius thumped the table, making his laptop jump. "The Cult of the Sun God was conceived by the pharaoh Akhenaton, who forcibly converted all of ancient Egypt from their long-held pantheistic religion to his new god, Aten. His guards slaughtered the priests of the old religion and defaced all of their temples and effigies, destroying millennia of worship in the space of a few years." Leaning forward in his enthusiasm, he said, "That was when the Nightkeepers fled Egypt—the survivors, anyway. Most of them were killed in Akhenaton's religious 'cleansing,' but a few survived. Those survivors eventually made their way to Central America, where they stumbled on the Olmec, who were just beginning to centralize, and were ripe for the teachings the Nightkeepers brought. Over time the Olmec, with the Nightkeepers' help, eventually bloomed into the Mayan Empire. It's . . ." He paused, then said, "It's perfect. It all fits. Just look at the time line."

Dead silence greeted that pronouncement.

For a second, Anna thought she caught a glint of satisfaction in Desiree's eyes, but the dragon actually sounded sympathetic when she said, "That was what we were afraid of, Lucius. Given that, along with the disciplinary problems you've had in the past, your mediocre GPA, and the general lack of substantiated evidence underpinning your thesis, it is the opinion of this committee that you should not be granted the degree of doctor of philosophy in art history at this time."

Anna wasn't altogether surprised, but the punch of it still drove the breath from her lungs. When she got her wind back, she said, "I wish to formally appeal this decision."

"Of course you do," Desiree said, sounding as if she couldn't care less. "The request is noted." Shuffling her papers into a pile, she rose, indicating that the meeting was over.

She and the others filed out, leaving Anna and Lucius alone in the conference room. He hadn't said anything since Desiree had made her decision. Anna would've thought it was shock and denial, except that neither of those things was in his face. Instead he looked . . . pissed. Resentful. Like this was somehow her fault.

"What's that glare for?" she snapped, annoyed.

"Please. Like you don't know." He stood, towering

over her, and for the first time she was aware of him not just as a man, but as someone significantly bigger than she. "I just got mowed down in the cross fire of the art history department pissing contest you and the Dragon Lady have going. You think I should be happy about that? Spare me."

He gathered up his papers and the handouts the others had left behind, shoving them into his knapsack with jerky, angry motions.

Anna stood. She wanted to go to him, wanted to touch his arm, hug him, something to bridge the gap that'd grown between them. *What happened to us?* she wanted to say. *What happened to you?* But it didn't take an *itza'at* seer or a mind-bender to know he wouldn't welcome the contact or the questions. There was something seriously bad going on with him, far worse than she'd suspected.

"Lucius, what's wrong? You can talk to me." She reached out but didn't touch him, just made the gesture and left it up to him whether to step toward her or away.

Something flashed in his eyes: guilt, maybe, or sadness. But it was quickly swept away by disbelief, then mirth. "Do you actually not know? Is it possible you're really that dense?" He moved toward her, but didn't take her proffered hand. Instead he leaned in and said in a low, angry voice, "Think about it, Anna. The crap with Desiree started right about the time you came back from your little mental-health break in New Mexico, and your not-so-saintly husband swore off other women, right? You do the math."

He straightened and jerked the knapsack over his shoulder. Tucking his laptop under one arm, he strode away, not looking back.

Oh, hell.

Anna didn't move; she couldn't. She was trapped, not in the soul-searching that should've followed Lucius's revelation, but in something that was a thousand times worse because it came with pictures and a sound track.

The vision caught her unawares, slamming through her subconscious blocks as if they were nothing, hammering her with the sounds of lovemaking, and the sight of her husband and Desiree twined together in the sort of raw, unabashed sex that Anna didn't remember having had with him in years. Shock blasted through her. Heartbreak. She'd known he'd had a lover, had dealt with it as best she could when they'd reconciled after the fall equinox. But seeing it, seeing the look on his face as he . . . She couldn't bear it.

"No!" She clawed the air, slapping at the images that were buried deep in her soul, in the seat of her magic. "Gods, *no!*"

Pain seared the skin between her breasts, where the skull-shaped effigy rested. Inert in the months since Strike had returned it to her, the pendant's power flared now, hot and hard. More images crashed through her, snippets of them together, sometimes naked, sometimes not. To her surprise she realized it was worse seeing them together clothed, strolling arm in arm along streets she didn't recognize, telling her that they'd traveled together, that his frequent business trips hadn't been all business.

On some level she'd known that, accepted it. But she hadn't known—and damn well couldn't accept—that it'd been Desiree. Her boss. Her nemesis. Worse, Anna's gut—or maybe the magic?—told her that Desiree's undeclared war on her was more than jealousy or jilted love. The bitch thought she was still in the running . . . which meant she had some reason to think it. Dick had left the door open, damn him.

"No." This time the word was little more than a broken sound, a sob that hurt Anna's ribs as the burning power drained and the images faded. Eventually she became aware of her surroundings, aware that she was in a conference room with the door open, and there were people passing by in the hall.

New grief tore through her at the realization that the safe security of her "normal" job was as much an illusion as her "happy" marriage. She'd forsaken her brother and the responsibilities of her royal blood in order to be a regular person and be married to the man she loved, yet that life was coming unraveled just as the Nightkeepers were reconnecting.

Fate, she thought. *Destiny. There are no coincidences.* This was the gods' will, their way of punishing her for turning her back on her duties, their way of reminding her where she belonged.

"I give up," she said to the gods as her heart cracked into a thousand pieces, each sharper than the last. "You win."

She crept to her office, moving slow, feeling sore. Grabbing her purse, she headed for her car, a four-year-old Lexus that Dick kept wanting her to trade in for something newer and shinier. Once she was on the road, she turned away from home. Or rather, she turned away from the home she'd made with her husband and headed toward the one she'd grown up in. The one hundreds of people had died in, though she had survived, a small piece of her always wondering why she'd been spared and other, better, more dedicated Nightkeepers hadn't.

Sometimes the phrase *the will of the gods* didn't even begin to cover it. But, she thought through a sheen of tears as she hit the highway and put the hammer down, Skywatch was a stiff fifteen-hour drive away. Maybe by the time she got there, she would've figured out what the hell she was doing with her life, and why.

After the thoroughly weird moment when Alexis had come out of her statuette-induced fugue, Nate shut himself up in his three-room suite in the residential wing of the mansion, ostensibly to get some work done for Hawk Enterprises. That was bullshit, though: first, because he was making zero headway on *Viking Warrior 6* and had been for some time, and second, because his real motivation had been to get the hell away from the crowd and away from Alexis's puzzlement.

She'd been looking at him the way she had right after they'd broken up, like she didn't know what'd just happened, or why.

Sure, he'd given her a reason back then—several of them, in fact, starting with, "It's not you, it's me," and ending with, "My life is too complicated right now to start something serious." All of which had been true, as far as it went, but it hadn't begun to touch on the reality, which had been more along the lines of, "You scare the shit out of me," and, "I want to make my own choices and can't get enough distance from all the crap that's flying around in our lives right now to figure out if we're good together or just convenient." He'd just told her it was over, and hadn't let her see that the decision tore him up, made him mean and surly, not because he'd known it was better for both of them that way, but because it sucked knowing she was a few doors down the hall and he'd given up the right to knock. Hell, he'd not only given it up, he'd taken it out behind the woodshed and shot the shit out of it, all in the name of free will. *Goddamn it.*

None of which explained what'd happened with the Ixchel statuette, he reminded himself when a low burn of lust grabbed onto his gut and dug in deep. And the here and now was what he should be concentrating on, not what'd happened in the past.

What the hell had Alexis seen in the barrier? Obviously he'd been in whatever vision she'd had, and from the way she'd been looking at him he had to figure it'd been a sex fantasy. Which meant . . . ?

Damned if he knew, but as far as he was concerned, it changed nothing.

"So stop thinking about it and get the hell to work," he muttered, glaring at his laptop screen. The storyboard for *Viking Warrior 6: Hera's Mate* had been three-quarters done on the day Strike had shown up at Hawk Enterprises, asked Nate about his medallion, and given him his first taste of magic. Now, because he'd dumped a bunch of shit out of the middle, the game was less than half-finished, and he wasn't sure he liked what was left.

Hera was a goddess and a hottie, a leader of her people, a magic user and a prophet. She deserved—hell, demanded—a mate who was worthy of her, and one who could kick ass just as well as, if not better than, she could. The gamers needed a strong, interesting character to get behind, and Nate needed to give her a fitting match. And yeah, maybe—probably—he was projecting, but so what? He was the boss. He could get away with crap like that, as long as he produced.

Right now, though, he wasn't producing. The hero that his head story guy, Denjie, and his other writers had come up with originally had been a solid character the gamers would've liked well enough. Problem was, Nate didn't think Hera would've given him the time of day; the dude had been an idiot, with a vocabulary of approximately six words that weren't swears.

Hera, for all her ass-kicking prowess, had a spiritual side as well.

So Nate had taken over the project and blown up the guy's story line. While he was in there, he'd morphed the hero from blond to dark, and taken him from meat-head to something a little more refined. He'd ditched the guy's name—who the hell thought Hera would fall for someone named Dolph? *Please.* He'd put Hera and Nameless together, let them fight it out a little, and then, just when things had been getting good and the two of them were teaming up to go after the main bad guy . . . Nate had stalled.

He knew what ought to happen next, what the story-board said should happen next, and it sounded like a pile of contrived, clichéd shit.

"Get a grip on yourself," he said to himself, or maybe to the characters that lived inside the humming laptop. "Contrived, clichéd shit sells; it's a fact of life. The gamers aren't looking for originality; they want something that looks familiar but a little different, something challenging but not impossible. You've done it a hundred times before. What makes this any different?"

He didn't want to look too closely at himself to find the answer, and damn well knew it. Which was why, when there was a soft knock at the door to his suite, he was relieved rather than annoyed, even though he had a pretty good idea who it was going to be: his *winikin* coming by for another round of *This Is Your Life, Nate Blackhawk.*

Sure enough, when he opened the door he found Carlos standing in the hallway.

"Hey." Nate stepped back and waved his assigned *winikin* through the door. "Come on in." He didn't figure he could avoid the convo, so he might as well get it over with. Maybe they could even get a few things settled. Or not.

Carlos was a short, stocky guy in his mid-sixties who wore snap-studded shirts, Wranglers, and a big-buckled belt with the ease of someone who actually was a cowboy, rather than just pretending to be one because the clothes were cool. His salted dark hair was short and no-nonsense, and his nose took a distinct left-hand bend, either from bulldogging a calf or losing a bar fight, depending on which story Nate believed.

On his forearm Carlos wore the three glyphs of his station: a coyote's head representing his original bound bloodline, the *aj-winikin* glyph that depicted a disembodied hand cupping a sleeping child's face, and a hawk that was a smaller version of the one on Nate's own forearm. If either Sven or Nate died, their glyphs would disappear from the *winikin*'s arm in a flash of pain. That was a sobering thought, as was the realization that back before the massacre, each *winikin* had worn one glyph for each member of their bound bloodline, in numbers so large the marks had extended in some cases across their chests and down their torsos, reflecting the might of the Nightkeepers.

Now each *winikin* wore a single bloodline mark, aside from Carlos and Jox, who each had two.

Carlos had escaped the massacre with his infant charge, Coyote-Seven, and stayed on the move as the *winikin*'s imperative dictated, making sure the young boy remained safe from the *Banol Kax*. Eventually, they had wound up in Montana, where Carlos had changed Coyote-Seven's name to Sven and taken a job as a ranch manager. Eventually he'd married a human woman and they'd had a daughter, Cara. By the time the barrier reactivated, Cara had been in her last year of college, her mother had died of cancer, and Sven had been wreck diving off the Carolina coast, all but estranged from his *winikin*'s family.

There was something there, Nate knew, having seen the subtle tension between Sven and Carlos, and the overt tension between Sven and Cara, who'd been pressed into service as the Sven's *winikin* when Carlos had transferred his blood tie to Nate. Not long after they'd all arrived at Skywatch, Sven had ordered Cara to leave, claiming he didn't need her, didn't want her. Cara had seemed relieved. Carlos had been devastated.

Quite honestly, Nate didn't even want to know that much, but it was damn difficult to avoid gossip in a place like Skywatch. Besides, he was pretty sure Sven's rejection of Cara—which was how it must've seemed to her dignified, tradition-first father—was part of what made Carlos push Nate so hard when it came to matters of propriety and prophecy, and why he found Nate incredibly frustrating.

"Have a seat." Nate waved the *winikin* to one of the two chairs in his small living room, which contained a couch and chairs, with a flat-panel TV stretching across one wall, and wire racks holding the latest gaming consoles of each format.

Carlos remained standing just inside the door. "What really happened today?"

Nate was tempted to fake misunderstanding, but that'd just draw out the pain, so he turned both palms up in a *who the hell knows?* gesture and said, "It was exactly how I told Strike and the others. Alexis touched the statue and blanked. I was the closest one to her, so I grabbed on to pull her away, and followed her instead. We were in the barrier for only a few seconds; then we were out. Nothing more sinister than that."

But the *winikin*'s eyes narrowed on his. "Did you actually see her in the barrier?"

"I'm not even sure I was all the way into the barrier," Nate said, going with honesty because there didn't seem to be a good reason not to. "I got a flash of the barrier mist, but never actually landed, and then I was back here at Skywatch. It was more like a CD skip or something, where the sound cuts out for a second and the music comes back farther down the line."

"Or," Carlos said slowly, his eyes never leaving Nate's, "maybe your mind chose to block off whatever you experienced."

"You think I'm hiding something?"

"Not intentionally, maybe. But Alexis definitely saw

something more, and she seems to think you did too. What if you did and can't remember it?"

Something quivered deep in Nate's gut, but he shook his head. "There are an awful lot of 'what-ifs' I could pull out of my ass around here. That doesn't mean any of them are true."

Carlos tipped his head. "Why are you fighting this so hard?" And by *this*, they both knew he didn't mean just the vision-that-wasn't.

"We've had this argument before. Neither of us ever wins," Nate said, dropping into one of the chairs, suddenly very tired of it all. He pulled on the chain that hung around his neck, withdrawing the hawk medallion from beneath his shirt.

His own personal amulet-to-be-named-at-a-later-date, the medallion was a flat metal disk etched on each side with a design that looked like the hawk bloodline glyph if he tipped it one way, a man if he tipped it another. It had been the only identifying thing he'd been wearing when he'd been dumped at Chicago's Lying-In Hospital, aside from the words *My name is Nathan Blackhawk*, which had been carefully printed on his forehead in pen.

It hadn't been until the prior year that he'd learned his abandonment had been shitty bad luck, that his *winikin* had died of injuries he'd sustained during the massacre, and hadn't been able to get a message to any of the other survivors before he'd died. Since each *winikin*'s imperative in the aftermath of a massacre was to keep his or her Nightkeeper charge alive and hidden, nobody had come looking for Nate. He'd dropped into the system, and from there to juvie, and then a short stint at Greenville for grand theft auto, before he'd straightened up and pulled it together to make himself into the successful entrepreneur he'd become.

He'd done that with the help of a social worker whose hide had proven tougher than his. Not the Nightkeepers, not the *winikin*, and not the gods. It'd been *his* choice to straighten out, *his* choice to succeed.

"Why don't you ever ask about them?" Carlos asked softly, and there was an *aha* look in his eyes that made

Nate wish he'd kept the medallion where it belonged: out of sight and mind.

"Because they didn't make me what I am. I did that."

"Are you so sure?"

"That'll be all for tonight," Nate said, his voice clipped with anger, which was pretty much how all of their convos eventually ended. But when the *winikin* turned and headed for the door, Nate cursed himself and said, "Carlos?"

The *winikin* turned and raised an eyebrow.

"Have you guys asked Alexis exactly what she saw?"

"Isabella is doing that right now," Carlos said, but with a look that suggested he would've rather had anyone else in the world be doing the asking. Which Nate could understand, sort of, because if Alexis sometimes acted like an overambitious brownnose, it was largely because that was what her *winikin* had raised her to be.

Which, Nate realized, glancing at his laptop as Carlos left the room, was one of the fundamental differences between Alexis and Hera: Alexis had a *winikin*, while Hera had grown up on her own. Just like he had.

CHAPTER FIVE

Vibrating with excess energy after a good meal and a short postmagic nap, Alexis headed for the pool an hour or so after dinner, intending to work off her frustrations. She could've used the gym that took up a good chunk of the lower level of the mansion, but that was where she and Nate had initially hooked up, the night after they'd each jacked into the barrier for the first time, gaining their bloodline marks and a serious case of the hornies. Which meant the gym and its ghosts were out.

Besides, she realized as she shucked out of her yoga pants and zippered hoodie and dumped them on a pool chair, baring her body in a decent one-piece, swimming a few hundred laps or so would not only wash away the nonexistent evidence of the sexual encounter she and Nate hadn't had, it would give her an excuse for the uncharacteristic aches in her inner thighs and the hollowness in her core.

The heated pool water was warmer than the air, and steam rose softly from the surface, making her think of the barrier mists, and Nate's insistence that nothing had happened.

"And you so need to get out of your own head," she said aloud, then dove in cleanly. After growing up very near the Newport beaches, with friends who'd brought her along to the country clubs as their guest, she was nearly as at home in the water as on land, and quickly fell into the rhythm of laps.

The pool was located at the back of the mansion in a rectangular alcove flanked on either side by the residential and archive wings, and fronted by the big glass doors of the sunken great room. The open side looked over the ball court, with the ceiba tree and training hall off to one side, the small cottages where the Nightkeeper families used to live off to the other. In the distance, lost in the darkness, the canyon walls were studded with Pueblo ruins she'd visited only once, staying away thereafter because the place gave her the creeps.

Nightkeeper traditions were one thing. Indian burial mounds were another. Besides, the pueblo was Rabbit's territory, and most of the Nightkeepers left the kid more or less alone, not because they didn't like him, but because he seemed to prefer solitude.

Relieved to let her mind skip from one thought to the next, as long as none of them were dark haired and amber eyed, Alexis was on lap number twenty when she heard Izzy call her name.

A large part of her wanted to keep swimming—or maybe dive down and hold her breath for a while, and pretend the rest of the world didn't exist. She just wasn't in the mood for conversation. But duty to—and love for—the woman who'd raised her had Alexis stopping to tread water. "Hey," she called softly to her *winikin*, who stood by the edge of the pool holding her robe and a towel. "You need me?"

Izzy nodded. "I thought we should talk."

The *winikin* was petite and ultrafeminine, with long dark hair caught back in a French braid that was as elegant as it was practical. Wearing trim slacks and a soft button-down that was about as casual as she ever got, Izzy looked put-together and in control.

In contrast, Alexis was a scattered mess. "I know," she said, but what she really meant was *damn it*. She'd wanted to avoid this convo, at least until after she'd gotten a good night's sleep, and preferably after she'd made the trip to New Orleans and acquired the sacred relic from the witch. Not only because they needed the artifact and the demon prophecy, but because she was hoping that spending the day alone with Nate would remind her why the two of them didn't work as a couple, namely that he was an arrogant, detached, egotistical jerk who didn't want any of the same things she did, didn't believe in the things she believed.

"Come on out. You'll shrivel." Izzy held up the robe and towel, her voice making it more of an order than a suggestion.

Alexis sighed and obeyed her *winikin*, mostly because there was no point in picking a fight just to blow off some steam. Her sense of peace was gone, her hope of burning through the restless, edgy energy pretty much shot. She might as well dry off and deal with Izzy.

The very thought gave her pause. Since when did she "deal" with Izzy? The two of them were closer than most mother-daughter pairs, and had stayed good friends through the ups and downs of teenagerdom and life thereafter. They'd dealt with things together, not one against the other, even after Izzy had revealed the truth about Alexis's parents and her role as protector and conscience, not just godmother.

But as Alexis climbed out of the pool, shivering as the crisp February air rapidly chilled the water on her skin, she realized that she and her *winikin* were back on opposite sides of one of their few true disagreements, a battle they'd thought had turned into a moot point months ago: the issue of Nate Blackhawk.

"Thanks." Alexis took the towel and dried off, then pulled on the robe, which was a thick terry-cloth indulgence with a pleasing nap and drape. Belting it securely at her waist and pulling the lapels close across her chest, needing the sense of being clothed, of being armored, she sat in one of the plastic chairs that was set around the long poolside table that served the Nightkeepers for everything from picnics to councils of war.

Izzy sat opposite her, folding her hands one atop the other. "Okay, no more evasions. What did you really see when you touched the statuette?"

Alexis thought about continuing to avoid the question,

but knew from experience that she wouldn't be able to hold out very long. Izzy wasn't just gorgeous and graceful; she had a sort of sixth sense when it came to her charge, an almost preternatural ability to tell when something was—or soon would be—bothering her. So instead of ducking, Alexis said, "Were Gray-Smoke and Two-Hawk lovers?"

There was a beat of shocked silence before Izzy said, "Absolutely not—they could barely stand each other, and she loved your father. Why in the gods' names would you even think something like that?"

Because when I dream, I can't tell if I'm myself, my mother, or someone else, some sort of me existing in a parallel reality where I grew up so much better than I did in this one, Alexis thought, but didn't say, because she didn't want to get into the dreams. Hell, she didn't really want to get into what'd happened earlier in the day. Gods knew, she hadn't fully processed it herself. But because she depended on Izzy for perspective, even when she didn't agree with the other woman's opinion, she said, "I've been getting . . . I guess you could call them flashes of a man and woman together. Sometimes I think it's me and Nate, but other times it's different, like it's us but not."

The *winikin*'s eyes sharpened. "These flashes are sexual in nature?"

"Um. Yeah." Quickly, feeling beyond awkward, Alexis sketched out the scene she'd found herself in earlier that day, describing the stone chamber and the water, skimming over the sexual details for both their sakes.

Izzy frowned. "Maybe it wasn't Blackhawk. Maybe it was someone else and your brain filled in the last man you were with."

"Meaning if I hadn't slept with Nate, it would've been Aaron?" Alexis thought of the charming prick she'd dumped just before Izzy revealed to her that she was a Nightkeeper. She tried to picture Aaron Worth, heir, philanderer, and world traveler, in the vision she'd had while touching the statuette of Ixchel, and failed miserably. "Maybe," she said, but she wasn't buying it.

A new gleam had entered Izzy's eyes. "You should

have Jade pull some of the *itza'at* spells for you. Your aunt and a couple of cousins had the sight.''

"I'm not a seer. I don't have a talent beyond the warrior's mark.''

"You don't know that for sure.''

"If I'm an *itza'at*, then it wasn't a case of my brain plugging in my latest lover," Alexis countered, fixing her *winikin* with a look. "Which probably isn't what you wanted to hear.''

Izzy looked away, refusing to comment. In the distance a coyote howled, sounding mournful and alone.

"You ready to tell me what you've got against Blackhawk?" Alexis pressed, though she'd never gotten far with the question before. "You raised me to want to be the best at everything, right? So why wouldn't you want me allied with another Nightkeeper? Gods know my magic could use some help.''

"He's untrustworthy," Izzy said, though Alexis got the distinct feeling there was more to it than that. "He already tossed you over once. Why would you go back there?''

"Lack of options?" Alexis said wryly, though she didn't mean it, not really. What was—or rather had been—between her and Nate had always been way more complicated than simple chemistry. She'd known his medallion before she'd ever met him, and had a feeling he'd recognized her on some level, though she'd never gotten him to admit it. And while their temperaments and priorities were very different, the sex had been easy . . . and phenomenal. Why shouldn't she wonder whether it was worth another try, especially after her vision?

But Izzy wagged a finger at her. "Don't settle.''

"But the magic—''

"I taught you better," the *winikin* interrupted. "Find your own magic. Don't put that on a mate, or you'll only be disappointed.''

For a second Alexis thought she saw something in the other woman's expression. "You sound like you're speaking from personal experience. Would that be you or my mother?" When the *winikin* said nothing, Alexis knew she'd hit a chord. Pressing, she said, "Is this about my father?"

She bore her mother's bloodline name and glyph, not her father's, which was highly unusual, and Izzy always avoided mentioning the man who'd sired her, except to say that her parents had loved each other. All Alexis really knew about her father was that he'd been a mage of the star bloodline, and he'd died a few months before the massacre.

"He has nothing to do with this or you," Izzy said, her expression going grim. "He was a good man who wanted only the best for you and your mother." But then her face softened and she reached across the picnic table to grip Alexis's hands in her own. "Just please promise me you won't act based on any of these visions until you've talked to somebody about them."

"Like who? In case you haven't noticed, part of the reason we're having trouble figuring out what the hell happened today is because we don't have a seer. Which means I can't exactly ask a seer."

"The eclipse ceremony is in a couple of days. Anna will be here. Talk to her."

Anna was an *itza'at*; it was true. But she couldn't control her visions, and really, really didn't like talking about magic. Not exactly a primo source of info. But Alexis nodded, mostly to appease her *winikin*. "Fine. I'll talk to her."

"And you won't make any decisions until then?"

Alexis snorted. "Nate and I are headed to New Orleans tomorrow to buy a knife from a wannabe witch who calls herself Mistress Truth. We'll be lucky if we don't kill each other on the plane ride, never mind finding time for some one-on-one." Still, she felt a kick of excitement at the prospect of the trip, and the thought of Nate seeing her at her best—negotiating a purchase. Which just went to show that she so wasn't over him, despite what she kept telling herself.

"Promise me," Izzy said, her voice low.

"Fine, I promise I won't do anything about the vision," Alexis said, tempering it with a mental, *for now, anyway*.

Since her swimming mojo had been thoroughly disrupted, she exchanged good-nights with Izzy and headed back to her room to read over the references Jade had found to the Order of Xibalba. Sitting on the elegant gray sofa she'd had shipped down from the city, Alexis started reading the summary report Jade had pulled together.

Strike seemed to think the enemy mage might have something to do with the Xibalbans, while Jox kept insisting the order was nothing more than a bogeyman legend the Nightkeepers and *winikin* had used to scare the crap out of their kids and keep them more or less behaving. But eventually Jox had admitted that the legend, like so many others, was rooted in fact. The Order of Xibalba *had* existed, and its members had been seriously bad news.

More important, they'd been marked with a quatrefoil glyph that represented the entrance to hell. Which meant . . . what? Was the guy she'd gone up against a surviving member of the original order, or someone who'd gotten hold of their magic, maybe through a spell book or something? And if it was one of those things, what the hell did it mean for the Nightkeepers?

Unfortunately, the more she read, the worse it sounded.

Some of the references Jade had uncovered said the order had arisen from the Mayan shaman-priests themselves, who had been astronomers and mystics in their own right, aside from their association with the Nightkeepers. Other references suggested the order arose when a group of rogue Nightkeepers split off and began to teach the Mayan priests some of the Nightkeepers' spells, which was forbidden. When the Nightkeepers' king had learned of the betrayal he'd gone after the rogues and their followers, who had fled into the highlands and disappeared into hiding, emerging only on the cardinal days, when they practiced their dark arts.

After that point the stories converged to agree on one major point: Around the year A.D. 950, the Xibalbans— which was how they'd come to be known by that point— had somehow breached the barrier and unleashed several of the *Banol Kax* onto the earth plane. The demons had slaughtered hundreds of thousands of Maya, wiping out entire cities and putting the empire on the brink of collapse. The Nightkeepers had eventually managed to recapture the creatures and restore the barrier, but the damage had been done. The Mayan Empire had never recovered to the heights it'd achieved prior to the Xibalbans' attack, soon losing ground to the vicious Inca, Aztecs, and Toltecs, who had flourished with the help of the Xibalbans until the fifteen hundreds, when the Xibalbans convinced them to welcome Cortés and his conquistadors. The Nightkeepers warned that the conquistadors should be sent away, but their counsel went unheeded. The two decades following Cortés's landing had seen the deaths of ninety percent of the Maya, Inca, Aztec, and Toltec; the destruction of the Mayan writing system; and the slaughter of all the polytheistic priests. A few dozen Nightkeepers had escaped, and the Xibalbans had disappeared entirely from the historical record, which was largely why Jox and the others assumed they'd been wiped out.

Had they, like the Nightkeepers, hidden themselves, focusing on training for the end-time wars? Or had the order truly disappeared, meaning that the enemy mage was a new breed of danger?

Damned if I know, Alexis thought, flipping Jade's report back to the first page and starting to reread it more carefully, in case she'd missed something critical the first time through. As she did so, though, she knew she was just avoiding thinking about her convo with Izzy, and the fact that she and Nate were going to be doing the close-proximity thing the next day when they traveled to Louisiana.

They were flying commercial because Leah had long ago decreed that Strike's teleport powers were emergency-only. Which only made sense; they didn't know enough about the magic to predict its limitations. What if he had only so many zaps in him, and they used them up blipping off to get beer or something? Bad idea.

So it was Delta, first-class, nonstop, which almost made up for the fact that Alexis hadn't been able to talk Strike out of sending Nate with her as backup. It wasn't as though she'd been able to tell him the truth, either, because hearing about her dream-vision would've only increased the king's determination to throw her together with Nate, for two major reasons: one, because gods-intended, mated Nightkeepers were so much more powerful together than an unmated Nightkeeper alone; and two, because Strike himself had dreamed about Leah long before he met her, and vice versa, even though neither male Nightkeepers nor humans were supposed to be precogs or visionaries. The king was a big believer in dreams and portents, and he'd already made it clear that he thought Nate and Alexis would make a strong pair-bond, and that a relationship between them would be an asset to the Nightkeepers in the coming war.

"So sad, too bad for him," she muttered under her breath. "Because a happy couple we very definitely are not. Sex doesn't make a lasting relationship if the people engaged in said sex can't carry on a civil convo to save their lives."

"Then I take it you won't mind me adding a third wheel," the king's voice said from the doorway to her suite.

Alexis jolted, but stopped herself from an instinctive gasp and spin because she was always aware of how Strike saw her, what he thought of her, and how she could improve that impression. How she could make herself useful in an advisory capacity. He already had Jox's long-range perspective on Nightkeeper matters, and Leah was at his side to give him the cop's view and the female opinion. As far as Alexis figured, her best commodities were her business experience and negotiating skills. Either way, she knew she had some serious impressing left to do if she wanted to take her mother's place at the king's side.

Still, when she turned to wave Strike in, she wasn't sure she liked his wary expression, or the way he closed the door at his back, as though he didn't want anyone listening in.

"You're coming to New Orleans?" she asked, hoping it was that simple—and that much of an opportunity.

"Nope, sorry." Strike exhaled, looked around her carefully decorated room and shifting inside his T-shirt like he wasn't feeling right inside his own skin. "I want you and Nate to take Rabbit with you."

Squelching her knee-jerk *no way in hell*, Alexis went with a neutral hum while she processed the info and came up with only one good conclusion. "You want him out of the way."

Strike shook his head. "He's getting squirrelly and needs to get the hell out of the compound. That's all."

"No, it's not." Alexis kicked her feet up on the soft gray ottoman she'd bought to match the sofa, and folded her hands across her chest, thinking. "Given what happened today it's not a good time to be sending anyone who doesn't absolutely need to be off property, so there's a reason you want Rabbit gone." She sucked in a breath as she made an intuitive leap she was pretty sure was right. "Something's wrong with Patience and Brandt?"

Of all the current Nightkeepers, Patience and Brandt White-Eagle were special thrice over: once because they'd found each other long before the barrier reactivated, meeting in Mexico on the night of the spring solstice, and waking up together the following morning wearing their marks; a second time because they'd defied the teachings of their *winikin* by getting married and having kids; and a third time because those kids were twins, which were sacred to the Nightkeepers because of their abilities to boost each other's powers. The kids, Harry and Braden, hadn't been put through any of the ceremonies yet, in order to protect them from being detected by magic seekers, but they lived at Skywatch among the bound Nightkeepers, watched over by Patience and Brandt's *winikin*, Hannah and Wood, when Patience and Brandt were unavailable. Which they'd been more and more lately, Alexis had noticed, as though they were drawing away from the Nightkeepers—or each other—and didn't want anyone else to know.

"Wow," Strike said, shaking his head. "You got there fast." But he didn't deny that it was because of problems with Patience and Brandt, who had become Rabbit's main support system after Red-Boar's death. Instead the king went very serious and said, "I need you to keep Rabbit out of the way, and I need you to keep him safe."

The teen was important to Strike; they'd grown up together, albeit separated by fifteen or so years, and Alexis had a feeling Strike and Jox had picked up most of the slack Red-Boar had left in the way of nonparenting. Which meant that the request was a sign of trust. She tipped her head. "Are you asking the same of Nate?"

"I'm putting him on notice," Strike replied, making it clear he didn't intend to ask Nate for a damn thing.

Alexis knew she should've regretted the low-grade animosity that existed between the two men, but she didn't because it only helped her cause, and it wasn't like Nate wanted to be part of the inner circle. As far as she could tell, he didn't even want to be part of the outer circle. "I'm honored by your trust," she said carefully, "but are you sure it's a good idea to put him in the middle of all the New Orleans occult stuff?" She wasn't sure how the half-blood teen's magic worked—none of them were, except that it didn't always behave the same as Nightkeeper magic.

Strike sent her a long, considering look, then shook his head. "Damned if I know the right answer to that." He paused. "What I'm about to tell you comes in the strictest confidence, understand?"

Startled, she set aside Jade's report. "Of course."

"I'm pretty sure Rabbit's mother was a member of the Order of Xibalba."

Whatever Alexis had expected him to say, it sure as hell wasn't that. She looked down at the thin report Jade had slapped together on a group of magi that wasn't supposed to exist anymore, then back up at her king. "Holy shit."

He grimaced. "Yeah. Pretty much."

Alexis wanted to say *holy shit* again, but didn't figure it'd add to the convo, so she stayed silent, trying to process that new info. Finally she said, "I take it you got that from Red-Boar?" She didn't think being half-Xibalban was something Rabbit would've kept to himself if he'd known.

Strike lifted a shoulder. "Let's just say he didn't deny

it when I asked him directly. I think that was the main reason he didn't want to induct Rabbit into the magic, why he didn't want him trained as a Nightkeeper."

"And why Rabbit's magic is different, and sometimes dangerous." Alexis thought it through, nodding. "Yeah, it plays. That'd explain why things have been weird for Rabbit during the ceremonies." The first time she and the other new Nightkeepers had gone into the barrier, instead of them all transferring together like they should have, the trainees had gone one place within the gray-green nothingness, while Strike and Red-Boar had each been sent elsewhere. The second time, Red-Boar had been forced to use extra magic to keep them together.

"It could also explain why he's got more power than he should," Strike said, referring to the fact that Rabbit wore the pyrokine's mark and could call fire, but also showed hints of telekinetic talents, in that he could un-lock doors with a touch.

"I'm not sure I like how this sounds," Alexis said quietly, thinking of the enemy mage's powers, and how easily he'd wielded far more strength than she'd ever come close to touching. "You think the Xibalbans' magic is stronger than ours."

"Or Rabbit's a special case." Strike spread his hands. "Nobody knows. Besides, it's just a theory." But the way he said it made her think it was more than that.

"Damn." She sat for a second, then frowned. "If that's the case, why put Rabbit out in the field with us, especially given that this Xibalban—if that's what he is—is after the artifacts too? Isn't that taking a needless risk?"

"Not needless. Calculated."

She froze at the possibilities . . . and the complications. "You want to see what happens if we put Rabbit and the new guy in the same room?"

Strike gave a yes-no wiggle of his hand. "Hopefully nothing's going to happen. Best-case scenario, this Mistress Truth character sells you the knife with zero issues and you get your asses back here. Meanwhile I'll be having a little sit-down with Patience and Brandt, and make sure that what's going on with them doesn't turn into a thing."

Alexis didn't ask, didn't really want to know. She'd prefer to go on thinking that Patience and Brandt had the perfect marriage, the perfect love affair, because if the two of them, who fit together like halves of a whole, couldn't make it work, what kind of a chance did anyone else have? So she focused on the fact that Strike was in her sitting room, offering her a chance to prove herself. She wasn't going to screw it up. "I'll do my best to keep him safe, best-case or worst-case, *Nochem*."

He winced at the honorific for *king* in the old language—he was still settling into his title, just as the rest of them were still getting used to being part of a monarchy. But instead of telling her not to call him that, which was his usual response when one of them *no-chem*ed him, he said, "Rabbit's a good kid who's had some tough breaks. Use him if you can; protect him either way. To be honest, I'd rather keep him here, but he's eighteen and itching for a fight. If I don't send him somewhere soon I'm afraid he's going to go looking for action on his own, and I can guarantee he'll get into trouble if that happens." He paused. "Take care of him for me, okay?"

Alexis nodded. "I will." They shook on it and he headed for the door. But as the panel swung shut behind him, she couldn't help thinking that she might've just agreed to way more than she was sure she could deliver.

After his disaster of a thesis defense—and the way he'd gone after Anna in the aftermath—Lucius went for a walk, trying to burn off the restless, edgy anger that'd been dogging him for weeks now, maybe longer. By the time he looped back to the art history building, he was calm enough to feel seriously ashamed.

His father had been right all along: He was a loser. It'd just taken him longer than the rest of them to figure it out. But what else could he call himself when he'd singlehandedly torpedoed the degree he'd spent the last five—okay, closer to six—years working toward? Anna had flat-out told him not to mention the Nightkeepers, and what'd he done? He'd gotten in the Dragon Lady's face over it, even knowing—when apparently Anna hadn't—

that Desiree was in full-on woman-scorned mode, with Anna as the target. Worse, he'd compounded that monumental screwup by striking out at Anna. They might not be as close these days as they had been before, but that was no excuse. He'd been embarrassed and ashamed, and he'd lashed out.

Which meant he owed her an apology, he thought as he crossed the cement bridge leading to the partially concealed main entrance of the art history building—a squat, dark concrete shape right out of the seventies. Her first-floor office was locked, which probably meant she'd gone home for the night. He really didn't want to put off the apology until tomorrow, though; he'd screwed up too badly. But was calling—or driving out to—her house any better? It was late, and he wasn't the Dick's favorite person to begin with, never mind him having been the one to drop the Desiree bomb. Which meant . . .

Hell, he didn't know what it meant. He didn't know what anything meant anymore. Things that used to make sense didn't, and things that shouldn't have made sense kept seeming like they did.

"Damn it," he said, and headed for his small office because he couldn't think of a better alternative. When he got there he saw that the message light on the landline phone was blinking, which was weird. Anybody who was anyone would've called his cell. Unless it was official university business, he thought, gut churning. That'd probably be done by landline, by some dean's secretary deputized to tell him he was out on his ass.

Wishing he could pretend he hadn't seen the blink, he hit the button, braced for the worst.

"Meet me in my office in fifteen minutes," Desiree's voice snapped. "And come alone."

"Shit!" He checked the time stamp on the message and saw that he was already an hour late. It didn't matter whether she'd called to kick him out or give him another chance; being late wasn't going to help. When the boss called a meeting, you showed. Or at least made a good effort to show. Stomach clenching on too many awful possibilities to name, he headed for her corner

office. He wasn't sure if he was relieved or bummed when he saw that her lights were still on, the door open.

He knocked on the doorframe, and the Dragon Lady—*Dr. Soo*, he corrected himself—looked up from her seat behind a wide desk. He couldn't read her expression when she saw who it was. "Come on in."

Her office was professionally done up in rich-looking blues and golds, accented with accessories that reflected her specialty of ancient Egyptian art. He wasn't sure, but the delicate faience bowl set in a case just inside the door looked real. Not willing to chance knocking it over, he gave the thing a wide berth as he stepped over the threshold.

"Shut the door," she ordered, returning her attention to her laptop computer screen. Her tone didn't make it sound like she'd reconsidered her decision on his thesis—more like she was getting ready to kick him out. He was pretty sure she couldn't do that without Anna's okay . . . but then again, it was entirely possible that Anna had okayed it and hadn't had the guts to tell him herself, he thought on a low burn of anger that was both foreign and tempting.

"Sit." Again with the orders, but he wasn't about to argue. At least not until she said she was kicking him out.

He took one of two chairs set opposite her desk, both of which were made of dark, carved wood and somehow managed to be big and imposing at the same time that they were delicate and feminine. The chair creaked under his weight; that was the only sound in the room for close to five minutes, as she kept reading and he sat in silence, partly because he wanted to wait her out, partly because flapping his trap had already gotten him in enough trouble that day.

Finally the Dragon Lady hit a couple of keys and pushed the laptop away, then looked him up and down and up again, until he started twitching under her scrutiny. Just when he was getting ready to break the silence, she said, "You know something, Lucius?" She tapped one high-gloss nail against her lower lip. "I like you."

On a one-to-ten scale of what he'd expected to hear, that ranked about a minus fifty. "Excuse me?"

"I like you," she repeated, "which is why I'm going to do something I almost never do. I'm going to give you another chance."

If anyone else on the faculty had said that, he would've thanked the hell out of them, and then asked when they should reschedule his thesis defense. Given who he was talking to and what she'd been up to lately, his first and potentially suicidal response was, "What's the catch?"

Something flashed in her eyes—irritation or amusement, or maybe a bit of both. "It's not a catch; it's an opportunity to expand on the work you're already doing. If you pull it off, you'll be making a hell of a name for yourself, and you'll get your degree." When he said nothing, simply waited, she leaned forward, giving him a glimpse of the steel in her eyes and the edge of a lacy bra beneath her camisole. "I want you to prove that the Nightkeepers are real."

"You—" he started in surprise, then broke off as he got it. She hadn't tanked his defense to embarrass Anna. She'd done it because she'd wanted his research. Embarrassing Anna had been a side benefit.

Son of a bitch, he thought, not sure if he was disgusted or impressed, or a bit of both.

Legend had it that the Nightkeepers had lived with the Egyptians up until Akhenaton had gone monotheistic. If that particular legend were real, proving the existence of the Nightkeepers wouldn't just blow the doors off the field of Mayan studies, it could rewrite a big chunk of Egyptology. And even better—as far as the Dragon Lady was concerned, no doubt—proving the Nightkeepers were real would invalidate a big chunk of Anna's anti-end-time publications, putting a serious cramp in her forward momentum at the university, maybe even providing enough ammo to get her tenure pulled.

Bitch, Lucius thought, his anger cranking hard and hot. But beneath the anger was a stealthy slide of, *Hmmm . . .*

Anna had never supported his research on the Nightkeepers. Was she his priority, or was the research?

The Dragon Lady continued, "Tell Anna you need some time off to figure things out. I'll fund your travel as necessary, and you'll report directly to me."

"I won't do it," he said, but it sounded weak even to him.

"There have to be things you've wanted to try, but couldn't because she wouldn't sign off on them, things you figured you'd do once you had your own grant money." She paused. "What if you could do them now?"

I can't, he repeated, only what came out of his mouth sounded an awful lot like, "I shouldn't."

"Come on; name it. If you had to pick one line of evidence to follow, and you had decent travel money, where would you go first . . . Belize?" That was where the Nightkeepers who'd survived Akhenaton's religious "purification" had supposedly wound up, where they had—again supposedly—hooked up with the Olmec, who had just begun to develop a cultural identity that would become, with the Nightkeepers' help, the Mayan Empire.

In theory.

But Lucius shook his head. "No, actually. I'd start in Boston. There's this girl—" He broke off, afraid that he'd come off sounding like an idiot, like he was crushing on someone he'd talked to on the phone for, like, twenty seconds, just long enough to take a message. A girl who hadn't returned any of his calls in the months since.

But Desiree—she'd gone from Dragon Lady to first name in his head all of a sudden—said only, "What about her?"

He let out the breath he hadn't consciously known he'd been holding. Which made him he realize something else, too. He was actually considering taking her up on the offer.

It was disloyal as hell, yes, and he owed Anna better. *But really,* that low, mean voice inside him said, *how much* do *you owe her?* She'd shut him out, withdrawn, left him behind. It'd been her fault they'd had to reschedule his defense; if he'd turned in his thesis last fall, on schedule, he would've sailed through. But he'd been forced to reschedule because she'd done her little disappearing act, leaving for a few weeks at the start of the fall semester and returning a pale, strange version of herself. If she'd stayed put and soldiered on, he'd have his Ph.D. and probably some new funding by now, enough to follow the clues that Anna pooh-poohed at best, derided at worst. She'd never wanted to even entertain the possibility that the Nightkeepers had existed, never mind discussing whether they still did, and what it might mean on the zero date. And it wasn't just a closed discussion in her book; it'd never been a discussion at all. To her, the Nightkeepers were nothing more than a bedtime story.

But that doesn't make it okay to go behind her back, he told himself, feeling as though there were two sets of feelings at war within his head: one that said he should trust that Anna would appeal Desiree's ruling on his thesis, and another that said he hadn't been able to trust Anna to do anything for him ever since she'd turned away from him, cut him adrift.

Rubbing a thumb across the raised knot of flesh on his opposite palm in a gesture that'd become habitual since he'd acquired the scar in a night of drunken stupidity, he told himself that friendships waxed and waned, that it was only natural for Anna to pull away from a relationship that'd perhaps gotten closer than she was comfortable with once she and the Dick had reconciled. The only relationship she really owed him was one of thesis adviser to student, and she'd never shirked that duty. Or had she? She'd steered him safely through his project, true, but had she kept him too safe? Desiree was right that the person who proved that the Nightkeepers truly had existed would be able to write his own ticket.

As the scar began to ache with the beat of his heart and the sluggish pound of anger through his veins, Lucius started to think Anna hadn't been helping him at all. She'd been holding him back.

"The girl in Boston?" Desiree prompted, and the victorious glint in her eyes said she knew she had him.

"Sasha Ledbetter," Lucius answered. "She's the daughter of a Mayanist named Ambrose Ledbetter. Back in the mid-eighties he wrote a few papers on the end-time, one of which included a description of a Mayan shrine that nobody's ever seen except him." He took a breath, held it. And took the leap straight onto Woo-Woo Avenue. "I think it was a Nightkeeper temple. If I can get a look at it, if I can translate the hieroglyphs, I can prove the Nightkeepers existed. I'm sure of it."

She nodded. "So why not call him directly?"

"He disappeared last summer while doing fieldwork in the highlands. At this point he's presumed dead."

Desiree's expression sharpened. "And you think you can get his notes from the daughter?"

"I think it's a good place to start," Lucius answered, not willing to tell the Dragon Lady that he couldn't explain why; he just knew he had to see Sasha. When he'd heard her voice on the phone, something had shifted inside him. He didn't know why or what it meant. He knew only that he had to find her, had to see her.

Desiree said nothing, simply opened her center desk drawer, pulled out a black plastic square, and slid it across the desk toward him. "Then go."

He stared at the credit card, at his own name imprinted on it. "Since when does the university hand out no-limit AmEx cards?"

"It's drawn on one of my private grants," she replied, in a voice that said, *Don't ask.*

Apprehension shivered through Lucius. The part of him he recognized as himself knew he should stand up, walk away, and never look back. But that darker part of him, the part that said nobody had ever given him a major break before, that he deserved this one now, told him to take the card and book the flight.

A thin whine started up in his ears, making his jaw hurt, and the world went a little fuzzy around the edges. What was he supposed to be worrying about? *Oh, right.* Betraying Anna by accepting Desiree's offer of some grant money. But really, could Anna honestly object to his taking on a side project? It wasn't as though she'd been using him lately. Anna hadn't been doing much of anything in the way of research ever since Neenee took off. And, come to think of it, that lack of academic production probably hadn't helped his thesis defense any.

When he came right down to it, Desiree's offer might be his best chance of cutting his losses and moving on—a logic that felt both right and wrong, depending on which part of himself he listened to.

"I'll do it." He picked up the card and balanced it on his palm for a moment, then closed his fingers. On some level, a level far away from the man he'd once been, he was unsurprised to feel the plastic slice into his scarred palm, bringing blood to the surface. Not pausing to tend to the cut, he held out his bleeding hand to Desiree. "You can count on me."

When she shook his hand, the silver cuff she habitually wore on her right wrist slipped back, and he saw the edge of a bloodred tattoo that looked oddly familiar.

CHAPTER SIX

Nate had never spent much one-on-one time with Rabbit before. Not because he had anything major against the kid, but more because he'd been spending most of his downtime wrestling with the story line for *VW6*. He'd hung with Rabbit as part of a group, sure, and shot a game or two of nine-ball, but there'd always been other people around to blunt the kid's 'tude. Which was why, when Strike had told him the teen was flying to New Orleans with him and Alexis, Nate hadn't thought much about it. Heck, he'd been relieved that there would be a buffer between him and Alexis, a third wheel to keep him from doing something really stupid, like acting on the edgy sense of possessiveness that'd been riding him since the day before. He kept telling himself it was a delayed reaction to having rescued her from the enemy mage, and again when the statuette kicked her into the barrier. He was bound to feel protective after that—it wasn't as if they could afford to lose any of the magi. It was only natural that he'd want to keep her safe. It didn't mean he wanted to start up again with something that hadn't fit right before.

So he told himself to ignore the way his skin kept tightening every time he came within a yard of her, and the way the memories of the two of them together were suddenly too close to the surface of his mind, far more so than they had been in the months they'd been broken up. He swore he could taste her, and feel her skin beneath his fingertips, feel the weight of her breasts against his chest, and hear her cries as she came apart around him.

It's just the eclipse, he told himself as he followed her onto the plane. Carlos had warned him that his hormones would flare when the barrier thinned, and eclipses were among the most powerful astrological events in the Nightkeeper calendar. Sure, the lunar eclipse was still a few days away, but damned if he couldn't feel the hum of sex and magic in his blood. It made him think of Alexis when he should've been thinking about the mission ahead, made his nostrils flare when he caught the light hint of her scent on the recirculated airplane air, made his flesh tighten when she glanced back at him and he saw the curve of her jaw, the soft swing of her hair. He wanted to find someplace where it was just the two of them, wanted to bury himself in her, lose himself with her—

And he so wasn't going back there.

Focus, he told himself fiercely. He needed to concentrate on the mission, on improving the Nightkeepers' score against the enemy mage. They were even: The Nightkeepers had the Ixchel statuette, but the redhead had Edna Hopkins's artifact. If it took Nate, Alexis, and Rabbit traveling together to make the score two to one, then so be it. They just had to get the knife and get back. No problem, right?

By the time their plane landed in New Orleans late that afternoon, though, he was seriously wishing he'd been flying solo. Alexis was barely speaking to him, answering his occasional questions with short, clipped monosyllables, and spending the rest of the time studying the report Jade had prepared on the knife, Mistress Truth, and the French Quarter. And Rabbit was in full-on punk mode, with his hoodie pulled most of the way over his face and his iPod buds jammed in his ears, making it clear he'd rather be anywhere else, with any*one* else. He'd been pissy about being ordered out of Skywatch, which didn't make much sense to Nate, who would've thought the kid'd be jonesing to see some action by now.

Deciding to ignore them both, Nate tossed his carry-on bag in the trunk of the first cab he saw, and made a point of sitting up front with the driver.

When he rattled off Mistress Truth's address at the outskirts of the French Quarter, though, the driver gave him a funny look. "You sure about that?" the cabbie asked as he pulled away from the curb and headed them into the stream of vehicles exiting the airport.

Nate focused on the guy, noting the edge of a tribal tattoo at his neck, partly hidden by his shirt. "Yeah. We've got an appointment at the tea shop."

The driver glanced over, and his voice was a little too casual when he said, "If'n you want your leaves read, you should go to my cousin's place. She does palms too, and she'll give you a break if you tell her I sent you."

Nate tensed. "What's wrong with Mistress Truth's?"

The other man's eyes slid away from his. "Nothing. Just trying to give family some business." He reached over without looking, palmed his Motorola, and chirped home base to announce the pickup and his destination, then turned up the dance music on the radio in a clear signal that the convo was over.

Nate would've pressed, but from the set of the driver's jaw he figured he wouldn't get far. Stubborn recognized stubborn. He half turned back to look at Alexis, who lifted a shoulder as if to say, *What can we do?* It wasn't like going to another tea shop was going to get them the knife. It was Mistress Truth or bust.

They traveled the rest of the way in silence broken only by the mindless syncopation coming from the radio, until the driver rolled them to a stop in front of a jazz club. "We're here."

Actually, they were more like four doors down, Nate saw, and tried not to wonder why the driver didn't want to stop in front of the tea shop. If the guy was trying to give him the creeps, he'd done a pretty good job.

Nate paid the tab and added a tip. When the driver made change he included a card for his cousin's place, but didn't say another word, just gave a two-fingered salute and pulled back out into traffic.

"Smells funny." Rabbit wrinkled his nose as he looked around.

"Can't argue that," Nate said, staring after the cab.

"You should've told him to wait," Alexis said, her tone carrying a distinct edge.

Nate ignored her snippiness. It didn't seem to be easing, which made him wonder whether it was more than delayed shock. But even if it had something to do with her vision of the day before, something to do with the two of them together, it wasn't like he could—or would—do anything to ease the tension for either of them. So he shrugged and said, "Somehow I doubt he would've waited, tip or no tip. Seemed like he was in a hurry to get out of here."

He took a long look around, trying to figure out why. The narrow street was cracked and heaved in some places, patched in others. Probably leftover hurricane damage, he figured, which might also explain the funky odor Rabbit had mentioned, which smelled like a cross between a bad air freshener and used sweat socks. The block they'd come to looked like most of the others they'd passed on the way: pieces of it old, pieces new, all of it vaguely fake-seeming, as though the contractors had tried to slap a gloss of cool over it, and missed. Mardi Gras had been a few days earlier, and confetti edged the street, lone wisps of streamers and colored dots that'd escaped the street sweepers lying now in the gutter, their once-bright colors gone drab.

The exterior of the jazz bar was slicked with a fresh coat of paint and sported a shiny new sign, but the next two places down were boarded up. Beyond them was the tea shop, which took up the corner of the block. The star-studded sign confirmed the cabbie's implication that the place might call itself a tea shop, but the actual tea was ancillary to fortune-telling, palmistry, and other supposed magical practices. The shop was plain-fronted, with a facade that looked older than even those of its abandoned neighbors. Instead of being shabby, though, it seemed sturdy, as though the floodwaters had passed it by.

Or not, Nate thought, mentally dope-slapping himself

for buying into the mystique that'd no doubt been painted on by the same contractors who'd done the rest of the block.

"We going in or what?" Alexis asked, then moved past him and headed for the store without waiting for an answer. Rabbit slouched along in her wake, and when he looked back at Nate he had a big old smirk on his face, like he was enjoying the tension between them.

"Punk," Nate muttered, and stalked after them both, passing them and shouldering through the door to the tea shop so he was the first one in. As he entered, he braced himself for the smell of death or the sting of dark, twisted magic.

He didn't get either. He got a tea shop.

It was bigger inside than it'd looked from the street. Large glass display cases flanked the door and ran along a central aisle, and chairs were grouped around small round tables behind the counters, set up for readings. And tea, he supposed. He could smell it in the air, an earthy mix of herbs that bore little resemblance to the Lipton his social worker, Carol Rose, had insisted he drink whenever they met.

That memory, though, hit hard when he smelled the herbs. He'd been tough and mean, hardened by his experiences in juvie, with defenses cemented in stone by what he'd seen and done—and avoided doing—inside Greenville. But lucky for him, Carol Rose had been tougher and meaner, and had refused to be scared off. She'd been the making of him as a man, and damned if he couldn't see her face right there in front of him, when he knew full well her pack-a-day habit had caught up with her six years earlier.

"Hey." Alexis tapped his shoulder. "You going to stand there all day?"

"I—" He broke off, shaking his head as Carol Rose's image disappeared in a swirl of tea-scented leaves. Seeing nobody in the small storefront, he stepped aside. "Yeah. Come on."

When the door swung shut behind her and Rabbit, a bell chimed in the rear. The paneling at the front of the store was light-toned wood, and the display cases were filled with low-key arcana: decks of tarot cards, incense and burners, and mass-produced voodoo dolls aimed at the tourist market. The big windows at the front of the store let in the light, and the whole effect was pleasant enough, if bland. Beyond that, though, the room darkened to a maze of tall bookcases set at crazy angles to one another. Nate couldn't see the back wall, but the echoes told him that there was nearly twice as much space in the darkness as in the light.

The setup made the place feel like two entirely different stores. The front was a safe zone, where tourists could do their thing and come out feeling as though they'd scraped the surface of the local occult community. The rear of the store was where it was really at, though. No doubt about it.

"Stay here," Nate said. "I'll be right back." He headed toward the bookcases.

Half a second later Alexis and Rabbit followed. Big surprise. He didn't bother to order them to wait until he'd checked things out, though, because he didn't figure it'd work. Besides, once he was past the first row of bookcases the light dimmed significantly, and damned if it didn't feel like the walls closed in a notch. He knew it was probably an optical illusion or the power of suggestion, but it made him think the three of them were better off sticking together, just in case.

The first two rows of cases held the usual assortment of woo-woo texts and themed day planners, exactly the sort of tourist crap he would've expected. The next few contained some legit-looking crystals and some crazy clay blobs. By the time he passed the fifth row of cases and realized the store was way bigger than he'd thought at first, he was into shrunken-head territory, and gut instinct had him on alert. He didn't feel power, per se, but there was a definite sense of danger, though he wasn't sure if it was real or if he'd talked himself into it based on the scenery.

Moving deeper into the gloom with the others breathing down his neck, he paused when he caught a hint of motion in his peripheral vision, there and gone so quickly he might've missed it if he hadn't been watching. "Mistress Truth?" he called softly.

"Keep coming," a deep, yet feminine voice responded from up ahead, which meant she hadn't been the source of the motion he'd seen. Filing that, he did as he was told, passing the last row of bookcases and stepping into a space that was at once both open and deeply shadowed, and appeared empty.

"You want the knife." One of the shadows moved, taking on the form of a dark-haired woman wearing a hooded black cape over a purple velour tracksuit. She was average height, average weight, with regular features that weren't particularly noteworthy until he got to her eyes, which were dark and intense, and sent a nasty twitch through his gut. *Don't turn your back on this one,* said his warrior's mark, or his own gut instincts. Maybe both.

"We brought cash," he said, wanting the deal done and them out of there. "Where's the knife?"

"Here." She withdrew the weapon from a pocket of her robe, balanced it on her palm, and held it to the light.

At the sight of it, something inside Nate went still. The ancient artifact was polished black obsidian, carved from a single piece of stone. The blade was maybe nine inches long, the haft slightly shorter, and carved with a repeating motif he didn't recognize, at least not consciously. Something inside him recognized it, though, and the recognition brought a surge of possessiveness. He had an obsessive, overwhelming urge to reach out and grab the thing, but held himself back, remembering what'd happened when Alexis touched the Ixchel statuette.

Even as he did so, a burn of satisfaction raced through him. They'd gotten there in time. The Xibalban—or whatever the hell he was—hadn't beaten them to the knife.

"Looks good," Alexis said, moving up to face the self-proclaimed witch. "I believe we agreed on twenty grand?"

The corners of Mistress Truth's mouth turned up. "Technically you offered twenty and I said I'd think about it."

"You also agreed to give us right of first refusal," Alexis added pleasantly, but with a thread of steel in the words.

"Did I?"

"You know you did." Alexis's voice went cool, and Nate got a really bad feeling, really quick.

Mistress Truth lifted a shoulder. "Maybe that was before I knew there was another interested party."

Shit, Nate thought, and would've moved forward if Alexis hadn't waved him back. "We'll double the offer," she said.

The older woman's eyes glinted with avarice. "He offered fifty."

"Then we'll give you a hundred," Alexis retorted without missing a beat. "Here and now, and let's get it done."

Mistress Truth pursed her lips. "Let me think about it."

Which Nate knew really meant, *Let me call the big redheaded guy for a counteroffer,* which so wasn't an option—not because Nate cared what they paid for the thing, but because he had no intention of losing to Red again.

Which begged the question of why the other mage wasn't there already. He'd already shown that he could 'port. Why hadn't he just zapped in and grabbed the knife?

Well, he hadn't, so that gave them an opportunity they couldn't afford to walk away from. Nate shifted to his left, then caught Rabbit's eye and gave the kid a little nod, sending him a few steps to his right, so they were flanking the wannabe witch.

He was just about to move in when Alexis said, "My offer expires in two hours." She turned away, headed back toward the light. "Come on, guys." She walked out, leaving the room's single exit wide-open.

Mistress Truth looked straight at Nate and smirked. "You three should really get on the same page, you know."

Having lost the element of surprise—and not sure he'd ever really had it—Nate followed Alexis out, with Rabbit at his heels. Nate crowded close to her and hissed, "What the hell was that?"

"It's called a strategic retreat. And you're not the negotiator here."

"Fuck negotiating," he said succinctly. "We should grab the knife, leave the cash, and get the hell out of here."

Her eyes went cool. "We don't all have the same set of flexible ethics as you, Nathan. And we can't hold ourselves out as the saviors of mankind if we run around acting like street thugs." She said the last very softly, letting him know that she too knew they were being watched. But if she was sharp enough to catch the furtive movement in the shadows, how could she not see that they were setting themselves up for disaster by leaving now?

Unless that was what she wanted to have happen.

Suddenly convinced there was something else going on here, something he wasn't aware of, Nate growled, "Exactly what the hell are you up to?"

"Later," she said as they moved from the bookcase labyrinth to the front of the store. She indicated the door. "Let's get out of here. This place gives me the creeps."

But when they hit the street, Rabbit wasn't with them. Nate cursed under his breath and was just about to go back in when the kid came through the door with a strange look on his face.

"What's wrong?" Nate demanded.

Expression blanking, the teen shrugged. "Nothing. I thought I saw . . . nothing. I'll take first watch." He turned away, heading across the street to a nearby bakery as though the only thing on his mind were chowing a couple of beignets, not setting up a surveillance post that faced the tea shop.

Alexis watched him go. "Creepy kid," she said after a moment.

"Why?" Nate snapped, irritated. "Because he's a half-blood? Watch it, princess, your *winikin*'s showing."

Her eyebrows climbed. "What's up your ass?"

You, he wanted to say. *The witch. The ersatz Xibalban. All of it.* The entire setup stank, just like Edna Hopkins's cottage had. His blood buzzed with anger, with impatience. He wanted that knife, hated that they'd just walked away from it, and resented his growing suspicion that Alexis had an agenda he hadn't known about. How the hell was he supposed to watch her back if he didn't know the whole plan? "You want to tell me what the hell's going on here?"

"It's an experiment." She paused, looking at him out of the corner of her eye, gauging his response when she whispered almost soundlessly, "Strike thinks Rabbit's mother was Xibalban. He wants to know if he reacts to the redhead's magic."

Stifling his first response, which involved the words *fuck* and *me,* Nate snarled, "So this isn't just a recovery mission; it's a science-fair project? Jesus, what kind of prioritization is that? Strike's off his rocker."

"We need information," she said, but avoided his eyes.

Shit. This wasn't the king's plan. It was hers, or maybe a bit of both. "What are you doing, Alexis?" Nate kept his voice low, but reached out and took her hand, feeling a buzz of contact that was a potent mix of sex, magic, and memory. He hung on when she would've pulled away, and said softly, "Talk to me."

She lifted her chin. "Consider this an extended job interview."

"You're not going to earn the king's trust by being stupid," Nate said, letting go of her hand because he wanted to keep holding on. "Think it through. We go back in there, steal the knife, and bring it back to Skywatch. Mission accomplished. What more could Strike ask?"

"That's the sort of thought process that got you thrown in jail, isn't it?"

The universe went very still. "Don't go there."

Something flickered in her eyes—regret, maybe, or nerves—but it was quickly gone, leaving coolness behind. "Sorry," she said, sounding unrepentant. "The point is

that I'm not going to get what I want by doing the mini-
mum. I have to prove that I'm ready for more, that I'm
ambitious and aggressive."

"That sounds like something Izzy would say."

"*I'm* saying it," she replied evenly, but then her expression softened. "Look, I know you want to follow
your own path; I get that, and I'm not asking you to buy
into something you don't believe in. But the thing is, I
do believe in fate and destiny, and I'd be honored to
follow my mother into an advisory position. I'd appreciate it if you'd help me out."

Translation: *You owe me.* And the thing was, Nate
realized, maybe he did. He'd slept with her when the
pretransition hornies had hit him hard, and he'd broken
it off when the urges waned. In reality there'd been
more to it—a whole shit-ton more—but she didn't know
that. All she knew was that he'd used her when he'd
needed to get his rocks off and dumped her when the
mating urge leveled out. So yeah, he probably did owe
her. And if the payback was him helping her impress
the king by getting both the knife and an idea of whether
Rabbit's magic reacted to the redheaded mage, then so
be it.

"Okay." He nodded. "Fine. I'm in." He still thought
it was a piss-poor idea. But he also knew her well enough
to figure she'd try it with or without his help. "Come
on. I guess we watch and wait."

He headed for the coffee shop where Rabbit had disappeared to, and he didn't look back.

In the small café, Nate and Alexis sat together at a
table so small that their knees bumped beneath it, while
Rabbit sulked at a stool by the window, shoveling in
calories at a rate of about a thousand a minute, in the
form of beignets, lemon squares, and coffee-laced hot
chocolate. All three of them had decent views of the
alley that ran around the back of Mistress Truth's shop,
leading to the rear exit. If anyone came or went from
the tea shop, they'd see.

The waiting, Alexis soon found, was the hardest part.
Or rather, waiting with Nate was, because he was crowd-

ing her, getting inside her space, under her skin. And he wasn't even trying to, damn him.

Her dream-vision of the two of them making love in the underground temple had undone the four months' worth of forgive-and-forget she'd managed to build up since their relationship ended. She wanted to scratch at him for dumping her, for not remembering what her gut told her actually *had* happened between them in the stone chamber. At the same time, she wanted to be skin-on-skin with him, wanted to ride him, race him, roll with him like they'd done before, when they'd packed more than her prior lifetime of sex into a couple of short months that'd ended long before she was ready.

And she wanted, more than anything, to get a grip on herself.

The writs said that what had happened before would happen again, and boy, was that the truth. As hard as she'd tried to do otherwise, she'd put herself right back where she'd been too many times before—dealing with an ex on a daily basis and having to pretend it was no big deal. Before, it'd been her clients, wealthy men who had wanted her for her business acumen as much as for her body, and had generally been bored with her body long before they were finished with her stock tips. When she'd broken up with Aaron after catching him below-decks on his yacht with a bimbo twofer, she'd vowed to do better the next time.

Yeah, that worked, she thought, glancing at Nate, only to find him looking back at her. Their eyes connected, and the punch of remembered heat was tempered with a twist of regret. Maybe it was the magic of the coming eclipse, which was thinning the barrier and strengthening the sexual pull that'd been there from the beginning. Or maybe it was their close proximity, or the vision. Whatever the reason, even though she and Nate were sitting still, unspeaking, she suddenly felt naked beneath his gaze. Vulnerable.

Excited.

Damn it.

"There," he said suddenly, leaning forward. "In the shop. Something's happening."

They rose and moved to flank Rabbit's vantage point at the front of the coffee shop. There was motion inside Mistress Truth's place: blinds being drawn, and a pair of shadows moving behind them, backlit by a glow of warm illumination that was too steady to be candlelight, too dim to be the shop's fluorescents. The quick February dusk had fallen, showing the figures clearly—one was Mistress Truth, the other far too small to be the big redheaded man. "Two shadows," Nate said. "The witch and whoever else was in there watching us."

Alexis shot him a quick look. She'd thought she'd been imagining the sensation of being watched. Apparently not.

"I saw her," Rabbit said, "I think." At Nate's look, he elaborated, "My age, maybe a year or two older. Thin, dark hair, black eye."

Alexis asked, "As in she had dark eyes, or she had a shiner?"

"A shiner. Looked like someone clocked her good." The teen shifted on his stool, shrugging restlessly inside his clothes.

Maybe the caffeine was catching up with him. Or maybe it was something else, Alexis thought as she caught a buzz of power off him, a whiff of smoke. *Oh, hell,* she thought, looking past the teen and catching Nate's eye. Her stomach dropped when he nodded that he'd sensed it, too.

The kid was jacked in and jacked up, and far too twitchy for his own good. Typically hair-trigger on a good day, Rabbit was wired to blow. He must've been more excited than she'd thought about the prospect of some action. Or else it really was the caffeine—who the hell knew with his powers?

The king had ordered her to keep Rabbit safe first and foremost. Learning more about his magic was secondary. Which meant she so wasn't putting him in front of the Xibalban now. Not like this. The kid was a loose cannon leaking way more power than he ought to be. Add that to the hormonal explosives that came with being eighteen and having a Y chromosome, and bad things could happen way too easily.

"Hey." Nate put a hand on the teen's shoulder. "Take a deep breath and chill."

Rabbit practically exploded off the stool, shooting backward and landing in a defensive crouch. *"Don't,"* he said on a whistle of breath, "touch me." He stood there for a second, ribs heaving, then looked around and went brick red when he realized he'd quickly become the center of attention in the café, and a couple of big dudes in the coffee line were looking like they were thinking about getting involved.

"We're cool," Nate said, holding both hands up in a gesture of *no harm, no foul.*

"Yeah." Rabbit sent the would-be Good Samaritans a filthy look as he slouched back onto his stool. "Nothing to see here."

"Sorry for the commotion," Alexis put in, and waited until most everyone had gone back to their own business before she glanced over at the teen. "You need to work on your blocks if you're pulling this much power already. The eclipse isn't for another forty-eight hours."

"The witch is leaving," Nate said quietly.

Alexis looked over in time to see Mistress Truth hustling through the front door of the tea shop, wearing a big purple jacket over the same purple tracksuit she'd had on earlier. Bracing herself for a fight, Alexis said, "Rabbit, listen—"

"I think I should stay here," he interrupted, then swallowed hard. His voice was shaky, his color was off, and heat crinkled in the air around him. "I'm not feeling so good. I'll wait here until you get back, maybe call Strike for a pickup if I start feeling too shitty."

Which so wasn't what she'd been expecting. "I . . . uh. Yeah. I think that'd be best."

"We've got to go if we're going," Nate said as a dark sedan pulled up in front of the tea shop and Mistress Truth climbed in. "Unless you want to stay here with Rabbit?"

She ought to, she knew. She'd promised to keep him safe. But Rabbit shook his head and waved her off. "Go. I'll keep out of trouble. Honest."

As Nate headed out to the street and flagged a cab,

Alexis wavered. Finally she said, "Okay. I'm going to hold you to that."

Telling herself it was the right call, she bolted after Nate and jumped in the cab. As the vehicle headed through the French Quarter in pursuit of the dark sedan, Nate glanced at her. "You sure he'll stay put?"

"Yeah. He promised." Whatever she might think of Rabbit, a Nightkeeper's word was his bond.

It wasn't until they were a good five minutes down the road that she realized that Rabbit had said *honest . . .* but he hadn't actually promised her a damn thing.

CHAPTER SEVEN

After Rabbit watched Nate and Alexis get in a taxi and do the "follow that limo" thing, he waited ten minutes or so, in case Mistress Truth circled the block to check on the tea shop before driving on. It was what he would've done in her place . . . especially since he was almost positive she'd left the knife behind.

He wasn't sure why the others hadn't noticed her lack of a power signature—maybe they hadn't seen the rippling magic coming off the knife in the first place? Either way, he was glad to be rid of them, because he badly wanted to get back inside that shop. There was something in there calling to him: maybe the knife, and yeah, maybe the girl. Either way, he'd played it right and the coast was as clear as it was likely to get.

It was pretty much full-on dark by the time he left the coffee shop and headed across the street, though *dark* was a relative term given the frenetic lighting of the French Quarter. Already bodies were piling up in the jazz club four doors down from the tea shop. The music and the crowd had spilled out into the street, but to Rabbit the partying seemed tinged with desperation, as though the locals were both tired of Mardi Gras and not quite ready to let it be over yet.

He slipped through the crowd unheeded. Thanks to a recent growth spurt, he was close to five-ten now and had finally broken the one-fifty mark. Still, at times like this it was an advantage being small and average-looking. The full-blood Nightkeepers couldn't blend to save their lives. Rabbit, on the other hand, barely got a look as he wormed his way through. A couple of glances headed his way when he went for the door of the locked-up tea shop, but the interest level faded fast when he made a show of fumbling with a set of keys. Nobody needed to know they were the keys to an ammo locker out at the Skywatch gun range, especially when a quick touch had the lock giving way.

His fledgling telekine skills were one of the things that set him apart from the full-bloods—no true Nightkeeper had multiple nonspell talents—but that was the one area where being a half-blood was actually an advantage. Nobody knew where the limits were on his magic, and he sure as hell hadn't bumped up against them yet. He knew it made some of the others—especially the *winikin*—nervous when he experimented or did something he shouldn't have been able to do in their limited view of the world, but he didn't care, not really.

They could have their suspicions. He had the magic.

He let himself into the front room of the tea shop, with its glass cases and tables for two, one of which held a single kerosene lantern that provided thin yellow light. He didn't see any surveillance or catch the faint background hum of electrical power going to a security grid. There also weren't any of the magic prickles that warned of spell-cast wards, but he hadn't expected there to be. He'd figured out pretty much right away that Mistress Truth was a poser; she had props from half a dozen so-called "magicks," yet the only thing that'd held actual power was the knife.

She had the trappings but didn't know what to do with them, and he was kind of disappointed. From the way the taxi driver'd been acting, he'd halfway hoped they were onto something interesting, something'd that'd disprove the Nightkeepers' bloody-minded insistence that the only workable magic was theirs. Rabbit's gut told him there were other types of magic out there, and that his mother had used it. That would explain why his power was different, stronger. If he could figure out who she'd been and how her magic had worked . . . well, it'd be a hell of a benefit come the zero date, if nothing else. As would gaining possession of the artifacts bearing the demon prophecies, he reminded himself, forcing himself back on task when a part of him wanted to just stand there and absorb the weird energy within the tea shop.

Wait a minute . . . energy?

The buzz was new since before, he realized on a spurt of adrenaline. Something had changed in the air. Damning himself for daydreaming when he should've been paying attention, he tensed and cast his senses outward, trying to pinpoint the alteration and its source. It wasn't magic, precisely. He didn't know exactly what it was, but he liked the way it feathered across his skin and curled inside his chest, and the way everything tightened and lit up, as though he'd inhaled the promise of sex along with air.

"It's okay," he said softly, somehow knowing it was the girl with the worked-over face. "I won't hurt you."

"Yes, you will, but you won't mean to," came the whispered answer. The sound seemed to come from all around him, and the lamp suddenly cut out, plunging the room into darkness lit only from the neon out on the street.

Rabbit heard movement and the rustle of clothing, and knew she was waiting to see what he would do next. Showing off, he held out his hand, palm up, and whispered the word that was burned into his soul and woven into the fibers of his being: *"Kaak." Fire.*

A red-gold flame flared to life, warming his palm and lighting the room.

A shadow moved over by the first row of bookcases, and the girl stepped into the bloodred light. She wasn't smiling, but her eyes were clear and unafraid as they met his. "Nice trick."

The red firelight faded the bruise to a faint smudge and sharpened the contrast between her pale complexion and her straight black hair, dark lips, and dark blue eyes. She was wearing low-rider jeans and a tight hoodie that'd been cropped off just above her waistband to show a strip of flat stomach and a starburst tattoo centered on her navel. She was lean hipped, slight, and tough-looking. And, Rabbit realized with a start, she was gorgeous. Somehow he'd missed that earlier, or maybe he'd gotten it but hadn't quite grasped the actual degree of her hotness. He'd been mostly focused on the shiner and the slump of her shoulders, the whipped-dog air he knew all too well from back in high school, when he'd been the daily target of three of the biggest bullies in town. He'd recognized the victim in her because like knew like. Now, though, she was straight shouldered, with her chin up and her eyes assessing, as though she were measuring him, trying to figure him out. She didn't look put off by the magic, but didn't look impressed, which meant that either she'd seen real magic before, or she'd seen so much of the fake stuff that she was automatically assuming the fireball was an illusion.

Rabbit had been prepared for the victim. He wasn't so ready for the girl who faced him now, unafraid. He was even less ready when she withdrew the carved obsidian knife from the back pocket of her hip-hugging jeans and balanced the blade on her palm. "You want this?"

Power sang in the air and made him think about being a hero, about proving that he wasn't as much of a fuckup as everyone thought. He nodded, his throat going dry. "Yeah. I want it."

She nodded, and her expression firmed. "Take me with you, and you can have whatever you want."

Nate hung on to the door handle in the backseat as their cabbie—a twentysomething who was thrilled with his "follow that car" fare—gleefully chased the dark sedan carrying Mistress Truth along the twisty streets of the Quarter. Eventually the sedan pulled up in front of the closed, locked entrance of an aboveground cemetery. Nate and Alexis's driver parked a block over and down, looking sorry that the ride was over.

"Let me guess," Alexis muttered. "She picked the location."

"She doesn't seem the sort to miss the opportunity for some drama," Nate agreed as he paid the driver, adding a twenty so the guy would wait.

They got out of the cab and worked their way back, making like tourists by holding hands and gawking at the carved marble pillars and ornate iron grillwork of the fence surrounding the cemetery, even though it was late and the area wasn't exactly a primo stop on the haunted walking tours.

As they neared the cemetery the sedan rolled past, heading back uptown.

"Think it's headed out to get our Xibalban?" Nate said, more thinking aloud than really asking.

"He can 'port," Alexis said with a bit of *duh* in her voice.

Nate would've argued that Strike didn't 'port everywhere he wanted to go, but didn't bother because he didn't want to buy into the fight. And yeah, he knew damn well it wasn't really a fight that was looking to spark between them, not this close to the eclipse. The electricity that pulsed on the night air was way more sex than anger, or maybe a mix of the two. Part of him was annoyed that his body had no problem buying into the destined-mates thing. The rest of him didn't give a crap about that, just wanted her against him, underneath him. And she was feeling it too. He could see it in the pink blush that crept up her long throat and high-boned cheeks when he caught her looking, and when they brushed up against each other as they walked, still holding hands.

"It's a one-way trip," she said, and it took him a few seconds to realize she wasn't talking about the two of them; she was talking about Mistress Truth and the limo, and she had a point. The sedan's departure suggested that whoever hired it didn't expect the wannabe witch to need a ride home.

"Come on." He sped up, and they came into sight of the cemetery entrance just as the witch's purple-jacketed figure disappeared through the arched gateway.

Nate and Alexis followed. The cemetery gate opened onto a main drag paved in pressed white gravel, with offshoots leading away at right angles, intersected by narrower pathways running parallel to the main drag, creating a regular gridwork of roads crisscrossing around straight rows of monuments and elevated crypts, all built well above normal flood height. There'd no doubt been some serious posthurricane rebuilding necessary, but in the moonlit darkness Nate saw no sign of the destruction or repairs. The cemetery looked secure in the silence. Peaceful. For now, anyway.

"There she goes," he said as their quarry stopped at an angel-topped crypt, fiddled with the lock for a moment, and then stepped inside. "Wonder if that's the family home?"

"I think—" Alexis broke off as the air suddenly rang with the rattle of foreign magic, and they heard the pop of displaced air from up ahead. "Come on!"

Nate wanted to grab her and shove her in a crypt until it was all over, but she wasn't his to protect, and she was a good jump ahead of him. Adrenaline flared and he started after her, pulling the nine-millimeter he'd checked with his luggage and hoped he wouldn't need. "Wait up," he hissed. "Wait for—"

But they were already too late. A dark shadow passed through the crypt entrance well ahead of them. A second later the witch screamed, the sound high and terrified, followed by a masculine roar of anger, then another scream, cutting off to a gurgling rattle.

"Shit!" Nate put his head down and ran, pushing past Alexis and barreling into the crypt.

The big redhead had the witch up against the back wall of the crypt, holding her off her feet by her throat. He had a stone knife in his other hand, its tip against her temple.

It was a stone knife, yes, and it was Mayan. Maybe even Nightkeeper. But it wasn't *the* stone knife.

The witch had switched blades, Nate realized, and the big guy was pissed. "Drop it!" he ordered, leveling the nine-millimeter. "These are jade tipped." He didn't fire, though, because ricochet would be a bitch in the stone chamber.

The witch's eyes locked onto him, relief warring with terror as her mouth pulled back in a voiceless plea for help. The enemy mage ignored the threat and dug the knife in a little, until a drop of blood welled and tracked down Mistress Truth's temple. "Where's the real knife? Back at the shop?"

She shook her head wildly, then nodded, spraying tears, spittle, and terror.

"Drop her now!" Nate shouted, sidestepping so he had half a prayer of nailing the redhead without killing the witch too.

The mage looked at him, disgusted. "For fuck's sake, you could've taken the damn thing earlier. That's always been the problem with you people. Too many fucking rules."

Magic clapped, brown smoke detonated, and mage and witch disappeared. Nate stood for a second, stunned. There had been no rattle of gathering magic, no pop of displaced air, yet his gut told him that they hadn't gone invisible or anything like that. The redhead had 'ported back to the shop.

Back to where Rabbit was waiting, jacked up on magic and angst.

"Come on!" Nate grabbed Alexis's hand and practically dragged her out of the crypt to their cab. They piled in and he told the cabbie to take them back to the tea shop ASAP, while she whipped out her cell and speed-dialed Rabbit's phone, punching it to speaker.

After five rings it kicked to voice mail, and Rabbit's recorded voice said, "I'm not here."

Then the line went dead. There was no beep, no nothing. Only silence.

Rabbit thought he was handling the negotiations pretty well. After a flash of panicked certainty that he was going to fuck this up the way he'd always fucked up pretty much anything else important he'd ever tried to do, he forced himself to slow down and focus. Think.

He'd let the girl—she'd said her name was Myrinne—keep the knife. Okay, actually she'd refused to hand it over, but he hadn't pressed. He had, however, insisted that they get their asses out of the tea shop. Myrinne hadn't argued; she'd just put her hand in his and let him lead her through the streets of her own neighborhood, looking for someplace loud and crowded. As they walked, she told him a bit about the other guy who'd wanted the knife, namely that he called himself Iago, and had actually identified himself as Xibalban, and promised to share his magic with the witch in exchange for the knife.

"He'll kill her," Rabbit said.

Myrinne said nothing, just pointed to a pizza joint across the street. "Let's go in there. It's usually pretty quiet this time of night."

Quiet was an understatement, Rabbit decided. The place was empty except for the guy behind the counter. Rabbit snagged a table in the corner and put his back to the wall, feeling nerves and power vibrating through him. When the guy headed toward them with menus, Rabbit ordered a couple of Cokes and told him they'd need a while.

Make that a long while.

Under the bright fluorescent lights, Myrinne's shiner stood out loud and clear, angry and purple-black, with spider tracks of broken veins edging the white of that eye.

Seeing that he was staring, she jerked her chin up and glared. "What're you looking at?"

"Did the witch do it?" he asked, knowing they both knew exactly what he'd been looking at. "Is that why you want to come with me?"

At first he wasn't sure she was going to answer, because she sort of locked up and hunched over, as though she weren't sure how much to tell him. But then she said, "Yes, she clobbered me. But no, that's not why I need you to take me with you. It's because of the dreams."

Something tickled the hairs at the back of Rabbit's neck. "What—" He broke off as the door to the pizza joint slammed open, and a big biker-looking guy with reddish hair strode through, looking pissed. He was dragging Mistress Truth along behind him.

Adrenaline kicked Rabbit's system even higher when he realized it was the Xibalban. Iago. Rabbit knew it like he knew his own name—not just from the description, but from the power that churned off the guy, murky brown and shit-strong.

Mistress Truth pointed at Myrinne. "That's her. She must've stolen it!"

Heart hammering up into his throat, Rabbit scrambled up and shoved Myrinne behind him. "Out the back," he snapped, pushing her in the direction of the door. "Hurry!" He didn't wait to see if she'd followed orders; he was too busy scrambling to call the fire magic, a shield, telekinesis, whatever the hell magic he could get his hands on, because he had a feeling he was going to need all of it and more.

Panic kindled in his gut, alongside excitement and a whisper of, *It's about time.*

"I don't want any trouble in here," the pizza guy snapped real quick. When nobody paid attention to him, he ducked down behind the counter and came up with a Louisville Slugger. He was halfway around the passthrough, weapon raised over his head, when Iago flicked the fingers of his free hand and said, "You're leaving now."

The guy got a blank look on his face, turned, and walked straight out the door. Rabbit froze too. *Holy shit.* This guy had some serious magical 'nads. He wasn't just a 'port; he could mind-bend too. What the hell else could he do?

Rabbit had a feeling he was about to find out, because Iago was headed in his direction, moving fast.

"Take this," Myrinne whispered, pressing something into Rabbit's hand. The feel of the stone haft and a serious buzz of power told him it was the knife. Then he heard footsteps and the slam of the back door.

The enemy mage slowed and stopped, and opened his fingers so Mistress Truth dropped in a heap on the floor, weeping softly. The big guy smiled mockingly. "Don't be a hero, kid. Hand it over and you'll live to report back to your father."

The taunt broke over Rabbit, chasing some of the terror with hurt, and the mixture of resentment and grief he couldn't seem to get past no matter how hard he tried. He closed his fingers over the knife and felt the blade bite into his palm, felt the blood flow. "News flash, asshole: Living isn't going to get me a convo with the old man. Dying will."

The blood sacrifice jacked him in; he stuck the knife in his belt and felt the barrier connection flare through him, starting in his bones and radiating outward, buzzing in his skull.

"Don't do it," Iago warned.

Rabbit would've told him to go fuck himself, but he couldn't find the words amidst the sudden spinning in his brain. Something was happening to him. A crazy pressure was crawling inside his skull, rooting around and taking him over, and then sudden rage poured through him, hot, angry joy, and the thrill of power. *Burn them,* something said deep inside him. *Burn them all.* He fought the impulse, but it quickly became a compulsion, an overwhelming need to destroy.

Blood riding high even as a small piece of him screamed, *Stop!* Rabbit clapped his palms together, dropped his head back, and shouted, *"Kaak!"*

The ancient word called the fire, called the gods, called a detonation that blasted through the room, laying waste to everything in its path. The front of the pizza joint blew outward in a hail of glass and superheated air. Flames lunged from Rabbit to the walls and ceiling.

Alarms wailed and people out on the street started screaming, shrill calls of, "Fire!" and, "Call nine-one-one!" and, "Hey, somebody's in there!"

At the center of the conflagration, completely untouched by the fire, Iago held out a hand, baring his crimson-marked forearm. "Give me the knife."

The order grabbed onto Rabbit, dug into him. *Give me the knife.* The words twined around his soul, twisting and caressing and making him want to do exactly that. *The knife,* his instincts said, *the knife, give him the knife.* Just as he hadn't wanted to call the fire, not really, he didn't want to give up the knife. But to his horror, he saw his bloody hand stretch out, saw his fingers open to offer up the bloodstained blade.

He's a mind-bender, he screamed inside his own skull. *Fight it, fight!* But he couldn't. He could only stand there while Iago grabbed the knife, gave him a middle-fingered salute, and disappeared, taking Mistress Truth with him.

Then there was nothing but the fire, and the screaming inside Rabbit's head as the world went dark, and he collapsed.

The door to the tea shop hung open. Nate was about to jump out of the cab, a really bad feeling knotting the pit of his stomach, when he smelled the smoke. That decided it for him. Lunging back into the taxi, he slammed the door and snapped, "We need to be where the fire is."

"Will do!" the cabbie shouted, and floored it, lost in some sort of James Bond fantasy and unaware that the reality was so much worse.

Alexis's expression tightened when a siren split the air, starting low and mournful and climbing to a shriek. "Damn it."

"Call Strike," Nate said. "We're going to need a quick exit. And have him bring Patience."

He took it as a bad sign that she didn't argue the need for the emergency evac 'port, or for Patience's talent of invisibility. Worse was the sight he caught when they rounded the next corner: glass blown out into the street, and most of a block aflame. *"Shit."*

He was out of the cab before it stopped moving. Aware that Alexis was right behind him he spun and snapped, "Stay here, and this time I fucking mean it!"

She called his name as he turned away, but he didn't look back. He headed straight into the flames, shouting, "Rabbit? Rabbit, goddamn it, answer me!"

There was no answer but the roar of fire. He sucked in another breath to try again, and pain seared his lungs, the foulness of smoky air grabbing on and doubling him over in a fit of coughing. He staggered onward, though, passing tables and chairs that had already burned to skeletons, as though they'd been liberally dosed with napalm.

Goddamn it, he was going to be seriously pissed if he died saving the kid's punk ass from fire he'd created himself and didn't have the chops to control. "Rabbit!" he shouted, his voice breaking.

And thank the freaking gods he got an answer, more a groan than any words, but it'd do. Staying low and holding what was left of his shirt across his mouth, Nate headed that way, not bothering to test the floor or worry about the flaming timbers overhead, because if he didn't move fast they were dead anyway.

"Keep talking!" he ordered, and heard another groan. Two more steps and his foot snagged on something and he went to his knees, kneeling atop a semiconscious Rabbit. "Got you," Nate said, voice cracking on smoke. "I've got you."

But who has me? he thought as he grabbed onto Rabbit's hoodie and jeans and started dragging the kid in what he thought was the direction of the door. The answer was, *Nobody.* He'd have to make it on his own, like always. But the room was spinning and the floor was pitching beneath his feet as he staggered onward, dragging Rabbit's limp body. He missed his next step and went down to his knees, then fell forward. He couldn't breathe, couldn't think, couldn't even feel the fire anymore. The flames were cool, licking across his skin like a lover.

He saw her face in the flames, saw her reach through the madness to touch him. But instead of the soft love she had in her eyes when he imagined her time and again—Hera, Alexis, one and the same—she looked terrified, resolute. And as she reached for him, someone else hurried past her and bent down to grab Rabbit. Then Nate felt the fantasy actually touch him, felt the jolt of contact, and he knew it wasn't a dream at all. Alexis had come after him.

And there was a damn good chance she was going to die right along with him.

Fuck! He grabbed onto her wrist, used it as a lifeline, and pulled himself partway up. He was aware of Strike slinging Rabbit over his shoulder. Then the king turned back and went for Nate's other side, so they were braced one against another, and it was all or nothing: Either all four of them made it out, or they died together, taking a quarter of the Nightkeepers' strength with them. And destiny or not, Nate wasn't letting that happen, wasn't letting Alexis lose herself trying to save him, not ever.

Together the Nightkeepers struggled from the burning building.

They made it out—barely. Just when they got clear of the door the whole place came down with a crash and a skyscraper-high gout of flame. Then Patience was there, grabbing onto the king and invoking her talent, and all five of them went invisible.

There were a few startled cries from bystanders who thought they'd seen what they couldn't possibly have seen, but the invisibility trick was quickly lost amidst the chaos of a four-plus-alarm blaze. Then golden magic flared, and the buzz of a teleport surrounded them. Nate barely had time to brace himself before he was jerked sideways and went flying into the gray-green nothingness of the king's 'port magic.

Nate held on to Alexis on his left side, Strike on his right. It hurt to breathe, to blink, to think, so he just hung there for a second in the gray-green nothingness of the barrier and let himself be dragged along. Then, with a bang of displaced air, Skywatch's great room materialized around them.

They zapped in maybe a foot off the floor and hovered for a second before gravity took over. In that second Nate realized his skin was burning and his lungs were seized with smoke. Instead of landing on his feet he hit the floor and curled up, hacking for all he was worth, trying to breathe. He fought back a scream and it came out as a groan.

"Nate!" Alexis dropped down beside him, her hands hovering in midair, as though she wanted to touch him but didn't dare. He didn't know whether it was meant as comfort, to reassure herself that he was alive, or, hell, to remind the king that she'd been an important part of the rescue, but Nate found it to be a nice moment nonetheless. And for a few seconds, as the coughing eased and the Nightkeepers' accelerated healing started to do its thing, he let himself relax and pretend she'd come after him because he mattered, not in the grand scheme of the Nightkeepers, but to her personally.

"Thanks," he said, though it came out as more of a croak.

She went still for a moment, and he was expecting a dig or a snappy comeback, so he was surprised when she said only, "You're welcome." And then she touched him, laying her palm against his scorched cheek so she could send him a wash of warmth and power, and an edge of softness he hadn't known he needed until just then.

Once Nate was asleep—okay, so he'd passed out, but who could blame him?—Alexis stepped back so Carlos and Jox could carry him to his room and get him cleaned up. She badly needed a shower too, but instead she found herself crouching down beside Rabbit, opposite Strike and Leah.

The king's face was streaked with soot and burn marks, the latter of which were already most of the way healed. But the strain and worry didn't ease; they wouldn't, Alexis knew, until the teen awoke.

"We left him behind so he'd be safe," she said softly, feeling guilt dig deep. "We didn't know the witch would come back to the tea shop." Which didn't explain why Rabbit had been three blocks away when he'd called the fire magic. But it also didn't own the full responsibility she carried. "I should've listened to Nate," she said, her shoulders sagging beneath the failure. "When the witch refused to sell us the knife outright, he wanted to steal it and get back home. I convinced him to wait. It's my fault."

But the king shook his head. "You didn't do this. The redhead did."

Rabbit stirred and whispered something from between cracked lips.

Strike leaned in. "Come again?"

"Iago," Rabbit said, his voice a dry rasp. "His name is Iago. And you were right; he's Order of Xibalba."

Leah stiffened. "How do you know?"

"Myrinne told me. Iago offered the witch a deal." The teen exhaled and faded again.

"Who the hell is Myrinne?" Strike demanded, voice rough with worry.

Alexis said, "If I'm guessing right, a dark-haired girl with a shiner; I think she may be the witch's apprentice or servant, maybe her daughter."

"Which means she probably knows what she's talking about. Shit. Order of Xibalba." He shared a complicated look with Leah, one that excluded Alexis and the rest of the world.

Leah nodded. "Yeah. Problem."

"I'm sorry I lost the knife," Rabbit said, his cracked voice painful to hear.

"Not your fault either," Strike said with a look at Alexis. He reached out to touch the boy, then hesitated and let his hand fall. "Heal up. We'll talk later."

At the king's word, Jox came in to tend the boy. Strike rose with a soft curse and headed out of the room, with Leah following. The cop-turned-queen paused at the archway leading to the louvered hall and raised an eyebrow at Alexis. "You coming?"

Alexis stalled, confused. "I don't . . . I didn't . . . what?" Treacherous hope unfurled. "You want me in on your meeting? Even though I screwed up?"

"At least you tried something," Leah said, her blue eyes cool and assessing, not giving away a thing. "You interested in maybe trying something else, or at least talking strategy?"

Alexis was filthy and sore, and a weak, feminine part of her really wanted to check in on Nate, but all of those things could wait. The toehold to an advisory position, the one thing she'd wanted ever since this all began, was being offered to her. She took a tentative step in Leah's direction, aware that the king was standing behind his mate, waiting for Alexis's decision.

She paused a moment longer, then lifted her chin and nodded, accepting her mother's place—her rightful place—among the king's council. "Count me in."

CHAPTER EIGHT

"Today is not a good day to travel this road," said Abe, the guide Lucius had hired to lead him into the Yucatán rain forest. The vague warning was the fifth he'd given in the past hour, as he and Lucius trekked along a nonpath through the heart of the jungle.

Lucius wasn't sure if the guy was trying to spook him, or if he really thought the gods had slapped a big old cosmic Keep Out sign across their path. But if anyone was going to get the omens right, it was someone like Abe, who was in training to become a Daykeeper, a shamanistic tradition the modern Maya had retained from their long-ago ancestors. Centuries of push-pull between Christianization and tradition had given birth to a blended religion that nodded to Christian themes while retaining many of the old ceremonies and beliefs, including the Daykeepers, who were in charge of the multiple Mayan calendars and their associated prophecies and portents.

According to Abe, those portents indicated that the spirits of the rain forest were restless, and wanted Lucius out of their 'hood.

Normally Lucius would've given in. Anna had taught him early on that a Mayanist worked within the local community, even when studying the ancient glyph system that was no longer practiced in the modern day. If she'd been there, she would've turned back on warning number two or three. She wouldn't've kept going until Abe broke out in a light sweat and his eyes went wild around the edges. But Anna wasn't there, and Lucius had no intention of turning back. Something was pulling him onward, drawing him along the faint pathway one of Ledbetter's grad students had mentioned seeing in his notes. The old coot had been secretive about the site, the girl had said; he'd nearly bitten her head off when he realized she'd seen the journal entry.

That was what she'd told Sasha Ledbetter when she'd come looking for a clue as to where her father had gone. And Lucius, thanks to Desiree and her magic AmEx, had followed, more than four months after Sasha had flown south, and fallen off the map, just like her old man.

Logic said that Ambrose Ledbetter and his daughter had perished, probably taking with them whatever Ambrose had known about the Nightkeepers. But Lucius needed to know for sure.

As though in answer to his thought, the wind picked up, moaning through the top level of the leafy canopy in an eerie descant. *Okay, that's creepy,* Lucius admitted inwardly. *Doesn't mean I'm quitting, though.*

Abe planted himself in the middle of the nonpath and jammed his machete into the loam. "We're going back now."

"It was just the wind," Lucius said, because really, there was nothing to suggest otherwise. The birds and critters were still doing their thing, and the sun still dappled through the canopy, though slanting a little lower in the sky than it'd been when they left the Jeep at the place where the narrow footpath intersected the muddy track that passed for a road. The air hadn't changed. Nothing was different.

Yet at the same time, something *was* different, he realized suddenly. There was a hum in the air that hadn't been there before, subsonic, almost a buzz running beneath his skin.

"I'm not going back," he said before he was even aware of having made the decision.

"I am." Abe stepped away and spit on the ground. "Good luck."

The loogie wasn't a sign of disrespect, Lucius knew, but rather the exact opposite. Moisture was precious in the Yucatán, where water ran entirely underground, coming to the surface only at circular openings, fallen-through sinkholes called cenotes. The spittle was a sacrifice. A blessing.

Or, more likely, a gesture of, *Gods be with you, dumb-ass*.

The Daykeeper left the machete and his canteen and took off, humping it back down the trail at more than twice the speed they'd made forging forward.

"Thanks for your help," Lucius called, figuring there was no need for hurt feelings. He had plenty of supplies, a GPS unit, and a satellite phone for emergencies. He could see the path—more or less, anyway—and figured there was a good bet that the temple site he was looking for was somewhere up ahead. He was good to go.

Yet his feet wouldn't move.

He stood there as the sound of Abe's retreat faded into the background jungle chatter, and he was completely frozen as the two halves of him pulled in diametrically opposite directions. The logical part of him, the part that'd absorbed Anna's training and already couldn't believe he'd gone behind her back like this, wanted to go with Abe. The Daykeeper knew his shit. If he said the signs were wrong, then the signs were wrong and it was time to leave.

The other part of him, though, the part that brought him strange, twisted dreams in the night, dreams that curled with fire and tasted of blood—that part of him wanted to grab the machete and keep going. The temple was up ahead; he could feel it, practically see it. There was no reason to turn back now and every reason to keep going. And then he *was* moving, though he couldn't have said why or how; he just knew he had the machete in his hand and was using it to widen the narrow trail, pushing through the densely packed vegetation, wading through an ocean of green.

Five minutes later he saw the first sign of civilization he'd seen in hours, and it wasn't modern. The carved stone pillar lay on its side, broken into three pieces along the seams where the stacked sections had been sealed together.

Called stelae, such pillars had been the Maya's billboards. In the ruined city of Chichén Itzá, they were grouped together by the hundreds in the Hall of Pillars, and had offered up everything from local proclamations and records of political changes to histories and legends. Elsewhere—including the burbs of Chichén—stelae were scattered farther out, standing alone, sometimes in the seeming middle of nowhere, a testament to a culture that might be long gone, but remained alive in its writings. Those scattered stelae had typically been more along the lines of road markers . . . or sometimes warnings.

Feeling a creepy-crawl heading down the back of his neck, Lucius knelt beside the stela and swiped at the encroaching vegetation, which had grown only partway up to cover the carved limestone. *Can't have fallen that long ago,* he thought as the heady excitement of fieldwork cleared his brain a little. *Would've been covered otherwise.*

If it'd been any more overgrown he might not've seen it. As it was, the only reason he'd noticed the white-hued stone was because he'd had to hack around a section of denser brush. It was a happy coincidence that he'd stumbled on the thing. Or maybe it'd been fate. The Nightkeepers hadn't believed in coincidence, after all.

Using the flat of the machete to scrape away some thorny, clinging vines, he uncovered a swath of carved stone. It took a second for the sight of the main glyph to register. When it did, he stopped breathing.

He'd found the screaming skull.

It was the one glyph he'd needed to prove his thesis. The one glyph he'd been unable to conclusively identify from actual writing samples.

"Holy shit." He'd been so sure it existed, had been pretty sure he'd found it at least twice before, but Anna had torpedoed his translation the first time, and the second time . . . well, back then they'd still been friends and he'd taken her at her word that it was really Jaguar-Paw's laughing-skull glyph. In retrospect, he had a feeling she'd Photoshopped his digitals to make sure of it. And wasn't that a nasty suspicion?

A faint warning bell chimed at the back of his head, a brain worm that said the thoughts weren't his own, and neither was the anger. But as he knelt there and the damp worked through the fabric of his breathable nylon cargo pants, the rage took root and started to grow.

He'd trusted her, and she'd blocked him at every turn. *I'll show her,* he thought, pulling his camera out of his pack and taking a dozen snaps of the stela, and the telltale glyph that symbolized the Nightkeepers' involvement in the zero date, and their vow to protect mankind. In theory, anyway.

"No theory about it," he said, rising to his feet and shouldering his pack, the weight feeling far lighter than it had only moments earlier as the certainty flowed through him. He was almost there, almost at the end of years of searching for something the experts said didn't exist. The stela had been a marker; he was sure of it. And maybe a warning, but he couldn't bring himself to care, just as he hadn't been scared off by Abe's talk of bad omens.

The thrill of excitement drew him onward, the promise of discovery, the mystery of what the hell'd happened to Ambrose Ledbetter, and the burning certainty that he had to find Ambrose's daughter, Sasha.

Lucius had e-mailed Ambrose once or twice about his end-time theories, but the old coot had stonewalled him, and their one in-person meeting had been more of a midconference snarl in passing from Ledbetter than an actual meeting. Lucius hadn't even known Ledbetter had a daughter until Sasha had phoned the glyph lab looking for Anna. Yet it was Sasha's voice he heard at the back of his head as he hacked his way along the thin trail, and her picture, which he'd downloaded from the Web page of the high-end restaurant where she worked, that he held in the forefront of his mind. She was pretty enough—okay, gorgeous—but it wasn't her looks that he'd focused most on. There had been something about her eyes, something about their shape and intensity. That something had sent a chill down his spine and kicked some serious heat into his bloodstream, driving him onward.

He wasn't expecting that she'd be at the temple, was actually hoping he didn't find her there, because if he did, odds were he'd be looking at her remains. But if luck—or fate—was with him, then he'd find a clue to where she and Ambrose had disappeared to.

The background hum of the rain forest—bugs or something, he didn't know what—rose as the sunlight went from afternoon slant to predusk dimness. He knew he should make camp, but something pushed him to keep going—a lighter patch up ahead, maybe, or perhaps simply the certainty that he was close, so close to his destination.

And then he was there. One second he was hacking at clinging green fronds, and the next his machete broke clear. Expecting his rote-mechanical swing to meet resistance, he stumbled forward when it hit only air, and wound up in a small clearing that was barely the size of his apartment kitchen.

A gap in the canopy let through a shaft of light from the setting sun, and the beam shone bloodred on a carved stone doorway leading into the side of a hill. Only it wasn't a hill, he realized after a second. It was an unrestored ruin, a pyramid that had succumbed to a thousand years of zero maintenance and been reclaimed by the land. Vegetation had covered all the stone with leaves and clinging vines, with the exception of the doorway, which gleamed almost new-looking in the fading light. It was a stone arch, with the cornice and lintelwork that the Maya stoneworkers had put into regular use by the height of the empire. They might not've had the wheel or known how to work metal, but they'd been pretty damn untouchable when it came to rock.

This wasn't just Mayan, though. There was an elongated elegance to it, one that reminded him of another pyramid-building culture on the other side of the world, one that had faltered into despotism after the Nightkeepers left and the sun god Aten held sway.

A faint shimmy started in Lucius's gut and worked its way out from there. High above him parrots called to one another and loose-limbed monkeys played tag in the gathering dusk. Down at ground level, though, there was strange stillness, and a hum that touched the air. Rubbing his scarred palm, which ached from all the machete work, he took a step toward the doorway, almost expecting it to disappear, for him to wake up and find himself in his crummy apartment, in the middle of his lame-ass, going-backward life.

But it didn't. He was really there, and so was the doorway.

"Here goes nothing," he said, scrabbling in his knapsack for his flashlight. Clicking it on, he took a couple more steps, passed beneath the lintel—

And nearly fell straight into nothing when the floor dropped out beneath him.

He saw the pitfall in time—barely—and stopped at the edge, where interlocking stones formed a tunnel that descended at an acute slant, ending somewhere deep in the earth, beyond the reach of his flashlight beam. Adrenaline spiked and he stepped back a pace, but the stone didn't give way beneath him. The trap had already been sprung.

From the scrapes in the dirt, it hadn't been triggered all that long ago, either. Rain had wiped the tracks within the first ten feet or so of the entrance, but beneath his own footprints he could see another set. Damned if they didn't look like the same kind of boot treads too, only smaller, as though the person who'd been there before him was a woman, or maybe a teen. Wearing trekking boots of the sort favored by fieldworkers.

His stomach did a nosedive as he shone his light downward once again. "Sasha? Are you down there?"

There was no answer. Not that he should've expected there to be. She was a chef, not a field archaeologist, which suggested the boot prints weren't hers. Besides, like it or not, whoever had gone down, they'd done it before the rains, which meant a couple of months at least.

Lucius felt a beat of grief for whoever it'd been, along with relief that he had a good reason not to go down there. Clamping the flashlight in his teeth, he edged around the pitfall, not letting out his breath until he was safe on the other side and there was no sign of a second booby trap. *Not yet, anyway,* he thought. But the presence of the first trap was oddly encouraging: It suggested there was—or had been—something in the ruin worth guarding.

"So onward we go," he said, talking to himself because it was too damn quiet inside the low tunnel that narrowed beyond the pit trap. Using the flashlight to check his footing, he worked his way deeper into what he suspected wasn't the ruins of a temple that'd been built up from the ground, but rather one that'd been dug into the earth itself. The tunnel sloped slightly downward as he walked, and the air was damp and chill.

Once again he saw evidence of someone else having been there ahead of him fairly recently. Two someones, in fact: A man's wide-footed tread was marked over with a woman's print. Oddly, though, the woman's print didn't match the tread Lucius had seen near the booby trap. If he figured the prints he was following now belonged to Ambrose and Sasha Ledbetter, then who had made the first set? And why weren't there tracks leading back out? That in itself seemed pretty damn ominous.

"Doesn't matter," he told himself. "Keep going." So he did just that, heading deeper into the Nightkeeper temple. Because that was where he had to be.

The walls of the tunnel were uncarved, but the stonework was meticulous, and the vibe . . . well, the vibe deep in his gut told him he'd found what he was looking for. He just needed some sort of proof to bring back to Desiree. And Anna.

At the thought of Anna, a complicated mix of guilt and resentment bloomed in his chest. For a second his old crush on Anna surfaced, making him feel like total shit for doing what he was doing, the way he was doing it. Then the hum rose up once again, blunting the fear and the grief and the guilt, making him numb to everything except the footprints that led him on, and the tunnel closing in around him.

Then, without warning, the shaft dead-ended at a pile of rubble. But it wasn't just any rubble he saw in the yellow light of his flashlight beam. The debris had been cleared and stacked into a shrine of sorts, and a crude teepee had been formed of lashed-together sticks. And atop it sat a human head. Lucius reeled back, gagging at the sight and the sudden stench of rot and death. But even his response to finding the skull felt muted, as though the hum in his bones were overriding his natural instincts. Leaning closer, he inspected the thing. Strips of skin and flesh were still adhered in places, though creatures and time had done some serious damage. Still, though, he could see that the skull had once sported long gray hair; some of it was still caught back in a leather-laced ponytail.

He'd found Ledbetter, or part of him, anyway. But where was the rest of him, and who had placed his head so elaborately? Why?

He figured the shrine had probably been an effort to mimic the pyramidal piles of skulls, called *tzomplanti* that the Maya had built at the height of their sacrificial practices. They had piled the heads of their sacrifices one atop the next and left them on platforms or at the city limits as a warning to their enemies. *This is what we'll do to you,* the *tzomplanti* had signaled. *Be warned.* But who had this warning been intended for?

"What happened to you, old man?" Lucius whispered, his voice echoing oddly. "Where's Sasha?"

The second set of feminine footprints was there too, smudged and scuffed over the top of the bootprints, but the dust was really messed up at that point, churned up amidst rust-brown splashes he had to assume were blood. Strangely drawn by the stains he crouched down to touch one of the bloodstains with his fingers, and felt a tingle when he made contact. It was almost as though there were two of him inside: One wanted to touch the blood and the skull and see if the tingling grew stronger; the other wanted to keep looking and see if there was any evidence of where Sasha had gone from there.

Forcing his fingers away from the bloodstains, he swept his flashlight in a low arc, stopping when he came across two new sets of footprints in the dust at the edge of the cave-in. They looked like the marks from . . . men's street shoes and a pair of high heels?

"You're shitting me." But even after he'd blinked a few times the marks were still there. He hadn't seen them anywhere else in the tunnel; nor did they seem to lead beneath the piled rubble. It was as though whoever belonged to the footprints had just appeared out of thin air, then disappeared once they'd done what they'd come to do. Which was just ridiculous. There had to be another explanation. He didn't know what, but there had to be. So he kept looking, sending his flashlight beam arcing from one side of the tunnel to the other, hoping to hell the literal dead end wouldn't turn out to be a metaphorical one too.

Then the flashlight beam glinted off something, there and gone so quickly he almost missed it. But when he repeated the action he got the same gleam again. More important, he got another glow farther down the tunnel, then another. There were mirrors on the walls, he realized. Rather, they were highly polished spots on the stone angled precisely so they caught the light and bounced it from one to the next and then on again.

The Egyptians had used metal mirrors to bring sunlight into their tombs and pyramids, Lucius thought as excitement kicked through his bloodstream. The ancient Maya, on the other hand, had worked by torchlight. The presence of the mirrors in the temple was another confirmation of the crossover, the connection from one continent to the next, one people to the other. But it was so much more, because for them to have bothered polishing the stone mirrors, there had to be something to see.

And it's probably on the other side of the damn cave-in, he realized, his stomach dropping in acid disappointment. *Unless* . . . he thought, jumping into the myth with both feet, not sure when he would hit bottom, *what if it's starscript?* The Maya had sometimes used moonlight to hide secret text within public carvings. The Nightkeepers had used the stars.

Holding his breath, he turned off his flashlight.

It was damned eerie standing there, alone in the darkness waiting for his eyes to adjust, knowing that Ambrose Ledbetter's skull was only a few feet away. He found himself saying quietly, "I promise that I'll find her. I'll protect her. I swear it on my life."

The words came out of nowhere, as did the urge to close his hand on the machete blade so it scored his palm across the thick ridge of scar tissue. Realizing he'd done exactly that without meaning to, he closed his eyes, balled his bleeding hand into a fist, and repeated the vow.

His blood dripped to join the other stains, and the hum in the air went silent.

When he opened his eyes once again he was surrounded in silver light, starlight that had reflected in from the distant entrance. And right in front of him were words picked out in starlight that hadn't been there for his flashlight.

It's starscript, he thought, floored. *It's real.*

Sweat broke out all over Lucius's body at the magic of it. This was confirmation, if he'd needed it, that he was in a Nightkeeper temple. But that wasn't the most shocking part. No, the thing that blew him away and set him back on his ass was the words the starscript spelled out. Not glyphs, not ancient Mayan. It was freaking written in English.

"Ledbetter," he breathed. "Fuck me." The old goat had left a message. In starscript.

It was an address.

Had Sasha read the message? Was that where she'd gone? Or had the owners of the other footprints taken her before she got the message? He refused to consider the alternative: that she'd been killed and her head was rotting on a skull pile somewhere else in the ruin. She had to be alive, had to be, though he didn't know why the hell it was so important for him to believe that.

Breathing shallowly through his nose, he fought the shock, fought the buzz, and ignored the questions. Riding the excitement of the starscript and the thrill of the hunt, he pulled a notebook and pen out of his knapsack and scribbled down the addy. He didn't know who or what was there, but he sure as hell intended to find out.

Anna might've told Strike that she'd catch an earlier plane and work on translating the starscript at the base of the Ixchel statuette, but after the cluster-freak of a thesis defense, along with Lucius letting drop that Desiree had been Dick's mistress, Anna had needed the drive time from Austin to New Mex. She'd driven until she'd cried herself dry and moved on to exhausted, and then she'd flopped at some motel in the middle of nowhere and slept until she woke up. Which meant that by the time she got to Skywatch, it was just about the same time she would've been arriving if she'd kept her original flight.

She'd needed the time alone, though. It wasn't as if she would've done the Nightkeepers any good arriving early and all stuck inside her own head. While she couldn't say she'd come to any earth-shattering decisions along the way, at least she was vaguely centered, which she needed to be, given that the lunar eclipse was less than twenty-four hours away. Her mental shields might be slammed and locked, preventing her from seeing good, ill or anywhere in between, but she could still feel the magic growing stronger as the time passed, as the miles passed. Finally, as she pulled into the circular driveway in front of the mansion that Leah had named Skywatch, Anna had a feeling she could break through the barrier if she chose, and see the future if she wanted to. Which she didn't. Not ever again.

"Which means the only thing I'm really contributing here is glyph geekage," she said aloud. "So I should shift my ass and get to it."

Still, it took her a long moment to get out of her Lexus. She'd parked out front instead of in the big garage, figuring she should make it clear from the get-go that she wasn't staying. She was just passing through again, fulfilling her promise. But parking out front had the downside that it aimed her toward the front door, and the plaque that Leah had given Strike as a kick in the ass the previous fall when he'd refused to step up as either king or leader, trying to deny the inevitable.

That was the thing about destiny, though. Somehow the bitch always caught up with you.

Sighing, Anna stopped with her hand on the doorbell and glanced at the plaque. The name Skywatch was engraved above an etched line drawing of a ceiba tree, very like the one that grew behind the mansion, rising from the ashes of the hundreds of *winikin* and Nightkeeper children who had been killed during the Solstice Massacre. There was no reason the rain forest–dwelling ceiba tree should've been able to survive in the desert canyon; nor had it been planted by any human hand. It had sprung from the ashes of the dead as a symbol. A reminder.

It played the same role on Leah's plaque, along with the words below it, which spelled out the motto the ex-cop had given them. Written in modern Mayan, it spelled out the three cardinal tenets the modern Nightkeepers had vowed to live: TO FIGHT. TO PROTECT. TO FORGIVE.

Except that Anna wanted to do none of those things. She just wanted to be left alone.

Sighing at the thought, and at the self-pity that had turned into too familiar a friend of late, she stopped herself from ringing the doorbell and pushed open the front door instead. She drew breath to shout a hello, knowing that Strike and Jox were expecting her, because she'd called from the road.

The greeting died in her throat when a ghost stepped into the front hallway, one that had traveled in time.

She knew his fierce eyes from her childhood, the slashing blade of his nose, and the high cheekbones. She knew the shape of his skull where he'd shaved his hair close, leaving faint bristles behind. He was slightly taller than she, and lean-hipped with youth beneath worn jeans, broad through the shoulders like all Nightkeeper males, with muscles to match the warrior's mark he wore on his inner forearm, along with his bloodline and talent glyphs.

"Red-Boar," she whispered, though she wasn't sure

the words actually came out aloud. But did it really matter? Fantasy, figment, or spirit—surely it could read her mind?

"Hey, Anna," the apparition said, only the voice was wrong. And then the ghost shifted from one foot to the other and slipped something into his pocket, and the air around him changed and she saw that it wasn't the father at all. It was the son.

"Rabbit." This time her voice had sound and shape, leaving her lungs in a rush. "You've grown." It wasn't just the size of him, either. His face was different than it'd been in the fall, which was the last time she'd seen him, because she'd made an excuse to skip the winter solstice ritual.

He half turned, and jerked his head in the direction of the great room. "Strike's in there."

"Thanks." She was seriously unnerved by how much he looked like the young man his father had been, back when she was a girl and the Nightkeepers had numbered into the hundreds. She moved to pass the teen, then stopped when she saw the rough patch of a partly healed burn that twisted its way across the side of his neck, then down beneath the undershirt. She sucked in a breath. "What happened to your neck?"

He raised a hand reflexively to touch the spot. "Long story."

Standing near him, she caught a strange smell. It was the odor of smoke and blood, but it wasn't that of incense and ritual sacrifice. More like a house fire, though there was no sign of damage aside from the scar, which would fade in time, courtesy of their healing magic. "I can make time," she said. "I'd like to hear it."

She hadn't known Rabbit well as a little boy. She'd been in full-on teenage rebellion mode right about the time Red-Boar had reappeared in her, Strike's, and Jox's lives, towing a toddler he'd refused to give a proper name or bloodline ritual. She'd been reeling from the horrifying loss of her parents—and her entire world structure—and she hadn't made it easy for anyone to like her, never mind love her. Not long after Red-Boar's return, she'd taken off for college. After thoroughly embarrassing herself, of course, but Rabbit didn't ever need to know that she'd once propositioned his father.

Still, the history was there. The link was there.

"Why do you care?" Whereas Rabbit had been in perma-sullen mode the previous fall, now there was an actual edge of curiosity in the question.

"Because we're both on the outside looking in."

He seemed to consider that for a few seconds, then nodded. "Fair enough." He didn't say yes or no and she didn't press, but as she followed him into the great room she felt a little less alone than she had only moments earlier.

When she reached the main room of the mansion, she found the rest of the Nightkeepers and the *winikin* waiting for her, taking up the sectional sofa and a bunch of chairs, with the remainder sitting at the bar near the kitchen, or sprawled on the floor. All twenty of them. Back before the massacre, the entire complement of Nightkeepers and *winikin* wouldn't have fit in the mansion, never mind the great room. There were so few of them now. Too few.

"Anna." Her brother rose to his feet and crossed to her, arms outstretched. "Welcome home."

She returned Strike's hug and didn't correct the *home* thing, mostly because that'd been the upshot of her soul-searching road trip: She didn't know where home was anymore. She'd thought it was with Dick, had wanted it to be, or thought she did. But how badly could she want it if learning the ID of his mistress had sent her running? The affair was over and done with, and they'd been making efforts to rekindle the romance in their marriage. She should've stayed and either talked it out with him or found a way to let the past stay in the past.

But everything that's happened before will happen again, her suspicions put in, using the Nightkeepers writs to give form to her fears. He'd been unfaithful at least once before; what was to say he wouldn't do it again? Worse, her gut told her that Desiree was after her because he'd given her reason to think their affair still had a chance. How could she reconcile all that?

She couldn't, which was why she'd come to Skywatch. And, she realized as she leaned into the solid bulk of her brother, who had grown even larger with the responsibilities of being a mated man, and a king, she'd needed her family, such as it was. "Hey, baby brother," she said, pressing her cheek to his. "What'd I miss?"

There was a snort from up on the bar stools, where the *winikin* were sitting, overseeing their charges. "What didn't you miss?" parried Jox, the man who'd been as much of a father to her as her real father had been even before the massacre.

Moving slowly, feeling the ache of too much thinking and driving, Anna disengaged from Strike and crossed the room to hug the royal *winikin*. She sketched a wave at Leah and hitched herself up on the bar behind Jox, so she was sitting with the *winikin* rather than the magi. She smiled at the others, who all looked pretty much the same as when she'd seen them last—young and big and gorgeous, and just starting to come into their powers. "Am I interrupting?"

"We were actually waiting for you," Strike said. "Command performance." He handed her a sheet of paper marked with a string of hand-drawn glyphs.

She frowned at the copied inscription. "What's this?"

"The starscript off the Ixchel statuette. We had good starlight last night, and figured this'd save time, given that you didn't wind up getting an earlier flight."

"Long story," she said, echoing Rabbit's earlier words to her. "Okay. Give me"—*an hour*, she started to say, but even before she could finish the thought, the glyphs were rearranging themselves in her brain, forming pictures first, then words.

She didn't know if it was a vision or something else, but the crimson power of the royal jaguar bloodline flowed through her, sweeping her up and carrying her along. Her vision washed red, then gold, and when the mists cleared she could read the inscription as though it were written in English, plain as day.

"Anna," Strike said, crossing to her to grab her shoulder and give her a shake. "What's wrong?"

She batted him away. "Nothing. It's just . . . Nothing." She let the paper drop, because the words were burned in her brain. "To paraphrase, it reads: The first son of Camazotz succeeds unless the Volatile—" She broke off.

"Unless the Volatile does what?" Strike pressed.

"That's it. You must've missed some glyphs."

But he shook his head. "That was all of it. I'm certain. Which means . . ." He trailed off. "It means we're missing a piece of the statuette. Fuck."

The obscenity was echoed by another of the magi, one whom Anna didn't know as well as some: Nate Blackhawk. The dark, handsome Nightkeeper muttered something else under his breath, then shot a look at Alexis Gray, with whom he'd been involved the year before. They must've come to some sort of truce, Anna realized, because Alexis met his eyes and nodded, her lips twisting in a smile that held zero humor when she said, "Current score: bad guys, two; Nightkeepers, zero-point-five. Looks like we've got another artifact to find."

Anna nodded. "And it'd help if we figured out what exactly this Volatile is supposed to be and how it works."

"That much we managed to do," Strike said, tone dark. He glanced at Jade, indicating that the archivist had been the one to find the record.

"And?" Anna pressed.

"It's a damned shape-shifter."

After the meeting broke up, Nate headed out along the narrow, rocky path that led from the training compound to the small Pueblo ruins high on the cliff face at the back of the box canyon. He needed some time alone to deal with the frustration that rose exponentially with each minute that brought them closer to the lunar eclipse. They were down to less than twenty-four hours and counting, and he could practically see magic in the air and smell sex on the breeze.

Or was it that he had sex on the brain? Either way,

it was all he could think about. He was hard and horny, and pissed off at learning that the Ixchel statuette wasn't complete. How had they missed seeing that a portion was broken off? The overturned basket or whatever the goddess sat atop had a flat side they'd assumed had been left rough on purpose, but now it was looking like a fracture plane, damn it. Which meant . . . what? They didn't even know what the missing piece looked like. How the hell were they supposed to find it?

"For fuck's sake," he said aloud, trying to gain control over the irritation, which he knew was as much about the magic as real anger. Then he heard footsteps coming up the pathway behind him, and the anger redirected itself, going from fury to a raging heat that he had even less control over. He knew who it was instantly, not through magic, but because the quick, self-assured stride could've belonged to no one else but Alexis. The warrior-princess.

When she rounded the corner, the sight of her was a kick in his chest. She was lovely in the moonlight—not soft, never soft, but the angles of her face and jaw combined into a mysterious effect, one that made him think of secrets and shadows, and the things they'd done to each other in the dark of night.

The eclipse fire rose up, threatening to take him over, to make him do things he wouldn't do otherwise. "What do you want?" he snapped, temptation roughening his voice.

She hesitated. "Carlos is looking for you."

"You didn't come all the way out here to tell me that."

"No." She lifted her chin in challenge. "I came to see you."

Holding himself still was a struggle. "Bad idea."

"Probably. But don't tell me you haven't been thinking about it." She glanced up at the sky, where the moon shone nearly full. "It wouldn't have to mean anything, or take us back where we were before. We could agree that it's just the barrier talking. The magic."

Which was exactly what he didn't want it to be between them. Heat flared in his veins, a sharp-edged howl of lust and need, but he dug his fingernails into his palms and forced his hands to stay still when they would've reached for her. "Tell Carlos I'll talk to him in the morning," he said, rejecting her offer by not mentioning it.

She stood there for a long moment, limned in moonlight. Then she turned and walked away, leaving him sitting alone in the night by the burial ruins of an ancient people much younger than his own. He was still there, dry eyed, exhausted, and lonely, when the sun came up and the eclipse day dawned.

The final hours before the eclipse both dragged and flew. As the day wore on, Alexis could feel the tingle of the barrier reaching out to her, making her crazy. Which was pretty much her only excuse for what she'd done—or rather tried to do—the night before.

Her cheeks burned at the memory, even though she'd already tortured herself throughout a long, sleepless night. She kept picturing the look on Nate's face—total disinterest with a liberal dose of annoyance—as she'd pimped herself out, offering strings-free eclipse sex. What the hell had she been thinking? She hadn't been; that was the answer. She'd simply gone back to old, bad habits.

She'd been the one to go looking for Nate that first time, just as she'd been the one to go after Aaron, and the guy before him, and the one before that, ad infinitum. She was usually the aggressor, the one who gave chase, mostly because she aimed so far out of her own league. And yeah, sometimes she got turned down. But not like this. Never like this. She was becoming *that* girl, the one everyone else pitied because she kept going back to the ex who hadn't treated her all that well in the first place. She not only took the booty call when the phone rang; she was the one doing the dialing. And where had it gotten her? No-fucking-where.

She was pathetic.

"Damn it," she muttered, pacing away from the window of her small suite, shrugging against the chafe of her weapons belt as resentment dug, not just against Nate but against all of them. She was pissed off, and jealous of the other Nightkeepers, who'd headed out to the training center to blow some shit up. Their powers were all ramping up as the eclipse approached. Her powers—what she had, anyway—had stayed flatlined; only her hormones had ramped. Which was just so not fair. Her mother had been a powerful mage, for chrissake. How come she'd lost the magic lottery? Was it because her father had been relatively weak? Izzy had implied that his minimal talents were why she carried her mother's bloodline name and mark; her parents had been trying to ensure that she had the best chance of gaining power, of being someone.

So far that hadn't exactly worked out, which was another thing that had anger spiking. What if—

Take a breath, she told herself. *This isn't you. It's the barrier.* The magic was making her nuts.

Stalking into her bathroom, she gave herself a once-over, knowing it was nearly time to meet the others for transpo to the intersection for the eclipse ceremony. The combat clothes she wore had been her mother's; Izzy had pulled them out of storage and made the necessary repairs once Alexis had graduated from the midnight blue robes of a Nightkeeper trainee. Alexis would've preferred to go with modern clothes, but it'd meant so much to Izzy that she hadn't fought it. The pants were basic black, and loose enough at the waist that Alexis could wear them at her hips, but tight enough at the legs that she looked like a chick rather than a drag queen. The shirt was black as well, made of heavy, stretchable fabric, and the cuffs were worked with intricate sprays of blue and white stone beads that were arranged in stylized designs symbolizing the smoke bloodline.

Looking at her face in the mirror, Alexis tried to see the woman from the vision, tried to see her mother in herself. And failed.

Where Gray-Smoke had been willowy and elegant in every picture showing her, Alexis was sturdy and . . . well, not elegant. Where her mother had had high, narrow cheekbones and a delicately pointed chin, Alexis's face was broad and anything but delicate. Almond-shaped eyes didn't match wide and round, and hazel didn't match blue.

They had nothing physically in common, and even less

in terms of magic, yet they were bound by blood, and perhaps by destiny.

"What if I don't ever find my magic?" Alexis whispered to her own reflection. "What if I fail?"

For a second her reflected image fogged up and wavered, as though it might answer, as though she'd drawn on the barrier to pull scrying magic she didn't know how to manage. Then she blinked and the picture solidified, and she realized it wasn't magic at all. It was tears. And she was being a wuss. She was supposed to draw strength from the barrier on the peak days, not cringe away from it. But with her streaky hair pulled back into a practical French braid and no makeup on, she felt exposed. Cool currents of air touched her body, tightening her skin and making her too aware of the brush of the heavy fabric and the weight of what was to come. Once Strike 'ported them to the safe house near the ruins of Chichén Itzá and they descended into the sacred tunnels below the ancient city, they were going enact the transition ritual and support Patience in her bid to become a Godkeeper, with Brandt as her Nightkeeper mate. And if that brought another slice of jealousy, nobody else needed to know how small Alexis really was, how petty.

There was a quiet knock at the door to her suite, followed by Izzy's voice calling, "You just about ready, princess?"

Don't call me that, Alexis wanted to snap. She didn't, though, because she knew the spiky irritability was the magic, nothing more. And besides, Izzy had called her that long before Nate had turned it into a sneer. The *winikin* meant it as an endearment, a reminder of what Alexis was meant to be. And maybe that was part of the problem. The pressure and expectations came from her bloodline, from her family's history. Not from her own potential for a damn thing. In a way she didn't belong here any more than she'd belonged at the Newport Yacht Club, and she kept wondering why nobody seemed to see it except her.

"Coming," she called in answer to her *winikin*, forcing herself to shove the insecurities deep down inside, in a locked section of her soul she opened only rarely, when she was down and needed to feel even crappier about herself. Or on days like today, when other people were depending on her and she wasn't sure she'd be able to produce enough power to help.

"You can do it," she told herself. And went out to face the lunar eclipse.

CHAPTER NINE

When Alexis reached the sunken great room at the center of the mansion, she found that the others were there ahead of her. The air hummed with magic and nerves. Strike stood with Leah on the raised platform that ran around the sitting area. The rest of them, both *winikin* and the Nightkeepers, stood on the lower level, shoulder-to-shoulder, looking up at their leaders.

As Alexis took her place with the others, working herself as far from Nate as she could get, Strike nodded and said, "Good. We're all here."

A soft golden glow surrounded the king and his mate, growing stronger when Strike reached out and took Leah's hand. The Nightkeeper's human queen might not have magic on a day-to-day basis, but when the peak days came around, look out. She and Strike together channeled the powers of the creator god Kulkulkan, who had serious skills.

Alexis suffered another tug of envy. Not just at the magic, but at the connection between the two of them, and the soft, intimate look they shared for half a second before turning to the business at hand. Which, in a way, was as much about love as it was about war, because the next god to come through the barrier would most likely offer its powers to a Nightkeeper female who had a strong mate at her side.

Alexis glanced over at Brandt and Patience. They

stood close together, holding hands and pressed together at hip and shoulder, looking like they'd worked out whatever had been worrying Strike the other day. This time envy tugged stronger at Alexis's heart. Was love so much to ask for?

"Okay, gang, here's how it's going to work," Strike said. "We'll link up and I'll use the boost to teleport all of us to the new site. We'll drop in the house, not the forest, because the house ought to be secure."

The Nightkeepers—or rather Jox—had purchased a run-down rental property in the Yucatán over the winter and retrofitted it with a kick-ass security system and emergency supplies, so they could use it as a staging area for trips down into the sacred tunnels. The move had become necessary when the Nightkeepers' previous passageway to the tunnels leading to the sacred intersection had been destroyed during the equinox battle. Luckily for them—though gods knew it'd been more fate than luck—Leah had known of a second access point near a small house her parents had rented on vacation when she was a child.

Though finding the entrance during the summer solstice of '84, amidst the massacre itself, had marked Leah and her younger brother and had eventually cost her brother's life, it'd also meant that the loss of the first passageway hadn't been the disaster it would've been otherwise. Gods forbid they couldn't get to the intersection and undergo the transition ritual, because the legends said the Godkeepers would be the first and best defense standing between mankind and the *Banol Kax* when the end-time came.

At the moment they didn't even have one full Godkeeper, though. Which meant they had some serious catching up to do.

Strike continued, "Once we've secured the perimeter, the warriors will go down while the *winikin* and nonwarriors stay topside and cover the entrance." The king made it sound matter-of-fact, even though it was a serious breach of SOP.

Traditionally, the *winikin* stayed back at the training compound and watched the Nightkeeper children. But with only the twin boys to watch over and too few warriors, Strike was pressing everyone into service. The female *winikin* would protect the twins back at Skywatch. The four male *winikin*, along with Jade, who hadn't received the warrior's mark or the attendant fighting prowess, would be heavily armed and tasked with keeping watch for Iago and his ilk, or any other sign of danger.

Alexis had argued along the lines of tradition, but Strike and Leah had overruled her. Still, the debate had helped them clarify a few fail-safes, so she felt like she'd at least added to the convo and justified her place on what was coming to be known as the royal council.

Leah took over, saying, "When we've reached the temple chamber, we'll link up. Strike and I will take whatever boost we need to man the defenses. The rest of the power should go to Patience and Brandt for the Godkeeper ritual."

Strike's expression, which had been serious all along, went deadly intense. "We need this, people. We need a true Godkeeper, and we need her now." He looked straight at Patience as he said, "With a Godkeeper's power, especially if we get another of the war gods, we might be able to get ahead of Iago, maybe even attack him on his own turf. Without it, we're vulnerable."

A chill skimmed down Alexis's spine. Without meaning to she glanced over at Nate. He was staring at the king, his jaw locked, and something told her his thoughts were elsewhere.

But where? And why?

"Any questions?" Strike asked, then quirked a humorless smile. "I suppose I should rephrase that: Any questions I'd have a prayer of answering? Didn't think so. Okay, let's link up."

Without further discussion the Nightkeepers pulled their ceremonial knives from their weapons belts and drew the blades across their palms. Alexis stared at the thin line she'd just carved in her skin, watched it go from shocked white to red, then well up and spill over. She felt the kick of pain and power, the shimmer of magic just out of reach, a wellspring of it that she could touch but couldn't really tap into, as though something were blocking her, keeping her from reaching her true potential. Or else that was wishful thinking and she was already as strong as she was ever going to get.

"Ready?" Sven asked from her left side, holding out his bloodied palm in invitation.

Alexis nodded and grabbed on. The power boost hummed through her bones as she reached out to clasp Patience's hand on her other side, continuing the circle of Nightkeepers. The *winikin* formed an outer circle, touching the magi so they'd be included in the 'port magic, even though they didn't add to the boost. When the circle was complete except for Strike and Leah, the royal couple stepped in and finished the connection.

When they did, the power whiplashed through Alexis, untold magic using her as a conduit, though not a wielder. She threw her head back and let her body arch into it as the world tilted sideways, then accelerated when Strike triggered the 'port magic.

Everything went gray-green, and mist whipped past. Then the universe decelerated around her, spun sideways, and slammed into the soles of her feet.

The air changed, going humid and earthy, and a room materialized around her, whitewashed and sparsely furnished in Early Particleboard, with a couple of serapes thrown around and a red velvet mariachi hat hung on one wall in a weak effort at local color.

Welcome to the Yucatán, low-rent style, Alexis thought. She'd been to the safe house once before, during the winter solstice, but hadn't noticed the lame decor so much. Maybe it bugged her now because she'd been making a real effort to brighten up Skywatch. Or maybe, she acknowledged, she was looking for something to focus on other than the ceremony.

Strike's low whistle caught her attention, and she looked to her king. He sent Jox and Michael to a locked back room that was filled with surveillance monitors, and gestured for the rest of them to wait. When Jox signaled the all-clear, Strike waved the Nightkeeper warriors out of the house, leaving Jade and the *winikin* males behind. Jade looked simultaneously relieved and miserable as the others filed out. She was the only one of them lack-

ing any fighting magic. The only other Nightkeeper lacking the warrior's mark was Anna, but although the king's
sister wasn't able to call upon her *itza'at* seer's powers,
she'd proven able to boost any of the others with her
power, so she was going with the warriors as backup.

Alexis sketched a wave at Jade on the way out, thinking that it might suck being on the low end of the warriors' talent range, but at least she was a warrior and
not a librarian.

It was cloudy outside, providing an unexpected conti-
nuity with the weather where they'd come from, but the
similarities pretty much stopped there. Where the land
surrounding Skywatch was arid and red-cast, with little
wildlife beyond the occasional hawk, snake, or coyote,
the Yucatán was lush and verdant, and before Alexis
had gone three steps she'd been bitten by a buzzing in-
sect. Parrots called to one another through the trees despite the gloom and the darkness, and monkeys chattered
from farther away.

Giving a second low whistle, Strike sent them into the
forest along the narrow path they'd scouted, cleared, and
then hidden again a few months earlier. It led through
the trees to a squat stone temple made of simple blocks
fitted together. The structure was uncarved and unadorned
from the outside, almost forgettable until they stepped
through the low doorway. The inside of the unprepossess-
ing structure was a rectangular room that during the day
looked like nothing much, with little more than a few
badly eroded carvings. At night, though, when the stars
were bright, the walls showed instructions for opening a
secret passageway that was viable for only an hour on
either side of an equinox, solstice, or major event like
an eclipse.

There were no stars tonight, and the writing didn't
glow quicksilver-bright, but the spell was already familiar. Strike and Leah knelt together, pressed their bloodied palms to the stones at the back of the narrow temple
space, and recited the ancient words in synchrony.

When the doorway opened Alexis hung back a little,
partially so she could scan the forest for any sign of
trouble, and partly so she could avoid being too close to

Nate as Strike and Leah led the Nightkeepers down the narrow passageway, and the others started falling in, moving single-file toward the sacred chambers, lighting the way with cheap flashlights.

Magic hummed in the air, heating Alexis's blood and setting up vibrations where they didn't belong, drawing her to a man whom didn't want her, and who she didn't want. *Liar,* her inner voice chided, but she ignored it and took up a position at the back of the line, with only Michael behind her. He always took the rearmost position, because he was the best among them at shield magic. Very few spells worked down in the tunnels, but the shield did, and it could buy them valuable time if they were attacked.

Which left Alexis feeling like a spare wheel, because her shield was for shit.

And you so need to get over yourself, she thought fiercely, not sure where the negativity was coming from, but figuring it had to do with the eclipse, and the things that had happened—real or imagined—between her and Nate over the past week.

The tunnel sloped gently down, and as the small group moved onward, the sound of running water quickly became audible. They would parallel the river all the way to their destination, which was a rectangular altar room deep beneath the ruins of Chichén Itzá. There they would initiate the ceremony, and if—gods willing—a god accepted Patience as its keeper, she and Brandt would in theory get their asses zapped into the circular chamber where Strike and Leah had first met. Now buried beneath a shit-ton of·rubble, the sacred chamber was where the Godkeeper ceremony was supposed to take place.

In theory, anyway. In practice, the Nightkeepers had performed the same calling ritual during the winter solstice, and had returned to the surface without a Godkeeper. There was no guarantee that this time would be any different.

When they reached the temple, which was fairly plain, save for sconces set at regular intervals and a large *chacmool* altar that took up most of one end of the chamber, they set their flashlights on the floor and reblooded their palms. Alexis barely felt the pain through the humming that'd taken up residence in her brain. The buzz was one of warm urgency and temptation, though she couldn't have said what it was tempting her to do.

Joining up again, the Nightkeepers spoke the words necessary to jack into the barrier: *"Pasaj och."*

Alexis felt the kick of power, felt the split in her brain as part of her went into the barrier and part stayed behind. As planned, Patience began reciting the Godkeeper spell as the others boosted her power. The intersection was a weak spot in the barrier, supposedly created when the Xibalbans had called the demons to earth in the first millennium A.D. There, the earth, sky, and underworld were very close together, though the skyroad was long and winding by comparison to the hellmouth. As such, the intersection was where the Nightkeepers gathered for their strongest spells, especially those designed to call a god. Yet at the same time it opened the way for a demon as well, which was why Strike and Leah joined up and called on their god, Kulkulkan, to cast blockade magic and help keep the *Banol Kax* from coming through the portal formed by the Godkeeper spell. As they did so, the king and queen were surrounded by a golden shimmer: the light of love, and of the gods.

Alexis turned away from them, her throat closing on a beat of grief for what could've been, yet wasn't. Telling herself that she was an important part of the battle regardless, she opened herself to the magic, reciting the Godkeeper spell in her head only a beat after hearing it in Patience's sweet voice, supporting rather than ascending, following rather than leading.

Then, suddenly, she wasn't following anymore.

Sudden urgency gathered in Alexis's chest and mind, grabbing onto her. She gasped as the power hum increased, then her lungs vised on the exhale. Suddenly she couldn't breathe, couldn't scream. Panicking, she opened her eyes, not having realized she'd closed them until that moment. She looked for help and latched onto Nate, saw the surprise on his face, the concern. He said something; she didn't catch what it was, couldn't hear him over the humming, yearning buzz. She could hear Patience, though, could hear the spell, could feel it grabbing onto her.

Sudden pain tore through Alexis's hand, though she'd sheathed her knife. She yanked her hands away from the magi on either side of her and looked down in horror. Blood ran from her palms, pooling on the floor and then running uphill to the *chac-mool*, where it streamed up the lines of the rain god's carved body in defiance of gravity. The blood collected in the bowl the statue held in its lap, pooling there.

Then, as she watched, the blood flared to fire, though none of the torches around the perimeter of the room were lit.

"Alexis!" She thought it was Nate's voice calling her back, thought it was his hands that reached out to grab her as she walked toward the fire, called by her own burning blood. She caught his hand, pulled him along with her. She knew this wasn't what he wanted, and her heart clutched a little at the pain brought by that knowledge. But the humming wouldn't be denied, compelling her to lean over the flames and inhale a deep lungful of the sacred smoke.

And the world she knew disappeared.

•

CHAPTER TEN

One moment Nate was in the altar room, doing the spell-casting thing, and the next thing he knew, he and Alexis had somehow gotten their asses zapped into the buried chamber. And that was so not a good sign.

"No, goddamn it!" he shouted. "You've got it wrong. You don't want us; you want Patience and Brandt!"

His words bounced off the curving walls of the circular stone chamber, which were carved with scenes of sex and sacrifice, as befitted the intersection where the earth, sky, and underworld touched one another in an unstable three-way joining that fluxed with the stars and the moon. At the top of the walls, near the ceiling, human skulls were carved protruding from the stone, their jaws agape in silent screams. Torches were set at regular intervals, with incense-burning braziers hung above. The moment Nate and Alexis had appeared in the space, flames had sprung to life, lighting the chamber and the altar that sat in its center, not a *chac-mool* this time, but a flat slab with manacles that could be fastened to the wrists and ankles of a spread-eagled victim.

The cuffs weren't original to the chamber, Nate knew; they'd been put there by the *ajaw-makol* who had sacrificed Leah's brother to reawaken the magic, then tried to sacrifice her to bring the barrier crashing down. But even though the cuffs weren't vintage, they made a hell of a statement, one that pretty much said, *Bleed here. Die here.*

"Oh, shit," Nate breathed, panic gathering in his chest—not for himself, but for the woman who both was and wasn't the girl of his dreams. The Godkeeper ritual required death and rebirth, and a sexual sacrifice on the altar of the gods. "Lexie," he began, taking a step toward where she stood.

She was staring at the room's single doorway, which was a flat slab of rock, dropped down to seal the circular chamber. From Strike's description of the Godkeeper ceremony he and Leah had just barely survived, the slab didn't respond to normal magic, only to the will of the gods. There was no way out unless the gods saw fit to send them back to the altar room.

"I'm sorry," she said without looking at him. "I know this isn't what you want."

"It's—" He broke off, because she was right. He didn't want to be a mated protector—didn't want to be mated, period. He didn't want the responsibility of being Nightkeeper to her Godkeeper, when he wasn't even sure he wanted her. Or, more accurately, he knew damn well he wanted her—he just wasn't sure for how long, or whether he wanted her, or a fantasy woman who looked like her but acted totally different.

Alexis was still talking, but her voice was lost beneath the roaring that built in his blood. An image slammed into his brain fully formed, with sight and sound and touch and taste. In it, she was bent over the altar as she was now, with her hands pressed flat, as they were now. Only in his waking fantasy she was naked, and he was coming into her from behind.

He'd taken two steps toward her before he could force himself to stop, force himself to lower the hands he'd raised to strip her harsh combat clothes away. Warned by the sound of her harsh, rattling breaths, she spun to face him. He expected her to smack him across the jaw or, knowing Alexis, throw a full-on roundhouse for his thoughts.

But he was wrong, he realized when he saw the flush

riding high on her cheeks and the glitter in her eyes. She wasn't pissed. She was aroused.

"Bad idea," he managed to say as she advanced on him, still fully clothed, but wiggling inside those clothes in a way that reminded him of before, when they'd been lovers and blamed it on the magic.

She shook her head, seeming lit from within with excitement, with a power he'd never seen in her before as she said, "The world needs a Godkeeper."

"Patience and Brandt are married," he countered, telling himself to move away. But his resolve wasn't as strong as it needed to be. It was weakened by the humming in his blood, the sparkle of power in the air, and the feel of her against him when she rose up on her toes so they were eye to eye. Mouth to mouth.

Unable to do otherwise, he touched his lips to hers. She leaned into him, opening herself to the kiss. The moment she did the chamber shuddered and heaved around them. And began to descend.

Nate cursed and hung on to her as the floor dropped beneath them. *No, goddamn it!* he shouted in his skull. *Not us, not her!*

He knew the theory: For a god to enter a Godkeeper, she had to be close to death, which brought her close to the gods. Then it was up to her mate to bring her back with the strongest of physical magic: the act of love. The sex would bind both man and god to the woman, linking them in an unbreakable three-way partnership.

To be chosen was the greatest honor in Nightkeeper lore. Yet if he'd been a teleport, he would've zapped them both the fuck out of there the moment the chamber started dropping down into the water table. He didn't want this, didn't want to be involved in a screwed-up cosmic business arrangement that exchanged sex for power. But the gods didn't seem to care what he wanted, or whether he was ready for a mate, for the responsibility. He was a conscript, plucked up and press-ganged into a position that Brandt was so much better suited to, with his wife as his mate.

"The gods are fucking crazy," he snapped, bracing his

legs when the inconstant motion of the chamber rocked the floor beneath them. "Where's the emergency exit?"

But the door was shut tight and there was no other way in or out. They were stuck there until a god's power brought them out again. Assuming, of course, that the transition spell worked, they didn't die in the process, and the god didn't get stuck between the planes, as Kulkulkan had done during Leah's transition. Which was a godsdamned lot of assumptions, as far as Nate was concerned.

Rock grated against rock as the chamber sped its descent. Alexis gave a low cry and clung to him, then seemed to realize what she was doing and tried to push away. He didn't let her break free, holding her close until she stopped struggling and sagged against him, breath shuddering.

"I'm scared." Her words were muffled in the fabric of his shirt, and nearly drowned out by the sound of the subterranean river that was being diverted by ancient mechanisms and magic, to fulfill the need of the gods.

"So am I." He wrapped his arms around her, cursing the gods for taking away their free will, forcing them into a union they'd tried once before and failed to make work. He and Alexis weren't prepared for this, hadn't ever thought it would be them going through the ritual. He could only assume the problems between Patience and Brandt went deeper than he'd thought, or else the gods wouldn't have bypassed them. Hell, if he and Alexis were better candidates for the spell, then the White-Eagles' marriage was in serious trouble.

The chamber finished its grating descent, coming to rest with a resonant thud and a shudder. Scant seconds later jets of water burst from the carved skulls at the perimeter of the room. The skeletal mouths screamed the water, dousing Alexis and Nate instantly with fire-hose pressure and cold. There was no preamble, no steady build like the one Leah had described. This was a mad rush to fill the chamber. Either the gods were impatient or something was very wrong, Nate thought.

As in *the fucking chamber's broken* wrong.

It wasn't entirely clear how much of the die-and-be-reborn trick of the sacred chamber was magic and how much was thousand-year-old engineering, and that was a seriously chilling thought, because if whatever was in charge of the water flow had been broken in the cave-ins the tunnels had suffered during the fall equinox, then the chamber might not drain the way it was supposed to when the transition spell was complete.

Game over, he thought as the water climbed past his knees.

"What if this whole place is broken?" he said softly. The water was to their upper thighs now and the pressurized jets continued screaming from the skulls high above.

"It isn't," she said without hesitation.

"You don't know that."

"I have faith."

"You *want* to have faith," he contradicted, feeling dread curl. "But it's too simple to say that what has happened before will happen again, or that it's not a sacrifice if it's easy. What if all that's bullshit, just like every other religion out there, just a construct used to frame some commonsense rules?"

She looked as though she pitied him. "It must suck to be stuck inside a belief system like yours."

"At least I've got a system," he snapped. "You just let your *winikin* tell you what to think." Inside, though, something said, *What are you doing?* He was being a jerk; that was what. And he was doing it because he was scared. The water was cool, almost cold, reaching past his chest and threatening to buoy him off the floor. He let out a breath. "I'm sorry. I take it back. I'm being an ass because I'm not sure what else I can do."

"I don't think there's anything we *can* do at this point." Her words were matter-of-fact, but her eyes were wide and scared, and she was trembling. Then the water snuffed the torches, plunging them into darkness. She gave a short scream, then muffled it.

He caught her arm and drew her close, making sure they could find each other in the darkness. The water wasn't glowing, and there wasn't any noise or wind, which didn't match up with how Strike and Leah had described their experience. Those details only added to his worry that the chamber mechanism wasn't working right.

If this was the end for them, he didn't want the last thing between them to be anger. Softening his voice and gathering her close, he whispered, "I'm sorry, Lexie."

Her voice went hollow and very small. "Me too."

Working by feel and instinct, he found her lips with his in a kiss that was part apology, part wish that things had, in the end, been different for them.

Then the water closed over both their heads. He couldn't hear the incoming rush anymore, couldn't hear beyond the pounding of his heartbeat, couldn't feel much of anything in the cool numbness except her lips against his. She hung on to him, her fingers digging into him for a moment, then two . . . then loosening and falling away.

Wishing he'd done it differently, that he'd been a better man all along, he held Alexis close and pictured the woman of his dreams. He whispered her name and let himself imagine the impossible as he kissed her and let out the last of his air, resigning himself to death.

White-gold light detonated in his skull. And then he was falling.

Alexis returned to herself slowly, as if awakening from a deep sleep, though her body didn't feel like she'd been motionless for long. She was aware of being wet through, and a little cold, with a hard stone surface beneath her and a heavy weight pressing on her from above. Water dripped somewhere nearby.

She cracked her eyes to find amber torchlight reflecting off carved stone walls, and Nate sprawled across her, motionless. For a second she thought she was dreaming again. Then she saw that the chamber was curved rather than rectangular, and the dripping noise came from droplets of water trickling from one stone to the next, rather than from an underground pool. More important, she wasn't alone in her skull. There was a tiny kernel at the back of her brain, warm and sparkling with colors. When she focused her attention on it, though, it dimmed and grew distant.

Come back! she thought, quick panic sparking her fully awake. But it hadn't gone away, she realized after a moment; it'd moved lower, the warmth shifting and the sparkles dispersing until she thought she could feel each nerve ending as a separate entity, an individual thought. Even as she reveled in the sensation, another came to her, the feel of Nate shifting against and atop her. He was sprawled facedown with his cheek on her belly, his arms loosely encircling her hips, and his big body more or less centered between her legs. The realization of their intimate positioning sparked the warmth to a blaze, and when he turned to look up at her, dragging the faintly roughened skin of his jaw across the sensitive skin above her navel, she saw the same heat reflected in his eyes.

"It's the magic," she said, her voice cracking around the edges. "The god."

But Nate shook his head. "If I'd seen you in Newport, I would've wanted you long before I'd ever heard the word *Nightkeeper*."

She would've argued, would've demanded an explanation, but he surprised her by casting a mild shield spell, one that pressed against her, held her pinned. The magic caressed her skin, sending ripples of excitement and power rolling through her, the pleasure holding her captive as much as the spell itself. Then, before she knew what he'd intended, he moved down her body, somehow taking her combat pants to her knees as he put his lips to her, his clever tongue delving deep and slicking her sensitive folds, which were already swollen and ready for him.

Alexis cried out and arched against him, or would have, but the shield kept her flat, binding her to the stone floor of the sacred chamber hard enough to excite but not hurt her. They had played with restraints once or twice before, but not like this, not so she could feel his magic. The power was brutally erotic, as were the touch of his tongue and hands as he simultaneously drove her up and held her down.

The kernel of colored light within her expanded, reaching outward and straining toward a distant, unseen goal. She writhed as pleasure suffused her, sent her outside herself, hurtling through time and space to a world of hue. The spectrum surrounded her, light and color combining into tangible shapes and audible sounds. On one level she was aware of Nate's mouth leaving her, and his big body moving up to cover hers. Another part of her, though, was caught, spinning out in a world of blue and gold, with ribbons of color twining around her, trailing from her in all directions.

She was in the sacred chamber with Nate; but she was in the sky too, in the realm of the gods. She saw them, impossibly beautiful, impossibly colorful. She was one of them, yet not, just as she was herself, yet not.

Then the shield spell was gone and she was free to move. She didn't go far, though, only enough to roll with Nate and rise above him. He was naked now, and so was she, their sodden clothing piled off to the side. The earth and sky combined within her for a second, letting her see his face, letting her see his reservations and his needs. Her heart cracked and bled at the knowledge that he didn't want this, that he was sacrificing himself for a cause he didn't fully embrace, compelled by the magic rather than choice.

Perhaps he saw her sadness, maybe just saw her hesitate; either way, he reached up, rising up to meet her, to cup her face in his hands and look into her eyes. "It's okay, princess," he said, and for the first time in many months, maybe ever, the term didn't sound like an insult coming from him. It sounded like an endearment. Like a love word. "We'll make it work."

"Yes." Somehow they would, she knew. There was no other option.

Letting herself sink into that promise, she touched her lips to his and let him guide her down, let his hard length fill her, stretch her until he was seated to the hilt. The feel of him inside set off a chain reaction of pleasure, each pulse showing a different color behind her eyelids as she let them drift shut.

"Lexie," he said, his voice ragged on the syllables, his palms bracketing her hips, his fingertips digging into her skin.

"Yes," she said again, because there didn't seem to be anything more to say as she leaned over him, shifting so the sensitive tips of her breasts brushed against the hard contours of his chest and her lips aligned with his as she began to move against him.

He countered the rhythm with his hands and hips, bringing new pleasure, new colors that wrung a moan from her as the ribbons of light spiraled inward, contracting around her body in a swirl of heat and power, pleasure and madness.

It was as though she were hovering above them, locked in a prism, looking down on them both, locked together in sex and madness. But she was also within herself looking out, seeing Nate's eyes hard and hot on hers, feeling the clench of his hands, the thrust of his body. Then the world spun as he grabbed her and rolled them both and rose above her to quicken the pace, pistoning against her as his eyes went distant and glazed.

Can you see the colors? she wanted to ask, but didn't, because it was all she could do to hang on and lock her legs around him and rise up to meet him halfway, driving the pleasure higher, and higher still.

The orgasm grabbed her and held her poised at the precipice for a long moment. Blue and green flashed through her, and orange-red. Then Nate's eyes sharpened and locked on hers, and it wasn't about the colors anymore, wasn't about the god-power that flowed through her, at least not entirely. It was about the two of them, about the connection they'd always found through the sex, if nowhere else.

He thrust fully into her and stayed there, pressing against her inside and out, and sending her over the edge.

She arched and cried his name as the throbbing pulses swept her up, tightening her around him and drawing him in, holding him fast. There were no more colors, no more god; there were only the two of them and the feel of his hard, slick flesh and the tight bands of his arm as he held her, pressed his cheek against hers, and cut loose with a low, rattling groan that didn't sound like her name.

They held on to each other, shuddering and bucking, gripped by a force that simultaneously anchored them and sent them beyond themselves.

Eventually the pulses slowed, then faded to echoes, to rainbow tremors that floated through her, warning her that everything had changed. The kernel of power was gone from the back of her brain. In its place was a hum of connection, not to the barrier, but someplace beyond, some*one* beyond.

Gods, she thought, then corrected herself. *Goddess.* Because there was no doubt in her mind that she was connected to a female entity, one that was lush and bountiful, a goddess of the sky, the light, and all the colors of the rainbow. *Ixchel,* she thought, the name a soft sigh in itself.

As if aware of her thoughts, Nate levered himself away from her, rolling onto his side and propping himself on one elbow, gloriously male, gloriously naked and unashamed. His medallion glinted in the firelight as he took her right hand and turned it palm up in his own, baring the place where her sacrificial scar had already closed, the healing impelled by the magic. "Show me," he said softly.

She didn't know where the word came from, or how he knew to ask, but she said, *"Kawak."* Rainbow. And a glimmering colored light appeared in her hand.

The magic didn't rise in her, but rather flowed from the sky to her outstretched fingers, through the conduit connection at the back of her brain, kindling a glow that started as a firefly pinprick and quickly expanded to the size of a softball, then flickered from white through each of the colors of the rainbow, slowly at first, then cycling faster and faster until the hues melded together once again, going blue-white.

"It's beautiful." He closed his fingers over hers, folding her hand shut and extinguishing the magic.

"But not very practical," she said, starting to get a trapped, panicky feeling at knowing Strike had wanted a war god. "Pretty lights won't do much against the *Banol Kax*."

"Don't," he said, tightening his grip. "Not yet. For right now, just enjoy it." He shifted and touched his lips to hers, murmuring, "Let's enjoy this."

"We can't." She held him off, though she was strongly tempted to give in to the heat, to the one thing that had always been easy and right between them. "We have to go back."

She didn't question whether they could return to the others, or how. She could feel the power inside; it would undoubtedly decrease some as the barrier thickened with the passing of the eclipse and the skyroad was once again separated from the earth. But for now, for this moment of magic, she had no limits.

She and Nate pulled on their soggy clothes, putting themselves back together as best they could. She tried not to think about the others seeing them, and knowing what had just happened. But sacrifice and sex were the cornerstones of the magic, particularly the Godkeeper ritual. There was no shame in it.

Even as those thoughts swirled in Alexis's brain, she felt the presence of the goddess, her quiet reassurance, not in words but in a wash of love that told her she could do this, she could. Knowing it, believing it, she turned and touched her lips to Nate's. And the gods, feeling them together, sent them back to the antechamber to be reunited with the Nightkeepers . . . bringing the rainbow goddess, Ixchel, with them.

Nate told himself he was braced for the stares, told himself it didn't matter what the others knew, or thought they knew. What was important was what'd just happened to—and between—him and Alexis, and how they went on from there. But when the gods zapped the two of them back to the antechamber and all eyes snapped to them, he realized he wasn't really braced for the attention . . . and he didn't have a frickin' clue where he and Alexis were headed.

A glance at his forearm showed that he'd been tagged with a new glyph he had to assume was the goddess's mark. There was no *jun tan*, though. No sign that they were officially mated, which was a relief.

The power—shimmering gold and rainbows—cut out when they landed, leaving him and Alexis swaying on their feet. He looped an arm around her waist so she wouldn't stumble and fall, and felt the familiar kick of heat that always came when he touched her. Only the heat was subtly different, stronger and richer, and laced with undertones of color and temptation.

Her taste was imprinted on his neurons, and he could smell their mingled scents on her skin, on his own. The musk, the sex, the goddess . . . all of it bound them together.

Uncomfortable, he let his arm drop and stepped away from her, so they stood apart when they faced the Nightkeepers, and their king.

Strike looked them both over, and didn't seem reassured by what he was seeing. "You guys okay?" he asked, but they all knew he was asking so much more than that.

"Better than okay." Alexis stepped forward, her face seeming simultaneously softer and edgier, as though the god-power had tightened her jawline and darkened the rims of her blue eyes, but plumped her lips and smoothed the corners of her mouth and her brow. She looked like herself . . . only more so.

Nate wasn't sure whether the changes were new and god-wrought, or if they'd been a gradual shift he hadn't noticed. Either way they looked good on her, and resonated within him, as though he'd seen this new Alexis in another time and place. Which didn't make any freaking sense whatsoever.

She cupped her palms and smiled, and light kindled in her hands. Where before she'd needed blood and chanted spells to summon a weak fireball, now it sprang to life instantly, without blood or word, growing from a spark to a conflagration, not just the red of a Nightkeeper or the gold of a god, but both those colors, along with the greens and blues and purples he'd seen from her in the sacred chamber, all the colors of the rainbow.

"Ixchel," Leah said, coming up to stand beside Strike.

The gold of the creator god sparked in her eyes through the magic of the eclipse connection.

The imperfect human Godkeeper faced the true God-keeper for a moment that hung suspended in time. Then the queen bent and spit at Alexis's feet in obeisance. Moments later Strike did the same. Then each of the others did the same, as the Nightkeepers welcomed the goddess into their midst.

Nate held himself apart, standing near Alexis because he couldn't not be near her, but distancing himself at the same time. Nobody seemed to notice or care, though, because—for now, anyway—the goddess's protector was ancillary.

"Thank you," Alexis said. Her face shone with power and joy, and the colors from the fireball had extended to touch her, limning her in rainbows. She looked at Sven, the goddess power somehow prompting her to pick him out of the others. "Congratulations."

Surprise flashed across his features, then pride. He held out his forearm, showing that the indecipherable talent mark he'd worn since the previous fall had changed, resolving itself into a glyph that was very like Strike's, yet not. "I'm a translocator," he said. "Which pretty much means I can teleport inanimate shit without touching it." But though his words might be deprecating, his eyes shone and his shoulders were square beneath his combat duds.

Alexis next turned to where Patience stood, with Brandt beside her. "I'm sorry." This time Nate was pretty sure it was Alexis the woman, not the goddess, who was speaking.

Patience shook her head. "It was as it was meant to be." She was holding Brandt's hand, her grip tight, as though she were fighting not to let go. She glanced at Nate, then back to Alexis. "Better for it to be the two of you right now."

Better for whom? Nate wondered, then wished he hadn't, wished he could just let events unfold. But un-ease dogged him as the Nightkeepers headed topside to collect Jade and the *winikin*, and they all linked up once again for the trip home. As the teleport magic kicked in, an echo in the king's voice reached them all, a thought he'd no doubt meant to keep private, or just between him and Leah, but had been broadcast through the bloodline link: *What good will rainbows do against Camazotz?*

PART II

SATURN AT OPPOSITION

Saturn is strongly associated with time. In the Dresden Codex, one of only four surviving Mayan texts, the movement of Saturn is used to help set the interlocking Mayan calendars, including the Long Count. At opposition, Saturn is at its closest point to the Earth.

CHAPTER ELEVEN

February 9

Lucius nearly killed himself trying to find the location the starscript had directed him to. Granted, he probably should've gotten a room in Albuquerque instead of pushing on into the darkness, but it was like something was driving him, keeping him going well past his natural reserves. He wasn't tired, though he knew he damn well ought to be. He hadn't been chugging caffeine, didn't even remember the last time he'd eaten anything, yet he was fully alert, and his body felt strong, supple, and ready for action.

Excitement buzzed through him at the thought that he might be close to finally meeting Sasha, finally putting a face and body to the voice on the phone, maybe even getting answers to some of the questions that plagued him. Oddly, he wasn't really thinking of Desiree's challenge or the doctorate, though he'd phoned in the day before and told the Dragon Lady where he was headed. Those things—and the university—seemed far away, and inconsequential.

What mattered was the strange light coming from the thin, iridescent corona surrounding the eclipsed moon, which had turned a bloody orange-red, and his headlights, which lit a faint track that optimistically called itself a road. He hung on to the steering wheel as his rented four-wheel-drive vehicle dropped into a pothole and bounced out again, and an ominous thumping noise started coming from the undercarriage. He didn't care, though. All he cared about was getting to the end of his journey.

Then, finally, he topped a low ridge and saw a glitter of lights below. Hitting the gas, he sent the SUV slaloming down the backside of the ridge. Ten minutes later he was driving through the open gates of what turned out to be a fricking palace, a mansion of sandstone and marble and shit that looked totally out of place in the middle of butt-fuck nowhere.

The gates swung shut behind him, sending a shiver down his spine. But that didn't stop him from parking by the front door and climbing out of the SUV. *Sasha might not be here,* he cautioned himself. *You're probably setting yourself up for some mondo disappointment.* But he thought not.

He'd followed Ledbetter's directions and found an oasis. He hoped that she'd done the same.

He saw a surveillance camera tracking him as he headed up a flagged walkway, under a pillared awning supported by columns that looked like their maker had gotten stuck halfway between Intro to Ancient Egypt and Mayan Architecture for Dummies. Nightkeeper influence, he was sure of it.

The air hummed with a strange, discordant sound—something his gut told him was ancient magic. Nightkeeper magic. Logic said his gut was taking a hell of a flying leap on that one, but his gut told logic to fuck off, because deep down inside he knew he was right. He'd found the Nightkeepers. And not just proof that they'd existed in Mayan times, either. He'd frickin' found the home base of their modern-day descendants.

Again with the logic leap. Again with the certainty.

His pulse was pounding as he lifted a hand to knock. Then, when the door swung inward, his heart quite simply stopped at the sight of the woman standing in the ornate entryway.

It wasn't Sasha, though. It was Anna.

"Lucius," she said on a long, sad sigh. "You shouldn't be here."

Holy shit, was all he could think. Shock and guilt swirled around, hammering at each other in a hell of a mental joust, as too many details that'd refused to gel in the past suddenly resolved themselves into an impossible, improbable certainty.

His boss was a goddamned Nightkeeper.

Anna could not freaking believe what she was seeing, even though the surveillance system had forewarned them of the visitor, and Strike had recognized Lucius. He'd ordered Jox to open the gates and told Anna to go meet her student and bring him inside, on the theory that it'd be better to contain the damage than try to avoid someone who'd shown up in the Nightkeepers' sphere one too many times for coincidence.

Even forewarned, though, it was a shock for Anna to have him standing on the doorstep of Skywatch, his eyes wide and a little wild. She was also surprised, once again, to realize that he'd gained mass and muscle, and wasn't her scrawny, geeky grad student anymore.

Which didn't even begin to tell her what the hell she should do about him. She was exhausted from the drain of the eclipse ceremony. Her brain was spinning from the gods' choice of a keeper, and the identity of the goddess who'd bound with Alexis. And now this.

"You shouldn't be here," she said, but she didn't tell him to leave. It was too late for that. Stepping back, she waved him in. "Come on."

He stood rooted, white-faced in shock, but she saw something else beneath the surprise. Resentment. "Why didn't you tell me?" he grated.

"Because it's none of your business." Though that was only because Red-Boar had mind-blocked his previous experiences with the Nightkeepers and the *makol.* Or had he? she thought, not wondering whether Red-Boar had neglected his work, but rather whether somehow Lucius had overcome the mental blocks. Frowning, she asked, "How did you get here?"

He stared at her for a long moment, looking like the guy she'd known for going on six years now, but also looking like the man he'd become since the prior fall, harder, tougher, and far more secretive. Then, doing a bad Anthony Hopkins impression, he said, "Quid pro quo, Clarice." He stepped past her into the entryway of Skywatch, adding over his shoulder, "You show me yours and I'll show you mine."

Three steps inside the door, he stopped dead at the sight of Strike, who was looking big and mean.

The king scowled and said, "That's so not how it's going to work."

Anna knew her brother was pissed off—not just because of Lucius's untimely arrival, but because they had themselves a Godkeeper but weren't really sure how the goddess of weaving and rainbows was supposed to help them, and because Nate and Alexis's relationship was far from stable, making him fear complications. That, and they were all dragging with postmagic hangovers. They should be chowing down on foods heavy in protein and fat and then heading straight to bed, rather than dealing with an unwanted guest and the questions and dangers his arrival was sure to bring.

Which meant the king was sporting a serious 'tude. Instead of backing off, though, Lucius shot his chin out. "Who the hell are you? And where's Sasha?"

"We're looking for her," Anna said, figuring there'd be time later to figure out why that'd been his first concern. She stepped between them when it looked like Strike was going to lash out first and ask questions later. "This is my brother, Strike," she told Lucius, then paused and added, "He's the jaguar king of the Nightkeepers."

Lucius didn't back down, but his color drained some. "Fuck me."

"No, thanks." Strike leaned in. "Get this straight. You don't belong here. We don't want you here. But you're here, and that's a big godsdamned problem for us. Given that you showed up at the tail end of the eclipse, I'm going to have to assume that some of the shit that went down last fall is breaking through, which makes you an even bigger problem."

Lucius glowered. "Look. I don't know—"

"Shut. Up." Strike snapped. He was starting to sway a little, suggesting that he'd burned through all his reserves and then some in the battle to maintain the barrier's integrity during the eclipse ceremony. Anna should know—she'd leaked him as much power as she could, but knew he'd forced himself not to take too much during the struggle. Which meant she was in way better shape than he was. Leah, on the other hand, was already asleep.

Knowing there was a good chance her brother was close to losing his temper or passing out, or both, Anna said, "We can figure this out tomorrow, after we've all had a chance to recharge. I'll take responsibility for him."

Strike turned on her. "And how do you plan to do that? You're just as wiped as the rest of us."

"Jox can—"

"No," her brother said, doing the interrupting thing again—a habit of his when he'd hit the end of his energy reserves. "We'll lock him downstairs in one of the storerooms." When she would've protested, he fixed her with a look. "Be careful or I'll decide Red-Boar was right in the first place."

"We had a deal," Anna reminded him. "His life for my return to the Nightkeepers."

"Hasn't been much of a return," he pointed out, sounding more tired than snide. "And that was then; this is now. If he's retained some memory of what happened, or worse, he's regained some *makol* magic—because how else could he have found this place?—then the deal's off." He paused. "I'm sorry. I have to do what I think is best."

Jarringly, that last statement echoed back in Anna's brain to an argument she'd overheard between their parents, when their father had spoken of leading the Nightkeepers to battle and their mother had counseled patience.

Scarred-Jaguar had done what he'd thought was best, and look what had happened. Strike was a different sort of man, a different sort of king. But was he different enough?

"Fine," she said, backing down, because it wasn't really important where Lucius spent the night. The larger issue of his fate wouldn't be decided until the next day, or maybe farther out than that. "I'll lock him downstairs."

"Have Jox help you," Strike said, not saying outright that he didn't trust her to do what she said, but pretty close to it.

"Go to bed, little brother." She turned her back on him, because she didn't like the dynamic that was developing, the way they kept jarring against each other over the smallest of things, never mind the bigger ones. She and Strike had been close as children, distant as teens and adults. With so long apart, she supposed it stood to reason that they wouldn't be able to fall right into an easy accord. That didn't stop her from feeling like there was something wrong between them, something he was keeping from her. But, knowing she wasn't going to figure it out running on empty, she turned back and grabbed Lucius's arm. "Come on."

He let her lead him through the first floor and down to the lower level of the main house, which held the gym on one side and a series of storerooms on the other. At the bottom of the stairs, he dug in his heels and pulled away from her, his expression accusatory. "Okay, Anna. Start talking."

Running pretty close to the edge of her own temper and energy reserves, she said, "I don't have to. You're the one who's trespassing."

"And you're about to imprison me. Who's breaking more laws, d'ya think?"

Refusing to go there, she said, "How did you find me?"

He hesitated, and for a moment she thought he wasn't going to answer. Then he said, "I wasn't looking for you. I was looking for Sasha Ledbetter. Are you sure she's not here?"

"Positive. Why would you think she would be? And again, how the hell did you find Skywatch?" Then she paused, thinking it through. "You followed Ambrose's trail to the haunted temple, didn't you?"

Just prior to the equinox battle, Anna and Red-Boar had tracked Ambrose Ledbetter to a sacred clearing, where they'd found him buried in a shallow grave. He'd been killed and ritually beheaded. At first they'd thought the *makol* had killed the Mayan researcher for the blood-power of the sacrifice, and to keep the Nightkeepers from asking him about the Godkeeper ritual. However, once Anna and Red-Boar had dug up the older man's remains to move him to a more appropriate burial site, they'd seen that his right forearm had been a knotted mass of scar tissue, as though the skin had been burned or cut away . . . exactly where a Nightkeeper's marks would've been.

Originally, they'd surmised that he might have been a Nightkeeper who'd been disgraced and cast out before the Solstice Massacre, somehow without Jox or Red-Boar knowing about it. With Iago's arrival on-scene, however, it seemed more likely that Ledbetter had been a Xibalban, perhaps one who'd seen the light and defected as the end-time drew near.

Maybe.

The PI, Carter, had been unable to learn much about Ledbetter beyond the common-knowledge stuff available through his university, and the fact that he had a daughter—or maybe a goddaughter, depending on the source of the info—named Sasha. Anna had tried to contact the young woman right after the fall equinox, got one missed return phone call, and then the girl had effectively dropped out of sight. Strike hadn't even been able to lock onto her for a 'port. The Nightkeepers had assumed she'd been killed too, and had turned their focus to other matters.

Now Anna wondered if they'd been too hasty on that one.

Lucius nodded. "Yeah. I saw the temple." His eyes changed. "Those were your bootprints just inside the door, weren't they? The ones that disappeared into the pitfall?" His eyes sharpened, went feral. "What was down there?"

"Nothing good," she said faintly. After reburying Ledbetter's headless corpse at the edge of the forest, she and Red-Boar had split up to look for the Nightkeeper temple they suspected Ledbetter had discovered. In finding it, Anna had been . . . she still didn't know how to describe it, though "partially possessed" was probably close enough . . . by a *nahwal*, which never should've been able to exist on the earth outside of its normal barrier milieu. Under its influence, she'd cut her wrists in sacrifice, nearly bleeding out before Red-Boar had managed to carry her into satellite phone range and call for help. Since then, none of the Nightkeepers had been back to the ruin, which they'd taken to calling the haunted temple because of the *nahwal*'s odd behavior. Without access to Red-Boar's mind-bending skills, which he'd used to pull her back when the *nahwal* tried to drag her into the barrier for good, Strike had decided there was too much of a risk. Anna had been scared enough of the place not to argue, but if Lucius had been there, if he'd seen something she and Red-Boar had missed . . .

"I found Ledbetter's head," Lucius answered, his voice going ragged. "And the address of this place, written in starscript. There were signs of a struggle, footprints that didn't add up." He swallowed hard. "I hoped Sasha read the 'script and came here. Since she didn't, and since nobody's seen her since she went south . . ."

When he trailed off, Anna finished, "Either the Xibalbans grabbed her from the haunted temple, or she's dead. Or both."

"Xibalbans?"

"I'll tell you later." *Maybe.* "What else did you see in the temple?"

He glanced along the basement hallway. "You going to lock me up?"

"I have no choice."

"Then I didn't see anything."

"Bullshit."

He raised an eyebrow, and something faintly malevolent glittered in the depths of his eyes, which were greener than she remembered. "Prove it."

Frustration slapped at her. "Damn it, Lucius." She was too tired to deal with this now, too drained.

Without being told, he headed for the first of the doors on the right, then paused and looked back. "This one?"

"Two down," Anna answered, knowing there really wasn't much more to say. She followed him to the store-room, which Strike had outfitted as a holding cell back when he'd planned to imprison Leah rather than letting her sacrifice herself. Her incarceration had lasted approximately five minutes, until Rabbit had let her out and Red-Boar had lured her to the Chaco Canyon ruins, where he'd tried to gun her down in cold blood, thinking to save Strike from repeating his father's mistake by choosing love over duty and dooming them all. In the end, though, Red-Boar had died for loyalty and love of his king. That sacrifice had washed away all the other sins.

And why do you keep thinking of Red-Boar? Anna asked herself with a stab of guilt. She'd called her husband from the road and made some excuse about her meeting being moved up a couple of days, and hadn't talked to him since. In the meantime, her heartache had eased some and logic had returned. They'd dealt with the affair already, and were working to move past it. And there was nothing concrete to suggest he'd encouraged Desiree. There was no reason for her to be thinking of another man. Especially one who was not only dead, but had been an asshole when he was alive. He'd had his reasons, but still. . . . She made a mental note to call Dick when she woke up the next morning. Maybe they could plan to take some time away when she got back.

"It's not as bad as I expected." Lucius shrugged at the accommodations. "No worse than fieldwork."

Tearing her thoughts from Dick and Red-Boar, Anna looked at Lucius and saw a stranger. Feeling fatigue drag, she said, "I'll come for you in the morning."

"Yeah." He turned away, and didn't look back as she shut and padlocked the door and set the key on a shelf nearby. Then, just to be on the safe side, she set a magical ward that a human could pass through, but which would stop a magical creature in its tracks.

In theory.

*   *   *

Lucius heard the key turn in the lock and knew he should feel trapped, knew he should be freaking right the hell out. Hello, mental overload. The Nightkeepers not only *had* existed, they still did, and Anna was one of them. He had his proof, had his doctorate, if he still wanted to play Desiree's game. But there was more here than just that, wasn't there? The convo out in the entryway suggested that the other Nightkeepers already knew about him somehow, that Anna had bargained for his life. How, exactly, had he missed that?

At the same time, though, that part of his mental process seemed dull and foggy, less important than the building burn of anger that rode low in his gut, telling him that she'd lied to him, that she'd made a fool of him. That she needed to be punished.

At the thought, the single light in the small room flickered.

Great. Lucius scowled up at the fluorescent tube. *Just what I need, wonky wiring.* Or maybe that was the idea. Maybe there'd be an "accidental" electrical fire in his cell, taking care of him while retaining some sort of plausible deniability if Anna complained to her brother about his death.

Not that she'd be likely to, he thought. The anger built, sparking heat into his veins as he paced the small room, past a narrow cot and a bucket that served as the so-called amenities. Anna had enjoyed being around him back when he'd been a student, a newbie. The more he'd learned, though, the more he'd questioned her conviction that the Nightkeepers were a myth, the less she'd wanted to be around him and the more she'd tried to narrow his research focus, directing it away from the Nightkeepers. Even now, understanding why she'd insisted he leave the issue of the Nightkeepers alone, he couldn't forgive how she'd pulled away from him when he'd started questioning her translations and interpretations. More than ever, he was convinced that she'd altered his files, removing the vital screaming-skull glyph and weakening his thesis work.

Rage washed over and through him, hammering in his skull like pain. Like pleasure.

"Damn it!" Lucius dropped to sit at the edge of the low camping cot, which gave a rickety squeak under his weight. He dug his fingers through his hair, rubbing at his scalp, which had tightened with the beginnings of a headache at best, one of his very rare migraines at the worst. And it wasn't like he had any way to ask for an aspirin.

His head spun and nausea churned, and he saw a flash of green, strange and luminous. It cleared when he blinked, but the afterimage stayed burned on his retinas for several seconds.

Deep inside, a small voice asked, *What the hell is happening to me?* He didn't feel like himself, didn't know where the anger was coming from, the pain. He should've been psyched to have found the Nightkeepers. And now that he understood what Anna had been wrestling with, he should've been relieved to know why she'd been strange around him lately. He should've been sympathetic, maybe even excited that they could move to a new level of trust now that he knew.

Instead, he wanted to snap and tear at her, wanted to hurt her. And that was so not him.

Curling onto his side, he moaned low in his throat, crossed his arms over his abdomen, and wrapped himself in a self-hug, feeling alone and angry. Out of control. The pounding in his head gripped him, took him over. He slapped for the light switch and plunged the room into darkness, which was a blessed relief.

The surface beneath him spun and dipped, and he longed for unconsciousness, reached for it when it came. But as he dropped off, a fragment of thought that felt more like his own than any of the others swirling in his head warned him that he'd forgotten something important, something that he needed to tell Anna immediately. But the thought, and the compulsion, slipped away as the green-tinged darkness rose up and claimed him.

Alexis was flat-out exhausted by the time the eclipse night edged toward the next day's dawn. She'd eaten and showered, and knew she should sleep for half a day or so, allowing her body to recharge from the magic and get accustomed to the conduit she could feel at the back of her brain, granting her access to the goddess Ixchel. But it was that last bit that kept her awake.

She was a Godkeeper; how crazy was that?

She tried not to think of the look on Strike's face when he'd learned that she, not Patience, had become the Godkeeper, with Nate as her mate, and that the goddess Ixchel had gained a foothold on earth. He'd been pleased, sure, but not overjoyed. She'd wanted—needed—the king's approval, and hadn't really gotten it. Which was why she couldn't sleep.

Or so she told herself. But when the knock came, she knew exactly who stood outside her door, and the true reason she was still awake.

Wearing her robe, her hair still wet from the shower, she rose and crossed the sitting area of her three-room suite to answer. Her suite had the same layout as those of all the other single Nightkeepers, aside from Rabbit, who lived in his father's cottage. Her place was the nicest of all of them, though. She'd redone it right after Nate dumped her, in part because there had been too many memories of the two of them together in the room, which they'd used almost exclusively. He'd never invited her to his suite, and had ducked the issue when she'd asked. She was proud of how her space looked now, all vibrant colors and lush fabrics, and suffered a small twinge of nerves as she waved Nate through, and a larger flash of irritation at the part of herself that cared what he thought.

When she opened the door, though, nothing much else mattered except the sight of him. He'd showered, too; she could smell a hint of soap and moisture, with the rich undertones of arousal and magic. He was wearing dark pants and a dark button-down shirt undone at the throat to show the glint of his chain, with dress shoes, their laces tied in perfect knots though it was nearly dawn and they were both still up from the night before. On another man the outfit might've looked stiff and formal. On Nate it looked like what it was: the uniform of a wealthy self-made man who was comfortable with himself and in control of his environment. He'd traded his designer glasses for laser surgery a few months earlier, for the benefit of fighting, so when his eyes met hers they were unshielded by dark frames or glass, though his expression remained as inscrutable as ever.

In that moment, standing at her door, he looked less like the mage and warrior he'd become, and more like the successful businessman who'd shown up at Skywatch in a stretch SUV the prior summer. He looked like the men she'd dated all her life, only more so. And she'd sworn off those men, hadn't she?

Rhetorical question, she thought. *You're a Godkeeper now.* And the gods had chosen Nate for her shieldmate.

Nerves pulsing beneath her skin, she stepped back from the doorway, nodding for him to follow. "Come on in."

He took a quick, dark look around the cream-and-teal upholstery and Bokhara rug, and curled his lip. "You've got expensive taste, princess." His edgy energy rode the air between them, warning that he'd come for a fight.

Stung, and pissed because it wasn't like she'd chosen the new direction their lives had swerved over to either, she jerked up her chin and glared at him. "It's not your money, so why do you care?"

Reaching out, he pushed the door shut, closing them in together. Suddenly he was very near her, his energy surrounding her, angry, sexual, and very, very male, tempting her to reach out and touch.

"No," she said aloud, surprising herself. Surprising them both. She stepped back, putting a distance between them that seemed much wider than the few feet she'd created.

He went very still. "No to what?"

"To this." She pointed from him to her and back. "To us. I don't want it to be like this."

His brows furrowed, his eyes darkening with irritation. "This from the original author of the company line? What happened to 'we need to do this for the Nightkeepers and mankind' and all that crap? Was that just—"

"Stop it," she interrupted sharply. "Don't you dare."

There was silence between them for a few heartbeats, and then he spread his hands in a thoroughly masculine gesture of *I'm clueless*. "You're going to have to help me here. This isn't what I want or how I wanted it, but I'm willing to try if you are."

And if that wasn't the least romantic statement ever, she didn't know what was. But that was the point, wasn't it? Sex between Nightkeepers wasn't always about romance; sometimes it was strict necessity. The thing was, she wasn't just a Nightkeeper. She'd been raised in the human world, and had human values too. And one of those values included not having sex with a man who shouted the wrong name when he came. Which, when she'd played it back in her head, she realized Nate had done in the sacred chamber. "Who is Hera?"

He stilled. "Where did you hear that name?"

His tone was all the confirmation Alexis needed. She closed her eyes on a slap of pain, of shame. *Goddamn it*. She'd been the other woman and she hadn't even known. She forced herself to meet his eyes, and kept her voice level when she said, "From you . . . in the moment, so to speak."

Now it was his turn to wince, only he didn't. He just kept looking at her as though weighing a major decision. After a long moment, he held out his hand to her. "Come with me."

The action pulled back his sleeve to reveal his marks, both old and new. If it hadn't been for the rainbow mark, she might've kicked him out. Hell, if there'd been a MAC-10 handy, she might've shot him. That was how furious she was over his deception, how disgusted she was to discover that she hadn't just repeated old patterns by falling for a wealthy, too-slick charmer who hadn't fallen as hard or far; she'd dropped right back into the familiar rut of falling for the cheater, damn him.

But the rainbow glyph reminded her that this wasn't just about her heart or her anger. It was about the Nightkeepers too, and the goddess. It was about the end-time war and the new part she was apparently destined to play.

"Shit." She scowled at him. "Fine." She didn't take his hand, instead marching past him with her chin up and the burn of tears in her eyes.

The hallway was deserted; all the others were undoubtedly sleeping off the magic. Hell, she should be, and so should Nate. But she had a feeling that the restless, overtired energy that had kept her awake until his arrival was driving him, as well. She could feel the power of him at her back as he followed her the short distance to his suite.

She paused at the door, turning and raising an eyebrow. "You sure about this? Big step for you, inviting me back to your place."

Before, when they'd been together, she'd figured he'd kept her out of his space because he was a private sort of guy, and because the communal living at Skywatch made him want to guard a space that was his alone. Now, knowing there was someone else, she had a sneaking suspicion she knew what she'd find in his rooms: pictures and mementos, evidence of his other life.

Been there, done that, hadn't meant to ever do it again. Then again, the writs said that what had happened before would happen again. She just hated proving it this way.

Reaching past her without a word, Nate opened the door and let it swing wide. He nudged her. "Go on. You asked."

Yeah, she had. So she headed into his suite, braced for pictures of him with another woman, the trappings of a man she didn't know, the private life he hadn't yet managed to leave behind.

Instead she got bachelor quarters.

The walls were still the stark white all the residential rooms had been painted after the renovations necessitated by the destruction of the Solstice Massacre and the decay from the compound's having sat empty for twenty-four years. The rug was the same neutral beige the contractors had laid down, and there wasn't much in the way of furnishings in the main room aside from a couple of big chairs that offered far more in the way of comfort than style. A gigantic flat-screen TV took up one wall,

and wire racks on either side were crammed with electronics. More electronics, a laptop, and a jumble of notes
took up the low coffee table that was the only other
piece of furniture in the room.

There was no artwork or pictures, nothing personal
about the room. There was nothing that spoke of the
Nightkeepers, either, she realized, which fit with his personality but gave her a weird shimmy in her stomach
when she realized just how detached he'd remained from
it all. Sure, she was pretty heavy into the symbolism, but
even total-slacker Sven had put up a couple of framed
coyote posters and bought a hand-loomed Navajo throw
with a repeating coyote-and-cactus motif. Nate's sitting
room, though, didn't have a hawk in sight, as though he
were trying to cut himself off from the bloodline, from
his Nightkeeper identity.

She'd known he didn't want to be there, not really,
but she figured he'd been working through it. Now she
realized that wasn't the case at all. He hadn't even
moved in, really; he was just marking time.

Turning to look at him, she found him standing just
inside the door, which he'd shut at his back. His eyes
were dark and hooded; his expression gave nothing away.
She raised an eyebrow. "You wanted to show me something?" Glancing at the closed bedroom door, she added,
"If it's in there, the answer is no."

"Really?" He sounded only mildly interested, but his
body was strung tight with tension. "Could've fooled me
a few hours ago." He crossed to her, predator-quiet,
getting inside her space and leaning close, so she could
feel his body heat and the promise of the power they
could create together.

She steeled herself to push him away when she wanted
to grab him and drag him close. But instead of reaching
for her, he moved past her, snagging a remote control
off the coffee table and using it to turn on the TV.

The entire wall lit, going blue for a second, then flashing to the static intro screen of a gaming console. He
leaned down and hit a couple of buttons on the laptop,
and a new graphic popped up: a decent-looking intro
screen to what she guessed was a computer game. She

didn't know much about gaming, but this one had a front panel that showed a dragon-prowed Viking ship, its occupants locked in battle with a variety of mythological creatures. A storm slashed across the scene, blurring the details, and the title read: *Viking Warrior 5: Odin's Return*.

She glanced at Nate. "One of yours?"

He looked surprised. "You knew?"

"I know you own Hawk Enterprises, which develops computer games for a couple of larger distributors." She also knew his approximate net worth, and the location of the condo he used every other weekend when he returned to Denver for "business" she now suspected was named Hera.

He looked more amused than upset. "You did a background check."

"Jox already had the basics." She didn't mention that Izzy had brought her the info behind the royal *winikin*'s back. Izzy had wanted Alexis to know about Nate's criminal record, had wanted to stress that the members of the hawk bloodline weren't realiable—that Nate wasn't a proper match. To the *winikin*'s annoyance, Alexis had been more interested in his life outside the Nightkeepers, and what kept drawing him back to Denver. The file hadn't contained that info. Now she was halfway wishing she'd hired someone to do a deeper check, one that'd included known associates.

He frowned. "If you already knew, then why did you ask who Hera is?"

"The info didn't mention a girlfriend." The last word stuck in her throat.

"That's because she's not exactly a girlfriend." Hesitating only briefly, he tapped another key, skipped over what looked like an animated introduction to the game, complete with lots of blood and guts, and fast-forwarded through a scrolling legend of the *A long time ago, in a galaxy not so far away, blah, blah* variety. When he stopped fast-forwarding, the screen showed a computer-generated image of a stacked, Valkyrie-big woman wearing what amounted to a leather-and-metal bikini that left zero to the imagination. "This is Hera."

It took a moment for the surprise to penetrate, another for Alexis to look past the horned helmet and see the resemblance.

Then she froze, because it was way more than a resemblance.

She could've been looking into a computerized mirror, one that reflected her physical appearance exactly down to the pixel, then added an edge of the *go to hell* confidence she'd always wanted and never quite managed to project. The woman in the faux Viking costume could've been Alexis's twin. Or rather, she could've been the woman in the dream-visions, the one who was a better version of the real Alexis.

Shock flared through her. "Who modeled for this?"

Did she *have* a twin? Excitement spiked at the thought, because the Nightkeepers revered the twin bond. But that excitement drained quickly in the face of knowing that a twin wasn't something Izzy would've kept secret. But if not a twin, then what?

"There was no other model," Nate said grimly.

Alexis went very still. "You based this on me?"

"Nope. The first *VW* game came out four years ago." He grimaced, looking partly proud, partly uncomfortable. "For what it's worth, Hera has a huge following. Mostly of the under-twenty gamer variety, but still."

"I don't get it," she said numbly, but she was very afraid she did. Afraid . . . and rapidly getting angry at the realization that he'd known her long before he'd met her, and had hidden the connection. Narrowing her eyes she said, "How in the bloody blazes of hell can you design something like this years before you met me, yet *not* believe in destiny?"

"I never said I didn't believe it, just that I wasn't going to roll over for it."

She waited for more. Didn't get it. Fisting her hand on her hips, she prompted, "And?"

He exhaled a long, frustrated breath. "Look, do you think I'm comfortable with this? Trust me, the answer is a big old 'not.' Hera is . . . she's a fantasy, an amalgam of all the stuff that tests high in market research, along with a few of my own preferences. She was living inside my head years before I started working on the first *VW* game, and she's been with me on a daily basis ever since. She's got a fan club, for chrissake."

Alexis didn't like the way he was talking about this computer construct as if she were a real woman, and suspected she was seriously going to hate where this was going. "Tell me about her," she said carefully.

Not looking at her, he said, "She's brash and bossy, she's a top fighter, she can do low-level magic . . . and she's big and loud and scary, and pretty much guaranteed to rip the balls off of any guy who gets in her way." He glanced at Alexis now, and she couldn't read the emotion in his eyes when he said, "She looks like you, or you look like her; I'm not sure which is more accurate. The first time I saw you, when I came looking for Strike and you opened the front door, I couldn't believe what I was seeing."

"That was why you fainted?" She'd always wondered about that, why a big, tough guy like him had done the eye-roll-and-drop thing about thirty seconds after he'd stepped through the front door of Skywatch.

"That was dehydration," he said, sticking to the story he'd maintained ever since the incident. But something in his voice suggested there had been a good bit of shock in the mix, as well.

Alexis just stared at the TV screen, which was so big that her—or, rather, Hera's—image was nearly life-size. "You can create something like this, years before we met, and still deny that we're supposed to be mated?"

"Just because Strike saw Leah in a dream doesn't mean *we're* meant to be together," he said quietly, answering the question she hadn't asked.

She told herself not to ask, but it came out anyway. "Why not? We're good in bed. Am I really so awful outside of it?"

He exhaled a long, slow breath. "That's not what this is about."

Which didn't answer her question in the slightest. "Then what *is* it about?"

He was staring at Hera when he said, "I don't do well with the idea of sex as a commodity."

Everything inside her went still. "I don't remember offering to pay you."

"But you'd be trading sex for power. We both would be." Something in his eyes said he wasn't talking solely about Nightkeeper magic, and the idea unnerved her.

She didn't say anything, didn't know what to say, because it was both true and untrue. For her, the sex was a joy and a revelation, but yeah, it was also a means to an end. And when she looked at it that way, she got a strange, squirrelly feeling in the pit of her stomach.

"Besides," Nate continued, "I don't do well being told what to do." His expression, and the locked-tight rigor of his muscles, suggested there was more to it than even that, but she wasn't sure she had the strength to keep fighting him right now.

"That's an understatement." Her voice came out a little choked as the held-off exhaustion started to hit. She was suddenly tired and sore, and so depressed she could barely think straight, never mind getting the rest of the story out of Nate, and trying to understand where he was coming from, and where they could go from there. Besides, why bother? she thought, realizing she'd made her decision without being aware of it. She was done trying to make it work with him, done trying to meet the gods halfway. Nate didn't want her, plain and simple. Or rather, he wanted her body, but not much else about her, and she was finished trying to fight that fight.

"For what it's worth," he said softly, "I'm sorry. I wish it could be different."

"Me too." To her mortification, the words came out choked with tears. She spun on her heel and headed for the door.

"Alexis, wait."

She stopped, but didn't turn back. "What." It wasn't really a question.

"What are you going to do?"

She swallowed hard, knowing what she had to do, and hating it. "You don't want to work within the prophecies? Fine, then neither will I. I'll find myself another protector. That'll let you off the hook."

"Who?" His eyes were dark and angry, but he didn't seem at all surprised, which meant that he'd been thinking about it, too, about how, if she took another one of the guys as a lover, she might be able to transfer the protector's bond. Maybe.

The fact that he'd already gone there in his planning was an added blow, but she didn't let him see it, saying only, "Well, my choices seem limited to Sven and Michael, don't they? Izzy approves of the stone bloodline, so I guess I'll start with Michael and see what happens."

Figuring that was as good an exit line as she was likely to get, she slipped through the door, closing it behind her and hoping he wouldn't follow, because she was too tired to argue anymore.

She headed back to her suite, knowing she couldn't do a damn thing until she got some sleep. Tomorrow would be soon enough to choose her new lover, she thought, and tried not to let the idea echo hollowly in her heart as she shucked off her clothes and dropped into bed naked. Soon she was asleep.

And in sleeping, she dreamed of Nate, the man who wore the matching mark that proclaimed him as hers, but wouldn't let himself be caged.

CHAPTER TWELVE

Nate was pissed off enough that he couldn't get to sleep even though his body badly needed rest. He lay awake on his bed, staring out the window at the shadow of the ceiba tree, dark against the darkness. The canyon night was cool, the AC off, so he had the window cracked to let in the air. A breeze brought the faint howl of a coyote.

He didn't have a good reason to be pissed, he knew. He'd gone to Alexis's room intending to have pretty much the convo they'd wound up having. Granted, he'd meant to offer himself for the sort of sex-only protective relationship she was now looking to find somewhere else, and logic said her theory was better. That didn't mean he liked the plan, though.

In fact, he fucking hated it.

He despised the thought of her with Michael, loathed the idea with both halves of himself, the magic and the man. He was logical enough to recognize that it wasn't fair, and to know he didn't have the right to block her from taking on one of the other Nightkeeper males if he wasn't willing to be what she needed. That didn't dampen the rage, though. If anything, it made it worse.

He cursed aloud, feeling raw from the fight with Alexis, and guilty that he'd called Hera's name in the moment of orgasm. Worse, he wasn't sure which one of them he'd betrayed. Which was just fucked-up beyond

words, and made him think he should maybe have a chat
with Jade, who'd been a therapist of some sort back in
the real world.

At the thought of Jade, he wondered what she'd say
if Alexis wound up taking Michael as her lover. Jade
and Michael had been together in the months between
the bloodline and talent ceremonies, in much the same
way as Nate and Alexis had been. Actually, Jade and
Michael had been more open about their relationship,
more prone to public displays of affection until they'd
gone their separate ways. They seemed to get along well
enough in the aftermath, but the Nightkeepers were a
small fighting unit, and their quarters were close. What
would happen if the singles started trading partners?

Nate tried to imagine it, and just got more pissed off.

Torturing himself, poking at the raw spot, he tried to
imagine what it'd be like if Michael turned Alexis down—
hard to imagine, but what if?—and she hooked up with
Sven. The youngest of the male Nightkeepers, Sven
came off more like a college party animal than a warrior.
He'd been a little more serious about his training since
the equinox battle, and his rank within the Nightkeepers
would undoubtedly shift now that he had the translocator's talent mark. The rank might matter to Alexis, as
might her desire not to mess with the dynamic between
Jade and Michael. Still, though, Nate couldn't see her
being attracted to Sven's surfer-dude 'tude or the relatively low rank of the coyote bloodline.

"So probably not Sven," Nate said aloud, feeling
something loosen in his chest, only to have it tighten
back up when his thoughts circled back to Michael,
whom he could picture all too easily being to Alexis's
taste, not the least because he and Nate resembled each
other: They were both tall and dark, both stylish in their
own ways, and both came off as wealthy. In Michael's
case, though, Nate suspected the money was only surface-
deep. More, he had a feeling that a background check
that went a level or two further than the one Jox had
done on each of them might turn up something seriously
dark and dangerous, something that Alexis belonged nowhere near. Nate didn't have any evidence to back up

his hunch, though. It was just a guess, based on a couple of overheard snatches of the telephone convos Michael invariably took in his private rooms, and the fact that of all of them, Michael had shown the least desire to leave the compound and return to the real world they'd left behind.

I should have Carter look into him, Nate thought, then cursed himself for the impulse. Michael was a Nightkeeper, a teammate. He deserved better.

They all did.

Realizing he wasn't any closer to sleep than he'd been when he lay down—in fact, feeling even more alert and awake now that he'd worked himself into a mental lather—Nate groaned and swung himself out of bed. Dragging a T-shirt on over a pair of gym shorts, he figured he'd head downstairs for a workout, hoping to exhaust himself into a stupor. Unfortunately, that was pretty much the same plan he'd had the evening after the bloodline ceremony, when he'd gone to the gym hoping to tire himself past the perma-boner he'd acquired with his first link to the magic. Instead Alexis had come looking for him, and they'd become lovers.

And that so wasn't what he wanted to be thinking about right now.

Cursing himself, he headed out of his suite and down the residential hall, toward the stairs leading to the basement. He was halfway there when a scream split the air.

Alexis! He knew it was her, knew it in his gut, and was running for her door before the sound died off.

Images flashed in his head—not visions, but a mix of the things he'd seen and the ones he feared: scenes of Iago grabbing her and 'porting her someplace he couldn't follow; scenes of her lying limp, bleeding out from sacrificial cuts in a long, rectangular chamber he didn't recognize, one that his brain must've conjured to fill the need for a dark and creepy setting.

He hit her door at a run, twisting the knob and using his shoulder, slamming the panel inward with such force that it banged against the inner wall hard enough to break the stopper and dent the drywall. He didn't care about the door, didn't care about the growing clamor of voices out in the hallway as the others responded to the commotion.

"Alexis!" He pushed through into her bedroom, slapping at the light switch on the way through, his heart in his throat with a half-recognized conviction that she'd be gone, her bed empty.

But she was there, sitting bolt upright in bed with the sheet clutched just above her nightshirt-covered breasts. Her skin was pasty pale, her eyes glazed, seeing nothing. His initial spurt of relief at seeing her there in one piece fled quickly when he realized she wasn't tracking, hadn't noticed his arrival.

His first impulse was to grab and shake her, but the memory of being drawn into her link with the Ixchel statuette had him staying clear and raising his voice. "Alexis, snap out of it!"

She didn't even blink.

Others were starting to come into the room now: Strike and Leah first, followed by Jox and Izzy, and then Michael, whom Nate really didn't want to see just then. Nate forced himself to block them out, though, as he reached out and gripped Alexis's wrist. When he wasn't immediately sucked into the barrier, he said, "Come on, Lexie," deliberately using the intimate nickname. He was partly hoping she'd hear it and know who was calling her back, partly wanting Michael to hear it and know Alexis was his, even though Nate knew the territorial urge marked him as a complete shit. "Wake up. It's just a dream."

That was so wrong it wasn't even funny, because he was rapidly learning there was no such thing as "just a dream" in the Nightkeepers' world. Which was probably why he never dreamed. His subconscious wouldn't let him.

The lie worked, though. Somehow it worked. Alexis stirred, and her pulse cranked up beneath his touch. She blinked and focused on him, then looked past him to where most of the resident Nightkeepers and *winikin* were crammed in her bedroom, expressions ranging from *what the hell?* to *oh, shit*.

Bright spots of embarrassment stained her cheeks. "I

screamed, didn't I?" When she closed her eyes for a second, Nate saw the pain she was trying to hide.

"What did you see?" he asked quietly, aware that he was still holding on to her wrist, and she'd curled her hand around to grip his forearm, linking them palm-to-mark.

When she hesitated, Leah said, "Would you like us to leave?"

"No," Alexis said, too quickly. Her blush went darker and she pulled away from Nate, scooting higher up in her bed so there was a sizable gap between them. "No, you should all stay and hear this."

It stung that she didn't want to be alone with him, didn't want to lean on him, but that was what he'd wanted, right? He didn't get to bitch about getting his way.

"The dream?" Strike prompted, his eyes intent on her, no doubt because of all of them, he was the biggest believer in dreams and their portents.

"I saw . . ." She shuddered and looked at Nate, then away, staring out the window and the gathering dawn when she said, "I saw Gray-Smoke and Two-Hawk; I'm sure of it this time."

The logical part of Nate would've asked, "This time?" because he hadn't known she'd seen their parents before this. But the other part of him, the closed-off, judgmental part, had already turned away, blocking off acknowledgment of the past. He didn't care what his father had done, who he'd been. The circumstances had been beyond his parents' control, granted, but that didn't change the fact that they'd been nothing more to him than DNA donors.

It was Strike who said, "What else did you see?"

That implied he already knew about the visions, which just irked Nate more. If Alexis had kept this from him, what else was she keeping secret? But even as he wondered that, the rational part of him knew that it wasn't like he'd encouraged sharing.

"They were in that long, narrow stone chamber," she said slowly. "The same one I saw when I touched the statuette." She bit off the word, making Nate wonder what she wasn't saying.

Anna pushed through the crowd, moving between Nate and the bed, subtly easing him away. She shot Strike a look, and he started clearing the room.

"Go on," Anna urged Alexis. "You saw your mother. What else?"

"I— Wait," she said breaking off when Strike herded Michael toward the door. "I want him to stay."

Nate muttered a curse and fought to stifle a flash of rage he had absolutely no right to feel.

Strike glanced from Nate to Michael and back, but raised his hands in surrender. "Okay. Michael stays." But the look he shot at Nate promised a serious convo to come.

Alexis nodded, then said, "In my dream, Gray-Smoke and Two-Hawk were at the altar, which was made of stalagmites mostly, carved with scales and rainbows. They were working some sort of ritual—at least, they started to. Then they broke off and started arguing about something."

"Did you hear the spell?" Anna asked. She was holding Alexis's hands in hers, and Nate suspected she was either leaking the younger woman power or trying to see her dream through the contact. "Or what they were fighting about?"

"No." Alexis paused and took a deep breath. "But here's the thing: It was the same chamber, only the altar wasn't the same. Well, it was, but there was a small door open on it, one that I didn't see before. Maybe it was a secret compartment? Anyway, there was a little alcove behind the door, and inside the alcove there was a small carving." Now she looked at Nate, their eyes locking. "It's the other half of the Ixchel statuette. I'm sure of it."

He nodded. It made sense that Ixchel would want them to find the other piece of her demon prophecy. Would've been nice if she could've beamed the missing text straight to Alexis or something, but he had a feeling none of what they were up against was going to be that easy. The gods had rules the Nightkeepers didn't understand any better than they knew the extent of their own magic, or the limitations of the Xibalbans and *Banol Kax*. "What else did you see?" he asked.

"Nothing much." She shook her head, grimacing. "There was this buzzing over everything, like interference. Static. I couldn't hear any of what they said, and they were still arguing when I woke up."

Strike shot a look at Nate. "Did you dream anything?"

"I was awake." He didn't think it necessary to mention that he didn't dream, or if he did, never remembered anything but the nightmares.

"Damn," the king muttered. "Anna, you get anything?"

The *itza'at* disengaged from Alexis, shaking her head. "Nothing. Sorry."

Nate didn't know whether that meant she had nothing to add from Alexis's vision, or she hadn't been able to pick it up at all. He cleared his throat. "Where does that leave us?"

Strike didn't hesitate before answering. "After the first Ixchel vision, I had Jade start searching for references to a temple like the one Alexis saw: a narrow rectangular room deep underground, water access the only way in or out, with a carved crowd scene looking toward a naturally formed throne."

Alexis straightened against the headboard. "And?"

"Last I checked she had it narrowed down to three possibilities. By now she may've gotten it figured all the way out."

"I'm going," Alexis said, her tone brooking no argument. "I'll leave as soon as she's sure of the location."

Strike nodded. "Of course. I'll transpo you and Nate once—"

"No," she interrupted. "I want Michael."

Nate hid the flinch as best he could. He'd known it was coming, of course, but that didn't temper the instinctive kick of rage.

Surprised, Michael looked from him to Alexis and

back. "Blackhawk?" he said, letting that one word ask several questions.

Michael was the only Nightkeeper to call Nate by his bloodline name; Nate had never been sure if it was intended as a sign of respect or a subtle dig. Whichever, it sparked his anger even higher now, but he throttled back the urge to rip, tear, and fight, knowing that this, at least, wasn't anybody's fault but his own. "It's fine," he said tightly. "Go ahead."

"You don't need his permission," Alexis snapped. "I'm not chattel."

Nate gritted his teeth. "Nobody said you were." Knowing she was safe—for now, anyway—and that the convo was likely to go downhill fast if he stayed put, he headed for the door. He brushed past Michael harder than necessary, a body bump of warning, and growled under his breath, "Anything bad happens to her—and I mean *anything*—and you answer to me."

Nate didn't wait for a reply, just stalked into the hallway, and from there out the back of the mansion. He was nearly dead from postmagic exhaustion, and knew he needed to shut it down, but he couldn't bear to go back to his room knowing that Alexis was nearby. Knowing she might already be making her move on Michael.

It would've been nice to head out to the Pueblo ruins and raid Rabbit's stash up there for a sleeping bag and enough of the Nightkeeper's fermented *pulque* to get seriously stoned, but Nate didn't think he could make it that far. Instead he headed for a nearer goal: one of the family cottages behind the mansion, where he figured he could crash and sleep with a modicum of privacy, and without the sense that he was surrounded on all sides by expectations.

The small, four-room cottages stood in two neat rows of six each, plus one on the end to make lucky thirteen. Once, they had held the Nightkeeper families who had resided at the compound but preferred the privacy of a small house over the convenience of the mansion. Now all but one stood empty. Rabbit was staying in the cottage his father had once lived in with his wife and twin sons, back before the massacre. Red-Boar had allowed only minimal restoration and Rabbit hadn't changed anything, so the place was pretty much vintage. Jox had ordered the contractors to redo three more of the houses during the reno, on the theory that some of the resident Nightkeepers or *winikin* might want the privacy. Nobody had taken the offer, though, so the small structures stood vacant and unlocked, still smelling fresh and new inside.

The other nine cottages remained as they had been the night of the massacre, save for a new coat of exterior paint covering over where they'd been marred by smoke damage or the six-clawed scratches left by the *boluntiku*, lava creatures sent by the *Banol Kax* to slaughter the Nightkeepers and *winikin*.

Starting to feel seriously woozy, Nate headed for one of the redone cottages. He had his hand on the door-knob when something made him pause and turn away, then head for the cottage next door, which was the last one on its row. It was one of the ones that hadn't been renovated, and the door was locked, but something in his spinning, overtired brain had him crouching down and feeling through the fist-size pebbles in the rock bed beside the front step.

He found one stone that was unnaturally light and warm to the touch. When he flipped it over and felt the bottom, he found a sliding panel and, beneath that, a key.

Somewhere inside he knew it shouldn't have been that easy, that there was no reason for him to have known to look for the hidden key. That knowledge, though, was dulled by the dragging exhaustion, and a sort of compulsion that drove him onward, compelling him to unlock the door and let himself inside.

He didn't even turn on the light, just stumbled across the eat-in kitchen, headed for the living space that separated two small bedrooms. There was nothing strange about his knowing his way around; the floor plans were the same in all the cottages. There was, however, something seriously weird about the fact that when he was halfway across the living room, he pitched forward and

let himself fall, knowing there would be a couch there
to catch him.

He landed face-first on cushions he shouldn't have anticipated, which should've been dusty but weren't. Then
there was no more strange familiarity, no more warning
bells inside telling him he shouldn't be there, that he
should've stayed in one of the renovated cottages or,
better yet, in his plain-ass suite in the mansion.

There was only the darkness. And finally, dreamless
sleep.

The day after the eclipse, Rabbit was up early and
feeling surprisingly okay, given the amount of magic he'd
pulled during the ceremony.

He dragged on clothes at random—it wasn't like anyone cared what he dressed like—and hooked up his iPod.
The tunes were more habit than anything at this point;
he was getting sick of the music, not needing the constant thump in his head when there was so much else
going on up there.

Lately he'd been leaving the music off, and had discovered an added bonus: Most everyone thought he
couldn't hear them when he had the earbuds in. Okay,
so maybe he'd reinforced that by playing deaf once or
twice, but why not? It never hurt to have added intel,
especially when Strike and the others—and his old man
before them—had made it crystal-clear that he was on
a need-to-know basis, and, more often than not, he
didn't need to know.

So he'd played deaf. And he'd listened. That was how
he knew that things were still wonky with Patience and
Brandt—like he couldn't have guessed that from being
around them, and from the fact that the goddess had
chosen Alexis—*Alexis*, for fuck's sake—as being prefera-
ble to Patience for a Godkeeper. Which was just wrong
on so many levels he couldn't even count them.

Patience was kind and steady, a warrior with a conscience. Alexis was . . . well, she wasn't steady, that was
for sure. He wasn't an aura reader, but ever since that
cluster-fuck in New Orleans, whenever he got within
spitting distance of her his arm hairs reached for the sky

and his stomach jittered. He didn't know what it meant, but he knew he didn't much want to be around her these days.

When he beelined from his cottage to the mansion for breakfast, though, he soon learned that wouldn't be a problem. Alexis and Michael—Michael? WTF?—were headed out as soon as Jade locked down the location of some temple or another. Not only that, but Anna's grad student, Lucius, the one who'd nearly gone *makol* before the last equinox, had shown up past midnight, looking for some chick Rabbit had never heard of. The guy had been given the hospitality of one of the downstairs storerooms for the time being, poor bastard.

Jox passed along all of that info over breakfast—the royal *winikin* wasn't big on gossip, but he didn't mind talking some, and he made a hell of an omelet, especially when the others were still sleeping off the magic.

Once Jox ran out of things to say about the Michael-for-Nate mate switcheroo, Rabbit said, playing it real casual, "What's Strike doing about Iago. Do you know?"

The casual part must not've come off like he'd hoped, because Jox sent him a sharp look. "Why?"

Rabbit shrugged. "Just curious."

"Then ask him yourself." The *winikin* nodded past Rabbit's shoulder. "Hey, boss. Breakfast?"

"And lots of it." Strike took the bar stool next to Rabbit at the big kitchen island and leaned both elbows on the marble countertop. "What's up?"

The king was wearing a schlubby gray sweatshirt and jeans. The sleeves of the shirt had fallen back to reveal his big forearms, and the marks he wore on his inner right wrist: the jaguar, the royal *ju*, the teleport's glyph, Kulkulkan's flying serpent, and the *jun tan* beloved mark signifying his mated status. It was an impressive array on an impressive forearm, and left Rabbit feeling small and inconsequential, which he hated like poison, because it was pretty much his fallback status.

Taking a deep breath, trying to play it like it was just an idea, like it didn't matter really to him one way or the other, Rabbit said, "I think we should have the PI tag Mistress Truth's credit cards, phone, and bank accounts." His heart drummed in his chest, from nerves and need.

Strike's gaze sharpened. "Why?"

"Myrinne got away from the fire; I know that for sure. But you said yourself you couldn't get a 'port lock off my description. There's no answer at the tea shop, and the bartender down the road said the place has been closed since the fire. Nobody back in New Orleans is looking for Mistress Truth too hard, because she scared the shit out of the neighbors, and the cops are way busy already." And Rabbit hadn't pushed because he hadn't wanted to make too much noise, in case Myrinne needed to keep it on the down-low. "I think Myrinne might've made it back to the shop and lifted Mistress's plastic." It was what he would've done, and even from their short meeting he knew the girl had survival instincts.

"Maybe," Strike agreed, nodding his thanks as Jox hooked him up with a mug of coffee. "But we need to find Iago, not Myrinne."

Speak for yourself, Rabbit thought, but knew that wasn't going to get him very far with Strike, especially not with Jox listening in. "She's important."

"To who, you?" Strike shook his head. "Forget about her, kid. Or if you can't forget about her, then do your best to help us get through the next few years and then go after her with my blessing. Hell, I'll even help you look."

"She said she'd been dreaming."

Strike went very, very still. "Of you?"

Rabbit shook his head. "Skywatch. She nailed it too, right down to the tree."

"Well, shit." Strike sighed, pinching the bridge of his nose the way he did when he was trying not to admit he had a headache. "That complicates things."

"We have to find her," Rabbit insisted, not sure why or how he knew, but positive that it was nonnegotiable. Call it fate, destiny, or hormones, he had to see her again.

"I'll call Carter." Strike fixed him with a look. "But let us deal with it, okay? I don't want you involved."

A chill creepy-crawled down Rabbit's neck. "Why not?"

Strike's expression said, *Because you're a fuckup half-blood and I don't trust your magic for a second.* But aloud he said, "Because we don't know what we're dealing with. Given her association with the witch, there might be something in there that we don't want inside Skywatch. Hell, for all we know this whole thing is a setup. I'll find the girl, but until we know her story, I don't want you anywhere near her. Got it?"

The too-ready anger that Rabbit battled on a daily basis flared before he was even aware of it building. Heat coursed through him, flooding his veins and begging to be set free. Forcing himself to remember where he was—and who with—he fought the temptation, tried to cap the anger. Knowing it was rude, he tapped the iPod on and popped one of his earbuds in, hoping the thumping backbeat would drown out the rage. It helped some, but not enough, and the fury had him snapping, "That's fair. You and Anna can have your human pets, but I can't?" He knew he'd gone too far the moment the words left his mouth.

Strike set his jaw. "Watch yourself, kid."

"Or what?" He jumped off his stool and gave it a boot, sending it skidding across the floor to fall on its side in the kitchen pass-through. He fisted his hands and dug his fingernails into the ridged scar on his palm, keeping the fire in check, though just barely. "You going to ground me? I'm already stuck here. Going to take away my privileges? Don't got any. Take away my magic? Just fucking try it."

In the beat of silence that followed his shout, the scene froze in Rabbit's head as though he'd taken a snapshot or something.

He saw Strike sitting there, coffee halfway to his lips, surprise slapped atop the anger in his expression. Jox stood in the kitchen, his face a mix of disappointment and resignation. Those hurt some, because the *winikin* had mostly raised Rabbit while Red-Boar had lived in the past with his "real" family. But even at that, Jox'd always made it clear that Strike and Anna were his first and top priority. The frozen tableau was completed by Leah, who was framed in the doorway leading to the residential wing, looking pissed, which suggested that she'd heard him call her Strike's human pet. That pinched, because she'd always been pretty fair with him, but still. Why did Strike get to bring his girlfriend into Skywatch, but Rabbit couldn't bring his?

And okay, so Myrinne wasn't his girlfriend. But there was something there; he was sure of it. He just didn't know what yet, and wasn't going to be able to figure it out if he went along with Strike's plan.

Then Leah stepped down from the entryway and the scene snapped from freeze-frame to play, and Strike was getting up off his stool and advancing on Rabbit, his dark blue eyes hard and angry.

Rabbit braced himself to get his shit knocked loose. Instead the king stopped just short of him, his expression leveling out some when he said, "News flash, kid: I'm not your old man. I'm not going to ground you or call you names. What I am going to do is tell you to man the fuck up, stop thinking with your dick, and factor your teammates into this equation. You bring Myrinne here and things go south, what do you think happens?"

A big chunk of the anger died a quick death, but Rabbit couldn't back down, couldn't let it lie. "I have to find her. I can't explain it; I just know I have to find her."

"Yeah, I got that." Strike paused and traded a look with Leah before he said, "I'll have Carter look into it. Leah can call in a few favors too. Once they find her, we'll see what the situation looks like and figure out the next step from there."

"I want to go back to New Orleans," Rabbit said, feeling all itchy and tightly wound. "I can help look."

"I can't spare you for that. I need you in Boston."

Rabbit had braced for the argument, so it took him a second to reorient. "What's in Boston?"

"Jade's tracked down two more of the artifacts. Leah and I are working on one of them. I want you, Sven, Patience, and Brandt to go retrieve the other."

"Oh." Rabbit's gut churned. Strike wasn't just avoiding his demand to see Myrinne again; the king was also throwing him back together with Patience and Brandt. Bad sign.

"In other words, you think their marriage is either fixed now, or so broken that having me around them won't fuck it up any more than it already is."

"No! Never that." The protest came from Leah, who crossed the landing, righted Rabbit's toppled stool, and perched on it beside her mate. She took his mug and snagged a hit of his coffee before continuing, "We know how much they mean to you. We wanted to protect you, not punish you." She paused, letting him see the truth in her cornflower blue eyes. "We were trying to make things easier. I'm sorry you thought otherwise."

Shame coiled around the anger inside Rabbit, dimming the whole mess a little. He looked down at the floor. "Sorry about calling you Strike's pet just now. If it helps, you'd be something cool, like a rottweiler."

Amusement sparked in Leah's expression, and she lifted a shoulder. "No worries. I don't get mad. I get even."

Rabbit grinned some at that, and she grinned back, and the two of them, at the very least, were okay. In the moment of mental calm brought by forgiveness, his brain processed the rest of what the king had said. His head came up and he focused on Strike. "You said 're-trieve' the artifact. We're not buying it?"

"The thing's in a museum."

Rabbit grinned. "So what you really mean is that we're going to steal it."

Strike shifted, shooting a vaguely uncomfortable look at his ex-cop queen. "Yeah. That's pretty much the plan."

Rabbit nodded. "Cool. I'm in." As if there had been any question of it, really. He might be on the outskirts of the real action, and only a half-blood, but he was still a Nightkeeper. He did what his king said. That didn't mean he couldn't add on a few things, though. Like keeping in touch with Carter, and making sure he was the first one to get to Myrinne.

As far as he was concerned, that was as nonnegotiable as a fricking royal decree.

"Hello?" Lucius banged on the storeroom door again, hard enough to sting his hands, though the blows made little impact on the heavy paneled door. "Anyone? Hello? I need to talk to Anna. It's important!"

He didn't know what time it was, though he'd slept until he wasn't exhausted anymore, which suggested it was well into the day after his arrival. Maybe already too late.

He rattled the door against its padlock. "Anna!"

A sick feeling locked his gut. He remembered how he'd gotten there, remembered the shock of traveling in search of Sasha Ledbetter and finding Anna and the Nightkeepers instead, but his memories of the prior night were hazy and unreal, like they'd happened to somebody else. An angry, resentful version of himself. In the light of day—okay, in the light of a single fluorescent tube, but after a good night's sleep—he felt more like himself. And in getting his brain back online, he'd realized he'd left out a crucial detail when he'd been talking to Anna.

Drawing a breath, he thumped on the door again. "Hello! Can anyone hear me?"

The lock rattled on the other side, and an irritated male voice said, "Hold on to your ass. I'm coming."

The man Lucius had been the night before would've looked for a weapon and taken a swing at whoever was on the other side of that door. The guy who'd woken up feeling more at home inside his own skin than he had in a long time backed away and dropped down to sit on the edge of the cot, trying to look as unthreatening as possible.

Which was a good thing, he realized the second the door swung inward, because the guy who stood in the opening was below average in height and weight, in his late fifties, with peppered hair and a quick, economical way of moving . . . and he held a machine pistol with easy familiarity.

Lucius raised both hands in an *I'm unarmed; please don't mess me up* gesture, and said, "I come in peace." *Hope you do too.*

He was no gun expert, but the thing pointed at him looked like something out of a war movie, or maybe a cops-and-gangs flick, automatic and nasty-looking. The guy, on the other hand, didn't look nasty. He looked wary and drawn, as if he had a ton on his plate. Then again, that'd make sense. If Lucius had truly found the Nightkeepers, they had to be gearing up for the end of the world, the battle they'd spent generations preparing for. And if that wasn't a mind-fuck, he didn't know what was.

"You said you had a message for Anna?" the guy said.

"Yeah. I, uh . . . I'd rather give it to her personally." He had a feeling it wasn't going to go down big regardless, but didn't feel so comfortable telling it to Mr. Armed-and-dangerous.

"I'm Jox, her *winikin*. I'll give her the message."

Which might've been useful info if Lucius had any idea what the hell a *winikin* was. Whatever the guy's job description, though, he didn't seem inclined to go get Anna. Knowing that Anna and her brother—the king, and how screwed up was that?—needed to know what he'd done, and figuring their response was going to suck regardless of how the deets were delivered, Lucius said, "Fine. Tell her that Desiree bet me my degree that I couldn't find proof the Nightkeepers existed, and gave me the money to do it. I called her last night from the road and told her where I was headed."

Jox looked disturbed but not panicked, suggesting that the location of the compound wasn't entirely sacrosanct to the outside world. He said, "Who is Desiree to Anna?"

"Her boss at UT. Beyond that, you'll have to ask her yourself." He was so not going there.

Jox considered that for a long moment, then nodded. "I'll give her the message."

When he started to pull the door shut, Lucius said, "Wait!"

Jox paused. "Yeah?"

"Tell her I'm sorry."

"Knowing Anna, that'd work better coming directly from you," the guy said, not unkindly. Then he shut and locked the door.

He was right, too, Lucius knew. Thing was, at this

point he wasn't sure he believed Anna would accept his apology . . . or the help he planned on offering.

Alexis was just getting out of the shower when there was a knock on the door of her suite. As she toweled off and threw on last night's nighshirt and a pair of yoga pants, she was strongly tempted to ignore it, needing a few more minutes to herself.

It wasn't like she'd had much in the way of downtime to recharge after the eclipse ceremony. Between her fight with Nate and the dream-vision, she hadn't gotten to bed until close to three a.m., and she'd slept poorly, her dreams chasing her with sensory images of Nate and Michael, and heartache. They'd been real dreams, not visions—she was sure of that much—but they'd put her seriously low on REM sleep.

She'd planned on chilling in her sitting room for another hour at least. The knock came again, though, suggesting that whoever it was knew she was in there, and wasn't planning on being ignored. Sighing, Alexis crossed the sitting area and opened the door to find her *winikin* on the other side.

Izzy's expression lightened, though it stayed worried around the edges. "Why didn't you wake me last night? I can't believe I didn't hear the commotion." The *winikin*'s voice became reproachful. "You should've had someone come get me. I would've stayed with you."

"I know." Which was why Alexis hadn't woken her. Trying to avoid having to say that, she took the *winikin*'s hands in hers and gave them a squeeze. "I'm fine, honest."

Izzy looked at her long and hard before nodding. "If you say so." She stepped into the suite and pushed Alexis toward her bedroom. "Get dressed. Jade wants you in the archive as soon as you've had some coffee."

That had Alexis stopping and turning, her heart kicking on a burst of excitement mingled with dread. "She found the temple? We're going?"

Izzy nodded. "You leave for Belize in an hour."

CHAPTER THIRTEEN

"It's called the Actun Tunichil Muknal cave system; ATM for short," Jade said, indicating her laptop screen, which showed a series of photographs that were eerily familiar to Alexis.

The two women were in the archive, having a one-on-one about the likely temple site. The three-room library was quiet, the temperature perfect, the air crisp from the high-tech filter system Jade had requisitioned a few months earlier. The whole effect should've been restful, but Alexis couldn't settle. She was keyed up by the prospect of seeing the temple for real, and nervous about going with Michael, knowing she would have to proposition him if she wanted access to the goddess's power.

What was more, she wanted to talk to Jade, and make sure things were really over between her and Michael. She couldn't bring herself to start the convo, though. Not because of Jade, but because thanks to some of what Nate had said the night before, Alexis couldn't help feeling as though she were pimping herself out for the magic. She kept telling herself it wasn't really like that, at least not by Nightkeeper standards. But at the same time, she had to admit that by modern standards it was borderline.

Forcing herself to focus, Alexis peered at the Web site Jade had found. Seeing that the nav bar had buttons for tours and hotels, she frowned. "It's a tourist attraction?" That didn't play with her visions.

Jade gave a yes/no hand-wiggle. "Not on the level of Yucatán sites like Chichén Itzá and Tulum, that's for sure. Belize is sparsely populated, and has maybe a half dozen paved airstrips for the entire country. Not exactly a destination for the average tourist." She tapped the screen, her fingertip hitting a picture of a calcified human skeleton. "The ATM cave system is a stiff three-mile hike in from the nearest road. Unlike the Yucatán, Belize has aboveground waterways; there are three river crossings between the road and the cave system, and when you get there you've got to swim in. Because of all that hassle, though, the complex still has most of its original artifacts in place. Access to the cave system is tightly regulated; only a couple of groups have permission to bring tours through, and those cost."

"So you've gotta really want it," Alexis said. She looked at the pictures, then shook her head slightly. "I'm not sure. This looks similar to the dream-visions, but I'm not seeing an exact match." She couldn't tear her eyes away from the picture of the skeleton, though, couldn't help thinking the feeling she got from the photographs resonated too much to be a coincidence.

"This is your cave; I'm sure of it." Jade slid a bound book across to Alexis, then clicked on one of the Web site buttons, bringing up a cartoon map of the cave system on the laptop. "Have a look."

The book was open to an age-yellowed map that bore a strong resemblance to the one on the computer screen, except that the hard-copy map, dated 1873, showed several additional chambers off by themselves, connected to the others only by blue water trails rather than brown-marked pathways or gray-shaded tunnels.

The farthest chamber was a narrow rectangle with a serpent-and-rainbow altar sketched in at the far end, with a strange, looping figure extending away from it. The altar looked like a good enough match that Alexis felt the click she'd needed, followed by a burst of excitement mingled with unease. "Yeah. I think you found it."

She traced the blue waterways leading in. "We're going to have to swim in through a submerged tunnel?" She shuddered a little, but there was no question that she had to go.

"It doesn't look too far. Or at least it wasn't in the late eighteen hundreds. Jade paused. "There are two things you need to know before you decide you're definitely going, though."

"That doesn't sound good." Alexis leaned back in her chair and gave the archivist her full attention.

Jade tapped the date at the top of the page. "Does the map date ring any bells?"

Alexis frowned and shook her head. "Sorry. You're better at the history stuff than I—" She broke off, realizing why it should've connected. "Shit, that was when Painted-Jaguar's expedition went south. You're telling me this is the cache site?"

After the Civil War, with "civilization" encroaching westward and the various Native American cultures being squeezed into smaller and smaller settlements, the Nightkeepers had once again been subject to the pressures acting on their hosts—in this case the Hopi. By the 1870s, the Nightkeepers had numbered less than a hundred, and the survivors were starving. Times were grim, prospects dim, until an *itza'at* seer had envisioned a fabulously wealthy cache of Mayan-era artifacts secreted away in a Nightkeeper temple far to the south. A small group of the strongest remaining magi traveled through the hostile Mexican territories, eventually finding the temple and the artifacts within. The journey had been harsh, though, the trip back even worse, and only two of the original twenty Nightkeepers had returned, bearing the recovered riches of their ancestors.

They had sold off some of the artifacts immediately, and the proceeds had allowed the Nightkeepers to integrate into society. Their children were educated in human trades as well as Nightkeeper magic, and judicious investments, funded with artifact sales, kept them going for the next fifty years or so, while their numbers increased. In the twenties and thirties they'd liquidated the remainder of the artifacts—including those bearing the demon prophecies—to fund the construction of Sky-watch.

"This was the cache site," Jade confirmed. "Meaning that just because your dream-vision showed the statuette fragment in that hidden alcove, that doesn't guarantee it's still there. For all we know, your vision showed where it was before Painted-Jaguar discovered the cache."

"True," Alexis said, drawing out the word. "But I saw my mother and Two-Hawk with the statuette fragment, which would've made it sometime in the nineteen seventies or early eighties."

Jade countered, "Right, but we're not sure how the visions work, and whether they're going to prove fully accurate. What if your dream . . . I don't know . . . folded time or something, showing you parts of two different scenes in the same temple?"

"It's still worth looking."

Jade grimaced. "Which brings us to *numero duo* of the things I think you should know before you decide to 'port." She tapped the paper map, indicating the loop that extended beyond the temple chamber, and the unfamiliar glyph below it. "This seems to indicate that there's a loop of tunnel extending beyond the temple, under the waterline. The glyph is *och ja-ja*, which according to Anna has two translations: One is 'enter the water,' which is pretty benign, but the other translation is 'death,' which was often associated with entering a watery tunnel on the way to hell, sort of a reverse of the birth process."

Alexis fought a little shiver as she looked down at the glyph and the map. "As in 'you die if you enter the water'?"

"I'm thinking it's something like that. Booby traps, maybe?"

"Well, that's just great." Alexis fought the shimmy in her gut. "Note to self: Don't go into the tunnels beyond the temple room." Fortunately, she didn't see why she'd want or need to.

"You could call it off," Jade urged.

"And do what?" Alexis asked, faintly irritated. "It's not like I wouldn't rather be doing something else, you know."

"I know, that wasn't very helpful, was it? I'm sorry."
Jade rolled her shoulders. "I've been in a mood lately.
I'm just . . ." She shrugged. "I don't know. Frustrated.
Sick of working in here by myself, pretty much functioning as a human Google." She flicked the side of her
laptop. "I can't wait to finish scanning the last of the
books into this thing and get the computerized system
going. Then it'll be up to you guys to query and find
your own spells and stuff." She paused. "Then again,
once you can, I'll be pretty much useless, won't I?"

"No," Alexis said quickly. "You'll have more time to
concentrate on developing your magic."

"What magic?" Jade looked at her forearm, where
she had her bloodline and talent marks, but no warrior's
glyph. "The scribe's glyph is supposed to mean I can
create new spells, but it's not like there's an instruction
manual. I don't even know where to start!"

Seeing the opening, Alexis said, "What about, um,
boosting your power? You know, try some autoletting,
or . . . something else." *Like sex.*

Jade's lips twitched. "Don't worry, I already heard
you all but propositioned Mike last night. It's fine. Honest." She even sounded like she meant it.

"Are you positive?" Alexis pressed, feeling like total
crap. Theirs was too small a community for her to be
making waves. What was she doing?

*Getting away from a man who wants a woman who
looks like you, but doesn't act like you,* thought her
rational self, the one that'd suggested she switch partners
in the first place.

"I'm positive," Jade said firmly. She took Alexis's
hand and pressed her fingers. "Truly. Mike and I aren't
a good fit—he wants the magic, and I . . . don't. I really,
really don't." She looked almost surprised to have said
the last part, but added, "I'm not even sure I want to
stay here."

"Wow." Alexis rocked back, stunned. "What does
Shandi think about that?" Shandi, Jade's *winikin*, was
quiet and ultratraditional; Izzy held her in high regard,
which pretty much said everything that needed to be
said.

Jade blanched. "I haven't told her, and you can't either. Promise? I'm just thinking aloud. I don't really mean it." But that last part sounded more like rote than reality.

"I won't say anything," Alexis promised, but her brain spun while she gathered the references Jade had pulled together on Belize and the ATM caves.

As she headed back to her rooms, concern dogged her footsteps. What was happening to the Nightkeepers? They'd been a team during the equinox battle. Now, only five months later, they were bickering and scattered. How were they supposed to build an effective defense against Iago if they couldn't manage to get along on a day-to-day basis?

Complete the statuette, a voice whispered at the back of her brain. Alexis didn't think it was hers.

Stopping dead, she whispered, "Ixchel?"

There was no answer, save for a flicker of color at the edges of her peripheral vision. That and a renewed determination. She was going into the ATM caves, and she was bringing out the second piece of the demon prophecy. They needed to figure out the meaning of the partial inscription . . . and time was ticking down to the next cardinal day, the spring equinox, which was when Jade's *nahwal* vision had foretold that the first of the demon prophecies would be enacted. On that night, the magi would have to block the first of Camazotz's death-bat sons from coming to earth and fulfilling the next step in the end-time countdown. And she was going to help them do it.

Alexis felt a kick of excitement at the prospect of playing a major role, finally. But alongside that was nerves, because she wasn't her mother, wasn't a powerful mage or a mated Godkeeper. What if she screwed everything up?

Nate woke far later than he'd intended or expected, and didn't know where he was at first. Then he got his eyes focused, saw a plate-size copy of his medallion hanging on the wall, and knew exactly where he'd wound up. Exactly where he *didn't* want to be.

He flopped back on the sofa. "Fuck me."

Carlos had told him about his parents' cottage early on. Or more accurately, the *winikin* had tried to tell him about the place, and Nate had cut him off midsentence with a stern warning that he had no intention of looking back. He didn't blame his parents for how he'd grown up, hadn't blamed them even before he'd known the circumstances. But he'd done just fine without a family history up to this point, and didn't see the need to acquire one now. At least, he hadn't intended to. Now it was looking like his subconscious might've had other ideas, probably egged on by the eclipse, maybe some sort of collective hawk consciousness bleeding through the barrier. Or whatever.

"Gods damn it," Nate grumbled, and swung up to vertical on the sofa, which was seriously dated, but non-musty, making him suspect Carlos had sneaked in and done some cleaning, just in case Nate came for a visit. A long look around supported the suspicion; there was very little dust, and the air smelled suspiciously of Febreze.

The walls of the sitting room where he'd crashed were painted a warm putty color, and the floor sported an unfortunate shag rug a few shades darker. The sofa was beige and nubby, brightened with colorful pillows of red, green, and blue. Two large paintings hung on sturdy hooks on either side of the polished brass plate inscribed with the hawk-man emblem, giving the room a distinct personality.

Nate stood and headed toward the paintings, drawn particularly by the one on the left, which was a canyon scene that might've come from right outside the window, but was seen from an unusual angle, sort of a three-quarter helicopter's-eye view. He halfway expected to find it was a print, something done by an artist that Alexis's expensive taste would've recognized.

It took him a second to figure out that it wasn't a print, another for his brain to decipher the painted scrawl in the lower right-hand corner: *Two-Hawk.*

"Aw, shit," he said, then realized that everything he'd said so far in the little house had been a swear. But who could blame him? It wasn't like he'd wanted to be here, wasn't like he wanted to know anything about his parents. He knew all he needed to: His father had been the king's adviser, his mother a healer named Sarah, originally of the owl bloodline. They'd given him their DNA, a *winikin* whose expiration date had come way too soon, some bloodline magic, and a hell of a responsibility he wasn't sure he wanted.

So leave, he told himself. *Nobody's keeping you here.* Instead of about-facing it, though, he looked at the other painting, which was of a group of partially restored Mayan ruins seen from a similar angle as the canyon picture.

Then, when he couldn't put it off any longer, he planted himself in front of the oversize medallion, or whatever it was. The big metal plate shone dully in a shaft of sunlight coming through one of the windows, making the hawk figure seem to move. Pulling out his medallion, he compared the two. Same etching, same shift from bird to man and back depending on the viewer's angle. And that was about it. But they clearly matched; it had to mean something.

Feeling dumb, he touched his medallion to the plate on the wall, then laughed at himself when abso-freaking-lutely nothing happened.

"Admit it: The thing's just a chain. It's not a magic amulet." Somewhere in the back of his head, ever since learning of his heritage, he'd wondered whether the medallion was something more than an identifier, wondered if it had power. Granted, it hadn't shown any hint of activity during the cardinal days, and he hadn't been able to get anything out of it when he was jacked in, but still, he'd wondered whether one day it wouldn't suddenly wake up, more or less like the barrier had, and offer him increased magic, maybe a cool talent.

Now, staring at the plate on his parents' wall, he had a feeling he'd fallen prey to the gamer's fantasy of thinking the thing would turn out to be an all-powerful amulet to be named at a later date, when it was really nothing more than a decoration.

He started to swear, but bit it off and said nothing,

just turned away and headed for the door. He found himself glancing back at his father's paintings, caught himself wishing he'd been in that helicopter, skimming over the canyons and the Pueblo ruins, over rain-forest canopies and the mountain-shaped shadows of long-lost pyramids. But his early daydreams of becoming a pilot and flying free across the landscape, like his childhood fantasies of having a family, had long been lost to the practicalities of survival, of fighting for what he wanted and needed.

Forcing himself to shove aside the thoughts and questions the cottage had brought, feeling a low burn of anger that he'd even gone there, he stomped across the courtyard and past the pool to the mansion. He'd meant to head straight to the kitchen and put something in his empty stomach, but his feet—and the growing rage gnawing at his gut—headed him toward the residential wing instead.

He didn't knock, just barged straight into Michael's suite.

The other man was in the kitchen area, talking on the phone, which was no big surprise. He was wearing heavy black boots, worn jeans, and a plain tee. His too-long dark hair was pulled back under an unmarked ball cap, making him look far more like a blue-collar laborer than the jet-setting urbanite he usually played, leaving Nate wondering who the hell the real Michael Stone was, and whether the distinction mattered worth a damn.

At Nate's entrance he turned and clicked the phone shut without saying anything to the caller, and moved to block the kitchen pass-through with his big body. He said simply, "Let's not do this here."

"Too late." Nate slammed the door behind him and advanced across the sitting room, barely taking in the sparse furnishings, which were chrome and glass, and expensive. "And for the record, I don't give a shit what you've got going on in the outside world, or what you're hiding from, as long as you don't bring it back here."

Michael seemed to consider that for a moment, then tipped his head in acknowledgment. "Fair enough. I assume you're here about me and Alexis."

"There is no you and Alexis."

One dark eyebrow raised in speculation. "Is she aware of this fact?"

Nate barely hesitated. "She will be."

But Michael had caught the quick pause. His dark eyes narrowed. "As soon as you figure it out for yourself, right? Wrong. You've already done the hot-cold thing too many times, and she deserves better."

Hands balled into fists, rage riding him hard, Nate advanced on his fellow Nightkeeper. "And what, exactly, do you consider 'better'? You?"

"In some ways, yes." Michael unfolded from the doorway and advanced so the two of them were squared off.

They were similar in height, and both dark haired, but as far as Nate was concerned that was where the similarities stopped. Back in Denver he'd worn Armani suits and good silk ties, got his hair cut every month in the same damn style by the same damn stylist, and ran a business that half a dozen other people depended on for their livelihoods. Michael, on the other hand, kept his hair long and flowing, his jaw artfully stubbled, and wore his trendiness like a badge. He also, as far as Nate knew, had never held down a tax-paying job in his life. He was a playboy at best, a gigolo at worst, probably somewhere in between, and Nate's gut-check said the guy owed money to someone big and mean. The mob, maybe, or Vegas—which pretty much amounted to the same thing, depending on the circumstances.

The two men probably weighed about the same, but whereas Nate's bulk was mostly gained from a series of increasingly frustrated workout regimes, he rarely saw Michael in the gym downstairs, and had a feeling the other man's muscles might look good enough, but they were as soft as his pretty hair. Which probably meant it'd be a quick fight, but he could deal with that, as long as he got a few good licks in before his opponent went down.

Because there was sure as hell going to be a fight. He could see it in Michael's eyes and feel it in the tension that snapped in the air between them.

Still, though, fairness had him saying, "Look, I'm try-

ing to work it out, okay? I'd appreciate it if you give
me some room while I'm doing that."

"I'm sure you would." Michael paused. "Not gonna
happen. She's asked me to help her, and that's what I'm
going to do."

Nate gritted his teeth so hard he was pretty sure he
heard a molar give way. "Over my dead body."

"I was hoping you'd say that." Michael grinned, his
eyes lighting with a sort of unholy glory. Then he was
gone. He just freaking disappeared from the spot where
he'd been standing.

Nate stood for a second, gaping. Then, catching a hint
of motion out of his peripheral vision, he spun and
brought up his fists, but he was already way too late.
Michael was already in midair, performing some sort of
flying spin-kick that caught Nate in the temple and sent
him sprawling. Nate landed, cursing, on the glass-topped
coffee table. The glass didn't break, but one of the table's metal legs buckled, dumping him to the neutral-
toned carpet. He took a burn across his cheek from the
rug's nap, and that just pissed him off worse.

"No teleporting!" he shouted, and lunged for Michael
in a flying tackle aimed square at the other man's midsection.

Only Michael wasn't there when Nate arrived, meaning that Nate crashed into the wall instead, then took a
brutal chop across the back of his exposed neck.

"I can't teleport, asshole. It's martial arts," Michael
said derisively from somewhere behind Nate, who sagged
to his hands and knees as his opponent jeered, "I'd suggest you try it, but there's a certain requirement for
rhythm, balance, and tact, and you seem to prefer the
Viking throwdown."

Nate didn't know if his opponent had mentioned Vikings on purpose or not, but the reference kicked his rage
higher. The world clicked over to slow motion. Nate
stood and saw Michael standing there, saw his mouth
flapping as he danced on the balls of his feet, readying
for another judo chop or some such crap. Then Nate
had the satisfaction of seeing Michael's eyes go wide

when he threw a punch straight from the shoulder, right into his pretty-ass face.

The punch connected, the impact singing up Nate's arm. Michael's head snapped back and he went down on the coffee table, and this time the sucker buckled completely, its legs sticking out to the sides, making it look like a squashed chrome-and-glass spider.

Michael lunged back up with a roar, his fancy moves forgotten somewhere in a haze of testosterone, and the two men got into it for real, grappling and punching, staggering around the suite in an inelegant tangle as they fought for balance, for leverage.

Nate was aware of someone opening the door, taking a look at what was going on, then shutting the panel again in a hurry. He was pretty sure it was one of the *winikin*, but his glance at the door was nearly his undoing, because Michael got in beneath his shaky guard and connected with Nate's jaw, snapping his head back and making him see a rainbow of pain.

"Son of a bitch!" Nate dug in and landed a decent three-punch combination he'd learned in prison, as part of the *this is my ass, not yours* battles he'd been forced to fight every few months. Michael grunted in pain but gave as good as he got, and they both went down in the middle of the sitting room, rolling atop the flattened tabletop.

A chrome leg dug into Nate's kidney, and he roared and reversed their positions. His mouth was full of blood, bringing power singing through him, but he didn't touch the magic. He wanted the blood and pain, wanted to pound out his frustrations.

Michael, it seemed, had a few of his own frustrations to get out. They hammered at each other for a few more minutes, grunting and cursing, bodies slicked with sweat and spittle and blood.

Then, as though they'd planned it all along, they broke apart and flopped onto their backs, side by side, ribs heaving as they gasped like dying fish.

"Fuck," Michael said after a moment, "I needed that."

Nate laughed, then groaned when laughing hurt. "Shit.

Me too." He paused. "You're not going to the temple with Alexis, right?"

"Never planned on it."

"Okay." Nate stared at the ceiling. "What?"

Michael's chuckle was a split-lipped rasp. "I've crossed enough people in this lifetime already; I'm not about to start thumbing my nose at the gods. They picked you for her, and I'm not getting in the middle of that."

"Okay," Nate said again, hating that the whole destiny thing was actually helping him out this time. What mattered, though, was that he and Michael had an agreement, that he was going to have some room to figure out what the hell to do about Alexis. He probably ought to feel victorious or something, but instead he just felt hollow and sore. And hungry.

At the thought of food, his stomach gave a huge growl that got them both laughing again.

"I think that's your cue." Michael dragged himself to his feet, kicking a piece of chrome out of the way, then leaned down and offered Nate his hand. "Come on. Let's see whose *winikin* freaks out worse when he sees the state we're in. Five bucks says it's yours."

Michael's shirtfront was stained dark with blood, his lip split and puffy, and he was going to have a matching pair of shiners the next day. Then again, Nate figured the way his face was feeling—all swollen and strange— he probably looked about the same. He shook his head, though, as he let Michael haul him off the ground. "I'll take that bet. Carlos doesn't freak. He lectures."

"Only because he's worried about you."

"Don't start unless you want another beating."

"Bring it on." But Michael headed for his bedroom instead, pulling off his shirt as he went. He ducked into the bedroom and grabbed a clean button-down, then reappeared, waving a shirt in Nate's direction. "You want?"

"Is it as girlie as the rest of the shit you wear most of the time, or are we going landscaper for a reason today?"

"Fuck you." But Michael was grinning as he tossed the shirt, and as they headed out of the suite and down to the main mansion's big, fully-stocked kitchen together, Nate was feeling about as relaxed as he had since Strike showed up at his office and hung him off the side of the building to get his attention.

They didn't see anybody on the way through the mansion to the kitchen, which Nate figured was probably a good thing. But when, by the time they'd killed a gallon of OJ between them, they still hadn't seen anybody, they shared a look.

"I don't like this," Michael said.

"Me neither." Nate headed across the sunken main room for the sliders that led to the pool and the remainder of the compound out back. If the mansion was empty, then the courtyard or the training halls were their next best bets.

Sure enough, he could see in the distance that the Nightkeepers and *winikin* were gathered at the picnic tables underneath the ceiba tree.

"Nice of them to come get us," Michael muttered.

Remembering the *winikin* head-pop he'd seen in the middle of the fight, Nate said, "I think someone tried. We scared them off."

"Oops."

Taking a couple of bagels to go, Nate and Michael headed out to join the group. When they got into range, Strike waved them to a couple of empty places. He didn't mention anything about their bruises, just said, "Good. Now that we're all here, we'll get started. Anna?"

As the king's sister stood and moved to the front of the tables, Nate glanced around, making sure he knew where Alexis was, checking that she looked okay.

She looked better than okay, sitting at the far end of the table in a soft sweater that made him want to touch her. The sight of her kicked his body from tune-down to overdrive, and it only got worse when he realized she wasn't meeting his eyes, was looking everywhere but at him.

But although he might not like it, he couldn't blame her for having decided she was better off done with him. More, he didn't know what he was going to do about it. He had, however, just bought himself some time to think it through. Then again, it wasn't as if he'd managed to rationalize their relationship in the months they'd been together or apart. Why did he think he'd have any better luck now? If anything, adding the Godkeeper issue into the mix just made things worse. Alexis was the sort who would want—and deserve—a commitment. She would want to be mated, want all the marks and ceremonies that went with it. All the promises . . . and the constraints. And Nate didn't do constraints.

"Okay, people," Anna said, interrupting his mental logjam. "Here's the deal. Last night my grad student, Lucius, showed up here, having followed starscript directions left by Ambrose Ledbetter in the haunted temple where I was attacked by the *nahwal* last year. Lucius had followed Ledbetter's daughter—or possibly goddaughter—to the temple, where he found a great deal of blood, along with Ledbetter's skull. He followed the directions, hoping to find her here, and found me instead. Based on his description of the tracks in the dust near where he found the skull, and our inability to track down Sasha, it seems reasonable to think that Iago and a female accomplice snatched her from the tunnel. Strike has been unable to lock onto her for a teleport, so we have to assume she's either being held underground . . . or she's dead." Anna's rapid-fire delivery was clipped and flat, but Nate could hear pain beneath it, and guilt.

Jade said, "Did he see any other starscript while he was there?"

But Anna held up a hand. "Let's wait on the questions, please. There's more." She paused, grimacing. "Lucius's search was being funded, unbeknownst to me, by a woman named Desiree Soo, who is also my immediate boss . . . and my husband's ex-mistress."

A collective wince went around the group at that one, and Alexis made a soft sound of sympathy. "I'm sorry."

"Thanks," Anna said, but her eyes were dull when she continued, "Anyway, the upshot is that Lucius checked in with Desiree before he came here. He told her about the temple, about the signs of a struggle he'd found there, and about the starscript directions he was convinced had something to do with the Nightkeepers." Anna looked from Strike to Jox and back. "I don't know what, if anything, Desiree will do with the information, but she knows how to find Skywatch if she wants to."

Surprisingly, because he sure as hell never said anything during group meetings under normal circumstances, Rabbit said, "Why does she care about the Nightkeepers?"

"Lucius is pretty sure he saw the quatrefoil mark on her wrist," Anna answered. "She always wears a silver cuff, so I never noticed it. But he described the Xibalbans' mark without knowing what he really saw."

There was silence after that one, broken only by Rabbit's low, "Oh, shit."

Nate cursed under his breath as things suddenly got a whole lot more complicated. *Oh, shit, indeed.*

Anna nodded, expression grim. "She's been at the university for five or six years now, having come over from a top Egyptology position at another school. It was a bit of a shocker, actually; she took a demotion to come to UT and head up our section of the art history department. In retrospect, and with no false modesty, I can only assume that the Xibalbans somehow learned that I wear the jaguar glyph, and Desiree put herself into a position where she could watch me closely and see if there were other survivors. She must've tapped into my e-mail. That would explain how Iago knew to start searching for the missing artifacts—Jade and I have exchanged a few messages. We kept the conversation general, but it could've tipped him off, told him what to look for and where to start." She paused. "I'd apologize, but what would be the point? We didn't even know we had an enemy besides the *Banol Kax* until a few days ago. All we can do is go forward from here."

There was a murmur of agreement, and Nate found himself nodding along with the others. But at the same time his mind was racing, trying to use his gamer's strategies to figure out what the Xibalbans' next move would be. Iago now knew where to find them. Question was, what would he do with the information?

Rabbit sat on the outskirts of the group, practically vibrating with impatience. He wanted to get going, to get moving, to do something, anything. He was pissed that while Strike was busy worrying about what Myrinne might do if he brought her to Skywatch, Anna had screwed the pooch with her own human contacts.

Yeah. That was fair.

Continuing the meeting, Strike moved up the plans to send Alexis and Michael to Belize, and fast-tracked the timetable for the group heading to Boston. "Leah and I are going to 'port to Germany. Carter thinks he has a lead on the artifact linked to the seventh demon prophecy, and we're going to go check it out."

On the other side of the picnic table, Nate frowned. "All due respect, but are you sure that's a good idea? None of us is expandable, but we sure as shit can't do without you two." Nate looked like hell: His knuckles were scraped and swollen, and his face looked like it'd run into someone's foot a few times. From the look of Michael, sitting next to him, Rabbit could guess whose foot. He could also guess what they'd been fighting over.

Strike's glance at Alexis and Jox suggested that the royal council had already had a similar debate about the advisability of his going after the seventh prophecy.

After a moment, though, Strike answered, "The seventh demon prophecy involves Camazotz himself coming to earth, and there's some suggestion that it trumps the other six. If we can get our hands on the altar stone that bears the prophecy, we might be able to figure out how to block all seven of the prophecies at once, rather than screwing around dealing with them for the next seven cardinal days in a row." He paused, but held up a hand when Nate moved to speak. "And you're right, that doesn't mean it needs to be me and Leah going after the seventh prophecy. In fact, given that there's a pretty good curse associated with possession of the altar stone, logic might suggest that someone else should go after it. Except for two things. One, I'm damn well not sending one of you on an assignment because I consider it too dangerous to do myself. If I'm not willing to take the risk, then we find another way, period. And two, the altar stone is dedicated to Kulkulkan."

There was a beat of silence after that, before Nate

said, "Okay. Even I'm willing to admit that the god connection trumps logic."

"Glad you approve," Strike said, his tone making it
clear that he didn't really give a shit whether Blackhawk
liked the plan. "Moving on, I wanted to let you all know
that we've decided to send the twins away for the next
few months, until we have a better handle on Iago's
power and how much of a threat he poses to Skywatch."
The king nodded to a pair of *winikin* at the end of the
table. "Hannah and Woody are going to take them
someplace safe."

Rabbit straightened at the news and sent a quick look
over at Patience and Brandt. But they weren't reacting,
which meant they knew already. Hell, it might've been
their idea. Brandt hadn't wanted the kids raised in the
compound in the first place. Acid gathered in Rabbit's
stomach, both because the rug rats were leaving and
because nobody had told him to his face. Up until a
month or so ago, Patience and Brandt had treated him
like part of their family. The more the two of them had
argued, though, the less they'd seemed to want him
around. Now the twins were being sent away. What the
hell was going on? Were Patience and Brandt breaking
up for real?

"Don't do it." For a second, Rabbit thought the strangled words might've come from him. Then he realized
it was Jox who'd spoken. The royal *winikin* stood and
stared at his king, looking wrecked. "Don't send them
away."

Strike grimaced. "It's for the best. You know that."

"Please," Jox said, just *please*, as though having the
twins leave were the worst thing he could think to
have happen.

Rabbit didn't know what that was all about, but felt
sorry for Jox when Strike just shook his head, like the
decision was already made. Gods knew Rabbit had been
on the receiving end of that look about a zillion times
before. *Welcome to powerlessness,* he thought. *How's it
feel?*

But even though he hated the idea of the rugrats leaving, Rabbit had to admit that Strike had a point—if there

were questions about the security of Skywatch, better to split the Nightkeepers up as much as possible than have them all bunched together. When you were down to your last dozen, it wasn't always practical to stand and fight. The twins had purposely been held back from their bloodline ceremonies, which normally would've happened on the first cardinal day after their third birthdays. Without their bloodline marks and that connection to the barrier, they were essentially invisible to the *Banol Kax*. They'd be safer away than they were at Skywatch; that much was clear. What wasn't clear was why Jox was so upset. He should be happy it was a couple of *winikin* taking them, not a pair of full-bloods taking off and diluting their fighting force. Besides, Hannah and Woody were a couple; they'd give the kids as close to a normal family setup as possible, under the circumstances. But when Rabbit looked, he saw that Jox was gone, like he hadn't been able to sit there and listen to Strike after the king had made his call.

What was up with that?

"The rest of us will stay here and shore up the defenses," Strike continued, and Rabbit returned his attention to the meeting.

"Why not go after Iago?" Sven demanded. "We've got two gods on our side now. We should be able to kick his ass, especially if we do it on the next ceremony day, the Seville at Opposition or whatever."

"Saturn at Opposition," Strike gritted, glaring at Sven. "And you seem to be forgetting that we don't have a clue how Iago's powers work. So far we've seen him teleport and mind-bend, and his mind-bending worked effectively on a Nightkeeper, which is highly unusual." He glanced at Rabbit. He didn't say, *Rabbit's just a half-blood, though, which might explain his susceptibility*. But he thought it. Rabbit knew that for sure. The king continued, "Besides, we don't have a clue about the Xibalbans' strength yet. There could be just the two of them; there could be hundreds. We don't know nearly enough about them yet to think about going after them."

"So we're just going to sit here and wait for him to

come after us?" Sven asked, sounding annoyed. "What happened to the best defense being a good offense?"

"Offense doesn't always mean going after the other side," Strike said evenly. "Sometimes it means making the enemy do what you want, thinking it's their idea."

Nate narrowed his eyes, one of which was nearly swollen shut already and rapidly darkening to a bruise. "You want Iago to come here. Why?"

"Because we don't have a clue what we're up against," Strike answered. "We need to know what the Order of Xibalba intends to do between now and the end-time; we need to get an idea of their numbers and their magic; and quite frankly, I'd like to convince them that they don't have to like us, but that we're all better off if we live through to New Year's Day, 2013."

"And if their idea of a workable negotiation rests on our absence from the earth?" Nate pushed.

"Then at least we'll learn something about the enemy." Strike glanced at Anna. "Given that our location has almost certainly been compromised, I say we plan to use the potential security breach rather than whining about it."

"And Lucius?" Anna asked quietly.

"He stays locked up for now." Which wasn't really an answer. It was only a delay.

The meeting broke up soon after that. It was about time, as far as Rabbit was concerned, because everything they'd spent the past forty minutes going over seemed like it could be pretty much summed up as, "The king's going to do what he wants." Hello, history repeating itself. Strike's father had ignored his advisers and led the Nightkeepers to their deaths. What if Strike was in the process of doing the same? Was loyalty defined as going along with the flow, or, if it didn't seem like the flow was heading the right way, doing something to change it?

Rabbit wasn't sure, but he knew he didn't like the way things were headed, and he had an idea that might help shed some light. Waiting until he saw that Jade was deep in convo with Strike and Anna, he made tracks for the archive.

On the first floor, tucked around a corner and down a short hall, the three-room library held the collected knowledge of generations of Nightkeepers, as well as just about everything that'd ever been written by outsiders regarding the Mayan end-time prophecy and the Great Conjunction. Jade was almost finished organizing and computerizing all of it, but the system wasn't online yet. That was too bad, because Rabbit was pretty sure he could've hacked past the basic passwords she was using to protect the spells Strike had decreed off-limits without special authorization, namely his. Since the database wasn't finished yet, if Rabbit wanted one of those spells he was going to have to get his hands on the actual books, which were locked in the second of the three rooms. Lucky for him, locks weren't much of a challenge these days. His powers were growing faster even than he was letting on to the others, making it no strain when he slapped a palm on the door and concentrated and felt the tumblers fall into place.

As he pushed through the door into the second room of the archive, where the older books and a handful of nonperishable artifacts were kept, he told himself this was the right thing to do. It was his fault Iago had gotten the knife in New Orleans, so he owed it to Strike and the others to figure out how to get it back. And he owed it to Myrinne to make sure she was safe, because he knew what it was like when nobody gave a shit.

"Okay," he said to the rows of neatly shelved books in the librarylike room. "Will the three-question spell please step forward?"

He found the book he was looking for almost right away, recognizing the binding from last fall, when Strike and Leah had used the spell to figure out why she, a human, had sporadic power. Technically the spell was supposed to work only on the cardinal days, the equinoxes and solstices, but Rabbit was betting he could make it work for Saturn at Opposition. He was positive he could call the three-question *nahwal*, the spirit guide who would answer three questions per person per lifetime. Granted, the *nahwal* wasn't strictly bound to answer the questions in a way that made immediate sense, but it'd be better than nothing, right?

Strike and Leah had already burned their questions, and the theory was that the rest of the Nightkeepers were supposed to save their questions for stuff that would be important to all of them, mostly dealing with the end-time. But Rabbit was so not into socialism. As far as he was concerned, it was his life, his questions.

He was a half-blood, after all. He might as well live down to expectations.

Two days later Alexis was in the weapons shed located between the ball court and the firing range at the back of the compound, prepping for the Belize trip by loading her weapons belt with spare clips of jade-tipped bullets, when she heard the scuff of a footstep in the gritty, wind-blown sand outside.

She turned, tensing. "Hello?"

Nate appeared in the doorway, his big body blocking the gap and his energy filling the small shed. He looked darker, rougher, and more dangerous than usual, the bruises on his face having gone from raw red to dark. Sensual awareness prickled across Alexis's skin, shimmering inward to gather in her core and at the back of her brain, where the connection to Ixchel awoke at his proximity. *He's the one,* the goddess seemed to be saying.

Well, guess what? The goddess was wrong. He wasn't the one. He was an ass.

Alexis couldn't believe he and Michael had beaten each other up, couldn't believe neither of them would tell her why, though guessing was easy: She was the only thing that'd changed between the men. She wasn't flattered, either, though Anna and Jade seemed to think she ought to be. No, she was seriously annoyed. She figured it was safe to assume that Nate had gone after Michael, who'd fought back in self-defense. And that scenario was just asinine, because Nate was the one who kept distancing himself from their nonrelationship. He didn't have any right to be pissed at Michael. Not that either of them would talk about it, of course; they were sticking together in some sort of Neanderthal code of ethics that just made her more annoyed.

When Nate simply stood there in the doorway, looking at her, she snapped, "What do you want?" Belatedly, she realized he was wearing black on black, with a bulletproof vest over the top, strapped down with a stocked weapons belt. "Where are you going?"

"Belize." He moved past her and started collecting spare clips, turning his back on her.

"The hell you are." She would've yanked him to face her, but knew from experience that he didn't get yanked. So she moved around in front of him, forcing him to look at her. "Michael's going with me."

"Not anymore. Stone and I reached an agreement." He turned away from her again, pretending to check one of his weapons, though they both knew he kept his guns in perfect working order. They all did—Jox, their resident gun junkie, had drummed that lesson home early on.

Confusion and irritation fought for dominance within Alexis, and confusion won. "Nate," she said softly. "Look at me, please."

He stalled the busywork, standing still for a heartbeat. Then he turned toward her, his expression guarded. He secured the autopistol in its holster, then hooked his thumbs in his belt as he faced her, looking ready for anything.

Anything, of course, except what she needed from him.

"This is nonnegotiable," he said, as if a statement like that would actually end the discussion. "I'll play the god card if I have to, though I'd really rather not."

And he has a point, damn it, Alexis thought on a beat of sadness, of frustration. She knew Strike would back him up if it came down to it, as would the *winikin*. So she didn't try to fight the fight she knew she wouldn't win. She simply said, "Why?"

He flinched, looking like he would've preferred that she argue, but answered, "I need time."

Whatever she'd expected him to say, that wasn't it. "How much time?" she asked, not sure what he expected to figure out in the coming days, when he hadn't managed it over the past seven months.

"I don't know." He shifted, settling the Kevlar across his broad shoulders. "I'm working on it." Which didn't tell her anything, really.

She stood there and looked at him, really looked at him for the first time after having spent the past several months—and particularly the past few weeks—trying not to let herself look. He was brawny as ever, with a set of muscles she suspected he'd developed during the prison stint he refused to talk about, then maintained in the years since with workouts that seemed fueled as much by anger as a desire for fitness. His face was different than before, though, especially his eyes, which held a new determination.

When she'd first met him she'd seen a slick, powerful businessman who'd shown up in a stretch SUV. Now she saw a warrior-mage who had saved her more than once, a man who was trying to reconcile the person he'd been with the one the future needed him to become. He didn't like being told what to do, didn't accept anything at face value, including the attraction that'd bound them together from the very beginning. But for the first time he seemed to be accepting that the Nightkeepers needed more of him.

He was trying; she had to give him that. So, despite herself, she nodded slowly. "Okay, you can come to Belize. I'm not promising anything, though."

"Understood." He nodded to her belt. "You locked and loaded?"

She took a deep breath to settle the sudden flutter in her stomach, then nodded. "Yeah. I'm ready."

"Then let's get our backpacks and get rolling. Next stop, Belize."

CHAPTER FOURTEEN

Using one of the photos Jade had pulled off the Web as a visual anchor, Strike teleported Nate and Alexis to a point just outside the ATM caves. The three of them were linked hand to hand, with her in the middle and the men, holding autopistols at the ready in their free hands. The weapons proved unnecessary, though. They were alone, thanks to Jox, who'd cleared the site by calling to book a tour, paying a premium to ensure that his group would be the only ones allowed in the caves that day, and then bailing on the reservation without demanding a refund.

Pulling away from the men, Alexis let her hands drop to her sides and tipped her head back. "Wow."

There didn't seem to be much else to say. The place was fricking gorgeous. They stood in a small clearing near where a slow-moving river widened to a stone-strewn pool that fed into the mouth of an arching cave. Sunlight dappled through the leafy canopy high overhead, and everywhere she looked there were jewel-green leaves and growing things. The abundant fertility was a shock, after they'd come from the mostly red-brown plant and animal life in New Mexico's canyon country. Alexis had been to the Yucatán for the cardinal days and the eclipse ceremony, of course, but those had been furtive trips, in and gone during the night, under the cover of darkness.

Now she took a moment to fill her lungs with air that was moist and fecund rather than desert dry. She smiled up at the chitters and cries of wild animals high above. She saw the flash of colorful birds and dark, long-armed shapes playing in the trees.

"Howler monkeys," Nate said, coming up beside her. "I wouldn't recommend trying to make friends."

"No worries on that account." She turned back to Strike. "Thanks for the lift. We'll call you for a pickup." She patted her knapsack, which held the satellite phone that would form their main link to Skywatch. Granted, a satellite glitch had forced Red-Boar to carry a wounded Anna out of the jungle the year before, and had meant that Strike had barely reached them in time . . . but without a true telepath among the Nightkeepers, they didn't really have a better option than the sat phones.

Strike nodded. "Be careful. And good luck." He raised a hand in farewell. Power hummed in the air, sparking royal red for a second and then coalescing inward, snapping to nothingness as he disappeared, leaving Alexis and Nate alone outside the ATM caves.

According to Jade, all the signs pointed to its having been one of the Nightkeepers' most sacred caves. To the Maya and Nightkeepers, all caves had been sacred, as had mountains and rivers. Those three components together—a cave at high elevation, with a subterranean river running within—characterized the entrance to Xibalba itself. Most of the Mayan pyramids were built on that idea, with the sloping sides ascending up to an open platform, often with a boxlike room at the top that mimicked the mouth of a cave and led to tunnels heading back down into the body of the pyramid and even beyond, down to underground tombs, waterways, and sacred sacrificial places. In that way, the dead kings entombed within the pyramids had metaphorically acted out the journey through the nine-layered hell of Xibalba and out the other side, to join the gods in the sky.

Those pyramids were man-made, though. Places where the mountain-river-cave conjunction occurred naturally were considered even more special, and only the highest-ranking shaman-priests dared enter such caves, lest they anger the gods or *Banol Kax*. Even now, a thousand years after the main fall of the Classical Mayan Empire, when the ATM caves had ceased being a center of worship, Alexis could feel the importance of the site and the crinkle of magic on her skin. The power wasn't the gold of the gods, the red of the Nightkeepers, or the purple-green of the *makol* and *Banol Kax*. Instead, it was a pale, colorless magic, a wellspring to be used for good or ill. It was a neutral, waiting sort of magic.

Hopefully, it was waiting for them.

"Ready?" she asked, and headed down the shallow slope to the pool before Nate could answer, trusting that he had her back on this, at least. "Please tell me Jade was right on the 'not enough piranhas to worry about and you'll see the poisonous water snakes and fanged reptiles coming' thing."

"We won't be in the water too long," he said. "Watch your weapons."

"Right." She unclipped her belt and tucked it in her knapsack, which was lined and would supposedly be completely waterproof once she engaged the double seal at the top. With her possessions secured, she stepped into the pool and started wading toward the cave mouth, then wound up having to swim when the faintly squishy bottom fell away. It was only a short distance across to where her feet touched the bottom, and then she was wading again, passing under the stone archway of the cave mouth.

Nate was right behind her, unspeaking, his solid presence helping settle her. She wouldn't have admitted it to him for anything, but part of her was glad he was there instead of Michael. She and Nate admittedly had their problems, but she was comfortable with him, knew his body language and how he moved. Whether either of them liked it or not, they worked well together, at least on the physical level.

The ATM cave was like a cathedral at first, open and echoing with the slosh and slap of water as they waded onward. Rock formations flanked the waterway, larger, stubbier, and softer-edged than the ones she'd seen in her vision. Was that because of a difference in time frame, or would the stalactites and stalagmites grow sharper and narrower, more fanglike as they worked their way into the cave system? She didn't know.

When they reached a section where a dry-land trail opened up alongside the waterway, they climbed out and sluiced off what water they could, then pulled water-resistant flashlights out of the packs, clicking them on for light as they moved deeper into the caves.

Alexis glanced over at Nate and was surprised at the pensiveness written on his bruised face. "Not exactly your idea of fun?" she asked, keeping her voice low because of the echoes and the sense of being inside a sacred place.

"It's not that," he said, equally low. "It's . . ." He hesitated, looking at her, then let out a breath. "I spent the other night in my parents' cottage. It got me thinking."

"You . . . oh." She broke off. Of all the things she might've expected him to say, that wasn't one of them. "Wow. Do you, you know, want to talk about it or anything?" Not the most elegant of invitations, perhaps, but even as lovers they'd shared little in the way of deep convo.

He shook his head, but said, "Maybe later."

They kept going, and soon passed a cluster of flare-rimmed pottery jars. The size of two cupped hands joined together, the vessels had most likely held sacrificial offerings—water, perhaps, or blood, intended to petition the gods for the shaman-priests' safe passage into the sacred caves. Nate and Alexis didn't dare leave a bowl or carved offering for subsequent visitors to find, but they also didn't dare enter the inner caves without a sacrifice, so they blooded their tongues and spat in the river. Then, using copies of both maps, they worked their way from one cavern to the next, passing more offerings as they went. The sacrifices grew more elaborate as they moved deeper into the cave system; farther in, the pottery jars were larger and decorated with depictions of bats and howler monkeys, both which were thought to act as messengers between the earth and the underworld.

Moving even deeper into the caves, they passed human remains, the calcified bones of adults first, then infants, each carefully laid out in chambers with high, vaulted ceilings and giant limestone pillars. The waterway wound through the scattered offerings, some of which had been placed on carved altars or grindstones, while others were set in natural niches and alcoves.

The researchers who had ventured into the ATM caves had pointed to the sacrificial victims and offerings as the efforts of Mayan priests to reverse the droughts, wars and famines that had supposedly struck the region around A.D. 950, when so many of the great cities had been abandoned en masse, seemingly overnight. But Alexis knew the sacrifices were not, as the archaeologists believed, tributes made to the rain god, Chaac, in an effort to alleviate drought. They were evidence of the terrible magic the Nightkeepers had been forced to call on in order to drive the *Banol Kax* back to hell, after the Xibalbans had loosed the demons on the earth, dooming the empire.

In the final chamber, where the subterranean river seemed to dead-end in a deep pool, nine skulls were stacked in a *tzomplanti*, a skull pile that could be used as a marker or a warning. Nine skulls to represent the nine levels of hell standing opposite the thirteen layers of the sky, with the single earthly plane between them as a buffer. A battleground.

Checking the older map, Alexis gestured to the pile. "That's our marker. According to Painted-Jaguar and company, the tunnel is beneath the skull pile."

Nate nodded. "Let's dive."

Digging into their knapsacks, they pulled out pony bottles, which were small compressed-air tanks fitted with breathing masks that covered the nose and mouth. Sven, an expert diver, had outfitted them with the canisters and given them a quick demo. The brief writeup that went along with Painted-Jaguar's map indicated they could make it through the tunnel on a single breathhold, but they weren't taking any chances. They also donned goggles and traded their flashlights for waterproof miners' headlamps.

Not exactly the height of fashion, Alexis thought, winc-

ing when the elastic straps pulled at her no-nonsense
ponytail. She resealed her knapsack, but didn't put it on,
because Sven had advised them to carry the packs
hugged to their chests, as that could reduce the danger
of snagging on the tunnel sides. The safety precautions
had her pausing at the edge of the water.

"Problem?" Nate asked, coming up beside her.

She stared down into the dark depths, but a flush of
heat and a flash of sensory memory warned her that it
wasn't the swim she was worried about. She was unset-
tled by the thought of what they might find at the other
end of the tunnel. She was sure Nate had been part of
her earlier vision, could swear they'd actually been in
the chamber, not just a dream-version of it. But if that
were the case, would there be any evidence that they'd
been there together, that they'd made love in the temple? Would she see a boot scuff and know it was his, or
see something they'd left behind? Or what if being there
jolted the memory loose inside his skull? He swore he
never remembered his dreams, so maybe their shared
vision had gone to wherever his dreams wound up,
blocked off by his stubborn insistence that there was
nothing to be gained from the past, or from prophecy. If
so, then what would happen if he suddenly remembered
making love to her in that cave?

It doesn't matter either way, she told herself firmly,
trying very hard to believe it.

"Alexis? What's wrong?" He touched her arm, bringing a flare of warmth to her midsection.

"Foolishness," she said, dismissing the fears, and the
small wish that fantasy could become reality. She took
a deep breath and told herself to man up and get the
job done. "Let's go."

She combat-dropped into the water; he followed a few
seconds later, their splashes echoing in the stone chamber. Alexis held her knapsack across her chest, the straps
looped around the arm holding the pony bottle as she
adjusted her goggles and headlamp and took a couple
of experimental breaths. With all systems go and Nate
treading water beside her, she let herself sink beneath
the surface.

The water was silty and brown-cast, the suspended particles dampening her light within ten feet or so and making her feel very isolated. Very alone. Unable to stop herself, she back-paddled until she could see Nate's reassuring bulk in her peripheral vision. When he gestured, offering to go first, she nodded, grateful there was nobody else there to see her be a wienie.

He dropped down along the rock wall to where the dark shadow of a tunnel led away. When he reached the tunnel mouth he glanced back at her. She gave him a thumbs-up, though her stomach churned. He nodded, slipped into the tunnel, and started swimming.

Alexis stayed right behind him, trying not to stir up too much silt as she swam, but feeling seriously awkward with all the stuff she was holding. At about the one-minute mark she took a hit off the pony bottle and let her exhaled bubbles trail behind her. She told herself not to use too much of the air too fast. Then, moments later, Nate's light curved upward and disappeared as the tunnel ended.

Following, she saw him break the surface of an air pocket. In the water all around her, stalagmites thrust upward. Before she'd even surfaced, she knew they were in the right place, and the knowledge twisted her heart with lust, with regret at knowing the dream wouldn't be repeated. Why couldn't real-life stuff be as simple as it was in her fantasies?

Knowing there was no answer for that one, she kicked upward and broke through to take a deep breath. The air was okay, though it smelled of age and stale *copan* incense.

The long, narrow chamber was just as she'd remembered it, just as she'd described it: the crowd scenes carved on the parallel walls and the short side behind them, the flying serpent and the rainbows overhead, and the limestone pillars marching up to the carved throne at the far end. The torches were dead where they'd been lit before, but everything else was the same, even the way the water went clearer and warmer as they swam toward the throne.

"It's beautiful," Nate said, his voice rasping a little as

he drew close to the V-shaped stalagmites where the two
of them had made love in her vision. He touched one
of them in passing, and she felt a phantom caress glide
across her skin, as though he'd touched her, not the
stone. Then he was past the spot and climbing up on the
platform. Once he was up on the ledge, he turned back
and reached down to help her.

Alexis stared at his hand, then up at him, and saw
nothing. No memory, not even a hint of heat. He didn't
remember.

Swallowing back a ball of tears that came out of nowhere, she put her hand in his and let him pull her up.
They didn't speak as they ditched their knapsacks and
pony bottles in a pile, then pulled out the flashlights,
which were strong enough to illuminate the entire arcade. The artificial light seemed cold and wrong when
Alexis's memory said it should've been torchlight, magic,
and the twining colors of love. But maybe this was better. In the harsher light she'd be less tempted to confuse
the vision with reality.

In the vision there had been love. In reality there was
a job to do.

She waved Nate toward the altar. "Stand over there,
facing me."

He moved as she directed, but said, "Why?"

"Because that was where your father was standing."
The words were out before she thought how he might
take them, given that he was just beginning to even
admit that he'd had parents who'd lived and breathed
back at Skywatch, and had been a part of the life he
was living now.

But Nate said nothing. He simply took his place,
stone-faced.

"Gray-Smoke was standing here." Alexis moved to
her mother's place, but felt nothing. She wasn't sure
what she'd expected to feel—some sort of resonance,
maybe, or an echo of bloodline power. Instead she was
aware only of the press of stone against the bottoms of
her feet and the damnable pull that kindled whenever
she was near Nate, a combination of chemistry and the
goddess's power. "I wish I'd heard the spell they were

using," she said, then frowned. "Which brings up the question of why they were here in the first place." She'd been trying to figure that one out since her latest dream, and hadn't gotten anywhere. "I asked Izzy, but she couldn't even be sure when they went off together." She looked around. "Why here?"

It was more of a rhetorical question than anything, given that Nate was the antihistory buff. But he surprised her by saying, "They were trying to work a spell that would tell them whether or not Scarred-Jaguar's visions were real, and whether the gods truly meant for them to attack the intersection during the summer solstice of 'eighty-four.'"

For a second Alexis just stared at him. "How do you know that?"

"Carlos told me back when I first arrived, before he gave up trying to spoon-feed me the history."

Alexis tipped her head, considering. "What did he say exactly?"

"I was trying to ignore him, remember?" When she just waited him out, he lifted a shoulder. "He said the two of them went away for a few days right before the summer solstice. Said they were going to get proof, one way or the other. When they came back they were barely speaking to each other, acting really weird. They said the augury spell they tried didn't work."

"Or maybe it did, but it didn't answer the question they thought they were asking."

"None of which is really relevant at the moment," he pointed out. "We're here to get the statuette. In your vision, where was it?"

She stared at him for a long moment, trying to decide whether it'd be worth having the fight, and in the end deciding probably not, because she'd never get him to admit that studying the past informed the present. Letting out a long breath, she said, "Here." She turned and touched one of the limestone columns, a rainbow carved between two snakes. "It is—or was—behind here." But there was no seam in the carved stone, no pressure pad to open a hidden compartment.

"Blood," Nate said succinctly, and handed over his own knife.

The haft was warm from his body heat, the feel of it far more intimate than it should've been. She nicked her palm, pressed it to the carved column, and whispered, *"Pasaj och." Open sesame.*

She jerked her hand back, shocked when, just that easily, the stone puffed to vapor beneath her hand, revealing the alcove she'd seen in her vision . . . and the carving that would complete the statuette of Ixchel. Holding her breath, halfway afraid it too would puff to mist when she touched it, she reached into the hidden niche and grasped the stone fragment, which looked to be another chunk of the basket the carved goddess sat atop.

She exhaled a sigh of relief when it stayed solid, heavy and warm in her hand.

"Got it?" Nate asked, his voice suddenly sounding too loud in the echoing chamber.

"Got it, thank the gods." She withdrew the carving. The moment it was clear of the alcove, the stone pillar puffed back into existence and went solid. "Whoa." She touched the spot and felt stone where an empty space had been only seconds earlier. "That was pretty cool."

"Agreed." Nate dug into his knapsack and held out a T-shirt and a padded, collapsible cooler about the size of a six-pack. When she raised an eyebrow, he lifted a shoulder. "Figured we'd need something to protect it for the trip back."

The small gesture shouldn't have touched her. Because it did, she avoided meeting his eyes as she wrapped the carving in his shirt and tucked it inside the cooler, which she zipped up and held out to him. "You want to carry it?"

"Sure." Their fingers brushed as he took the cooler, sending a frisson of heat up her arm. From the sudden lock of his eyes on hers, she knew he'd felt it too. The sensual buzz between them kicked up a notch, and they both stood there, each, she suspected, waiting for the other to make the first move either toward or away.

Sudden urgency beat within her. She wanted him, wanted to take him inside her, wanted to couple with him in the water, braced against the limestone pillars while the slap of wetness and flesh drove them both higher, drove them beyond reason. But the man in her vision wasn't the one who stood opposite her now. The man in the vision had wanted her for herself. In reality, Nate didn't know what he wanted, except his freedom from everything and everyone . . . which was incompatible with her concept of family, never mind their responsibilities to the Nightkeepers.

Very deliberately, she let go of the cooler and stepped back. "Thanks. For taking the carving."

Eyes still locked on hers, he nodded slightly. "No problem."

And in that short exchange, far more was said than the actual words.

"Let's go." Working side by side, they repacked their flashlights and knapsacks and checked their pony bottles, which were still mostly full. Then they dropped into the water, clutching their packs, and headed out the way they'd come in. As Alexis submerged and kicked for the tunnel, once again following in Nate's wake, she had to brace herself against a sting of disappointment and a sense of failure.

They'd gotten what they'd come for, it was true. But she had the strangest feeling that she'd left something behind.

CHAPTER FIFTEEN

By the morning of day six of his incarceration, Lucius was seriously worried. He hadn't seen Anna in days. The only human interaction he'd had was with the *winikin* Jox, who brought his meals and could be leaned on to provide toiletries and requested snacks, but not much else.

Granted, it wasn't as though he were being tortured or anything—they'd upgraded his accommodations to a three-room suite on day two. The rooms had new-looking bars on the windows, an empty phone jack, and a sturdy lock on the door, but it had a bathroom and a small kitchenette, and comfortwise beat the hell out of his apartment back in Austin. But still, it was a prison.

He'd watched as much bad satellite TV as he could stand, and had fiddled with the gaming console and cartridges Jox had brought him. But he'd never been huge on TV, and he'd sort of burned out on gaming a couple of years earlier, so neither of those distractions held much in the way of appeal. Or, more accurately, what was outside the suite held so much more.

His window overlooked a freaking Mayan ball court. How could he not want to be out there? Ball courts were his all-time favorite type of ruin. Only this was no ruin; it looked like fairly new construction, like the Nightkeepers still played the traditional game after all these years.

Two twenty-foot-tall stone walls ran parallel to each other, and were open at both ends. The walls were intricately carved, and although he couldn't see the murals from his vantage point, he could guess what they looked like: scenes of ballplayers wearing the traditional yokes and padding, each vying to send a heavy rubberized ball—sometimes containing a skull at the center—through rings set high on the walls while members of the opposite team tried to stop them using any methods possible, fair or foul. The carvings might also show the losers— or sometimes the winners—being sacrificed in tribute to the gods, blood spurting from the stumps of their beheaded necks, the gouts turning to sacred serpents as they landed.

He would've given just about anything to be able to get down there and check it out. He also wanted to get a look at the kapok tree nearby, which must've had a serious irrigation system keeping it alive, because they weren't supposed to grow in the desert. There was the big steel building behind the tree, a firing range beyond that, and what looked like a set of Pueblo ruins at the back of the canyon. . . .

Frankly, he didn't care what he got to explore first; he just wanted to get his ass out there. He'd tried the door and window already, along with the vents and anyplace else he thought he might be able to break through, but had stopped short of busting up the furniture and using the shards to hack through the drywall into the next room over. Another couple of days, though, and he might give it a try.

He was trying not to blame Anna for deserting him; he'd blamed her for too much already, all but destroying a friendship that had once been very important to him. Besides, it wasn't just about the two of them, was it? His being there was undoubtedly a security breach of epic proportions for her people, never mind the way her brother had implied that he'd been involved with them once before and was already living on borrowed time.

Lucius really wanted to know what that was all about. But the strange thing was, he was curious but not mad, bored but not blaming anyone for it, which felt more like the him of a year ago rather than the guy he'd become over the past six months. Something had changed inside him since he'd come to the compound. He'd arrived all pissed off and ready to lash out, feeling like the victim, like the world was out to get him and he'd be better off striking first rather than sitting back and waiting it out. He'd been mad at Anna, mad at Desiree for sending him on his quest, mad at Sasha Ledbetter for not being where he'd hoped she would be.

Since then he'd had a serious reality check. Maybe it was seeing Anna and realizing what she'd been hiding from him, and partly understanding why. Or maybe it was just the time he'd had to do some navel-gazing and figure out what the hell was important. Anna was important, he'd decided. What she and the others were trying to do was important, because the end date was less than four years away. And, more than anything, he wanted to help. He wanted to be a part, however small, of the war that was to come.

His mother had always said he'd been born into the wrong time, that he should've been one of Arthur's knights, a hero in an age of heroes. He wasn't sure about that, but he knew there were some battles a man had to step up and fight no matter what.

"I may not be a Nightkeeper," he said aloud, "but with Ledbetter gone I'm the best-informed human they're likely to find. I can help with the research, if nothing else."

"I agree," Anna's voice said from behind him. "That's why I'm busting you out of here."

Lucius spun away from the window, shocked to hear another human voice after so many days of talking to himself. "Anna! How . . . Who . . . ?" Then her words penetrated, and he concluded with an oh-so-brilliant, "Huh?"

"Lucius, sit. Breathe." She waved him to the generic sofa that took up most of the generically decorated sitting area. Once he was sitting, she took one of the chairs opposite him and leaned forward, folding her hands over her knees. "We need to talk."

On the heels of shock came all the emotions he'd been

sorting through over the past few days, crashing into one another until his brain was a total train wreck of half-completed thoughts. Taking a deep breath, he blew it out again and said, "I'd say that ranks pretty high on the understatement scale."

Her eyes warmed a little. She looked good, he realized. Then again, he'd pretty much always thought she looked good. At least, he had until recently. Somewhere along the way he'd stopped noticing how her hair looked brown in one light, chestnut in another, and how her deep blue eyes seemed to look into a guy, seeing far more than was on the surface.

Had he changed or had she? Or had they both gone in different directions and wound up back in the same place once again?

She was wearing jeans and a soft blue shirt he didn't recognize, with long sleeves pulled down over her forearm marks. The yellow quartz skull-shaped effigy she'd started wearing the previous fall hung from a chain around her neck. The thing that got and held his attention, though, was the knife tucked into her belt.

Carved from black stone—obsidian, probably—it didn't look terribly old, but it sure looked sharp.

With his eyes locked on the knife, he said, "You mentioned something about busting me out of here? That wasn't a euphemism for something I'm not going to like, is it? Like telling a little kid that his sick old dog went to live on a farm?"

He expected a grin. Didn't get one.

"Here's the deal," Anna said, "and hold the questions until the end, at which point you're only allowed three. I know you too well—if I let you quiz me, we'll be here until the solstice." She paused until he nodded, then continued, "As you've figured, Skywatch is the Nightkeepers' training compound. What you probably haven't figured, and the reason that I've argued against the 2012 doomsday for so long, is that up until last summer I believed that the apocalypse had been forestalled. Twenty-five years ago my father led the Nightkeepers against the interplanar intersection, based on a vision from the god Kauil saying he could prevent the end-time. Instead, the demon *Banol Kax* came through the intersection and slaughtered the warriors, then sent their creatures here to Skywatch to kill the children. All but a few of the youngest Nightkeepers died."

Her voice shook a little and her eyes had gone a very deep blue, as though she were seeing something he couldn't. Lucius wanted to help, to comfort her, but he didn't dare interrupt, so he waited.

After a second she continued, "The power backlash sealed the barrier. We checked the intersection every cardinal day for years after, but it remained closed, and the magic stayed inactive. We truly thought the end-time had been averted."

"We?" he blurted, unable to help himself.

She fixed him with a look. "That's your first question." But she answered, "Me, Strike, our *winikin* Jox, and the sole adult survivor of the Solstice Massacre, a mage named Red-Boar." Her eyes went sad. "You met him last fall, sort of, but won't be able to remember it. He is—he was—a mind-bender."

Which brought up so many questions Lucius didn't know where to start, so he gestured for her to continue. "Go on."

"Well, the short of it is that there was one remaining prophecy dealing with the end-time, stating that certain things would happen in the final five years before 2012. Sure enough, last year a *makol*—a human disciple of the underworld—used some major blood sacrifices to reopen the barrier at the summer solstice. All of a sudden the magic was working again, and the end-time countdown was back on. Strike was forced to recall the surviving Nightkeepers, who had been raised in secret by their *winikin*. Since then, we've been going through crash courses in magic and fighting skills in an effort to whip together a fighting force capable of defending the intersection at each equinox and solstice, and capable of either somehow averting the end-time, or at the very least holding the *Banol Kax* in Xibalba when the calendar ends in December 2012, and the barrier falls." She paused. "There are thirteen Nightkeepers left on earth, counting a pair of three-year-old toddlers and a powerful freak show of questionable allegiance named Snake Mendez, who still has another six months before he's eligible for parole."

She fell silent, but it was a long moment before Lucius said, "Okay. My brain's officially in 'tilt' mode."

She sent him a warm look that recalled better days. "Join the club. You want to ask your last two questions now?"

"Sure. What's a *winikin*?"

"That's the most important thing you can think to ask?" she said slowly.

He grinned. "No. But it's been bugging me for almost a week."

After a serious eye roll, she said, "They're the blood-bound protectors of the Nightkeepers, descended from the loyal slaves who sneaked fifty or so Nightkeeper children out of Egypt when Akhenaton started killing polytheists. The single surviving adult Nightkeeper, who came to be called the First Father, led the slaves and children to safety, eventually ending up in Olmec territory. Knowing that history repeats, he put a spell on the *winikin*, binding them to the bloodlines they helped save and entrusting them with making sure the culture and the magic survived until 2012. In that way they became our partners rather than our slaves; they're bound to protect us and guide us, though they have no magic of their own."

Which totally dovetailed with the Nightkeeper myths Lucius had scraped together for the side project that'd slopped over into his thesis and then bitten him in the ass. It didn't explain why the *winikin* were never once mentioned in the mythology he'd uncovered, but that so wasn't the last question he needed to ask.

He took a deep breath. "Why are you telling me all this?"

"Now, that's the right question," she said approvingly. "The simple answer is because you're one of the best researchers I know, and our current archivist is actually a repurposed child psychologist. It's another monumental understatement to say she's floundering."

"If that's the simple answer, then there's a more complicated one," he said, careful not to make it be a question.

"That would be that I'm telling you a little about of our history and current situation so you'll understand what's at stake."

He grimaced. "A dozen or so Nightkeepers against the fall of the barrier protecting the earth from the forces of Xibalba? I'd say the stakes are pretty high." If, by pretty high, she meant insurmountable.

"Exactly," she said, as if he'd uttered the last part aloud.

"Which doesn't explain what you're going to do with me. The term 'busting out' implies liberation, but I don't see how freeing me helps, especially given what already happened with Desiree." He paused, then said, "For what it's worth, I'm really, really sorry about that. I don't know what came over me. It was like . . . I don't know. Like I was somebody else for a while. Somebody I don't like very much."

"We go on from here," she said, which wasn't the same as accepting his apology. "That includes my asking you a favor." She paused. "I want you to stay here and help us."

The offer took a moment to register. "Me? Help the Nightkeepers?" Excitement was a quick kick, tempered by the complications she'd mentioned. "Would I have to stay locked up?"

"Not in this room." Again with the nonanswer. "You'd have free run of the compound and access to the Nightkeepers, the *winikin*, and the archive, which contains a number of codices, artifacts, and original sources, along with commentaries from generations of Nightkeeper scholars, Spanish missionaries . . . pretty much everything ever written about the Nightkeepers and the end-time, along with some primary Mayan sources you won't find anywhere else."

His researcher's soul sang. *They have an archive!* Excitement zipped through him, lighting his senses. "What's the catch?" he asked, though there was no question that he was going to agree to whatever it was. He was being offered every Mayanist's dream—access to a previously unknown stockpile of information. More, he was being offered a part—however small—in the end-time war.

"I'm going to need an oath of fealty," she said.

"No problem. Where do I sign?"

"That's not exactly how it works." She drew the obsidian knife from her belt and balanced it on her palm. "It's more along the lines of a spell that binds us together, making you my responsibility. You would become my *k'alaj.*"

His brain kicked out the translation, and he said slowly, "I'd be bound to you? Like a slave?"

"Technically, yes. My bond-slave." Her eyes held his. "In practice, you'd be exactly who and what you are, except that you'd be restricted to the confines of this training compound, unless I'm with you or I give you a charmed eccentric granting passage through the wards surrounding the canyon."

An eccentric was a small ritual item, usually carved from stone in the shape of a god or animal. Stomach churning, Lucius tried to imagine himself wearing one around his neck, like a cosmic hall pass, or a collar with a rabies tag. "A slave," he repeated, hating the idea, the word. But there was more; he could see it in her eyes. "What aren't you telling me?"

She grimaced. "In binding myself to you, I'll be granting you my protection, but also making myself responsible for your behavior. The bond will give me a limited sense of where you are and what you're doing, and some degree of control over you. However, if you do anything to jeopardize or harm the Nightkeepers, it's my duty to find and execute you, and upon my return I will also be punished as suits your crime. Which is why, as you might guess, this spell has been enacted only a handful of times throughout the Nightkeepers' history, and then only with humans the bond-master or -mistress believe they can trust with their lives." Her eyes showed worry fear.

Lucius couldn't think of a response, couldn't think of much except, "Holy shit." He was going to be a slave. He'd be Anna's slave, and in service to the Nightkeepers, but still. A slave. He shook his head. "What do you mean, you'd have some control over me? Like a mind-meld or something?"

"Nothing that elaborate. I'd be able to send negative reinforcement through the bond."

He thought about it for a second, not liking any of it, but unfortunately able to see the logic from the Night-keeper side of life. "Would you promise not to use the bond on me?"

"I can't do that; I'm sorry." She paused, exhaling. "Look, this is the only way I could convince Strike to let you help." And by that he knew she meant "let you live." "He agrees that we need your research skills, but because of who and what you are, we can't risk letting you go free." She reached out and took his right hand and turned it palm up, then placed her own beside it to show that she had a scar to match his own. "You've already been marked by the *Banol Kax*. I'll tell you the whole story later, after the bond is complete. Suffice it to say that if you leave Skywatch without Nightkeeper protection, you'll be subject to influence by the *Banol Kax*. That can't be allowed to happen."

Lucius wanted to be able to laugh that off, but he couldn't. It aligned too well with the feeling of a dark cloud lifting off him over the past few days. On some level he didn't need to know anything more than that. "Shit."

"Yeah. That about sums it up."

He stared at his hands, not daring to look at her when he asked, "Why are you willing to risk yourself like this? If I'm connected to the demons somehow, what's to say I won't turn on you again, like I did by dealing with Desiree?"

"If you stay inside Skywatch, you'll be the Lucius I know and love."

The statement brought his head up as he thought, just for a second, that maybe the occasional flash of interest he'd seen in her eyes was for real.

But she shook her head. "Not that way. As a friend only. I owe you, though, in more ways than I can count. I traded my freedom from the Nightkeepers for your life last fall because it was my fault you crossed paths with the *Banol Kax*. I'm offering to bind myself to you now because I think you can help us, and because of our friendship. You let me lean on you when things got bad with Dick, let me wallow when I needed to, and kicked my butt out of the funk when it got to be too much."

He looked away. "I didn't tell you about Desiree."

"No, you didn't. But I can see how that'd be a tough judgment call . . . and I'm not sure much would've happened differently if I'd known she was Dick's mistress. It's a sucky situation, but it had nothing to do with you . . . and not much to do with Dick, either, if she is what we think she is. Besides, I'm dealing with it as best I can. Part of that involves your staying here and helping Jade when I head back home."

Lucius closed his eyes and tested out the idea of never going back to the university, and was surprised to find it didn't hurt that much. He had lots of friends but few close ones, and he could call home from Skywatch just as easily as from Austin. It wasn't as simple as that, of course, but the lure of the Nightkeepers overshadowed the other issues. He'd spent a big chunk of his life defending their existence. How could he not help them when asked?

He took a long, deep breath. "Okay. Let's do it."

She hesitated. "In the interest of full disclosure—"

"Will any of it change what has to happen?" he interrupted.

"No."

"Then tell me later." He nodded to the knife, his gut tightening in anticipation of pain, his brain blocking out the concept of servitude. "Do it." But when she lifted the obsidian blade, he said, "Wait. What about Sasha?"

She gave him a long look, but said, "We've reopened the search already. There's a chance her father was one of us, probably a better chance that he was Xibalban. Either way, we need to know where she is. Strike has his PI, Carter, looking for her, and also for the Xibalbans, on the theory that they probably know where she is."

"You won't give up on her this time?" Lucius pressed

as something tightened in his chest, making him feel that finding Sasha was somehow more important than the question of his own servitude. "You promise?"

"I promise." Without another word she slashed her own palm, then his. Pain slapped at him, wringing a hiss, but he didn't pull away, couldn't move. His body was locked in place, frozen by the sight of the blood that welled up and spilled over.

Gripping his bloodied hand in hers, she closed her eyes and rapped out a string of words he couldn't parse, coming so quickly, when his brain was more used to sounding out the syllables from glyph strings.

Something stirred beyond his being, a sense that there were things going on at a level he couldn't perceive. A sudden gust of wind slapped through the room, though the windows were closed. The disembodied gust blew his hair in his eyes and whipped around the two of them, forming a sharp funnel cloud with them in the center. Above the wind roar, a buzzing noise sang a high, discordant note.

Then Anna said a final word, and the world shifted sideways, tilting and swerving around him. He slid off the sofa, landing hard on his knees while Anna hung on to his hand. The note racheted up to a scream, and pain lanced through him, centered not on his bleeding palm but on his forearm. He cried out and bowed his head as something snapped into place around him, an invisible force that vised his body, then inside to grip his heart, which went still. The wind quit abruptly, leaving only silence inside his skull.

He couldn't even hear his heartbeat.

Panic gripped him, but he couldn't struggle, couldn't scream. He could only wait in the silence. Finally he heard it. *Lub.* Then *lub-dub.* Another, *lub-dub.* The beats stuttered and then sped, finally dropping into normal sinus rhythm. The moment they did, the force field disappeared, leaving him to sag back against the sofa.

He sucked in a shuddering breath. "Jesus Christ."

"Wrong pantheon," she said, voice wry. Shifting her grip, she lifted his arm and turned his hand palm up. He saw blood but no cut, only the scar he'd gotten last fall, ostensibly in a drunken kitchen accident that he now realized had been far more than that.

Awe gathered in Lucius's chest at the sight of the healed wound. "Magic," he breathed.

"Yep." She pushed his shirtsleeve up across his forearm, revealing something else, something that made his heart stutter in his chest when she said, "Welcome to the family."

His forearm was marked like hers, with two glyphs. One was the same jaguar she wore, only smaller. The other was the *k'alaj* glyph representing the back of a human hand and a length of rope or sinew: the "was bound" mark, used for slaves and captured enemies . . . and sacrifices.

He took a deep breath. Let it out. Looked at Anna, the woman of his dreams, who was now his mistress, and not in the way he'd wished. "Okay, boss," he said, doing his best to act like everything *was* okay when he wasn't yet sure that was the case, "take me to your library and tell me what I'm looking for."

"That's easy," she said. "We want everything you can find on the Order of Xibalba."

His heart, so recently knocked off-kilter, took another stutter step. "You're kidding me."

"Wish I were."

"The order's real too?" It was a little like learning that not only was the Loch Ness monster real, so was Godzilla.

Anna nodded. "Worse, we're pretty sure Desiree is a member."

"Desiree is—" He broke off, slamming his eyes shut as an awful gulf of guilt opened up inside him. "Please tell me you're kidding."

"Still not."

"Shit." He opened his eyes and looked at her. "I'm so fucking sorry."

"We're dealing with it."

"I'm surprised your brother didn't have me thrown into the Cenote Sagrado," he said, naming the huge sacrificial well at Chichén Itzá.

"I promised him you'd behave."

"I will," he said fervently. "You have my word."

"I don't need your word. I have your blood oath." She bared her forearm, where she too had gained a new mark, a closed fist. His heart shuddered as he recognized *ajawlel* . . . the slave-master's mark.

Once Anna had handed Lucius over to Jade in the archive, she went in search of her brother. She found him in his and Leah's quarters, the expansive royal suite once shared by their parents.

Anna hesitated at the double entry doors, assailed by memory.

She'd been fourteen on the night of the Solstice Massacre, which meant she had fourteen years' worth of childhood memories from Skywatch. Strike had been only nine, and his mind had blocked off the bulk of his early years as a defense. Unfortunately, she hadn't been so lucky. Maybe it was because she carried the seer's mark, maybe because of the five-year difference in age. Whatever the cause, she'd been unable to outrun the memories, her brain choosing to block her power rather than the past.

Ever since her partial return to the Nightkeepers, she'd dealt with the memories by staying at Skywatch as little as possible, and avoiding the spaces with the most ghosts . . . like the royal suite. Now she forced herself to knock on what she still thought of as her parents' door, and made herself push through when her brother's voice invited her in.

"It's me," she called, standing just inside the royal suite and trying to concentrate not on the memories but on the differences, the new decor and the way the walls had been painted, the floors stripped and redone, all part of Jox's efforts to exorcise the ghosts.

"I'm in the altar room," Strike said, his voice echoing from a door off to her right. "Come on back."

Although the royal couple's shrine of private worship was pretty much the last place on earth Anna wanted to be, she forced herself down the short hallway leading to the ceremonial chamber. She couldn't make herself step inside the tiny room, which was little more than a closet with stone-veneered walls and a gas-powered torch in each corner, with a *chac-mool* altar against the back and a highly polished obsidian mirror on the wall.

Strike stood in the center of the small space, on a woven mat marked with bloodred footprints facing the altar. In ancient times the mats had symbolized a position of power or leadership; to stand on the mat was to claim the right to speak and be heard. Since then, among the Nightkeepers those mats had come to represent the king's right to speak to—and for—the gods.

Just then, though, Strike looked less like a god-king and more like a tired man, a former landscaper with a business degree and teleporting skills, who was in way over his head. He and Leah had made a try for Kulkulkan's altar stone in Germany, only to find that it wasn't where it was supposed to have been. Leah had stayed behind, following where the trail led, while Strike had come home alone to deal with the business of securing Skywatch against the Xibalbans. Anna knew that Leah could reach him instantly through the blood-link of their love, knew that he could 'port to her in a flash. He knew it too, but the separation was wearing on him, worrying him. His eyes were tired, his expression drawn.

Anna could relate.

Leaning against the doorframe to ground herself when the reflection in the mirror threatened to waver and show her things she didn't want to see, she said, "It's done."

Strike nodded. "He'll help?" But what he was really asking was, *Have you bound him as your slave?*

"Yes." She hated the necessity, hated the decision, but hadn't been able to argue either. In saving Lucius from Red-Boar's knife she'd taken responsibility for him. The binding ritual had simply been a formal extension of that duty. Or so she was trying to tell herself.

"And the other?"

"That's why I'm here. I wanted to make sure you hadn't reconsidered."

His lips twitched. "Wanted to see if I'd come to my senses, you mean."

"Something like that."

"Consider your objections noted."

Fat lot of good that would do in the long run, Anna thought, but inclined her head. "I'll make the call."

Feeling as though she were escaping from the room, if not the duty, she headed for her own suite, which was the same one she and Strike had shared as children. Jox had overseen the renovations, yielding a pleasantly neutral space with a few personal touches in the jaguar motifs of the art prints and small trinkets on the bamboo furniture. They'd all been placed by the *winikin*, not her, but they did serve to warm the suite, making it fairly comfortable for the short stints she was in residence, during the cardinal days and a few other ceremonial occasions.

Now she let herself sink into the soft, earth-toned sofa and dug out her cell phone. Dialing the main university switchboard from memory, she punched in an extension and waited through two rings, then three.

Just when she was wondering how much to say on voice mail, the line went live. "Desiree Soo speaking."

"I have Lucius," Anna said without preamble.

There was a startled pause before Desiree said, "You can keep him. He's served his purpose."

"That's what I want to talk to you about. We'd like to invite Iago to the compound for a parley."

Desiree's surprise was palpable, but she snorted. "Parley? What is this, *Pirates of the Caribbean*?"

"A meeting, Desiree, between your leader and mine. March thirteenth. And your agreement that the Xibalbans won't come after us between now and then."

"The day after Saturn at Opposition? What, you think your ancestors are going to come through and tell you how to get hold of the remaining artifacts? Keep dreaming."

Anna dug her fingernails into her scarred palms, determined not to let the bitch bait her. "Do we have a deal?"

"I'll have to get back to you on that one. Where can I reach you?"

"Leave a yes/no on my office voice mail. I'll be back in town tomorrow, the day after at the latest."

"Interesting." Desiree paused, then said sweetly, "Would you like me to let your husband know of your plans? Apparently he expected you back from your 'meeting,' "— there were obvious finger-quotes in the words—"the day before yesterday, and couldn't reach you on your cell."

"Don't trouble yourself; I'll call him," Anna said through gritted teeth, and cut the connection.

Once they'd figured out that Desiree was Xibalban, and had most likely been sent to the university solely to keep an eye on Anna, it was a logical extension to assume she'd gone after Dick for additional inside information, and probably for leverage. That didn't make his infidelity any less galling, but it made Desiree's part in it that much more insidious.

Hating that she'd bought into the bitch's manipulation, Anna dialed Dick's cell phone, intending to apologize for not checking in sooner. She couldn't tell him about Lucius and the Xibalbans, and would have to explain away the *ajawlel* mark as another on-a-whim tattoo, when he wasn't too crazy about the ones she already wore. But though there were so many things she couldn't tell him, so many little lies, she wanted to talk to him, wanted to hear his voice and remember her real life, and the man she'd made that life with.

When the call dumped to voice mail, though, she didn't know what to say. So she hung up without speaking and just sat there on the sofa, staring at the one personal touch that had found its way into her room, borrowed from the training hall with Rabbit's permission.

The boar-bloodline death mask might've been an impulse buy on Alexis's part, but Anna was grateful for the impulse, because looking at the mask made her think not of Red-Boar, but of the fact that in some cases, death was only the beginning of the great cycle, the start of the next life.

At this point she was starting to hope she got it right in her next life, because her current one was turning into a train wreck.

* * *

In the weeks following the trip to Belize, Nate felt like he was rattling around Skywatch, disjointed and out of step with himself.

He and Alexis had brought the carved fragment back and united it with the main statuette, and watched in awe while the pieces had knit, going molten and then seaming together with a hum of magic and color, creating an entire whole. Then they, along with most everyone else in residence at the compound, had gathered outside later that night. When the starlight had come, the full demon prophecy had been revealed.

Lucius had done the translation, because Anna had returned to her husband. The shaggy-haired grad student, who Jade said seemed to be alternating between fascination at being among the Nightkeepers and deep depression at being a slave, had parsed out the glyphs, copying them down on the kitted-out laptop Anna had sent from the university. Even before the program had confirmed the translation, he'd quietly intoned, " 'The first son of Camazotz succeeds unless the Volatile is found.' "

Which told them nothing new, really, and sort of made the cave trip seem like a waste.

Jade and Lucius's research had turned up a couple of references to the Volatile, indicating that he was male and a shape-shifter, which put him firmly on the bad-guy side of life, as far as the Nightkeepers were concerned. A great deal of post-Classical Mayan religious practices were based on the idea that their kings were gods, and capable of turning into sacred creatures, mostly jaguars. That, however, was due to the influence of the Order of Xibalba, which seemed to have worshiped a mimiclike shape-shifter that could take on many forms. The Nightkeepers, in contrast, wanted nothing to do with shifters, who had the rep of being fiercely independent at best, dangerously unstable at worst.

At the same time, the word "volatile" was also associated with the daylight hours and the levels of heaven. Which meant there was no telling whether the Volatile named in the demon prophecy was a Xibalban—maybe even Iago himself?—or something else. They weren't even sure the Volatile was a shifter; the info was that foggy. It was also perplexing that the demon prophecy discussing the Volatile had been written on the statuette of the rainbow goddess, yet didn't say jack about what Ixchel was supposed to do.

The facts that the rainbow goddess's statuette held the prophecy and that she'd formed the Godkeeper bond with Alexis suggested that Ixchel should be instrumental in defeating the first of Camazotz's sons . . . yet the prophecy directed them to the Volatile. Did that mean they were supposed to hand over Alexis to the Xibalbans? That was so not happening as far as Nate was concerned.

Alexis had become more and more withdrawn as the debate had dragged on. Nate had tried to engage her, tried to have a sit-down, but she'd been distant and had quickly excused herself each time. He couldn't blame her, really. And in a way her detachment was a bonus, because it had somehow weakened the crackle of magic between them, blunting the sexual energy. Maybe the statuette was somehow helping her channel the goddess's powers without his help. Maybe the magic was lessening as the barrier thickened, cycling between the eclipse and the approaching opposition. Or maybe he'd finally managed to gain control over his attraction to her, to the point that he could make a decision for himself, one that wasn't dictated by politics or power.

That should've made him feel better. Thing was, he didn't, not in the slightest. He was snarly and out of sorts, humming with an edgy energy that he didn't recognize. Working himself into exhaustion down in the gym didn't help; if anything that made his mood worse, with the added annoyance of sore hamstrings. Training didn't help; research didn't help. Hell, he couldn't even work on *VW6*; Hera was still stuck midstory, not sure if she wanted to partner with Nameless or behead him.

And yeah, Nate could see the parallels between the storyboard and his and Alexis's on-again, off-again relationship; he wasn't an idiot. Seeing it didn't mean he knew what to do about it, though. Which was why he headed out to the Pueblo ruins near dusk in early

March, five days before the opposition ceremony, needing some serious time to himself. Instead of going all the way out to the pueblo, though, he wound up detouring over to his parents' cottage, knowing that was where he'd meant to go all along.

When he opened the door and stepped through, he found someone waiting for him in the sitting room, and stopped dead. "Carlos." *Shit.*

"Are you ready to listen yet?" the *winikin* asked, making it sound as if he were willing to wait as long as he needed to, even though they both knew time was running out. The equinox was nine days after the opposition, and Alexis needed to have full access to the goddess's powers by then if she hoped to have even a prayer of battling the first of the foretold demons. That meant having her Nightkeeper mate's full support.

The operative word there being "mate."

"I can't pull hearts and flowers out of my ass just because it's convenient for everyone else," Nate snapped. "And for what it's worth, I offered. She turned me down. End of story." Okay, so technically he'd offered some fairly clinical, no-strings sex approximately sixty seconds before she'd asked him about Hera and realized she'd been a stand-in. Or was Hera the stand-in? Fucked if he knew; they were all mixed-up together in his head.

"I wasn't talking about you and Alexis," Carlos said mildly. "Although if you'd like to talk about the two of you, I'm more than happy to listen. I had twenty wonderful years with my Essie. I could probably teach you a few things."

"I don't," Nate said between gritted teeth, "want to talk about me and Alexis. I don't want to talk at all." But he didn't turn around and leave, either, just stood in the middle of the sitting room, glaring at his father's paintings. "Not everything that happened before will happen again, goddamn it. I don't need to know the history of my bloodline to be a warrior."

"Maybe. Maybe not." The *winikin* should've looked out of place, but somehow his snap-studded shirt and big old belt buckle fit into the subtle—albeit dated—elegance of the furnishings and decor.

Which, damn it, made Nate wonder about the others who'd sat on that same couch. His mother and father. Their friends. Hell, Alexis's mother had probably been there a time or two, if only to bitch at his father for something. He didn't know much about the goings-on at Skywatch prior to the Solstice Massacre, but it would've been impossible to miss knowing that Gray-Smoke and his father had spent a good chunk of their time as royal advisers trying to argue each other into the ground.

Kind of like him and Alexis. Not that he believed in history repeating itself. *Shit.*

Nate dropped down to the sofa and let his head bang against the backrest. He tried not to look at the paintings again, because he already knew from experience that he'd stare at them way too long if he gave himself the luxury.

"I've never even seen a picture of them," he said after a moment, damning himself because he knew he was losing the battle.

Carlos had the good grace not to do a victory dance, saying only, "Have you looked around?"

"Hell, no." Nate glanced back at the open front door and the fading light of freedom beyond. He'd been toying with the idea of trying the ball court and figuring out the game Lucius kept going on about. Maybe that'd help the restlessness. And, hell, it couldn't be much harder than basketball, right? The hoops were higher and set vertical rather than horizontal, but there was no dribbling to worry about on the pounded-dirt surface; it was mostly knees and elbows. He bet he could get the others into the idea, maybe use the game to burn off some frustrations.

He should get started now, he thought. But he stayed put.

Carlos rose. "Come on. I'll help you find some snapshots."

"No," Nate said again, but it was more of a plea than a denial.

The *winikin* ignored him and headed for the second bedroom. Unable to do otherwise, Nate followed.

And stopped dead in the doorway of a frigging nursery.

He didn't recognize the crib or toys, or the spinning mobile of stars and moons above the bed. He had no memory of the rain-forest scenes painted on the walls, or the birds of prey painted on the ceiling. But his gut confirmed what logic said had to be true: that this was where he'd slept for the first two years of his life.

It wasn't just any nursery; it was *his* nursery.

Sucking a breath past a punch of pain, he cursed and turned to retreat. Except his feet didn't move, planting him there in the doorway as Carlos crossed the room and opened a large closet, which was stacked with toys, clothes, and baby stuff on one side, neatly labeled boxes on the other.

"You snooped," Nate said, the words coming out on a wheeze. "You cased the joint before I got here."

The *winikin* didn't turn back. "You're a tough case, Blackhawk. I'll take whatever leverage I can get."

Which was pretty much what Carol Rose, his social worker, had said about him. She'd refused to take "fuck off and die" as an answer, and had ridden his ass until he straightened up and made something of himself. He was starting to get a feeling that Carol and Carlos had more in common than the similarities in their names. And that was simple fucking coincidence, he thought bitterly. Not fate.

"So what exactly do you want from me?" he finally asked.

"Nothing much." Now Carlos did glance back, and his lips twitched. "I just want you to help save the world."

It should've been a joke, probably had been meant as one, at least in part. But the *winikin*'s words shot straight to the heart of Nate's frustration, his pounding sense that he wasn't doing what he was supposed to be doing, yet he couldn't do what the others wanted him to. Letting his legs unlock, he slid down the wall just inside his nursery until he was sitting on the floor, his spine propped against the doorjamb. Looking up at the stand-in father figure he hadn't met until seven months earlier, he said, "I don't know how."

Rancher-practical, Carlos said, "I can't tell you how to feel or what to do. But I can tell you what's been done before, and how those before you thought, felt, and acted."

"Their history ended in 1984," Nate said, though the words came out less like a protest and more like a plea. "It's just not relevant today."

"Then you will have wasted a few hours listening to an old man's stories. Is that really any worse than going up to the Pueblo ruins and getting hammered on Rabbit's stash of *pulque*?"

"Busted," Nate said, and found a grin. Forcing himself to breathe, he waggled his fingers in a *bring it on* gesture. "Okay, *winikin*, you win. Introduce me to my family."

Which was how, as the quick desert dusk fell and day turned to night, Nate found himself staring at a snapshot of a tall, handsome man with eyes like his, wearing the hawk medallion around his neck, with his arm curved protectively around the waist of a dark-haired woman who had laughing, loving eyes, and an infant cradled in her arms.

CHAPTER SIXTEEN

Rabbit had lived in Massachusetts for a good chunk of his life, through the misery of junior high and high school, and then for a few months after graduation, up until the barrier reactivated and Strike and his old man had reopened Skywatch. So he pretty much felt like an ass that he'd showed up for the 'port to Boston wearing shorts and a light hoodie, and then gave Strike lip when he'd suggested a jacket. It'd been seventy and sunny in New Mex.

It was, however, thirty and pissing freezing rain in Boston. How had he forgotten the misery of early springtime in New England?

He couldn't bring himself to ask Strike to zap him added clothes, though, so he wound up standing in an alley around the corner from the MFA, shivering his frigging ass off while Patience, Sven, and Brandt went over the plan yet again. He was pretty sure really only Patience and Sven, with their talents of invisibility and translocation, were necessary for the actual op, but Brandt had refused to let his wife go off on her own, and Strike had wanted Rabbit out of the way, so all four of them were on the mission.

Strike hadn't actually said he wanted Rabbit out of the way, of course, but the subtext had been there. Which, Rabbit suspected, meant Carter finally had a lead on Myrinne, and Strike didn't want him to know about it. Tit for tat, Rabbit had done an end run of his own, tapping the Nightkeeper Fund for fifteen hundred bucks with Jox's blessing, claiming he needed a laptop upgrade. Instead, he'd pocketed five hundred and used a thousand to hire a PI of his own, one with a slightly different code of ethics than Carter. The PI, Juarez, had indicated that he'd have Myrinne's location by the end of the day, which had Rabbit alternately feeling hot and cold even in the pissing drizzle. He went feverish at the thought of seeing Myrinne again, clammy when he imagined going against a direct order from his king.

"Rabbit!" Patience said, voice sharp, as though she'd been trying to get his attention for a while.

"Sorry," he said, avoiding her eyes, because she knew him well enough to know what he was thinking half the time, and he did *not* want her knowing about Myrinne or the PI. "We ready?"

"If you are," Brandt grumbled, leading the way.

They headed for the museum entrance and paid the entry fee in cash, then followed the signs to the traveling exhibit of Mayan artifacts. The signage directing them to the special exhibit had a cartoonish rendition of a generic Mayan pyramid, with a glyph string beside it. The glyphs were visually interesting, granted, but Rabbit was pretty sure he saw the *at* glyph, which stood for "penis," and the *'we* glyph, which meant "eat."

He snorted. Somebody had a sense of humor.

"Focus, kid," Brandt muttered out of the corner of his mouth. "Don't screw this up for us."

"Bite me." A few months ago he never would've talked to Brandt that way, not after he and Patience had practically adopted Rabbit after Red-Boar's death, letting him stay in their big suite and trusting him with the twins and stuff. But things had been strained ever since a few weeks earlier, when Rabbit had walked in on a big-time fight and overheard Brandt pressuring Patience to leave Skywatch and take the rug rats with her. The last thing Rabbit had heard as he sneaked back out of the suite was Brandt saying something about all the time Patience had been spending with Rabbit. But when he'd said "Rabbit," what he'd really meant was "half-blood fuckup." That was what Rabbit's old man called him, what all the others thought of him.

Well, screw them.

Brandt pinched the bridge of his nose and exhaled a long, suffering breath designed to let his wife know how hard he was working to control his temper with Rabbit, who was more her friend than his.

"Knock it off, you two," she said without missing a beat, in the same voice she used on the twins when they were fighting. "This way." She kept a firm grip on Sven's arm, steering him through the first room of the Mayan exhibit, hanging on to him as though she thought he might bolt.

Good guess too, Rabbit thought, getting a look at Sven's pasty face. The mage was wide-eyed with nerves. Gods only knew why he was so freaked. It wasn't like they were getting ready to kill someone—they were stealing a bowl, for fuck's sake, and if saving the world wasn't a good enough reason for some five-fingering, Rabbit didn't know what was. Besides, if Sven's brand-new talent backfired and they set off the alarms or something, Patience could blink them invisible while they sneaked out and called Strike for a pickup. Worst-case scenario, like if the museum went into lockdown, they could hide and have Strike risk an interior 'port and pick them from inside the building.

Seriously, what was Sven's deal?

"Okay, this is the place," Brandt said, moving ahead of the others, bumping Rabbit on the way by in what might've been an apology, might've been a challenge. Or, hell, even an accident. He continued, "We're going to work our way around the room and pretend to look at the stuff. Sven? You ready?"

Way not, Rabbit thought, but to his surprise Sven nodded, and his voice was steady when he said, "Ready." His color had even come back. Looked like the dude had manned up, after all.

"Rabbit, you're on the door," Brandt continued, like they hadn't gone over the stupid-simple plan a thousand times back at Skywatch. "Keep an eye out for guards, and warn us if it looks like one's headed this way while Sven's making the switch."

They weren't even totally stealing the bowl; they were switching it with a comparable ceremonial bowl from Skywatch. They'd stashed the spare in an alley Dumpster nearby, because they hadn't figured it'd be a good idea to stroll into the museum carrying the replacement bowl. Hello, obvious. The idea was that Sven would translocate the bowl from the alley and switch it with the one they wanted. Which sounded great, but got complicated because it meant he had to split his brain and do a simultaneous double translocation, timing it perfectly so the motion detectors guarding the museum's bowl didn't register the change in the bowl's weight on the pressure pad of the display, Indiana Jones–like. In theory, anyway.

"You realize," Rabbit said to Brandt, "that if they've got audio-recognition software, you probably just triggered it by talking about the guards."

"I doubt they've got the technology." But the big man looked around a little, and waved for them to split up. Rabbit took his position in the far corner, where he could pretend to be studying one of the displays while keeping an eye on both of the doors serving the exhibit room. Patience, Brandt, and Sven wandered over to the display case containing the ornately carved bowl, where they lingered, waiting for the room to empty of most of the other museumgoers.

Come on, come on, Rabbit thought, the wait wearing on him quickly. Trying to figure out how long it'd take for whoever was manning the surveillance cameras to wonder why he was so interested in the display he was parked in front of—which was a blah fragment from a not-very-interesting mural at Tulum—he palmed his cell phone, checking the time for no particular reason.

Okay, he was checking for messages, so sue him. Brandt's voice whispered through his mind, saying, *Don't screw this up,* but Rabbit hit the "incoming" icon just in case.

There was a message from Juarez.

Excitement fired in his blood, bringing a hum of magic as he clicked over to the text. *Target was in N.O. two days ago,* the text read, followed by an address Rabbit didn't recognize. Feeling a kick of optimism, he started keying in a reply.

He was halfway through when an unfamiliar voice said, "Sorry, kid, no cell phones in—" The guard broke off two steps inside the room, locking on Sven, who must've fucked up the translocation, because he had the demon prophecy bowl in his hands, rather than it being safe in the alley where he was supposed to send it. "Hey!" the guard shouted, going for a button on his belt first, and then rushing the thieves.

He was across the room before Rabbit broke from the shocked paralysis that'd gripped him the second he realized just how badly he'd fucked up. Before he could move or yell a warning, the guy had stun-gunned Patience, who dropped without a sound. Brandt roared a battle cry and decked the guard, who went down for the count, but the damage was already done.

Alarms shrilled and panels started grinding into place. And the Nightkeepers' fallback invisibility plan was a no-go.

Heart hammering, Rabbit jammed his phone in his pocket and started across to help, but Brandt shoved him aside. "Fuck off. You've done enough." He got his wife over his shoulder and grabbed Sven by the shirt, dragging him through the nearest door just before it clanged shut, leaving Rabbit behind.

Rabbit stood for a second, paralyzed, then bolted, barely making it out the other door. He was shaking and breathing hard, panic mixing with awful guilt. With Patience unconscious, the others were visible, vulnerable. He should double back around and find them, help them. But Brandt's anger cut through him, warning him that he'd finally done it, finally fucked up one too many times. Rabbit's hands were trembling when he pulled out his cell and speed-dialed home. When Jox picked up, he said, "Have Strike lock on Brandt and get them out, *now*." His voice broke, and tears were gumming up his vision, but he didn't care.

He hung up, chucked his phone in the nearest trash, and took off.

The day the Boston mission left, Alexis spent most of the day in her suite studying—she refused to think of it as hiding. She was reading up on the Godkeeper legends, which were woefully lacking in detail, and trying out a few selected spells to see if she could pull them off.

So far, that would be a no.

Her tactile senses were heightened, especially when it came to textiles and other woven things. She could touch a piece of fabric and know instantly where its weak spots lay; give her a piece of clothing and she immediately knew where its seams were imperfect, its design flawed. She saw new colors in the world around her, and was preternaturally aware of how the light bent slightly as it came through a window, how it refracted in a droplet of water dripping from her bathroom sink. And she knew at a glance where the women around her were in their biological cycles—hello, TMI. All of those were consistent with Ixchel's triad role as the goddess of weaving, rainbows, and fertility. But how the hell was any of that supposed to help her repel the first of Camazotz's sons during the vernal equinox in two weeks?

Alexis didn't have a freaking clue.

Back in the fall, Leah's bound god, Kulkulkan, had manifested as a giant winged serpent to fight the flying crocodile demon, Zipacna. Which had made some sense— flying monster versus flying monster. So what, exactly, was the goddess of rainbows supposed to do against a death god? And how the hell did the Volatile fit in? It would've helped if she could talk to the goddess and ask for info. That had been the hope going into the ceremony. Leah had gotten some thought-flashes from Kulkulkan, so they'd theorized that a true, full-blood Godkeeper might have a closer bond, one that allowed for actual conversation. Unfortunately, not so much. Which meant that so far Leah, with her flawed connection to the creator god Kulkulkan, was still more useful than Alexis as a fully bound keeper to Ixchel.

Granted, although she might be fully bound, she was functioning without her gods-destined protector. She'd stopped thinking of Nate as her gods-destined mate and gone with "protector" instead, because the more comfortable she got with her connection to Ixchel's subtle powers, the more the fabric of her own life took shape around her, letting her see that she deserved someone who wanted her, flaws and all, someone who loved every piece of her and asked nothing but that she love him back. Which, she realized, was sort of what Nate had been saying before, that sex and love shouldn't be a commodity used to pay for increased power.

She couldn't help thinking, though, that if he wanted her enough, needed her enough, then none of the power stuff would matter to him, and he'd take her any way he could get her. That meant he hadn't—and didn't—want her enough. Story of her life.

Aaron had liked her as a portfolio manager and arm candy in certain social situations, and most of his predecessors had been iterations of the same theme. Izzy loved her; Alexis was sure of that. But at the same time, she couldn't help wondering how much of that emotion was tied into the *winikin*'s ambitions, always wanting her to be the best and brightest, to live up to her bloodline and her mother's reputation. And Nate . . . hell, he wanted her sexually because the gods had hardwired him that way, whether or not he was willing to admit it. But the woman he truly wanted wasn't her. He wanted the warrior in his video game, the woman Alexis might have been if the massacre had never happened, if she'd been raised by her parents within the Nightkeeper system. But that hadn't happened, and the lives each of them had lived prior to discovering their true nature had made them too different from the people they should have been. Which meant she and Nate were almost—but not quite—a match.

A quick knock on the door jolted her out of her reverie. "Yes?"

"We've got a problem. You'd better come." It was Nate, sounding clipped and urgent.

His voice brought a buzz of heat and frustration, coming so close on the heels of her thoughts of him. But his tone warned that something was wrong.

"Coming," she called. Heart kicking against her ribs, she scrambled to her feet, dumping a pile of reference books on the floor. Pausing only to jam her feet in a pair of scuffs, she headed for the door, coming up short when she swung open the panel and found him standing in the hallway, waiting for her. He was wearing combat clothes, though no bulletproof vest or belt. Hesitating, she said, "Should I get my gear?"

He shook his head. "I was headed out to the shooting range when Carlos came for me. There's a problem with the team in Boston."

"Iago?" she asked immediately.

"Rabbit."

"Let's go." They hurried up the hall to the main body of the mansion. When they pushed through a set of swinging doors leading to the sunken main room, Alexis gave a low cry at the sight of Patience lying motionless on one of the big couches with Jox bent over her. Sven was sitting on the other sofa with his head in his hands; Carlos was trying to make him drink some OJ, only to be shaken off. Jade was hovering over the sofas, looking lost, with Lucius in the background behind her. The other *winikin* were in the kitchen, pulling together food, suggesting that serious magic was on tap. There was no sign of Strike, Brandt, Michael, or Rabbit.

"Where's everyone else?" Nate asked before Alexis could. For a moment there was no answer; then Sven dragged his face out of his hands and looked up, revealing a hunted, haunted expression. "They went back for the demon-prophecy bowl. I managed to make the switch, but I zapped it into my hands instead of out into the alley. A guard saw, and I lost the bowl while we were trying to get away from the cops. I fucking *dropped* it, and now we've got nothing."

"It wasn't—" Carlos began, but Sven shot to his feet and stood, swaying.

"It *was* my fault; don't you get it? I dropped the bowl and didn't go back for it. I was too busy running away, just like—" Now he interrupted himself, clicking his teeth over the words and saying instead, "It fucking *was* my fault."

Alexis, who'd never had much patience with breast-beating guilt trips, found herself crossing the room and taking the glass of OJ from Carlos. "Get him food," she ordered. Then she made Sven sit back down and pressed the juice into his hand. "Bottoms up," she said firmly. "You need the sugar after pulling off the double translocation."

"I didn't pull it off," he snapped. "I—"

"Dropped the bowl. Yeah, I get that. Thing is, you won't be any good for damage control if you're half-dead from a postmagic hangover. So drink the damned juice, and eat whatever Carlos brings you."

A little to her surprise, he complied.

Shifting her attention to Jox, she said, "What's her status?"

The *winikin* had a hand on Patience's wrist, tracking her pulse. He shook his head. "One of the guards Tasered her, and she's always had a bit of an arrhythmia. Kicked her heart off rhythm pretty good, but it seems to be settling now."

"Does she need to get to a hospital?"

"I don't think so."

"Be sure," Alexis pressed, her voice hard.

Surprise flashed in Jox's eyes, but he nodded. "I'm sure."

A small piece of Alexis wondered why he knew about Patience's med history, and why he was hovering as if she were his charge, not Hannah's. But Hannah and Wood were away in hiding with the twins, so perhaps he'd become in loco *winikin* to Patience and Brandt. Besides, the surprise in the royal *winikin*'s expression reminded Alexis that it wasn't her place to be handing out orders; she wasn't in charge. She asked, "Where's Leah?"

Strike's mate had recently returned to Skywatch, un-successful in her efforts to find Kulkulkan's altar stone. The artifact bearing the seventh demon prophecy had dropped from the historical record after World War II, reappeared briefly in a private collection in Denmark, and disappeared again in the sixties, leaving the ex-cop frustrated as hell.

"I'm here, but don't let me stop you when you're on a roll." Leah came into view, wearing combat gear and a worried expression. She glanced at Jox. "Any word?"

"Nothing yet." He looked down, relief smoothing some of the frown lines when Patience stirred and her eyelids fluttered. "She's coming around. That's something, at any rate. Why don't we—"

A slap of concussion cut him off, and Strike, Brandt, and Michael appeared in the center of the room, in a flash of royal red and a hum of strong, pissed-off Nightkeeper magic.

"The bowl!" Sven lurched up, sloshing the dregs of his OJ. "Did you get the bowl?" But Brandt shook his head, his expression grim. Sven sank back down, whispering, "Gods damn it. The cops got it?"

"Worse," Strike said. "The place where it'd been stank of Iago's magic. I'll bet you anything the bastard was watching the whole time, and swept in and grabbed it when the plan went south."

Sven just kept shaking his head, looking shell-shocked, as if he couldn't believe he'd screwed up so badly.

Leah crossed the room to touch Strike's arm. "What about Rabbit?"

The king's expression went hollow. "There wasn't any sign of him. I couldn't even lock on for a 'port."

Silence followed that pronouncement. It wasn't dire news, necessarily, because Strike had already discovered that 'port magic often failed to lock onto a person if they were underground or within thick walls. That was why he generally kept the 'ports to open air. However, his inability to lock onto Rabbit could stem from a more sinister reason—like he was unconscious, or worse.

"Take me there," Leah said. "I'm good at finding people."

They shared a look, and Strike nodded. "Yeah. You are." He closed his eyes to initiate the 'port, which he needed to do these days only when he was trying to summon magic without enough of a power boost.

"Wait!" Alexis said, interrupting.

Strike's eyes popped open. "What?"

"Take this. Eat." She grabbed three of the protein bars Carlos had brought for Sven, who preferred them over chocolate or some of the other quick-energy foods the Nightkeepers gravitated toward. "We can't afford to have you 'porting low on calories."

He took the bars and nodded, and Leah's eyes gleamed a quiet thanks as the magic powered back up and they vanished, air rushing in with a pop to fill the space they'd vacated.

When they were gone, Alexis realized what she'd just done, and felt a flush climb her cheeks. "Did I just interrupt teleport magic to nag the king to eat?" she asked the room at large. "I can't believe I did that. I'm an idiot." Strike was a grown-up, and about ten times the mage she'd ever be.

"You're not an idiot," Jox said. "You're a royal adviser, and you just advised." He withdrew a palm-size eccentric from his pocket and held it out to her. "Strike asked me to pull it out of storage for you. I think he'd want you to have it now."

Alexis just stared at the small effigy for a beat, while tears lumped in her throat and scratched at the backs of her eyes. The eccentric was carved in the shape of an ear of maize, the lifeblood of their ancestors.

It was a twin to the one her mother had carried.

"If you'd rather wait until they're back—" Jox began.

"No," she said quickly, then again, "No. This is perfect." And it was, she realized. Although Strike might have given her the position because he knew how much she wanted it, Jox wouldn't have agreed if he didn't think she was worthy of being an adviser. The royal *winikin* was steeped in the old traditions, bound by them. If he was offering the eccentric, then the offer was real. The need was real.

She reached out and took the smoothly carved piece, which was warm from Jox's body heat. Dipping her head, she said, "Thank you."

A patter of applause from behind her was a surprise. She spun around and saw that Nate was clapping, and not looking the slightest bit sarcastic. The applause swelled as the others joined in. Jade and the *winikin* looked pleased; Lucius was clapping with the others, even though he shrugged when their eyes met, as if to say, *No clue what just happened, but congrats;* Patience was sitting up, her eyes clear and focused as she rested within the curve of her husband's arm, the two of them forming a unit despite their continued problems; and Izzy was front and center, her eyes shining, with maybe even the hint of a tear on her cheek. And in that moment it didn't matter how hard the *winikin* had pushed, or why. It mattered only that things had happened the way they were meant to happen . . . exactly as they had happened before.

And if that interpretation of the writs rang false in Alexis's head, she didn't stop to analyze, not then. She smiled at her teammates. "Thanks, guys. Just . . . thanks."

"Don't thank us too quickly," Jox said. "As both Godkeeper and royal adviser, you rank, which means you're in charge while Strike and Leah are off property. So what do you want us to do?" The look in his eye said it wasn't a casual question.

A glance around the room showed why. The Nightkeepers were warriors without a battle to fight, the *winikin* a support staff without real direction. They were worried for their king and queen, scared for Rabbit, and disturbed that they were so close to the vernal equinox and the deadline for the first demon prophecy, yet didn't have a clear plan or arsenal.

Join the club, Alexis thought, but knew that wasn't good enough. As part of the royal council, it was up to her to do something, say something. Granted, if she did nothing, they would go on as they had been, and nothing would truly be lost.

Except, perhaps, some hope. And she owed them that.

Thinking fast, she looked over at Lucius. "You can translate carvings, right?"

He looked startled at first; then his eyes took on a gleam of interest. He nodded. "Definitely." Glancing outside to where the dusk was still a few hours off, he said, "It'll have to wait a little if you're talking star-script, though."

"No, regular glyphs. I want you to sit down with the Ixchel statuette—Jade can get it for you out of archive lockup. See what you can make of the plain carved text. The auction house had translated the writing on the piece I bought and said it was a love poem, nothing spectacular. But maybe it'll take on a new meaning once it's read in its entirety, with the other piece. Maybe it'll give us a clue how to fight Camazotz or find the Volatile."

Or not, but it was something to try, anyway, something she'd only just now thought of, and wondered why they hadn't tried it before. But that wasn't fair, either. They were playing catchup to Iago, trying to map out the next few years without nearly enough information. It was a start, though. In the absence of any other semibrilliant ideas, Alexis didn't bother trying to order any of the others around, because she figured they were all grown-ups, and she wasn't much in the way of a leader. But as they dispersed, Patience, Sven, and Brandt to sleep off their exertions, the others to various tasks, she got a nod here, a "way to go" there.

Nate was the last to leave, and as he passed her he stepped in close. "Congratulations."

He touched his lips to hers before she'd guessed his intent, before she'd had a chance to brace herself. But there was no need to brace, no need for defense. Where before their kisses had been all about heat and need, this was about tenderness, about affirmation.

Weakened by surprise, she shuddered against him, let herself lean for a second. Then he eased away and looked down at her, his amber eyes intent on hers. For the first time she felt like his entire focus, as if he was seeing not just the outer shell of her, but actually seeing *her*.

Then he took a big step back, away from her, and tipped his head in a nod that was almost a bow. "I'm happy for you. I know this is what you wanted."

And he turned and walked away.

She stood there, torn between letting him go and calling him back. The kiss had been entirely different, almost like one she would've expected on a first date, an exploration rather than a possession. But what did that mean? Did it mean anything? She didn't have a clue, and because she didn't she let him go, watching where he'd been long after he'd pushed through the sliders, headed for the firing range.

Sensing that she was being watched, she turned and glanced toward the kitchen area, and found Jox standing there. "Well," she said on a sigh, "what now?"

She wasn't entirely sure if she was asking about the next step she should take as an adviser or the next step—if any—she should take with Nate, with the goddess, with the magic. She figured she'd let the *winikin* pick; she was open to suggestions at this point.

"Now we wait," he said, giving a vague answer to her vague question.

"Yeah," she said, dipping her head in a nod. "We wait. We watch. We do the best we can."

So the Nightkeepers and *winikin* waited, watched, and did the best they could. They waited until Leah and Strike came back, drooping with fatigue and defeat. They waited for Rabbit to contact them, growing more concerned as the days passed without any word from the teen, without Strike being able to connect to him with a teleport thread. And they waited as the hours and days passed, Saturn moved into opposition, and the barrier thinned. And as they waited, they did their best. Strike and Leah continued to search for the altar stone, only to be frustrated each time it seemed they were getting close. They had zero luck tracking down Iago, and there was still no sign of Sasha Ledbetter. Alexis practiced her magic, honing her shield and fireball spells, both of which glowed with rainbows. And she sat long into the nights with Strike, Leah, and Jox, arguing the options, until they finally settled on a calculated risk for the Saturn at Opposition ceremony.

Alexis, with Nate as her power boost, would travel into the barrier and attempt to work the three-question spell. That seemed like their only option for gaining the information they needed about the Volatile and Ixchel's defense against the first demon prophecy.

If they were lucky, the spell would work even though the opposition wasn't a cardinal day.

Back in New Orleans, far away from Skywatch, both in miles and in his head, Rabbit hunkered in a narrow doorway that smelled of old smoke. He scanned the street using all his senses—physical and otherwise—to make sure the coast was clear, then slipped through a wrought-iron gate that led to a series of interconnected courtyards that would bring him to the rear entrance of Mistress Truth's tea shop.

He'd been living there the past couple of days, ever since he'd bolted from the MFA and dumped his phone. With five hundred dollars cash in his pocket and a valid ID, it hadn't been difficult for him to upgrade his wardrobe and hop on an Amtrak headed south. With his telekine powers, it also hadn't been hard to bust into the tea shop and make himself at home, hoping Myrinne would check back. He was more or less safe and comfortable, and off the grid. The thing that sucked, though, was how much he missed being a part of something.

It wasn't that he missed Skywatch so much—it was a pretty cool place, but it was just a place. As for the people . . . well, he'd never spent much time away from Strike or Jox before, but they were both busy with their own stuff now, and besides, the compound was so big, he'd been able to go days without seeing them if he wanted to. He'd been living in his old man's cottage for the past few months, had gotten used to being alone. But after a couple of days of traveling, then shacking up in the tea shop, he'd realized that "alone" was a pretty relative thing back at Skywatch, where there was always somebody nearby, always something going on. In the tea shop he was totally solo. Granted, the streets of the French Quarter never actually quieted all the way down . . . but still, it wasn't the same as being back in the training compound. He found he loved the isolation during the day, when he could ghost around the neighborhood looking for Myrinne, or just spend a few hours poking through the witch's stuff. Most of it was crap, of course, but he'd gotten a power buzz off a few things, and had set them aside to fiddle with.

At night, though, things went quiet and his mind got very loud as it replayed what'd happened back at the museum. Brandt's anger had stuck with him, along with the knowledge that Patience had gotten hurt because he'd been fiddling with his text messages. Rabbit had bought a new phone and called the investigator, Juarez, to do some checking on the museum break-in, so he knew the others had gotten away from the museum. But the fact that Strike hadn't locked onto him for a 'port pretty much summed up where the Nightkeepers stood: *You've fucked up enough times, kid. Good riddance.*

Which meant he was on his own, at least until he found Myrinne. She'd checked out of the shelter Juarez had tracked her to, and vanished. The PI had told him to stay put, that he was on the case, but as the days passed, the stars aligned, and the barrier thinned, and Juarez kept telling him he'd have better news the next day, Rabbit knew what he had to do.

Screw the PI. He could find Myrinne himself . . . with a little help from the three-question *nahwal.*

CHAPTER SEVENTEEN

The Nightkeepers were a somber group as they prepared for the Saturn at Opposition ceremony.

And why not? Nate thought, frustrated. The score was Iago three, Nightkeepers one. Hell, for all they knew, the Xibalban had Kulkulkan's altar stone, along with the last two artifacts, a knife and bowl that Jade hadn't yet managed to track down, even with Lucius's help. The grad student was proving useful in other areas, though. His translation of the Ixchel poem hadn't added much to what they already knew—it was a love poem, and although it mentioned rainbows, there didn't seem to be any clues hidden within the text. That was assuming Lucius had the translation right, but Anna swore by him, so who was Nate to argue?

Lucius had been locked in the storeroom for the duration of the opposition ceremony, lest his connection to the *makol* reactivate when the barrier thinned. Nate felt bad for the guy; lockup was no fun, regardless of the situation. And although the slave bond had been a matter of necessity, Nate didn't feel good about the royal council's decision on that one, either. Then again, as far as Nate was concerned, the council could use an outside opinion. Leah might've started out as an antiestablishment type, but since being mated to Strike she'd been assimilated, Borg-like, into the Nightkeeper mind-set. Jox was an establishment guy all the way, Alexis was good at improving ideas that were already out there but wasn't an outside-the-box thinker, and Strike . . . well, as Carlos said, their king was his father's son—a stubborn dreamer with huge sense of duty and a heart that could send him in the wrong direction with the best of intentions.

Not that Nate was planning on volunteering to sit in on the debates and act as the voice of reason. Or rebellion, he thought, knowing he would be the maverick in the group, the one to counter all the history-steeped decisions.

Which so wasn't what he should've been thinking about as he followed the others into the sacred room at Skywatch. *Focus, dipshit,* he told himself. He and Alexis were about to try pulling some serious magic on a noncardinal day. He needed to get his head in the game.

The sacred chamber at Skywatch was a circular room located at the end of one of the mansion wings, decorated with intricately carved walls and a *chac-mool* altar like the one in the sacred tunnels beneath Chichén Itzá. Unlike the sacred chamber beneath Chichén Itzá, though, it was open to the stars and moon, which glowed through a glass-paneled ceiling. Where the cardinal-day ceremonies of the equinoxes and solstices were conducted down in the Yucatán, along with those celebrating high-magic events like an eclipse, the lesser ceremonies like Saturn at Opposition were held in-house at Skywatch. Personally, Nate thought they should've gone south anyway, given that he and Alexis were supposed to enact the three-question spell. Strike was banking on her Godkeeper powers to fuel the spell, but Nate couldn't see how it would've hurt for them to stack the deck even further by invoking the spell at the intersection. Not that anyone had asked his opinion, least of all Alexis, whom he'd seen less and less frequently as her duties increased.

He hadn't even realized how much time they'd spent together—or actively avoiding each other—until it wasn't happening anymore. He missed the contact, missed the arguments. And yeah, he knew it made him a prick, but it wasn't until she wasn't around all the time that he realized how much he'd enjoyed having her around.

Which made zero sense, given that he'd spent the past six months trying to drive her away, but there it was. He would've liked to talk to her about the things he was learning from Carlos about his bloodline, about his family. He wanted to hash over the inconsistencies he was seeing in some of the prophecies, and get Alexis's take on the Iago situation. But instead he held himself away, figuring he'd muddied those waters for far too long, and she deserved some space.

Whether or not there was distance between them, though, he knew the moment she came through the doorway into the sacred room. He could feel her energy on his skin and hear the hum in the air change in pitch, singing a high, sweet note.

She was wearing the black robes of a Nightkeeper warrior-priest, a long ceremonial regalia worked with stingray spines and shells, with pointed sleeves and a long hood. They were all wearing the robes over combat clothes, except for Jade, who wore scribe's gray and minimal weapons, and Strike, Leah, and Anna, who wore royal red robes over full combat gear.

But although Alexis was dressed like the others, Nate knew where she was every instant, even with her hood covering her streaky blond hair, and her back to him. He recognized the way she carried herself, the way the air seemed to shimmer in rainbows around her. And as she turned and glanced at him, he recognized the way his blood heated with the attraction he'd never managed to outrun or ignore.

She looked strong and tough, her movements graceful, as though she'd finally stopped wishing to be small and delicate and finally embraced the fact that she was an athlete, a warrior. Her high cheekbones stood out sharply, suggesting that she'd lost weight when he hadn't been watching, or maybe the magic and responsibility had burned away the last of the human softness, leaving the Valkyrie behind.

"Nate," she said finally, nodding and moving toward him, because one of them had to do something besides stare across the room.

"You look good," he said, forcing himself not to reach

out to her, because he'd given up that right rather than get into something he hadn't been ready to deal with, might not ever be. Nightkeeper sex wasn't about love; it was about power and necessity, and he'd played that game too many times already.

"You too," she said, though he had a feeling the return compliment was a formality. He was pretty sure he looked like shit. He'd been eating too little, working out too much, and working on *VW6* long into the nights, hunkered down in his parents' cottage, typing furiously.

The rest of the story had finally started coming together when he'd realized the source of his block. Hera hadn't totally clicked with any of the mates they'd sketched out for her—even Nameless—because she hadn't needed anything from them. Things hadn't started to flow until he'd hit on the idea of giving her a childhood trauma that had driven her to fight. Once she had that small chink in her armor, covering a larger vulnerability, he'd been able to bring the story line forward, which was why he'd been up way too late, way too many nights lately.

That and the realization that as Hera was becoming vulnerable, Alexis was growing into herself, becoming the woman she'd always wanted to be . . . and he wasn't part of that change.

"Alexis," he began, then stalled because he didn't know what the hell he wanted to say. The things he wanted were all tangled up in his brain with the stuff he knew were supposed to happen according to the gods, and that was crammed against things he knew didn't work for him, couldn't ever work.

Her lips turned up at the corners in a small smile that was more acknowledgment than emotion. "Yeah. I know."

"Okay, gang, let's do this," Strike said, breaking up their nonconversation, which was both frustrating and a relief.

At the king's gesture, the Nightkeepers took their positions, forming a circle within the circular room, with Strike and Leah standing with their backs to the *chacmool*. Because they were going to be enacting the three-question spell, Nate and Alexis stood outside the circle, one on each side of the altar.

With them outside the circle, Red-Boar dead and Rabbit still missing, the Nightkeepers' circle seemed very small.

"Ready?" Nate said, and Alexis nodded. She pulled her ceremonial knife and used it to blood her palm, then hesitated and held the knife out to him.

The act of using her knife to carve a bloody furrow in his palm seemed very intimate, and he held her eyes as he returned the knife and they joined hands over the altar. The background hum of magic sparked at the contact, jolting through him and lighting him up, sending his power higher than it'd ever been before, even when linked to the king. *Gods,* he thought, then amended it to, *Goddess.* Because that was what he was feeling: Ixchel's power. Alexis's power.

"You remember the spell?" Alexis said quietly.

Nate nodded. "Yeah. Let's do this."

They drew strength from the altar, and from the ashes of ten generations of Nightkeeper magi mixed into the mortar beneath the carved stone. They drew strength from each other, though he feared it wouldn't be enough. Too much divided them, when the Godkeeper's magic relied on the catalyst of her Nightkeeper mate.

Leaning on the magic they made together, and the humming pool of energy created by their uplinked teammates, they locked eyes and said in unison: *"Pasaj och."*

They blinked into the barrier on a flash of gold and rainbows, with none of the lurching, rushing sensation Nate was used to. One second he was in the sacred room at Skywatch; the next he was in the barrier, standing facing Alexis, their hands linked. They stood on a flat, faintly spongy surface that they couldn't see because gray-green mist swirled to their knees. The sky was the same gray-green, and the horizon—if there were such a thing in the barrier—was lost in the gray-green monotony of it all. Their entry to the barrier had been far smoother than ever before; before there had been a jolt, a rush, and a churn of nausea. But the barrier itself was the same as before.

"Wow. That was pretty painless," Alexis said, mirroring his thoughts. She dropped his hands and looked around, as if to verify that they were really in the barrier.

"Thanks to the king's adviser." Nate faked a bow in her direction.

"Thanks to the goddess, you mean."

It's all you, he wanted to say, but didn't. Instead he said, "Stage two?"

She nodded. "Stage two."

The three-question spell required petitioners to jack into the barrier, which meant that their physical bodies remained on earth—in this case, in the sacred chamber of Skywatch—while their incorporeal forms—their souls, for lack of a better term, though it made Nate cringe— entered the in-between gray-greenness of the barrier. Once there, the three-question petitioners had to perform a second bloodletting and another spell. Then, if Nate and Alexis had done everything right and had the magical chops to call the ancestor despite it not being a cardinal day, the three-question *nahwal* would appear.

That was the theory, anyway.

Nate reached into the pocket of his robe and withdrew a pair of stingray spines. He handed one to Alexis and kept one for himself. "I'm so not looking forward to this part."

"It's not a sacrifice if it's easy," she answered, para- phrasing one of the writs. Then she shot him a look and a sly grin, knowing how he felt about scripture.

Instead of answering, he stuck out his tongue, jammed the stingray spine into it, and ripped the barb free. Pain slapped and spiraled, so much sharper than the familiar bite of blade against palm. Blood flowed down his chin as Alexis did the same, hissing as she yanked out the spine, tearing flesh.

The magic might heal them quickly, but it didn't stop the pain.

Both a little shaky now, they joined hands, leaning on each other, and chanted the second spell, calling the three-question *nahwal.*

Alone in the barrier with blood running down his chin, Rabbit finished the chant that should have called the three-question *nahwal,* but nothing happened. So he said it again. And again. Each time he started the words in the old tongue he threw more magic into it, more of his own blood.

Maybe it wasn't working because he was alone, because it was the wrong day. Or maybe because he was nothing but a fuckup half-blood, like his old man had always said. But he refused to give up, because frigging Juarez still couldn't find Myrinne, and Rabbit's urge to get to her was growing by the hour, along with his conviction that she needed him, that she was important.

His body buzzed with the power and the pain as he said the spell again, taking the magic into him and sending it outward, summoning his ancestors' wisdom. He wasn't sure where he ended and the mist began. He was the mist and the mist was him, and he was all alone.

Then, suddenly, he wasn't alone anymore. The nearby fog thickened, coalescing into a vaguely human shape that stepped forward into the shadowless gray-green light.

The three-question *nahwal* looked like the bloodline-bound *nahwals* that had come to the trainees during the talent ceremony. Both types of *nahwal* looked pretty much like desiccated corpses that happened to be up and moving around; they had no nipples or genitals, and their eyes were pure black, with no whites or emotion. But where the bloodline *nahwals* were each forearm-marked with their bloodline glyphs, this one was unmarked. And although they were supposed to be emotionless, this one looked seriously pissed off, with V-grooved frown lines between its dead black eyes, and its fangs bared.

Shit, fangs? Rabbit thought on a jolt of fear and surprise. Why hadn't anybody mentioned the fangs?

Holding his hands away from his sides in a gesture of *I'm unarmed; please don't fuck me up,* he said, "Ah, um. Are you here to answer my three questions?"

The thing hissed and charged, reaching for him with hands that'd grown claws.

Rabbit let out a yell and dove to one side. He felt the breeze of the *nahwal*'s swipe, but no pain. He bounced up from the springy surface underfoot and spun to face his attacker. "What the hell?"

The thing apparently wasn't in the mood for convo,

questions or otherwise. It spun and lunged for him again, scratching and snapping, and howling with rage when Rabbit danced aside. Palming his father's knife, which he still wore on his belt, Rabbit dropped and rolled, coming up inside the *nahwal*'s guard and leading point-first when he stood. The blade cut through the thing's skin with little resistance, but deflected off bone and skidded aside. Which just pissed the creature off worse.

Roaring, its face contorted with rage and hatred, though neither was supposed to be in its repertoire, the *nahwal* spun and dove on Rabbit, grabbing his legs and driving him to the ground. They rolled together for a few frenzied seconds before Rabbit's control broke under the onslaught of battle rage.

Tipping his head back, he called the fire on a long scream of pain and magic: *"Kaak!"*

The gray-green sky split, and flames poured down to spear straight through the *nahwal*. The burning energy lifted the thing up and off Rabbit and tossed it aside. The creature shrieked and writhed, wreathed in flames as its skin and ropy flesh burned away.

"No!" Rabbit shouted. "Stop!"

He tried to call the magic back, tried to cut it off, to do something, anything to stop the fire from consuming the *nahwal*. But nothing worked. He could only watch as the thing's struggles slowed, then stopped, and the only visible motion became that of the greedy flames and the mists that swirled at the periphery of the blaze. Eventually—it'd probably been only a few minutes, but it felt like forever—even the flames guttered out. The gray-green mist moved back in to cover where the *nahwal* had been, and it was as though nothing had happened. Only it had, Rabbit knew, horror and guilt vising his chest and making it hard to breathe.

He'd fucking killed the three-question *nahwal*.

"It's not working," Alexis said, looking around the gray-green fog and not seeing a *nahwal*, not seeing anything except mist and more mist. "The opposition magic must not be strong enough to power the spell." *Or else we aren't.*

"Let's try it again and give it everything we've got." Nate's eyes were steady on hers, his grip firm.

Alexis nodded, not wanting to admit defeat. *Please, goddess,* she thought, *help us. Help your warriors on earth figure out what the hell they're supposed to do.* It wasn't the most eloquent of prayers, perhaps, but it was heartfelt, and she thought she sensed a little power bump at the back of her brain, a shimmer of color that might've been a response. "Okay," she said, reaching down deep and drawing on the magic. "Once more, with feeling."

They started reciting the spell again, and before they'd gotten past the second grouping of words in the old language, she knew something was different this time. She could feel the power gathering and expanding outward, could hear the hum of magic.

Then, without warning, the hum escalated to a scream and wind slapped at them, driving the mists to a frenzied funnel cloud in an instant and yanking them off their feet.

"Nate!" she screamed, grabbing for him as the gale knocked her back, ripping her hands from his.

"Alexis!" He dove for her, hooking her around the waist and flinging them both to the yielding surface beneath the wind-whipped mist. "Down," he ordered. "Stay down!"

He flattened her body beneath his and hung on tight while he cast around, trying to find a handhold to anchor them. She did the same, but there was nothing to hold on to but the moist squishiness of the barrier surface, formless and alien.

"I'm slipping," she cried, feeling the slick surface moving beneath her, feeling the wind grab hold and not let go. "What's happening?"

"The spell misfired." He shouted the words over the rising howl of the wind. "I can't find the way home!"

Cursing herself for not thinking, Alexis closed her eyes and pictured the sacred chamber back at Skywatch, imagining her and Nate on either side of the altar, the others forming a ring in the center of the circular room. Tapping the power of the barrier, she thought, *Na otot.*

The words, which meant "house" or "home," should've dropped her out of the barrier and back into her body.

They didn't.

"It's not working for me, either!" she cried.

They were moving in a circle now, being dragged along by the force of the funnel cloud as it reached down lower and lower still, coming for them. Worse, the funnel cloud didn't stretch up to the sky, but rather folded double so the spitting mouth, which bellowed mist and wind, was pointed downward, toward the underworld. Where it touched the barrier surface, the gray-green had gone black, suggesting that they were about thirty seconds from a one-way trip to Xibalba.

"The goddess," Nate shouted. "Call on the goddess!"

Fear rode Alexis, but the connection at the base of her brain had gone dim. Throwing power at the spot didn't change the background glow; prayer didn't make a dent. Knowing no other way to reach the goddess, Alexis turned beneath him and wrapped her arms around his neck and her legs around his waist, offering herself to the heat and the magic. Lust rose quickly, slapping a vicious whip through her body, a feverish demand that seemed sharper than before, greedier.

For a second she thought he might refuse her. Then he groaned, a harsh rattle at the back of his throat, and met her halfway in a kiss that was hard and hot and openmouthed. Something inside her said, *Thank the gods*, because this wasn't the reserved man he'd been in recent weeks, or the one who'd given her that single, sweet kiss to celebrate her advisership and avoided her since. This was the man she'd mated with, the one who was never far from her thoughts or dreams.

Lust revved her senses, making her achingly aware of the solid strength of him, the hard bulge of muscles beneath her gripping hands, and the good weight of him atop her. They kissed again and again, touching and tugging, finding their way through the ceremonial robes to combat clothes and the bare skin beneath. She arched into his touch as he found her breast and drove her up, his hands and mouth working together, bringing heat.

Leaning into the magic that came with desire, Alexis

called on the goddess, called on the powers of a Godkeeper.

Luminous green lightning split the sky, burning her
retinas, interrupting the build of magic. The funnel cloud
roared and twisted as if gaining strength from the lightning, which flared again and again as an ever-increasing
growl of thunder pummeled them. The firmament shifted,
jolting them. Wind pulled at their bodies, and Alexis
howled Nate's name as he was torn away from her and
up into the funnel.

"Nate!" She reached for him, but missed as he was
whipped away from her. *"Nate!"* She screamed for him,
screamed for herself as the funnel plucked her up and
tossed her in a wide arc. Her stomach lurched and fear
grabbed her by the throat when there was no answer.

Then she saw him up ahead, at the place where the
world went from gray-green to limitless black. Not thinking, not caring, she pointed her body in that direction and
pressed her arms flat against her sides, like a skydiver
aiming for a target midair. She arrowed toward him, crossing the intervening distance quicker than thought.

Halfway there she slammed into an invisible wall, one
that shimmered with rainbows when she touched it. The
moment she hit, the air went still on her side of the wall,
leaving her hanging motionless in gray-green nothingness
amidst deafeningly sudden silence. On the other side of
the invisible barrier the funnel spun unabated, drawing
Nate farther and farther away.

"No!" Alexis banged against the wall, drew her knife,
and tried to hack through it. She grabbed for her holster
but wasn't wearing it; she had come to the ceremony
unarmed, knowing their incorporeal selves would be
brought into the barrier wearing all that they wore on
earth, and thinking there was no reason to bring jade-
tips into the barrier. At least, there normally wasn't.
Now, though, she was under attack, and defenseless.
They had called the three-question *nahwal* and gotten
chaos instead.

Nate! her heart cried as the funnel spun him closer to
her for a second and she could see his face. He mouthed
something, and she knew in her gut that he was telling

her to get away, to save herself. But she couldn't. She just couldn't.

Flipping the knife so she held it by the blade, she sliced both her palms, cutting deep, letting the blood flow freely. Then she held her hands away from her in supplication, touched them to the invisible wall she instinctively knew had been put there by the goddess in order to keep her from being sucked into the funnel. But that meant the goddess was nearby, that she could act within the barrier. If that were the case, why wasn't she coming into Alexis?

The answer danced just out of her reach. Cursing the goddess, praying to her, Alexis tipped her head back and, compelled by instinct, or maybe a whisper from beyond, she cried, "*Takaj,* Ixchel!" *Come, goddess!*

As though Ixchel had been waiting only for the call, the conduit came to life and a starburst exploded rainbows at the back of Alexis's brain. Power flowed through her, passing out of her to the funnel cloud beyond. She was the goddess and the goddess was her. A contemptuous flick of her bloodstained fingers swept aside the rainbow-wrought shield that had both saved her and separated her from Nate. A word extinguished the funnel cloud. A gesture had an invisible hand plucking Nate's limp form out of the edge of nothingness, and bringing him to where Alexis hung in midair.

The rainbow surrounded them, bound them together as she touched him, felt the solidness of him, the reality of him. Closing her eyes, she imagined the sacred chamber and whispered the words that would send them home.

There was no lurch or movement, no sense of transitioning from one plane to the next. There was only a flash of gold and colors, and they were there, facing each other over the altar, hanging on to each other for dear life.

Impressions bombarded her. Snapshots. She was aware of Izzy and Carlos sitting cross-legged where the other magi had been, saw their expressions of delighted relief, heard them shouting for the others. She was aware of the stars and the moon overhead, aware that hours had passed when it had seemed like only minutes. And she was aware of Nate's fingers holding tightly to hers, and his eyes flickering open, showing confusion first, and then darkening with memory.

Moments later, the door flung open and Strike hustled into the chamber, followed closely by Leah and the others, who were all talking at once. But it was Nate's voice Alexis heard. He said, "You did it, Lexie. You called the goddess."

"Yeah." She smiled, tentatively at first, then wider as she realized the connection was there now, and fully formed where it had been nothing but a wish before. Joy lit her up from within, radiating outward until the air sparkled with the hint of rainbows, like light blurred through a subtle prism. "I did, didn't I?"

The other magi gathered around them while the *winikin* tried to push them back, saying something about food and rest first, questions later. But Alexis kept looking at Nate, and the rainbow joy dimmed slightly when she saw the knowledge in his eyes, and felt it in her own heart. The goddess had taught her to call the magic by herself, which meant she didn't need Nate anymore.

The realization should've been a relief.

It wasn't.

PART III

VERNAL EQUINOX

A day of equal light and dark, and the first day of spring. A time of change and growth.

CHAPTER EIGHTEEN

March 13

When Rabbit awoke the morning after the opposition, he found himself lying on a camping cot in a square, empty room that was paneled in wide, rough-cut pine boards. There were barred windows on each wall, through which he could see a cloudy gray sky and a smattering of pine branches. As he watched, a bright red cardinal bounced onto one of the branches and away, placing him somewhere north of the snow line, far from either Skywatch or New Orleans. The air was so cold that his breath fogged on each exhale, though he was covered in a couple of blankets, and warm enough.

Which was so not the point. What the hell was he doing in a camping cabin?

His head spun with the worst postmagic hangover of his life, and his body throbbed from his fight with the *nahwal.* For reasons known only to the gods, the magic healed cuts but not bruises.

"Screw the bruises. You're lucky to be alive after the stunt you pulled," a voice said from behind him.

Jolting hard in panic, Rabbit turned and scrambled to his feet in a single motion, calling the fire to his finger-tips in an instant. He took one look at the redheaded man sitting in a folding chair and let rip with the fire magic.

The flames stopped dead three feet or so from Iago's face, spreading along an invisible liquidlike barrier, shield magic the likes of which Rabbit had never seen before. Groaning with the effort, he increased the power, but though the fire magic roared higher, it still wasn't denting the shield.

"Cut the blowtorch, will you?" the other mage called over the crackle of fire. "I'm not going to hurt you. Hell, I'm the one who pulled your ass out of that funnel last night."

Rabbit called back the fire but kept it close to his fingertips as his heart drummed against his ribs and he tried to remember what'd happened after the *nahwal* collapsed. He came up blank aside from a wash of terror and the sound of his own screams. Ignoring the chill that brought, he demanded, "Where the hell are we? What do you want? And how did you know I was thinking about the bruises?"

"We'll get to all that." Iago leaned his chair back against the wall and stacked his hands behind his head, all casual. He was wearing black canvas flannel-lined pants, and heavy work boots that had tracked wet spots across the floor, along with a black turtleneck and a heavy blue fisherman's sweater. The sleeves had pulled some when he stretched his hands over his head, baring the bloodred quatrefoil on his arm. The mage's dark red hair was partially hidden by an earflap hat, which would've looked dumb if it weren't for his eyes, which were hard-edged emerald.

"You look like a lumberjack." Rabbit jammed his thumbs in the pockets of his jeans and whistled a few bars of the transvestite lumberjack song from Monty Python, pushing back the fear some with 'tude.

"Stuff it, kid. I was a bigger snot at your age than you'll ever hope to be." He paused. "Besides, the digs are only temporary. We've got a sweet homestead down south. We'll leave as soon as you're ready."

"How about I leave now and you go fuck yourself?"

Iago just rolled his eyes. "Hello? You've torched more real estate than a California wildfire, turned the museum job into a train wreck, and killed the three-question *nah-*

wal. If I were you, I'd be looking at my options right about now, because the Nightkeepers give fuck-all what happens to you."

"Shut up," Rabbit snapped, but his voice cracked on the words.

"It's not like they came looking for you when you took off, right? And that was before you nearly got the new Godkeeper and her mate killed." One reddish eyebrow climbed at Rabbit's confused look. "Oh, right. You were unconscious for that part. Congratulations, two of your former teammates tried to use the three-question spell right after you offed the *nahwal*. They got barriered instead. Barely made it out alive."

Rabbit pressed the heels of his hands against his ears as the guilt amped. "I said shut up!"

"Reality sucks. Get used to it." Iago stood and moved toward him. Rabbit tried to throw up a shield, but he'd lost the magic to emotion. Getting inside his space, the mage leaned down to him, his face so close that Rabbit could see the flecks of magic that flickered in Iago's green eyes. "I'm offering you a choice, kid. You want to switch sides, we're happy to have you. Otherwise you're going to be our guest until the equinox. We could use some powerful blood for the sacrifice we're planning."

"Fuck you," Rabbit spat, but all of a sudden his words were slurring and the floor was doing a slow roll beneath him. He couldn't tell if he'd just hit the end of his reserves, or if there was something else going on—drugs, maybe, or sleep magic. Either way, he was fading fast.

"Think about it," Iago said. "I'll have some food brought for you. No sense trying to figure it out if you're half dead." The mage headed for the door, which swung open at his approach. He looked back and smirked slightly at Rabbit, as if to say, *See how much more powerful I am than your precious Nightkeepers?*

"Wait," Rabbit croaked when he was partway out the door.

Iago turned back. "What?"

"Why me?"

That seemed to startle the Xibalban. Then he started laughing. "Have they honestly not told you? Gods, that's pathetic." He turned back, eyes alight with mockery. "Why do you think they're so afraid of your magic? Your mother was one of us."

The kick of emotion that hit Rabbit square in the chest and drove the breath from his lungs probably should have been surprise, only it wasn't. Something inside him said, *Of course*, as though he should've known all along, or maybe a piece of him had guessed long ago. "Oh," he said, only it came out more like a groan.

"Think about it, kid. I'm offering you a family, and more power than you could possibly imagine." Then Iago turned and left. Moments later the door swung shut and a lock clicked into place from the outside. A few seconds after that, Rabbit felt a buzz of unfamiliar ward magic settling into place, sealing him into the cabin.

He lay there for a long moment, unmoving, thinking about Iago's offer of more power than he could possibly imagine.

Well, Rabbit could imagine a whole lot of power.

As far as Nate was concerned, by inviting Iago for a parley, the Nightkeepers were just asking for trouble.

Strike thought it was imperative that they at least talk to the bastard, given how few Nightkeepers there were. Nate thought it was fucking stupid, and told the king that in so many words the day after the opposition ceremony, when he was still running hot on magic and frustration, and an edge of hurt that Alexis didn't need him anymore. He and Strike had gotten into it, had gotten loud, and then Alexis had waded in, shouting right back. Nate wasn't sure if she really thought the meeting was a good idea or if she just wanted to argue with him, but they'd gone at it for a bit before the king separated them and announced that he wanted Nate to be part of the group that would meet Iago outside the front door of the training compound, beyond the wards.

Which was why, two days after the opposition ceremony that'd nearly killed him and Alexis and had liberated her instead, Nate found himself standing beside her, with Strike and Leah on his other side. Anna was there too. She and the members of the royal council had spent a chunk of the prior evening hashing something out, so Nate had a feeling they were planning more than a simple parley, but he wasn't in on that piece of things. He was just window dressing, another body standing by the front gate, waiting for Iago.

Who was late.

"Maybe it's a trick," Nate said after ten minutes had turned to fifteen and there was no rattle of 'port magic in the air. "A distraction."

"Allowing them to do what?" Alexis asked. "If he had the ability and the desire to 'port straight into Skywatch, he would've done it by now." She didn't look at him; at least, he didn't think she did. It was hard to tell, when she was wearing a pair of three-hundred-dollar sunglasses that shaded her eyes and hid her expression.

"Isn't the whole point that we don't have a clue what he can and can't do?" he challenged.

Before she could say anything, Strike interrupted. "Incoming."

Moments later Nate felt it too: the rattle of magic that felt like Nightkeeper power, but wasn't. It geared up to a roar, displaced air exploded outward in a cloud of brown smoke, and Iago and a striking-looking woman appeared several feet away, zapping in with their feet planted on terra firma with no stumbling, no awkwardness.

Wearing hiking boots, jeans, and a white T-shirt, with a long black duster over the top, Iago looked like just another guy with a bit of cool on. But Nate saw disdain in his face, and thought how he'd promised the old woman in the doily cottage that he would make sure her killer was punished.

Iago's eyes skimmed over the Nightkeepers, pausing briefly on Nate as though feeling the hatred, or maybe seeing it in his eyes. Then he moved on, his message clear: *You don't scare me.*

No? Nate thought on a flare of anger. *We'll have to fix that.*

The woman at his side locked onto Anna immediately, and her lips tipped up in a small, mean smile. That'd be Desiree, then. Nate wasn't sure who she was to the Xibalbans, or why she was at the meeting, but one thing was for sure: Malice radiated off her in waves. Anna, in contrast, seemed detached, disinterested, standing there with her eyes unfocused and her hands jammed in her pockets. Which didn't totally make sense, given that she'd flown all the way to New Mex in order to go at it with her enemy on the Nightkeepers' turf.

"Nochem," Iago said to Strike, who stood slightly ahead of the others and had rolled up the right sleeve of his black T-shirt to reveal the *hunab ku*, the geometric mark of kingship that was located on his upper arm, where only kings and gods were marked.

"Call me Strike."

"Then I'm Iago." The mage looked past the king. As he did so, a faint rattle of background magic started up, an annoying buzz that made Nate's jaw ache. "I assume these are your advisers?"

"Yes," Strike said simply.

Nate quashed a knee-jerk protest. It didn't matter what they called him; he was just there to counteract some of Alexis's less rational ideas. That didn't make him an adviser.

Iago snorted. "Fine, I get it. You're not inviting me in for tea and cookies or whatever. You're the one who asked for a meeting, so let's meet. What do you want?"

Strike nodded. "Okay, here goes. Your order has gotten some seriously shitty press over the millennia, but I'm thinking that we may have a common goal at this point. Doesn't do you any good to have the world end any more than it does us. So I thought we might be able to come to terms, maybe cooperate. You've got some of the demon prophecies; we've got some of them. What if we combined our forces?"

Iago smirked. "You've got one of them, and I've got the other six, you mean. I should thank you for the last three, by the way. Your archives must've contained info that mine didn't, because I couldn't find Cabrakan's bowl, the Volatile's knife, or the Ixchel statuette for love or money until your archivist started Googling them and my filters caught the keywords." He grinned and flexed his fingers. "Gotta love the Internet."

Which unfortunately meant he'd already found Kulkulkan's altar stone, Nate realized, his gut knotting on anger and disappointment, made worse by the annoying subsonic buzz of magic. *Gods* damn *it.* But some of the other information was new, namely that the knife they'd almost gotten in New Orleans was connected to the Volatile. Which meant it was vital that they get the thing back.

"We have a common goal," Strike persisted. "Both groups want to stop the apocalypse."

Desiree shifted her attention from Anna to Strike and sneered. "You're trying to stop the inevitable."

"Perhaps," Anna said, and Nate got the distinct impression that she wasn't just talking about the end-time. "But what's the alternative? You think you're going to rule in hell? Think again. The *Banol Kax* don't deal that way."

"And how do you know that for certain? From your precious gods? Not exactly an unbiased source." Desiree bared her teeth. "Speaking of sources, how is Lucius getting along? Tell me, has he—"

"Enough." Iago's voice was quiet, but it silenced her immediately. Focusing on Strike, he said, "I have ten times your numbers, Nightkeeper, and I have the other six prophecies. Moreover, I'm not bound by the traditions that you are. We have no *winikin*, no writs. We've adapted. We've grown. We need nothing from you."

"Then why even bother to come?" Strike asked, his frustration obvious. "I fail to see—"

Automatic weaponry chattered behind them, coming from *inside* the compound.

"Son of a bitch!" Nate snapped, making the connection between the buzzing sound and the sense of magic. "He's overriding the wards. He's got someone inside the compound! *Bastard!*"

Without stopping to think, Nate lunged at Iago. With surprise on his side, he nailed the mage waist-high with his shoulder, sending them both to the ground. He wound up astride Iago, and got in three good punches before the chirr of dark 'port magic surrounded him.

Roaring, Nate grabbed on to the lapels of Iago's jacket and hung on, intending to go with him. He didn't have a plan, didn't have a weapon, knew only that he owed it to the old lady, to his king and his people. Seconds later he was flying through the air, slapped aside by an unseen giant's fist to land hard, face-first in the dust.

Iago and Desiree had vanished.

"Come on!" Alexis was dragging him up and along before he could get a breath. Strike and the others were gone, undoubtedly having 'ported into the compound the second the gunfire started.

It'd stopped, leaving ominous silence behind.

Nate and Alexis ran for the mansion together, dragging each other along. When they reached the main room he heard a babble of familiar voices all talking over one another, and followed the sound. He found the *winikin* and Nightkeepers gathered in the hallway outside the archive, with some inside the first room. He pushed through, with Alexis right behind him, and stopped dead when he got a clear view. "Oh, *shit*."

The archive was a disaster area.

It looked like somebody had unloaded two or three MAC clips into the bookcases holding centuries' worth of rare texts. Lucius was folded up in one corner, looking shell-shocked but alive, and clutching an autopistol. Jade was standing in the middle of the room with tears tracking down her face, her mouth open in an "O" of horror, a bullet-riddled book clutched against her breasts. The locked door leading to the second room hung from one hinge, and blast marks marred the doorframe.

Nate didn't even need to ask. He already knew.

"Ixchel," Alexis whispered, taking two steps toward the battered door and stopping. She raised her hand to her mouth, then let it fall away. She turned to Nate, reached out for his hand, and he felt her sorrow in the link of palm to palm. "They took the statuette."

"Yeah." He wrapped an arm around her shoulders, figuring their problems had been momentarily backburnered by the disaster. Glancing over at Strike, who looked royally pissed, he asked, "Was anyone hurt?"

The king shook his head. "No, thank the gods. And

we've still got all the translations from the statuette, right?" He directed the question at Jade.

It was Lucius who answered, "Yeah. And digital pictures from every angle, under both natural light and starlight, which means we still have a chance of figuring out how to block the first prophecy."

"It's not just the first one we have to worry about," Anna said, pushing through the crowd, looking way more connected and focused than she had during the meeting.

Strike stiffened. "You got something?"

"It wasn't easy." She pulled her hands out of her pockets. They dripped with blood and held crystals.

"Jesus, Anna!" Strike caught her hands in his, expression thunderous. "This wasn't what we talked about you doing. What the hell were you thinking?"

"That I needed to do whatever it took to punch through the mental blocks guarding my powers." She was pale, swaying a little on her feet, but she smiled. "I did it. I got inside his head. I saw what he saw."

"Jox, get in here," Strike snapped, and the crowd stirred as the *winikin* pushed through, took one look at Anna's hands, and started dragging her out of the archive.

But she dug in her heels and pulled away. "No, wait. Let me say this first. We're not just talking about a single prophecy anymore. That's why Iago wanted all the statuettes. He's not trying to stop us from defending against Camazotz's sons one at a time. He's going to use the artifacts to bring all seven of them through at once, during the vernal equinox. He wants to jump-start the end-time by a couple of years."

Which meant they had a week to mount a defense, or the next stage in the end-time countdown was going to be coming very early.

"Son of a bitch," Nate growled.

"We've got to find him," Leah said quickly, her face gone very pale. She looked at Strike. "Are you sure you can't lock onto him? What about Desiree?"

He shook his head. "No. I couldn't even lock on when

I was standing there, staring at them, which means they've got some way of fouling 'port lock, maybe a version of whatever they used to jam the wards." He glanced at Anna. "Did you see . . . anything else?"

They all knew he was asking about Rabbit. The teen's absence weighed heavily on the king.

"No, I didn't," Anna said softly. "But that doesn't necessarily mean anything good or bad." She held out her hands, where the deep sacrificial cuts were starting to heal. "I'm an *itza'at*, not a mind-bender or a 'path. Even if I were full strength and all the way trained, there's no guarantee that I'd have seen anything but what was at the forefront of his mind, which was the image of bringing all seven of the artifacts together during the vernal equinox."

Sven said from out in the hallway, "Gods damn it. If I hadn't dropped the bowl—"

"Don't," Alexis said firmly. "Don't anybody go there. We've made the mistakes we've made, and most of them have been because we haven't had enough information."

As usual, Nate thought but didn't say. Whether or not he bought into the writs, information loss was a recurring theme with the Nightkeepers, as they had been victimized by cyclical acts of genocide that had not only wreaked havoc on the population, but also pretty much cut off info transfer from one phase of their history to the next. For a culture that believed in the recurring nature of time and liked to say crap like, "What has happened before will happen again," the lack of forethought was pretty sad.

Or rather, he realized with a sinking, shimmering sensation, it was downright unbelievable.

"What is it?" Alexis murmured at his side, warning Nate that his face had betrayed his thoughts. Or maybe she'd picked up on something using the powers of the goddess—he still wasn't sure what she could and couldn't do. He didn't think she was, either.

"A repository," he said.

"Yeah, that was what Jade was just saying, how she'd scanned almost all of the books into the computer system, so this"—she indicated the bullet-riddled books—

"shouldn't cost us too much in terms of total information. Given that we can practically reproduce the statuette from the pictures and measurements we've got, this wasn't as much of a disaster as it could've been." She paused. "That assumes, of course, that all the statuette had to offer was contained in the carvings and starscript. I can't help feeling like we're missing something there, like maybe there's another layer of script somewhere that we didn't know to look for. Otherwise, why else was Iago so hell-bent on getting his hands on all seven of the artifacts?"

Nate only half heard her; his brain was locked on the idea of a repository. "Not a repository," he said. "Alexandria."

Alexis frowned. "As in Virginia?"

"No." He shook his head. "As in 'the library of.' I was just thinking how there's a central flaw in Nightkeeper thinking if we can be so badly derailed over and over again by catastrophic failures of the oral and written traditions." He barely even noticed that he'd used "we," where before he'd held himself apart from the Nightkeepers as much as possible.

Strike narrowed his eyes, considering. "You're thinking there's a hidden library somewhere down south."

Nate nodded. "Our ancestors cached artifacts. Why not knowledge?"

"Which would be great if we knew where to start looking." Alexis turned her palms up, indicating that she didn't have a clue.

"I know." Nate dragged his fingers through his hair, thinking. He turned to Lucius, grateful to see that one of the others had snagged the MAC from the shaken bond-servant, who was on his feet now, pale but resolute. Nate asked him, "You ever hear something that might've hinted at there being a hidden library?"

But Lucius shook his head. "Can't think of anything, but Jade and I can certainly check through the books and—" He broke off, scrubbing his hands across his face. "Or we could've if I hadn't just shot them to pieces. I can't believe I did that. I don't know what the hell came over me."

Strike and Anna exchanged a telling look.

"Wait," Alexis said, her voice excited. She turned to Nate. "You said it yourself when we were in the ATM caves: Why were our parents there before us?"

He furrowed his brow. "Because they were trying to find out—" He broke off as it connected. To Carlos, he said "When Gray-Smoke and Two-Hawk left, right before the massacre, are you sure they were casting an actual question spell?"

The *winikin* thought for a second, then spread his hands. "It was a long time ago." He looked behind him at the other *winikin*, then over at Jox. "Anyone?"

He got a round of head shakes.

Nate said, "What if they were trying to investigate the king's vision, not through magic, but by finding a cache of information, codices and such, that our ancestors had collected before the conquistadors started burning texts? We know they warned the kings against letting the galleons lay anchor, and we know they had prophecies warning of dark times ahead. Seems like a good time to stockpile." He paused, remembering the artifacts in the ATM cave system. "Or maybe they cached their books even earlier than that, back in the nine fifties, when the Xibalbans released the *Banol Kax* and the empire fell. That was when they cached the artifacts; why not a library too?"

Anna shook her head. "It's a good story, but you've got no proof."

"Actually . . ." Lucius said, "I may have seen something the other day, on that old map of the cave system." He cast around for a few seconds, then plucked a splayed-out book from the floor where it had fallen in the melee. He righted one of the chairs and used it as a desk, because the table was leaning on three legs, with the fourth broken off midway. After flipping through several battered pages, he stopped, tapping Painted-Jaguar's map. "Here. There's a glyph hidden in the drawing of the dead-end waterway beyond the temple. It could be the *jun* glyph, which stands for 'book' or 'folded codex'. "

Jade leaned close. "I didn't see that before."

The others crowded close to look. Nate didn't know the glyph, but he knew where Lucius was pointing, all right. He muttered an oath. "Don't tell me."

"It makes sense," Alexis murmured in return. "Why set booby traps if you've got nothing to protect?"

CHAPTER NINETEEN

After Strike finished the postattack debriefing, Lucius headed back to his rooms, dogged by a nagging darkness the likes of which he hadn't felt in weeks. He'd shot the shit out of the archive. How the fuck could he rationalize that?

He and Jade had been sitting together, dragging through the laborious chore of cross-checking the information from a set of scanned-in pages. A weird rattling sound had cut through the air, and seconds later a blond woman had popped into existence in the middle of the room, wearing combat gear and a soldier's stone-faced expression, and toting a nasty-looking machine gun. She'd taken one look at Jade and Lucius and opened fire.

He didn't know how he'd done what he'd done. He just knew that the moment he'd seen sweet, soft-voiced Jade in the path of fire, a strange, luminous green had hazed his vision, and his body had gone into hyperdrive. Or maybe the world had slowed down; he didn't know which. All he knew was that one second a line of automatic weapons fire had been walking its way across the archive toward Jade, and the next he somehow had the gun in his hands and was blasting away at the blond bitch. When the bullets finally ran out and the green haze cleared—he was a little iffy on the time line there, because he hadn't exactly passed out, but things had sort of shifted suddenly—the room had been full of people, the door to the second archive room was open, and the Ixchel statuette was gone.

And according to Jade, he'd shot the shit out of hundreds, maybe even thousands of years of texts, which might've been scanned already, but had been irreplaceable nonetheless. "How could I have done that?"

"You know how," Anna's voice said from behind him.

He squeezed his eyes shut and fisted his fingers around the raised scar on his palm. "You said the *makol* couldn't get to me through the wards."

After the slave-bonding ceremony, she'd told him exactly what had happened the previous fall, how he'd learned that she was hiding a codex fragment in her office, and had broken in and stolen it, influenced somehow by the *Banol Kax* even before he'd begun to read the transition spell. She'd described how she'd had a vision of him cutting himself and invoking the spell, and had contacted Strike and a senior mage named Red-Boar to help him. They had teleported to Lucius's apartment and found him most of the way turned *makol*.

As she'd spoken, he'd known he should've been shocked and horrified. But his only real thought had been, *Of course, how could I have forgotten all that?* He didn't remember any of it, not really. But everything she said had clicked at a gut-deep level, with a sort of cosmic "aha!" that labeled it as the truth. It explained why he sometimes saw things through a luminous green sheen, why he'd been out of sorts since last summer, and why he'd felt more like himself inside the compound, which was warded against *makol* magic.

At least, it was supposed to be.

"The wards went down during the parley," Anna said. "That's how Iago 'ported the third Xibalban, the blonde, into the archive, and how the *makol* got through to you just now."

He stared down at the raised scar ridge on his palm. "Fuck me." He closed his fingers over the scar, hiding it. "At least I didn't kill Jade." That would've been beyond unthinkable. Of all the surprises he'd found at Skywatch, his almost instant friendship with the shy archivist was by far the nicest. If he'd hurt her . . . "Does Strike think it's too dangerous to keep me in the compound now?"

"He's not sure," she said, both of them avoiding the point that if he was too dangerous to keep in the compound then he was too dangerous to be let free and there was really only one other choice.

"What do you think?" he pressed.

She looked at him long and hard before answering. "I think we can't afford to sacrifice any valuable allies at this point."

He knew her use of the word "sacrifice" was no accident. Horror mixed with anger within him, yielding a deep-seated resentment much like what he'd been feeling for months now. But the wards were back in place, which meant . . . what? Were these really his feelings, or had something taken root inside him in defiance of the Nightkeepers' shielding magic?

Oddly, the latter thought didn't bother him nearly as much as it probably should have.

"So what now?" he asked her.

"We're not making any hasty decisions," she said firmly, though that wasn't really an answer. "I'm flying back tonight, but call me if you need to. And if you start having flashes or whatnot, tell someone. Promise me you won't try to fight dark magic on your own."

"I won't," he said. But he didn't promise.

By day two of Rabbit's imprisonment, he'd become very familiar with the wooden rafters above his cot, and with the walls and floor of his one-room prison, which was locked and warded, not just with a spell to keep him in, but with one that blocked his magic. Which totally sucked.

He hadn't seen another human being since Iago left. He got fed twice a day, morning and night. He'd know it was chow time when he heard footsteps outside . . . and then the lights would go out, not in the cabin, but in his head. He'd freeze wherever he was, locked in place for a few minutes or so. Then he'd blink back in and there'd be food and whatever in the middle of the room, and he'd hear the footsteps moving away. Other than that . . . nothing. Which meant there wasn't much else to do but count splinters and get tangled up inside his own head.

He knew he should be trying to contact Strike and the others, knew he should be trying to find a way home, but some piece of him kept wondering whether Sky-watch was really home anymore. What was to say they even wanted him back? From what he could tell by look-ing out the windows, the cabin was part of a ramshackle, closed-down resort. He wasn't underground, wasn't in a warded temple, which meant Strike should be able to lock onto him for a 'port if he wanted.

He hadn't bothered.

That left Rabbit with a hollow ache in his gut, a burn of resentment in his heart. He'd depended on the Night-keepers for magic and family and they'd shut him out. But someone else was offering to fill the gap. So the next time Rabbit heard the crunch of approaching foot-steps, he shouted, "Don't freeze me, okay? I want to talk to Iago."

The world blinked out. When it blinked back in, he found himself standing just inside the door of another, larger cabin. His brain sent him three snapshots immedi-ately: the first was of Iago, standing opposite him in gray ceremonial robes; the second was of nine stone skulls arranged in a circle, facing a pale green ceremonial bowl; and the third was the sight of Myrinne, tied to a chair in the corner. Her ankles were bound to the chair legs, her wrists trussed behind her back, and she was limp. Unconscious, or worse.

Rage hammered through Rabbit, slapping aside any thought of family, magic, or working with Iago. He lunged for her, shouting, "Myrinne!"

And found himself hanging in midair.

"Don't be an idiot," Iago said. He raised his voice and called, "Desiree? I think we're ready for you now."

Cursing, Rabbit twisted, finding that he could move some within the force that held him aloft. His muscles strained as he fought to get free, fought to get to My-rinne. "Let her go, you bastard!"

The door opened behind Iago and a tall, exotic-looking

woman stepped inside, wearing a long, sleek leather coat and high boots. Her red-toned hair was pulled back from her face, and her perfectly made-up eyes were pale hazel, nearly inhuman.

"No!" he shouted when she started toward him, screaming again when she went straight past and reached for Myrinne.

"Shut it, twerp," Desiree said. Reaching inside her coat, she produced the ceremonial knife Iago had taken from Rabbit back in New Orleans. "Head and heart, or just bleed her out?" she asked Iago with zero emotion, like she was talking about squashing a bug.

"Head and heart." Iago nudged one of the carved skulls more precisely into alignment along the ceremonial circle. "We'll need all the juice we can get." He fixed Rabbit with a look. "Unless you're interested in doing some magic?" He gestured at the green bowl in the center of the circle, which had taken on a faint glow. "This is the bowl of Cabrakan, the earthquake god, and I have need of his services."

"Fuck you!" Rabbit lashed out at him, threw fire, then screamed when the flames bounced off the field surrounding him, burning his clothes and skin. Twisting against the invisible bonds, he howled as Desiree licked the edge of the knife, blooding herself.

Then Iago snapped his fingers and Myrinne awakened.

She blinked a few times, then tugged halfheartedly against the bonds like she already knew they were there. Then she saw Desiree and her eyes went wide and scared. Pulling harder, yanking at the ropes, she strained away from Desiree and the knife. She managed to skid her chair a few inches across the floor, then bumped into a wall. "Don't," she whispered, voice cracking. "Please don't."

But the cool-eyed woman advanced, taking it slow, drawing out the suspense—and the pleasure.

"For gods' sake, listen to her," Rabbit shouted. "Don't do this!"

Myrinne's head whipped around and she focused on him, her mouth dropping open in surprise, her eyes lighting with hope, then fear when she saw him hanging in midair. "Help me!" she screamed, straining toward him, her eyes glazed with terror. "Rabbit, help me!"

She'd remembered his name. That wasn't the most important thing just then, not by a long shot, but it mattered.

"No!" he shouted when Desiree lifted the blade and cut Myrinne's shirt away, then sliced her bra and parted the clothing to bare her torso for the first cut, the most important one. The magic worked best if the cut was a single slice just below the ribs, tracing their line and cutting through the diaphragm so the victim couldn't breathe, so she'd already be dying even as she watched her beating heart be torn from her chest.

Rabbit felt something rip inside him, as though it were *his* heart being cut out. "Okay!" he screamed as the ceremonial knife began its descent. "Okay, I'll do it. Whatever you want, I'll do it!"

"Hold," Iago rapped out.

Desiree didn't respond right away, taking a moment to carve a shallow slice in Myrinne's flesh, tracing a line where the real cut would've gone.

Iago snapped, "Damn it, woman, I said *hold*!"

Myrinne was sobbing—broken, hollow sounds that reached inside Rabbit and twisted his soul. Blood tracked down her belly, flirted with her tattooed navel, and soaked into the waistband of her jeans, flowing more with each sob.

Iago flicked his fingers, and the field surrounding Rabbit disappeared. Gravity took over and he fell with a shout, splatting inelegantly on the floorboards, face-first. He lay there for a second, gasping for breath, then struggled to his feet and stood, swaying. "Son of a bitch."

He wanted to rage, wanted to puke, wanted to wake up and be back at Skywatch and have it all be a bad dream. But it was far too real as Iago waved him into the center of the room.

The moment he crossed the skull-drawn circle, fire roared to life in the carved skulls, shooting several feet into the air and heating Rabbit's already scorched skin, making him want to scream with the pain, with the power. The magic was inside him, called by anger, beat-

ing at him, begging to be set free. But alongside the
familiar Nightkeeper fire was another power, a quiver at
the edge of his senses that tempted him, telling him that
all he had to do was let it inside and he would rule, he
would command.

Myrinne shouted his name on a broken sob, but he
hardly heard her, could hardly hear anything but Iago's
voice as the mage began to chant, starting down low and
bringing it up, calling the strange magic in words Rabbit
didn't understand but somehow did, as though they were
cousin to the old language he knew.

"Here." Desiree held out the carved obsidian knife
Iago had stolen from him in New Orleans. "You know
what to do."

And he did, though he couldn't have said how, only
that the compulsion ran through his veins like liquid fire
as he bared both forearms and began the ritual.

Rabbit had started the day a Nightkeeper. He would
end it something else entirely.

The ATM cave site looked the same as it had weeks
earlier. The vegetation was still vibrantly green, the parrots and howler monkeys were still doing their thing high
above, and the pool outside the cave still flowed slowly,
collecting in a swirl and then moving on, deeper into the
ceremonial cave system.

Nothing was different. Yet to Alexis, *everything* was
different.

She felt strange inside her own skin, as though her
bones had shifted and realigned while she'd slept. Nate
was different too. He seemed bigger and tougher, staying
close behind as they worked their way down to the pool,
shouldered their knapsacks, and started to wade, then
swim. The routine was the same, but the man had
changed.

He wore an eccentric now.

Her surprise that the king had offered him a second
adviser's position had been nothing compared to her
shock when Nate had actually accepted. He hadn't
looked nearly as thrilled as his *winikin*, but still. He'd

accepted, and wore the eccentric beneath his shirt and Kevlar, next to his medallion.

It shouldn't have made a difference that the position put them back on par, that it gave him equal weight in the adviser's council. But it mattered, and if that made her the small-minded, position-loving snob he'd called her on more than one occasion, then she owned it. The promotion—or maybe something else?—had him carrying himself bigger, and had his power revving just below the surface, so it sparked along her nerve endings, reminding her that she might not need sex with him to touch the goddess's magic, but that didn't mean she hadn't enjoyed the sex, didn't think about it. Didn't dream about it.

"That's different," he said from behind her, startling her.

For a second she thought he was talking about her dreams, which had stopped feeling like they were happening to other people, becoming just the two of them, alone together as they were now. Then she glanced back and saw him treading water and looking up to where the cave roof arched overhead. A huge crack ran with width of the cave, and several raw stumps showed where stalactites had broken loose and fallen.

She surveyed the damage. "Looks like it's holding well enough."

He nodded, but stayed pensive. "Hope nothing collapsed farther in."

"We'll deal with that if and when it happens. Let's keep going." Like there had ever been a question of turning back. If there was any hope that their ancestors had hidden a library beyond the submerged tunnels, then they needed to go after it, no matter what. The Nightkeepers were struggling too much, needed the knowledge too badly.

They worked their way onto dry land and continued onward from arcade to arcade, past the sacrificial relics and skeletons to where the realm of the modern researchers ended and that of the Nightkeepers began. They rearranged their packs, and donned their headlamps and masks, acting in tandem even though the air jarred with faint tension between them, partners slightly out of step with each other. Once Alexis was ready, she gave a quick thumbs-up and jumped in first, with Nate splashing down behind her a moment later.

She was only maybe a yard or two down the tunnel when the jangle she'd thought was tension grew to a rumble, then a roar.

Pressure slammed into her from all sides, forcing the air from her lungs, and she scrambled to keep hold of her pony bottle even as she turned to retreat. But Nate was blocking the way, urging her on, so she kept going, swimming deeper into the cave system as the water began to boil, then shake. Only it wasn't the water shaking, she realized a heartbeat later. The rocks around them were trembling, and the tunnel itself.

Earthquake!

CHAPTER TWENTY

Panicked, Alexis kicked for all she was worth, but up and down had gotten scrambled in her brain. She couldn't see, couldn't tell where anything was, where she should be going as the water swept her along. Then a thick stone column appeared out of nowhere, inches from her face. Screaming bubbles, she backpedaled, but Nate ran into her from behind and the world shifted hard. She slammed into the stalagmite and saw stars.

She heard Nate shout her name through bubbles and water. Then he was there, grabbing her, hanging on to her as the world went mad around them.

Up was down and down up. Something slammed into her upper arm and she gasped with pain, only then realizing that they weren't underwater anymore, that Nate was dragging her out of the temple pool, onto the narrow stone shelf, which heaved and plunged with the temblor. They were both working by feel; her headlamp and knapsack were gone.

"Hang on!" He pushed her away from the water and she bumped into a wall. Scrabbling with her fingers, she tried to find something to grab on to, some sort of anchor against the mad pitch of the surface beneath her. She found an edge, a handhold, and latched on, only then realizing that it was the stone altar, that they were on the wider platform at the short end of the narrow room. But the platform didn't seem as wide as it should have; water touched her toes, then her ankles.

"Nate!" she cried. "The water's rising!"

The earthquake faded, quieting the rumbling roar. Which was worse, in a way, because then there was silence, broken only by the sound of water trickling nearby.

Nate didn't answer.

She strained toward the pool, screaming, "Nate!"

There was a splash in answer, then his voice. "Here. I'm here." Coughing, he dragged himself up onto the platform—she tracked his movement by the slap of displaced water and the racking coughs, which echoed in the darkened stone chamber. "Sorry I scared you." Breathing hard, he joined her on the narrow ledge. "Come on." He took her hand and tugged. "Water's rising. We should get higher."

Together they climbed up onto the carved throne. As Alexis huddled against Nate's solid bulk, she couldn't help thinking that the throne had probably doubled as a sacrificial altar. Was that the end that awaited them?

Fear reached up to grab her by the throat, thinning her breath in her lungs. The water noise was increasing by the moment, going from a trickle to a steady stream, warning that they weren't safe yet. Far from it.

"The quake must've broken through to another waterway higher up than this one," Nate said, his voice a painful-sounding rasp. He shoved something into her hand. "Take this."

It was one of the flashlights. Relieved, Alexis fumbled it on. When the cone of yellow-white light sprang to life, she turned it toward Nate. He was sopping wet and bleeding from a cut above one eye. He'd lost his goggles but somehow kept his headlamp; it sagged down over one of his ears and had a cracked lens, and gods only knew whether it still worked. A huge rip cut across his Kevlar vest, probably where he'd been bashed into the rocks as she had been, and the tear drove home the fact that they'd likely both be dead if they hadn't been wearing their vests. Which was a hell of a thought. "Nice job hanging on to your knapsack," she said, nodding at the sodden lump.

He rummaged through it for a second. "Actually, I think this one's yours; it banged into me and I grabbed on. Same difference, though. Flashlight, satellite phone that won't do jack underground, weapons, and . . . water?" He pulled out a bottle of springwater and sent her a disgusted look, then pointedly glanced down below, where the water level was halfway up the carved throne and rising. "What, you thought we'd run out or something?"

She sniffed. "You want to drink out of a river in a foreign country and get parasites, go ahead. I'd rather bring my own."

"I don't know about you, but I think I already swallowed a couple of gallons, thanks."

She exhaled. "Okay, fine. It was stupid; I get it. Let's move on."

"Not stupid." He touched her cheek, her chin, his fingers warm despite the chill of the water and the soggy air. "Very you."

She wasn't sure how to take that, didn't trust the skirr of warmth that ran up her arm at the contact, or the contemplative look in his eyes. A piece of her said that if he was being nice to her now, when all they'd done was bicker or avoid each other for the past several days, that meant he didn't think they had a chance. Her voice was low and shaky when she said, "The tunnel collapsed, didn't it? There's no way out."

"I'll have to go back under and see," he said. Then, when she just kept looking at him, he nodded. "Yeah. I think so."

"The map didn't show another exit."

"Doesn't mean there isn't one." But his optimism was false and forced, and after a moment he let his hand fall away from her face and drew a deep breath. "I'm going back down. If nothing else, I think I know where I dropped my pony bottle." Not that there was any guarantee it'd still be where he'd left it, they both knew.

"There could be aftershocks."

"Probably will be," he agreed, but didn't say anything else, because that didn't change the situation.

Alexis turned her flashlight out over the gallery. The

beam showed that the water was most of the way to the top of the throne, with more streaming in every second, coming from a big split in the ceiling about halfway down the wall. It must've been a trick of the light that made the carved figures look as if they too were staring up at the cracked spot.

"Take this." She held the flashlight out to Nate. "You'll need it to check the tunnel entrances."

"It's water-resistant, not waterproof," he reminded her. "Might not survive." He didn't correct her use of the word "entrances," plural, because they both knew their best chance of making it out was getting into the library that—hypothetically, anyway—led off the dead-end loop, and hoping to hell it had a set of stairs leading out.

"We'll have to chance it," she said to both points, though the idea of being without light brought a serious shiver, as did the idea of swimming into the booby-trapped tunnel. "Besides, fireballs aren't the best light source, but they're better than nothing."

Rueful awareness flickered in his eyes. "Fireball. Shit." They'd both forgotten about the magic during the quake. A barrier spell would've gone a long way toward blunting its impact.

"We've only been practicing half a year." She lifted her shoulder in a half shrug. "It's not always going to come naturally." Which was an understatement. Even with the goddess's power, her magic tended to feel awkward and unnatural.

For that matter, where had the goddess been during the earthquake? she wondered. There had been no flash of gold and rainbows, no impulse to protect herself from the danger. Yet when she sent her senses to the back of her skull, she could feel the connection, alive and well. Which meant either the goddess hadn't thought she was in true danger . . . or she'd wanted the danger.

"Drowning," she said softly, looking around the chamber once again, this time seeing how similar it was to the sacrificial chamber beneath Chichén Itzá, not in size or shape, but in essence, and in the rising water. "The goddess didn't let us drown before. Maybe this is the same thing. Maybe she wants me—or us—to have another near-death experience."

Nate shot her a look. "You willing to bet on the 'near' part?"

She held his eyes for a moment, then shook her head. "No."

He flicked the switch on his headlamp a couple of times, but the small blub was dead, forcing him to take the flashlight. "I'll be right back."

She wanted to tell him to be careful, wanted to say . . . hell, she didn't know what she wanted to say, only that she wished so many things had been different between them, wished they'd been the people—the couple—the gods had meant for them to be. But none of those things really mattered just then, so she simply said, "Good luck."

He nodded as though she'd said all those other things instead. "Yeah." Then he was gone, slipping over the edge of the throne and wading across the short platform. He paused and looked back, and she raised a hand to give him a little finger wave.

Then he was gone, slipping into the water, leaving her alone.

She saw the light move down and away, diffusing in the murky water, which had gone nearly opaque from stirred-up silt. Soon the water glowed faintly, lit from beneath, but it was impossible for her to tell precisely where the light was coming from. Had the glow been still for too long? She didn't know, told herself not to panic. Not yet, anyway.

A hint of motion drew her attention upward. The faint illumination just barely lit the carved figures of the serpent and the rainbow on the arching ceiling, and the rippling of the water made the figures seem to move. Or was that for real? The air whispered of magic, and the connection at the back of her brain kindled a faint rainbow glow. "What do you want me to see?" she whispered. "I don't understand."

There was no answer in the trickle of water, no sign of success or failure from down below. Needing to do something, anything, Alexis spoke the necessary words and jacked into the barrier's power, finding it quickly in the holy place. Then, holding her palms cupped together, she called a small fireball.

It appeared immediately, and in the multicolored light she saw that the movement had been an illusion, that the serpent shape of Kulkulkan and the arching rainbow remained where they had been before. Or were they? She frowned, trying to decide if the serpent's head had moved closer to the crack that was letting in the water from above. No, she decided. It was her imagination. Wishful thinking that the carvings meant something, that the power of the feathered serpent Kulkulkan, wielded by her king and queen, was somehow meant to be joined with the goddess's rainbow, that together they'd be strong enough to fight Iago and the sons of Camazotz when the vernal equinox arrived. *Because if that's not the case,* she thought with a flare of anger, *then we're shit out of luck.*

She'd been raised to succeed, not fail. But what if the balance between success and failure wasn't in her hands anymore? What if it was up to the gods, or fate, or destiny?

"Then it seriously sucks," she said aloud, hearing her words echo in the chamber and thinking maybe she understood part of where Nate had been coming from all along.

She hadn't minded following fate's path up until now, because it'd pretty much led her where she'd wanted to go. She'd wanted power and position, had wanted to feel like she was part of something important. Finding out she was a Nightkeeper had more than fulfilled those needs, as had the training, and the way the magi had come together as a team during the fall equinox battle. But ever since then things had been different, seeming slightly skewed from where they'd been before. Or maybe she was the one who'd been changed, both by her experiences in battle and the failure of her relationship with Nate. She'd always thought it should've worked, *would've* worked if he could've been more flexible. She'd put the failure on him; he'd been the one to break it off, after all, and he'd been the one unable to put into words what hadn't been working for him.

Now, as the water crested over the top of the altar and wet her already sodden clothing, and her fist-size rainbow fireball cast colors on the walls of the ceremonial chamber, she had to wonder whether she was the one who hadn't tried hard enough. After so many failures with men like Nate—powerful and charismatic, big and strong enough to make her feel feminine, though not weak—maybe she'd been too ready to hide her feelings behind fate and destiny rather than claiming the emotions for herself. Maybe if she'd let him know how she'd felt about him as a person, rather than as a Nightkeeper or a stepping-stone to more power, he wouldn't have bailed so quickly.

Or maybe not, said her practical self, the part of her that'd lived through too many breakups to think this one had been any different. *Most likely he's exactly what he seems, thinks exactly what he says and says what he thinks.* Which was true enough. Nate was a guy's guy, and not particularly subtle on the best of days. Or was that her seeing him through a lens crafted by the other men, the ones who'd thought she was good enough for a fun time, but not forever?

"Goddess help me to know what's right," she whispered, cupping the rainbow close to her heart and realizing that for the first time in a long time—maybe forever—she didn't know what defined success.

Normally, Izzy would've told her what was right, because that was a *winikin*'s job. But how could a *winikin* know the will of the gods better than a Godkeeper? She couldn't, that was the answer, which meant the Godkeeper needed to look inside herself for the answer. Unfortunately, when Alexis did that, she saw nothing but a blank spot where certainty used to be, which left her feeling adrift, and so alone. Then the water moved in the center of the chamber, swirling around the few stalagmites still visible above the rising tide. The light brightened at that spot, and bubbles rose in a furious exhale as Nate kicked upward and broke the surface, holding not one, but both of the pony bottles aloft. "Found them!"

Finally some good news. "Way to go!" Alexis called, her words echoing in the filling chamber. "Do they both work?"

"Yep. The flashlight survived its dunking too, which is a bonus." He swam toward her, creating ripples in the water that trailed after him, turning to colors in the light from her fireball. He'd ditched the broken headlamp and held the flashlight in one hand, the air canisters in the other.

When he reached the altar, though, he didn't climb up to sit with her. He stayed in the water, his expression going grim when he said, "The main tunnel is completely blocked, as is the left-hand side of the loop."

Which, of course, was the side that didn't have the death glyph on it. Granted, that didn't mean there weren't booby traps, but still. She shivered involuntarily. "That leaves us with a lovely choice between braving the possible booby traps or sitting here until we run out of air and croak. Oh, joy."

There was no real need for discussion. Of course they were forging onward—first because there wasn't a better option, and second because they'd come to do a job. The earthquake hadn't changed that. So she extinguished her fireball and secured her bedraggled knapsack, knowing that the satellite phone and autopistol could wind up being vital . . . or useless. There was no way of knowing what waited for them up ahead.

Forcing herself to scoot to the edge of the throne, she dropped her legs into the rising water, wincing at the clammy chill. To her surprise, Nate stood on the ledge and moved between her knees, setting the flashlight and pony bottles aside so he could bracket her with his arms braced on the edge of the throne, one on either side of her. He was cold and wet, but his eyes were steady and kind, which sent a ripple of nerves through her, straight to her core, because Nate could be many things, but he was rarely kind.

If he was being sweet, he thought they were in deep shit.

"No mushy stuff," she said, ducking under his arm

and dropping down into the water, dragging the knapsack behind her. "Let's get going."

It wasn't until he'd nodded and passed her one of the pony bottles, and they were both sinking down in the water and heading for the right-hand tunnel with Nate holding the flashlight and leading the way, that she realized she'd done it again, done exactly what she'd just been telling herself she needed to avoid. She'd hidden a moment of emotion behind necessity, behind practicality. No wonder Nate didn't want to be around her anymore. She treated him like a convenience. Or was that yet another way for her to convince herself there was a chance for the two of them? she wondered as she kicked after him. How many rejections would it take her to figure out that it just wasn't happening for them?

Maybe at least one more, came the answer from deep inside her. Then Nate was passing into the mouth of the tunnel and she wasn't thinking about anything except the chill that gripped her as she followed and the rock walls closed in on her. They were ridged, natural and uncarved, like the tunnel that had led into the rectangular gallery, only narrower, closing in to within a foot of her on either side, meaning she had to cut down on her kicking strokes or risk banging rock. Up ahead she could see Nate reaching out and touching the walls, feeling his way along, partly to propel himself, partly to check for whatever had earned the death glyph on the map.

Nerves growing by the moment, she took too many puffs off the pony bottle and the world started to spin. She made herself slow down, calm down. There had been no sign of danger. Maybe the glyph had been a metaphor.

Nate swam on, breathing regularly from his pony bottle, though the bubble stream was growing thinner with each breath. Alexis had a feeling her bottle was running low, as well.

Then Nate stopped dead, tensing. After a moment he looked back at her and shook his head, then waved her onward and started swimming, moving fast now, tossing his empty pony bottle as he went. When she passed the spot where he'd stopped, her stomach knotted on a hard surge of disappointment at the sight of a narrow groove that cut all the way around the tunnel. It wasn't the channel that was bad news, though; it was the sight of the stone blade that had moved along the track to bury itself in the tunnel floor, and the silt-shadow of old bones beneath.

The good news was that Nate hadn't triggered the trap. The bad news was that they weren't the first to swim the tunnel.

Worse, when she took her next hit of air, she got almost nothing from the canister. Sucking hard, she took what she could, and kicked along after Nate, following the dimming flashlight beam.

They passed two more blade traps; both were triggered, though neither held bones. She cared less for them, though, than the building desperation as her lungs tightened with the need to breathe. Heart pounding, she started kicking harder as panic gathered. Then something grabbed her from the side and she nearly screamed out the last of her air. She didn't, though, and she struggled only momentarily before she forced herself to be still, knowing it was Nate.

A look showed that he was in a wider tunnel leading off the one they'd been in. The walls of the new tunnel were curved, lined with stone tiles that might have been carved and painted at one point in the past, but had been worn smooth and featureless by centuries—maybe millennia—of moving water. Magic crinkled across her skin, indicating that he'd unsealed the passageway. That was all she had time to notice, though, because he grabbed her hand and started kicking. She swam beside him, so they were linked and moving together, neither one leaving the other behind. Then, blessedly, she saw a shimmer up ahead, as the weakening flashlight beam bounced off an interface where water gave way to air.

Shouting a stream of bubbles, she and Nate kicked for the pocket, breaking the surface together and inhaling, gasping, choking on air gone foul with time and lack of good circulation. They clung to each other for a moment, just held on as relief crested and ebbed, and she began to believe they weren't dead. Not yet, anyway.

Unfortunately, that was the sum total of the good news, she saw as soon as Nate lifted the flashlight and panned the space they'd come to.

A set of stairs rose up from the water, four or five treads leading to a raised platform. The sides of the dais were carved with Mayan figures, not acting out scenes of battle or sport this time, but rather scenes of study, with men and women bent over codices and stretching up to work on carved stelae. At the top and bottom of each panel ran a repeating motif, a glyph of a hand holding a parrot-feather quill. It was the same mark Jade wore on her forearm: the scribe's mark, the mark of a librarian and spell caster. Which was the good news.

The bad news was that the platform looked empty from their vantage point.

"Gods damn it," Nate said. "Someone beat us here."

Alexis felt his frustration echo, felt her own rise to match. "Iago, maybe?"

"That'd explain why he's so much more advanced than we are." His voice was hollow and disgusted. Discouraged. Paddling to the start of the stairs, he climbed out of the water, then reached a hand back to help her up. "Come on. Let's see if the bastard left us anything."

Left unspoken was the other question, equally important if not more so: *Let's see if there's a way out.*

When they reached the top of the staircase, though, Nate muttered a low curse. The space had been stripped clean; hell, it even looked like Iago—assuming it'd been him—had swept on his way out. There was no evidence of a doorway, either. The walls were seamless painted murals on three sides, with the fourth open to the water, but no matter how hard they pressed or whispered the *"pasaj och"* spell, no secret passages revealed themselves.

"It's a dead end," Alexis said finally, trying hard not to let her voice shake.

"In more ways than one," Nate said, his eyes hard with anger. "Gods *damn* it. I'm sick of being two steps behind these bastards." He spun away and paced the edge of the platform, wheezing a little as the air in the closed-off space started to thin.

Legs giving out under the weight of the fear she'd
held off for as long as she was able, Alexis leaned back
against the painted wall and slid down until she was sitting
on the cool stone floor with her knees to her chest, her
body curled up in a protective ball. She wanted to ask
what they were going to do next, but didn't because she
figured his answer would be the same as hers: *I don't
know.*

"We could probably make it back to the other chamber on a single breath if we swim fast," she said.

But Nate shook his head. "For all we know, the chamber could be full up by now. At least here it doesn't
look like the water's rising. We should—" He broke off,
freezing midpace. "The chamber could be full up," he
repeated.

"Yes. And?"

"Where's the pressure going?"

"The—Oh, right," she said, remembering what little
she knew of fluid dynamics, most've which had come
from hanging out at the marina. "The incoming water is
displacing air, which has to be going somewhere, or the
water would stop flowing into the chamber because of
back pressure." She thought for a moment, then shook
her head. "You're right that there's got to be an outflow.
But we're way bigger than air molecules. Nothing says
we'd be able to get through."

"Maybe. Maybe not." He held out a hand, kindling a
small fireball. "The airhole would be a structural weak
spot, right?"

"You want us to blast our way out?"

"Would you rather stay here?"

"Hell, no." Wary hope kindling in her chest, Alexis
pushed herself to her feet and crossed to him. As she
approached, he let the fireball wink out. She stopped
very close to him and looked up into his eyes, which
were dark in the fading flashlight beam. "We're betting
on there being some air left."

"You see a better option?" he asked, his words a soft
touch of breath on her upturned face.

She shook her head. "No. I definitely think we should

try it, but I was wondering . . . what about a barrier spell?"

"To protect us after we let rip with the fireballs? Definitely."

"Well, that. But I was thinking more along the lines of casting one all the way around our bodies and seeing if it acts like a dry suit, keeping the water away from us and trapping a layer of air. It'd have to be a thin layer so we still fit through the tunnel, but it might hold enough oxygen to buy us time." Grim logic said they'd be out of air when they reached the cavern. If the space was completely submerged, they wouldn't even have a chance to try the underwater-fireballing theory.

"A shield like that would be a power drain," Nate said, but it was more of a comment than a real argument. He tipped his head in acknowledgment. "I think it's worth a shot."

They descended the short staircase side by side, and Nate kept a protective hand on the small of her back. Alexis wanted to lean into the touch, into the man, but she didn't because it wasn't the right time. She did, however, make an inner vow: *If we get out of here, I'm going to show him that I cared—and I still care—about him as a man, not just a mage or a mate.*

As if she'd spoken the thought aloud, he stopped and turned at the bottom of the stairs, and took her hand in his so their sacrificial scars lined up like a promise. Then he leaned in and touched his lips to hers. "For luck."

"For luck," she whispered when he drew back.

He palmed his ceremonial knife from his weapons belt, which had been damaged in the quake maelstrom, and cut his palm, then offered her the knife because she'd lost her belt altogether. She cut a groove along the raised ridge of flesh, welcoming the bite of pain because it meant that she was still alive, still fighting. Then she handed the knife back, and they both jacked in and called on their warriors' shield magic.

Alexis's shield appeared in a flash of color and a brilliant burst of power from the base of her skull. Nate stumbled back in surprise, and would've fallen into the water if she hadn't reached out and grabbed him. When they touched, the rainbow spread from her to him and back, and the shield spell strengthened far beyond where she'd been able to get it previously. *Thank you, goddess,* she thought, relieved by the help, and by the evidence that Ixchel hadn't deserted her entirely.

Sending her consciousness into the magic, Alexis shaped it around her body, then around Nate's, leaving a three-inch space between the shield and his skin, weaving the protective magic into a different form than it normally held, one with texture and flexibility. Soon their bodies were surrounded with a pulsating glow that was all colors and none of them at once, buoying Alexis with magic and light. But alongside the thrill of power was the knowledge that this was a one-shot deal, and they didn't have a plan B. *Please, gods, help us,* she thought, aiming the prayer toward the back of her skull.

Then she nodded. "Okay. Let's do this."

They dropped into the water together, submerged together, and stared into each other's eyes as they each took a breath inside their force-field dry suits. Alexis had to make herself inhale, as her eyes were telling her brain that she was completely underwater. But when she breathed, she got a lungful of the old, stale air trapped within the skin-shield. It would have to be enough.

Knowing they were already running out of time before they even began, they turned and kicked for the tunnel, moving fast. Nate pulled ahead, and Alexis cursed inwardly when that meant she had to fight the turbulence from his powerful kicks. Then she moved up and found a slipstream of sorts, and the going got easier. They flashed along the wider, smoother tunnel, then turned into the narrow half loop, which was dark and claustrophobic in comparison. The flashlight must've died for good, because Nate let it fall as he swam, and Alexis felt a jump in the barrier flow as he jacked in another level deeper and called up a fireball. The light kindled to life up ahead, boiling the water around it and sending a cloud of steam bubbles back along the tunnel. They popped when they hit the edges of Alexis's shield spell. For a moment she wondered whether they might help freshen the increasingly stale air inside her protective layer. They didn't, though, killing her quick thought of somehow using fireballs to boil water and generate an air pocket. It might be possible in theory, but they didn't have time to figure out the trick.

Then Nate's trajectory suddenly changed and he was shooting up and away. Alexis had half a second to think that the trip out had been so much faster than the one in; then she was following him and trying not to put too much stock into the hope that there would be air left up above.

When she saw his fire magic glitter off the interface between water and air, she started crying with relief.

The second her head broke the surface, she let go of the shield magic, gasping as the water rushed in on her, soaking her and chilling her in a slap that proved more invigorating than uncomfortable. Treading to keep her head in the air pocket, she squinted against the red burn of Nightkeeper fire. The situation wasn't good; their heads were nearly touching the carved ceiling of the long, narrow temple room, and water was still coming in from the cracked place near where the dragon's snout touched the rainbow in the overhead mural.

Wait a second, she thought. *What?* She was positive the carved entities hadn't been touching before; they'd been several feet away from the crack. She blinked and looked again, but the carvings didn't change. The images of Ixchel and Kulkulkan were touching each other, pointing to the crack. She was positive they'd moved somehow, but why?

Then she remembered the torches from her vision, and how the smoke had moved to a narrow fissure in the wall, halfway down the long side.

"That's it," she said, suddenly understanding. She pointed to the crack where the water was flowing in. "That's where we need to hit the wall. It's the weak spot."

Nate looked seriously dubious. "Sure, it's a weak spot, but there's nothing to indicate that there's air on the other side. The water could be coming from a fully submerged tunnel." But he swam to the spot and put his face near the crack, trying to hear or feel some sort of breeze that might suggest the air was going out the same way the water was coming in. After a long moment he shook his head. "I don't know. I think we should keep looking."

The top of Alexis's head nudged the ceiling as the water continued to rise. She tilted her chin up so she could breathe, and said, "Trust me. That's the spot."

His eyes bored into her, and for a second she thought he was going to refuse. In the end, though, he nodded. "If you're sure." He didn't ask how or why she knew; she had a feeling he didn't want to know. He swam toward her. "Let's get in the corner over by the throne. Remember, put your shield up right after we launch."

"Count on it."

Lit by his low-grade fireball, they swam to the short end of the room, where they found that they could stand on the altar itself and keep above water—for the moment, anyway. The window of opportunity was closing fast. In order to both stand on the throne they had to crowd close together, her back to his front, in a position that fit too well as far as Alexis was concerned, one that felt safe and sane, and revved her nerves, not just at what they were about to attempt, but also what she'd vowed to do if they made it out of there alive: try once more, this time letting him know that she wanted him for who he was, not just for the power they could make together.

"Ready?" he asked, his voice a low growl, his lips very near her ear.

"One more thing," she said quickly, as the water rose to her mouth. "When you shield, try to take as much of the air around your head as you can. Just in case."

He nodded. "Will do."

They didn't need to clarify what the "in case" would be, nor would it help to mention that if their fireballs broke through the weak spot and the water came rushing in, even the shields would buy them only so much time to enlarge the hole if necessary, swim through, and find another air pocket and a way out.

"Okay," she said, though he hadn't asked, "I'm

ready." She wanted to hold on to him, wanted to kiss him good-bye, wanted to ask him if he thought there would ever be a right time for them. But in the end she didn't do any of those things. She just leaned back a little, drawing strength from his strength, and readied her magic, stretching out her bleeding right palm and calling on the goddess for help, for luck. She felt Nate's magic rev up, felt it touch her own, and felt the two twine together for a moment, somehow becoming more than their sum. Twin fireballs grew from the weeping cuts on her and Nate's outstretched right hands, growing larger and larger, spinning and spitting and beginning to heat, though the flames didn't burn their users.

Alexis dug down, felt him do the same, and the fireballs grew and changed from a source of light to one of destruction. She closed her eyes and envisioned the weak spot, envisioned the carved serpent and the rainbow fleeing away from the cracked spot. Her power peaked, and the fireball flared to life.

"Now!" he shouted.

The fireballs winged through the air and hit their target, and the world exploded.

CHAPTER TWENTY-ONE

Alexis ducked instinctively, though they'd both yanked up their shields, bubblelike around their heads. Seconds later Nate shouted something and dragged her below the water, crowding her close to the throne wall, shielding her with his body and his magic.

A shock wave slammed into them, compressing Alexis's lungs even through the shield. A freight-train roar of explosion thundered around her. She cried out inside her small sphere of air and clung to Nate, who was hanging on to her, keeping her secure, keeping her anchored. Debris pelted them, pinging off the magic, and she felt Nate flinch, wondered if something had gotten through.

In the aftermath of the shock wave there was a rush of water, colder than the liquid surrounding them, stirring up a current, a tide, as the water moved from one chamber to the next.

They'd done something, she realized. But had they done enough?

Before the water had even begun to settle, Nate kindled a small fireball and urged her into the current. They had to swim hard at first, then less so, as the chamber they were in filled fully with water. And although that had been the plan, Alexis's heart kicked when she saw the last thin stream of bubbles escape through the hole they'd made.

"Follow those bubbles!" she said, and felt Nate's fingers tighten on her hand, which he'd clasped and held fast, as though he never intended to let go. And though she knew he'd let go eventually, she let herself lean on the feeling as they kicked toward the gap that'd opened up in the rock wall.

Regret twisted at the sight of the carved stone blocks shattered by the attack. The temple had stood for more than a thousand years, only to fall to the ancestors of its makers. But necessity was necessity, so she spared only a glance back at the narrow room she'd dreamed of, seeing that the carvings of the serpent and the rainbow had disappeared. Then she kicked upward, following Nate's tug on her hand, and the red-hued glow he held clutched in his outstretched hand. Moments later he extinguished the fireball, because they didn't need it anymore.

Instead, they swam up toward daylight, and freedom.

Later that night, back at Skywatch, exhausted, sore, and dispirited from the day's events, Nate avoided his teammates, bummed a sandwich off Jox, and hid out in his parents' cottage. He got his laptop up and running, but couldn't bring himself to write. Instead he lay back on the sofa and stared at the hawk medallion he wore around his neck. The one that—according to Carlos— his father had entrusted to his *winikin* just hours before king Scarred-Jaguar led his Nightkeepers to attack the intersection.

The flat metal disk caught the light when Nate turned it from side to side, making the man turn to a hawk and back again. Or, if he stopped it halfway, there was a point where the image was both hawk and man.

It was a symbol of the bloodline, he knew. A family heirloom, nothing more and nothing less. But for a few seconds earlier that day, in the moment that he and Alexis had stood together on the carved altar and called their magic together, he could've sworn he'd felt the amulet respond. There had been a frisson of electricity, a jolting sense of change, of connection—there and gone so quickly he kept trying to tell himself he'd imagined it entirely. Only he hadn't. He was sure of that much.

"Probably something to do with that wonky shield

spell," he said aloud, trying to talk himself out of the crazy thoughts that kept trying to shove themselves inside his head—gamer's fantasies about magic amulets and the last-minute discovery of powers that could save the world. Thing was, this was reality, or at least a cock-eyed version thereof, where men could do magic and orgasm was a pathway to prayer. Was it really so unbelievable to think the amulet was more than a decoration?

"It was your imagination," he told himself for the fourth time in the past half hour, and forced himself to tuck the medallion back inside his shirt, next to the frigging adviser's eccentric that he'd tried to give back earlier, only to have Strike tell him to keep it for now.

Which, goddamn it, meant he owed Carlos fifty bucks, because he'd bet the old bugger that he'd never be the king's man, as his father had been.

Well, fuck that, he thought sourly, forcing himself back upright on the sofa with his feet on the floor, and trying to make his eyes focus on the laptop screen. He was just doing the last read-throughs on the storyboard before he e-mailed *VW6* off to Denjie for programming and shit. The story was as close to perfect as he could make it, and it was time to let the thing go. Maybe even time to end the whole series, because he wasn't sure there was more story to tell. Hera's past had been uncovered and resolved, her mate found, wedded, and bedded—though not in precisely that order. She didn't need the quests anymore.

And that was a hell of a thought.

Nate was scowling at the screen, wondering if maybe he should pull back on the whole happily-ever-after thing, when someone banged on the cottage door. Figuring it was Carlos, come to see if he needed anything—and to do some more gloating—Nate called, "Go away; I'm not in the mood."

The knock came a second time. For all of Carlos's faults, he was pretty good about fucking off when told to fuck off, suggesting that whatever he'd come to say was important. Hoping to hell that it wasn't, because he couldn't stand any more drama today, Nate pushed to his feet and headed for the door, hissing against the pull of countless bruises from the day's events.

Those small annoyances fled the second he swung open the door and saw Alexis standing there. In their place flared heat and want, and a sense of the inevitable.

She was wearing loose light blue yoga pants and a cropped sweatshirt two shades darker, in deference to the chill of the night air. Unlike her usual put-together outfits, which dared a guy to peel them away layer by layer, this one was easy access, two items, maybe a couple more if she was wearing panties and a bra. He was betting not, though, because he knew the outfit, knew it meant she was in the mood. Before, it'd been a signal, a sort of cosmic *don't bother prettying it up with speeches; I need to get off.* Now, however, though there was heat in her eyes; there was something else, as well. There was warmth.

"Help you?" he asked, which was about all he could get out through a throat gone suddenly dry.

The year before, her answer would've been something along the lines of a coy, "I think we can help each other," and it would've been accurate. But now she paused for a second, then said, "Can I come in?"

The question hung in the air, becoming everything. Before, they'd mostly used her rooms, or a spare bedroom elsewhere in the mansion. If he invited her inside his parents' cottage, things shifted to a new level, a new degree of importance. If he invited her in, they would have each other, Nate thought, using the safe euphemism when his conscious mind couldn't cheapen the act to sex, couldn't call it making love. But more, they would do it with their eyes open to each other's flaws and the ways they didn't fit.

He cleared his throat, and yearned. "Why now?"

Her lips turned up at the corners in a sad, self-aware smile. "Because for the first time in a long, long time, neither of us needs anything from the other. This would just be us together, because we want to be."

Which begged the question of whether he wanted to be with her, despite everything. And the answer, damn it all to hell, was a resounding, stupid-simple *yes.*

So he stepped back out of the doorway. "Come on in." He probably should've said something way smoother, but what smoothness he possessed seemed to have deserted him. She didn't seem to mind, though. Head high, she marched through, not looking at him. Her cheeks were flushed, her eyes bright with excitement and, he suspected, nerves.

Or maybe he was the one who was nervous, and he was projecting like hell, knowing that if they had sex now it'd skirt the line of making a commitment he didn't want. It was bad enough he'd wound up a royal adviser. He wasn't letting the gods pick his girlfriend—or worse, his wife. He refused to use the Nightkeeper words of "mate" or *"jun tan,"* because he was a guy first, a Nightkeeper second. Or so he liked to think. The way things kept happening around him, exactly as the gods seemed to have decreed, he had to wonder about that. Problem was, he didn't exactly have a decent out clause in his contract. Hell, he didn't even have a contract; it was all blood and ancestors and destiny and shit.

And none of that mattered now, really. He'd already let her inside.

She stopped in the middle of the main room and looked around, unspeaking. He couldn't read her body language or her expression, and suddenly he realized he cared more than he expected to what she thought about him all but living in his parents' old place.

"You'll make some changes," she said after a moment. "I see you as more of a black-and-chrome sort of guy."

That surprised a snort out of him. "That'd be my office back in Denver." He wasn't sure it suited him anymore, though. Wasn't sure what the hell suited him except the sight of her in his space, and that was far from a comforting thought. So he went for light. "What, you don't think shag carpeting is me?"

"Carpet can be replaced." Her eyes lit on the paintings, and the oversize medallion. Like him, she was drawn to that wall, crossing to stand very near the painting of the Mayan ruins seen from above. "The rest of this place suits you, though, or what I've seen of it. It's

practical and stripped down, and there's not much in the
way of family pictures or mementos, but there's a sense
of latent power and . . . an honesty, I guess." She shot
him a look. "I don't always like what you say, but I
know that if you say it, you mean it."

He didn't know how to respond to that, or how to
deal with the possessive clutch in his chest at the sight
of her standing in front of his bloodline symbol. *Yes*, a
thousand generations of his ancestors seemed to say,
she's for you. This is meant.

Because he couldn't deal with that just then, and
maybe because he wanted her to see, he waved toward
the bedroom door on the right and said, "Have a look
in the spare room."

He followed her, stood too close to her when she
paused at the threshold and breathed, "Oh." Just that
one word. *Oh.*

It still caught him the same way too. His old nursery,
preserved intact for nearly twenty-five years, telling him
that he'd come from somewhere, that he'd been loved.
That love was in the boxed photos stacked in the closet
too, though he didn't want to show them to her now,
couldn't bear to go through them again so soon.

He wanted to shy away from the snapshots of his parents and his infant self, taken here and there around
Skywatch and elsewhere, pictures of his parents with the
other magi, his father standing slightly apart from the
group, pictures of Nate with other babies and Nightkeeper
children. The images were difficult for him to look at,
knowing that everyone in them was dead except him,
and because he'd spent his entire life not caring about
the parents who hadn't cared enough to keep him. It
probably should've helped to know that they'd cared,
and cared fiercely. But somehow it was worse knowing
that he should've been with them, or, failing that, with
a *winikin*, growing up like Alexis had, pampered and
groomed, always having someone to tell him that he
could do better, that he could *be* better.

It was worse knowing he should've grown up thinking
he was important, when instead he'd been taught that
he was nothing, that he had to scrap to survive, steal

when he wanted a little extra, and defend himself every second of every day.

Alexis seemed to sense at least part of that, though. She took his hand, threaded their fingers together, and squeezed gently. "I'm here because of who you are in this lifetime, not who you might've been."

He turned to her then, and lifted their joined hands so he could kiss her knuckles, where a faint bruise darkened the skin. "And I let you in the door despite who you are in this lifetime, because even though I keep telling myself I want something—and someone—else, it keeps coming back around to you. To us."

Her eyes flashed at that and her jaw went a little hard, but then she shook her head ruefully. "There's that honesty again. Refreshing, if not always complimentary." Then her lips turned up and she tipped her face to his. "Kiss me before I remember that you annoy the shit out of me and start to wonder why I'm here."

"You're here *because* I annoy the shit out of you," he said, then obliged by touching his lips to hers chastely, letting the contact kindle warmth as he murmured against her mouth, "You're here because I won't pander to you like the boys down at the marina, and because you know that I won't make promises I can't deliver on. I might be a gamer, but I'm not a game player."

She was silent for a moment, then settled against him a little and said simply, "I'm here because there's nowhere else I'd rather be."

Nate would've said something glib in response, but the words jammed in his throat, backing up against the realization that the same was true of him.

Before, he'd resented the demands of a bloodline responsibility he'd never asked for, never sought. He'd wanted to be back in Denver, working the life he'd built for himself, the one that played by familiar rules, with familiar people. The life he was good at. Somewhere along the line, though, that'd changed. Denver seemed far away. He knew he could be there in a few hours, faster if he asked Strike for a 'port. But the city—and the life he'd lived there—had dimmed in his brain, his new life as a Nightkeeper seeming so much more important now.

Granted it *was* more important on a save-the-world scale. But now even on a smaller, more personal scale, he realized that he didn't want to be back in the city. He wanted to be where he was: in his parents' homey, outdated bungalow with the woman he'd never managed to convince himself to leave all the way. Which, in all honesty, wasn't fair to either of them.

"I'm sorry," he said, the apology coming out of nowhere, from deep inside him.

Nonsequitur though it might be, she seemed to get it, shaking her head. "Don't be. We move forward. Everything that happens from here on out, whether good or bad, is new. It's just you and me, guy and girl. Humans, for what it's worth."

Which was so not like her usual rhetoric that he drew back. "What happened to the whole 'time is cyclical, what has happened before, blah, blah'?"

She smiled, and this time it reached her eyes. "We're not our parents. We were raised human. I think we've got the right to claim something for our own, don't you? Well, I claim this, for as long as it lasts."

He saw the truth of it in her eyes, and tasted it on her lips when he dropped his head for a second kiss, this one longer and moister, and bringing more heat to the moment. When it ended, he glanced out the window to where stars shone over the Pueblo ruins at the back of the box canyon. "I can promise you until morning, at least."

He'd meant it partly as a joke, but her eyes were serious when she said, "That'll do for starters." Using their joined hands to tug him along, she urged him in the direction of the bedroom, then stalled. "Um. Will this be too weird for you?"

"You don't want to do it in my parents' bed? What are we, sixteen?" The laughter felt good, as did the rush of heat and joy as he reversed their positions, with him urging her along. "Don't worry. Carlos made some changes once I started hanging out here. That includes the mattresses and bedding." Along with a few personal items he didn't bother mentioning, because, having made the decision, he was done talking.

He got her inside the bedroom and left the lights off, so the space was softly lit by the illumination coming through the door from the main room. The bedroom was sparsely furnished and decorated, as were the other rooms, but with the same few deft touches of character and magic. Another of his father's paintings hung over the bed, this one of a green sea and an achingly blue sky, a helicopter's-eye view approaching a verdant island of sand and trees, and a limestone cliff with a Mayan ruin at the top. The domed silhouette marked it as one of the ancient celestial observatories, where Nightkeepers and Daykeepers alike had tracked the movements of the stars and used them to tell the future and the past.

A shimmer of that same mysticism walked across Nate's skin as he stripped his shirt over his head in one yank, then tossed the garment aside and took Alexis in his arms and kissed her, letting his body tell her what he didn't always get right with words.

In response, she pressed her hands to his chest, touching his medallion, which grew warm with their body heat as she leaned into the kiss, opening to him. And as the night waned and became a new day, he took her to bed and they became, perhaps for the first time, lovers.

CHAPTER TWENTY-TWO

It wasn't until Anna had been back in the glyph lab for a few days following her quick trip to Skywatch that she finally admitted, to herself at least, that the balancing act wasn't working. Not the way she was trying to pull it off, anyway.

It'd taken some serious crystal magic to jump-start her *itza'at* powers and get a peek inside Iago's cesspool of a brain. She didn't regret the magic, but she sure as hell could've done without the aftereffects, namely the fact that she'd been unable to close the lid on the visions once she'd called them. Granted, she'd known that could be the outcome. She just hadn't known how much being a full-fledged visionary would suck. Even now, sitting at her office desk, she was bombarded with flashes and fragments, images of things that might have happened or might yet happen, made worse by the very nature of her work because she was surrounded by artifacts that resonated with her power, showing her things she didn't need or want to see.

How did it help anybody for her to know that the tiny *chac-mool* figurine she used as a paperweight had been carved by a wizened old man with two front teeth? Or that the painted bark strip that hung on her wall in a museum-quality frame was a clever fake? She already knew it was a fake; it wouldn't have been on her wall otherwise, for chrissake.

Worse, those pointless little details existed as a background drone to larger flashes and full-fledged visions, emotionally charged moments that would—or already had—happened to the people she interacted with every day. It was exhausting to be lecturing on the celestial significance of the four staircases of the pyramid at Chichén Itzá, and suddenly learn—in excruciating detail—that the guy third from the left in the front row had started the day on the receiving end of a world-class blow job. It drove her crazy to get the change from her take-out lunch purchase and know that her cashier was about a week away from getting his heart broken, though it was a relief not to see anything worse in his future. Because that was the really sucky thing about being an *itza'at* seer. No matter what the seer did or said, the future visions always came true. Always.

It was one of the numerous reasons she hadn't wanted the sight, had tried to fight it for as long as she had. If she couldn't use the damn talent as a tool to make things better, why put up with it? If she could've had someone get inside her skull and rip the magic out of her cortex— or wherever the hell it lurked—she would've. Since that wasn't an option, she did the next best thing: She worked on rebuilding the mental blocks, piece by agonizing piece.

She was slumped down at her desk, staring at the yellow quartz effigy that had belonged to her mother, and generations of *itza'ats* before her, doing exactly that, when the phone rang. It wasn't much in the way of an interruption, though. She was tired and heartsore, worried about Lucius, stressed about the upcoming equinox, and hating that so much of her normal life had become a series of lies designed to cover up her life as a Nightkeeper.

Glancing at the caller ID, she found a small smile at seeing it was Dick. The pleasure was bittersweet, though; they'd taken a few days away together, had even flown the brightly colored kites she'd bought as a surprise. It had been lovely and romantic, and vaguely awkward. The therapist had said that the more they acted as though the love were there, the more actual love would follow. And maybe there was something to that, because ever since their getaway it'd felt less and less like an act and more like the real thing.

She picked up on the third ring. "Hey, hon. I was just thinking about you."

"Hey back. I was calling to see if we're still on for tonight."

"Definitely," Anna said, though for a second she couldn't remember their having any plans. Then she thought, *Right. Dinner out. Eight o'clock reservations.* The drain of setting the mental blocks was making her woozy and forgetful, she thought, and scribbled down a note reminding herself to eat something.

"And you're leaving the day after tomorrow for that guest lecture, right?"

Guilt pinched at the lie, but there was no way she could tell Dick that she was headed down to New Mexico to hook up with the brother he didn't know about, who would then teleport her and a dozen or so other psi-powered warriors down to southern Mexico, where they were going to fight like hell to hold the line between the earth and the underworld when a bunch of heavy hitters tried to come through and precipitate the end of days.

Yeah. So not going there.

"It's just an overnight," she said. "I'll be back the day after." Assuming, of course, that she survived the fight, Iago hadn't succeeded in opening the hellroad, and there was still a university for her to return to. And the fact that those assumptions didn't bother her as much as they used to was just another sign of how tired she was, how strung-out and stuck inside her own jumbled-up head.

"Meet me at the car around seven thirty?"

"Will do," Anna said. That had been another one of the therapist's ideas, for them to commute together, given that they were both going to the same place on a daily basis. And she had to admit that it was kind of nice riding in and out with him. It gave them a chance to chat—forced them to do so—twice a day.

"See you then. Love you." As usual, he hung up before she could respond in kind. It used to annoy her, because it seemed like he was winning by getting the last word. These days she wondered if he did it because he was afraid she wouldn't say the words back. He was trying. They both were.

"Love you," she said, even though he was no longer there.

Then she hung up the phone, ignored her scribbled note about a snack, and got back to work, knowing that her life would be a thousand times better once she killed the background drone. Problem was, blocks were the sort of thing she would've learned after her talent ceremony, when her mother and the other *itza'ats* would've instructed her on the proper use and control of her talent. Normally she would've had her talent ceremony during the cardinal day right after she hit puberty. Since that had coincided with her father's attack on the intersection, the ceremony had been postponed . . . and then never happened. She'd finally gotten her *itza'at*'s mark, twenty-four years later, when Strike had dragged her back into the world she'd left behind. But the talent hadn't come with training or enlightenment, had barely come with added power, thanks to the subconscious mental blocks her brain had thrown up to stop the nightmarish memories of the massacre, which she'd seen through the eyes of not just one, but hundreds of dying Nightkeepers.

"Focus," she said aloud, and forced herself to concentrate on the quartz effigy that she'd set in the middle of her blotter. According to the sketchy records Jade and Lucius had been able to find, an *itza'at* should be able to use her crystal to form a reversible block, one that could be kept in place on a day-to-day basis and lowered for a vision quest. In theory.

In practice, she wasn't getting very far.

Don't be such a girl, a familiar voice whispered at the back of her mind. The sound had her shooting straight up in her chair and looking around for a ghost, though she knew that was beyond stupid. He wasn't there, wasn't ever there. He was nothing more than a memory, and not even a good one, at that.

"Damn it," she muttered, hunkering down with her chin on the edge of her desk and glaring at the effigy.

Amazingly, the quartz seemed to shimmer for a second, then started to glow from within. Excitement tightened her skin as carefully, very carefully, she sent a tendril of mental magic toward the crystal, and—

The phone rang, snapping her concentration. "Gods *damn* it!" she snapped, annoyed with the caller for calling, beyond annoyed with herself for forgetting yet again to forward the phone to voice mail. Grabbing the handset, she snapped, "What?"

There was a pause; then Lucius said, "I think you should come back to Skywatch." His voice grated, as though he were forcing each of the words.

Anna's fingers tightened on the phone. "I'll be there the day after tomorrow for the equinox ceremony. Is that soon enough?"

"I . . . don't think so." His words trailed off to hissing silence.

She understood then, and the bottom fell out of her world. Heart hammering against her ribs, she said, "I'll be there as soon as I can. And Lucius?"

"Yes?" The word was barely a sigh.

"I'm sorry." This time she was the one who cut the connection, then dialed the main number at Skywatch. After ordering Jox to update Strike, and for the two of them to clear Lucius's rooms of any sharp objects and lock him the hell in, she called the airline and paid a fortune to move her tickets up two days. She snagged the last seat on a flight that left in ninety minutes, and called a taxi to pick her up.

She was in the air by seven. At nine she realized she'd stood Dick up for their date. At ten thirty, she called home to apologize, but there was no answer.

At midnight she stood with Strike and Leah, looking down at Lucius.

He lay curled on his side, clutching his bloody hand to his chest, his eyes flickering from hazel to luminous green and back, as the barrier thinned with the approaching equinox and evil struggled to gain a foothold in Skywatch.

With Lucius locked up tight and a second layer of wards cast around his rooms, both to keep him in and to keep the *makol* out, the royal council adjourned to the kitchen to argue about what they should do with him. By the time Jox kicked them out of the kitchen so he could work on breakfast, and they'd adjourned to the royal suite to continue the battle, Alexis had been thoroughly reminded that Nate might be damn good in bed, but he could be seriously annoying and incredibly wrong when it came to matters of state.

They sat together on a love seat in the sitting room of Strike and Leah's suite, while the royal couple and Anna sat opposite them on a long couch. For the most part, though, the love seat wasn't feeling much love.

As far as Alexis was concerned, there was no excuse for maintaining a *makol* within Skywatch; it was too great a risk. She hated to do it, but had to vote for sacrificing Lucius. Leah agreed with her, which was a little surprising, given that the detective was a non-Nightkeeper herself, and had been under a similar threat of death only months earlier. But Leah was practical, and a cop, and was pretty firm on the idea that the needs of the many outweighed those of a given individual. Strike and Nate, on the other hand, wanted to keep Lucius alive and locked up through the equinox, on the theory that if he was human three hundred and fifty or so days a year, they could stand to lock him up for the duration of each solstice and equinox. Like he was some sort of werewolf or something, and there were only four full moons a year.

Granted, Strike's opinion was at least in part based on the fact that they didn't know exactly what would happen to Anna if her bond-servant were sacrificed. Some of Jade's info suggested she'd lose the slave-master's mark on her arm in a flash of pain, similar to what the *winikin* experienced when a Nightkeeper member of their bound bloodline died. Other references, though, suggested that the outcome could be far worse, especially because she was an *itza'at* seer. One even went so far as to suggest that she would experience his death over and over and over again, regardless of whether she was awake or asleep. Since that was pretty much what Anna had been through after the massacre, Alexis saw the king's point and sympathized with his concern for his sister. Unfortunately, since Nate agreed with the king, that left them deadlocked in a two-to-two vote, with Anna abstaining for obvious reasons and Jox maintaining that this was a matter for the magi, and a *winikin* shouldn't cast the deciding vote.

"I don't want to do anything that'll hurt Anna," Alexis said, feeling like they were going around in circles. "But it's simply not safe for us to harbor a *makol* in our midst. Just look what happened when Iago got one of his people inside. Do you really want to give the actual *Banol Kax* a foothold?"

"Lucius is locked up and double-warded," Nate countered. "We can keep him that way, and study him during the cardinal days, maybe come up with a way to cure him. The rest of the time he'll be free to roam the compound and help Jade in the library, just like he is now." He spoke to the group, but Alexis knew his words were aimed directly at her.

The air crackled between them, rife with energy. But it wasn't the same anger and frustration as before; this was a good energy, a productive energy that had developed in the week since she had gone to him as a woman wanting a man, and nothing more.

During the day they trained together, and advised the king and queen, taking opposite sides partly because their views differed that sharply, and partly because having a devil's advocate never hurt. They spent their nights together, usually in the cottage, which she liked for its privacy, and for the touches of home. The shag rug would have to go, of course, but the other kitsch had grown on her just as quickly as the idea of Nate as her lover and partner. They worked well together, loved well together.

And if she'd fallen hard while he was still seeing the sex as a nice side benefit, then that was entirely her problem, her choice. Her responsibility to deal with.

She shook her head, both at her own weakness for the slick, aloof ones, and to counter his point. "You're making Lucius sound like a pet we can stick in a kennel and let out when it's convenient. That's inhumane."

"So it's more humane to kill him now, without giving

him a chance to come out of it?" Nate's eyes narrowed on hers. "That's logical."

"From his perspective? Maybe not. But from the perspective of keeping the Nightkeepers safe, so we'll have the greatest possible number of warriors to hold the barrier and fight the end-time, then yes. It's the most rational answer." Alexis glanced at a too-pale Anna, hating the necessity, and said softly, "I'm sorry."

The king's sister grimaced. "What we need is a mindbender to exorcise the *makol*."

Nate held up both hands in a *don't go there* gesture. "The only one we know of is Iago, and not even I'm going to okay a plan that involves capturing him and somehow forcing him to fix Lucius. Besides, wouldn't it be more or less impossible to make a mind-bender like him do something? He could just twist us back around and make us think it was our idea to release him in the middle of Skywatch."

"Now, there's a cheerful thought." Alexis shuddered. "Too bad none of the others got—" She broke off as a new thought occurred. *"Oh, shit!"*

"Is that a good 'oh, shit,' or a bad one?" Leah asked.

"Potentially both," Alexis answered as adrenaline kicked. "After what happened with the library, a bunch of us were sitting around and brainstorming, trying to figure out how Iago does what he can do. Lucius was wondering whether Iago might not have far fewer talents than it seems. For example, during the parley he didn't try to force us to open the front door; he jammed the wards and the woman 'ported inside. So what if that means he didn't have access to his mind-bending abilities? What if he's actually borrowing some of his powers from the magi around him?"

The others took a moment to digest the concept. Nate finally broke the silence, saying, "Not a bad point, but it's academic, isn't it? It doesn't really matter where he gets the powers from, as long as he's got access."

"It does matter, though, if you think about who he was with when he showed mind-bending powers," Alexis said. "The first time was when he got the knife from Rabbit, and we're figuring that he probably used it again in the museum, to distract Rabbit and lure the security guard onto the scene at exactly the wrong moment, then later to make Sven drop the bowl and leave it behind." She paused. "Are we seeing the pattern here?"

Anna's eyes sharpened. "The peccary bloodline carries mind-benders." She paused. "You're thinking that Iago was borrowing from Rabbit?"

Leah exhaled. "But Rabbit doesn't—" She broke off. "You're right. It could be in his bag of tricks, like the telekinesis. He might not even know he has it yet, or didn't when he left." She nodded pensively. "If that's the case and we can find him, it's possible he could help rescue Lucius from the *makol*."

"That's assuming Rabbit's still alive," Strike grated, his face setting in pain. "We have no reason to believe that's the case. For gods' sake, I can't even get a 'port lock on him."

Alexis leaned in. "You couldn't get one on Desiree or Iago, either. What if they've got him and they're blocking your 'port?"

Strike's expression went thunderous. "Then we find them. And they're dead."

Rabbit and Myrinne had been locked up together in the warded cabin for nearly a week with no outside contact, and only a couple of jugs of water and a box of energy bars. Her bruises had faded, leaving her high-cheekboned face unmarked and lovely, though pale with nerves as they sat shoulder to shoulder up against the wall. "You're sure he'll come today?" she asked quietly.

"Tomorrow at the absolute latest. He'll want me for the equinox, which is the day after." Rabbit tugged at the grimy cuff of his sweatshirt, pulling it down farther, even though it already hid the new mark he wore on his forearm: the quatrefoil red hellmouth of the Xibalbans. He'd sold himself for Myrinne and didn't regret the transaction for an instant. They'd clicked with each other there in captivity. She was tough and bossy, with an edge of street cool, and she got him like nobody else did. She understood when he needed to be quiet. Heck, she'd shut him down once or twice when she'd needed her own space, and he hadn't minded. She couldn't do magic, but wasn't afraid of it, either, wasn't afraid of him. After being the odd man out for so long, it was a huge relief to Rabbit to have someone else out there with him.

They fit, they matched, just as he'd known they would when he'd first seen her and the restless, edgy part inside him had gone still.

They hadn't done more than hold hands, or curl close together to share body heat as they slept, but that much had been exactly right, calling to something deep inside him, letting him know that now that he'd found her, it was up to him to protect her. Which meant getting both their asses out of there and back to Skywatch. He no longer cared whether Strike was pissed at him. He just wanted to go home. Once he got there, he'd kiss whoever's ass he had to, promise whatever was necessary in order to claim sanctuary for him and Myrinne.

But first they had to get the hell out of the cabin and away from Iago, which was way easier said than done, given that the bastard had that whole fast-forward/pause thing going on.

Thing was, Rabbit thought he knew a way to neutralize Iago's advantages—some of them, anyway. He didn't know how he knew; he just did.

It all went back to the second day of his captivity, when he'd traded his magic for Myrinne's life. After making the deal, he'd followed Iago's orders, standing inside the skull circle and drinking his own blood from the ceremonial bowl that had been dedicated to the earthquake demon, Cabrakan. He'd screamed when pain racked his entire body, and again when he'd seen the hellmouth mark appear on his arm and he'd jacked in, not to the barrier, but to the first layer of hell.

Vicious, glorious power had whipped through him, and suddenly Iago had been inside his head, using him, forcing him to pray to the *Banol Kax*, to give himself to them. Through him, Iago had exhorted Cabrakan to collapse a cave down south somewhere. But even as the Xibalban had been using him, Rabbit had found himself catching thought snippets from the other man: impressions and images, emotions and bits of conversation. From them, he'd learned that Iago needed him for his wild half-blood magic, and was somehow using that magic against him through the quatrefoil mark, turning Rabbit's mind-bending powers inward, on himself.

Shock one had been learning that he was a mind-bender, and that the talent worked on other magi. Shock two had been realizing that Iago was a borrower, capable of siphoning another magic user's talents.

After he'd figured that out, Rabbit had gone digging a little deeper, taking his mind off what his body was used to doing. As he'd sat cross-legged opposite Iago with the bowl between them, working the dark magic, he'd learned that Iago's borrowing talent worked at close proximity with any mage, but better when that mage wore the quatrefoil mark, which was why he'd needed Rabbit bound to the Xibalban magic. Since Iago couldn't risk fouling the bonding process with a mind-bend, he'd needed Rabbit to take the mark more or less willingly. Having seen Rabbit and Myrinne together at the pizza joint and seeing that she was important, the Xibalban had located her, captured her, and then waited to grab Rabbit. He would've taken him from the museum, but Strike and Leah had shown up, looking for him and he hadn't wanted to risk their detecting the magic.

Even knowing that much had helped Rabbit, because it meant that at least they'd searched for him a little. It also gave him hope that they'd take him back . . . except for the part where Strike had forbidden him to bring Myrinne into Skywatch, of course, but he'd blow up that bridge when he got there. The first order of business was getting the hell free.

Then he heard it: the crunch of a footfall on the packed snow outside, too close, not giving him enough time to prepare.

"Shit!" Rabbit scrambled for the magic, lunging to his feet while Myrinne gasped and dove for the corner. Rabbit tried to latch onto Iago's mind, but he wasn't jacked in right; he was in the barrier, not the hell layer. Breathing fast, heart hammering in his chest, he tried again and failed. Another footfall came outside, and the doorknob rattled, and Rabbit shouted, "No!"

The universe blinked out. Then it blinked back in, and he was in another of the cabins, this one entirely bare save for a woman lying on the floor, bound in a rope cocoon. She was dark-haired and smooth-skinned beneath the bruises that marred her face and bare forearms. She was in her mid-twenties, maybe, wearing ragged, outdoorsy clothes, like she'd been grabbed in the middle of a camping trip. Her eyes were dim with drugs, but she was aware enough to be terrified.

"Please," she whispered, her eyes locked on Rabbit. "Please don't."

Iago swung the door shut behind him, closing them in.

"Son of a *bitch*!" Rabbit spun on him, his gut clenched with fear, with rage. He lunged at the other mage. "If you did anything to Myrinne, I'll—"

"Shut the fuck up," Iago said, effortlessly grabbing hold of his mind and shutting him down through the quatrefoil mark.

The Xibalban pulled the demon prophecy knife and blooded his right palm without a change in expression, then tossed the knife to Rabbit, who caught it haft-first, and blooded his palm similarly, all without wanting to.

Rabbit felt powerless. Impotent. Like he was fourteen all over again, and being pounded on by the bullies at school, the ones who called him Bunny-boy and teased him about his zonked-out old man. Only this was so much worse, because he wasn't just worried about saving his own ass anymore.

"As you've no doubt figured, I'll be needing your assistance the day after tomorrow," Iago said. "However, since there's no guarantee you'll live through the equinox ceremony, I thought I'd call on you beforehand to help me deal with a small problem." He clasped Rabbit's bleeding hand in his own, and the surge of uplinked power nearly lifted them both off their feet. The floor shifted beneath them, and the air crackled with fire magic, with transport magic, with all the borrowed talents the Xibalban held within him.

An invisible net tightened around Rabbit, binding his

limbs, his brain. It grew tentacles that dug into him, writhed through him, searching for something. He arched against the invading pressure and screamed at the top of his lungs, but the tentacles kept coming, kept searching. Then, as if one of them had plugged into a socket within his brain, suddenly he could see through Iago's eyes and Iago could see through his. They were two and they were one, with Iago in control, Rabbit shoved to a corner of his own mind.

He couldn't move, couldn't scream, couldn't do anything except watch as Iago used his body as a puppet, forcing it to focus on the dark-haired woman, forcing it to call on something Rabbit didn't know he'd possessed, a grayish intensity of magic he didn't recognize.

Then Iago and not-Rabbit spoke in synchrony, asking the woman, "Where is the library?"

Her drug-dulled eyes blanked for a second, and her mouth opened as though to answer, but only a strangled cry emerged, one that went to pain as the woman bit down on her own tongue and blood flowed. "I don't know," she said.

The gray haze in Rabbit's brain thickened, and he could feel the magic, feel the pressure as Iago and not-Rabbit said, "Tell us where your father hid the library."

"Fuck. You." Her words came from between gritted teeth.

Iago leaned on Rabbit for more power, dug deeper into the woman's mind for an answer. Grinning a horrible rictus of pain, she writhed against her bonds, emitting high, inhuman mewling noises that made Rabbit's blood freeze with horror at the knowledge that he was helping Iago torture her.

Stop it, he told himself. *Make him stop!* But he didn't know how to use his own mind-bending powers, hadn't known he had them until the Xibalban had pulled them to the surface.

The woman was screaming now, deep, raw cries that started at the back of her throat and rose up through the octaves, each one a little weaker than the last.

"Your father found the library and recovered it from the caves," Iago pressed in his and not-Rabbit's voices, their talents amplifying each other, the mind-bender and the borrower, locked together to break a human woman who was so much stronger than she should have been. "Where did he take the codices? Where did he hide them?"

She was beyond speech now, but speech wasn't necessary, because they were inside her head. Rabbit could see flashes of an older, gray-haired man, and a busy restaurant. And over it all was the refrain of a song, one that he almost recognized.

She was using the song to block the invasion, Rabbit realized, and was impressed. More than that, he was free to go after the magic, because Iago was pissed, and entirely focused on the melody that blocked the information he wanted. Hustling, Rabbit fought to track the grayish mist to its source, only it didn't seem to have a source; it was all over, all around him. And then, somehow, it was inside him, inside the small knot of Rabbit-consciousness that he'd managed to retain within the prison Iago had made of his mind.

He threw himself into the mist, took it within himself, and found the magic. Or maybe the magic finally found him, as it had done with fire and telekinesis. Either way, he grabbed for it, locked onto it, and threw it straight into Iago's head. *Stop!* he shouted mentally, as loud as he could, pouring all the power he possessed along the link. Barrier power, hell power, he didn't care; he just threw all of himself into the Xibalban, screaming, *Stop!*

Roaring, Iago yanked his hand away from their uplink and grabbed for his skull. "Get out!" But he didn't have control of the mind-bend anymore, so the words were just words.

Die! Rabbit shouted, beyond himself with hatred, with violence. *Die, you son of a bitch!*

Too late, he realized they were still connected to the woman. The command split between her and Iago, traveling the mind-bender's link to both of them. Iago fell with a crash and went still. The woman arched up with a soundless cry. Then she too went limp and motionless.

In the sudden silence—both inside his skull and inside the cabin—Rabbit stared at the bodies. He reached out trembling fingers to touch the woman, and exhaled a shuddering breath of relief when he felt the faint flutter of her pulse. Same for Iago. They were alive. Sort of.

He wasn't sure whether he should be relieved or disappointed. He hadn't wanted to kill the woman, but the world would be better off without Iago. Way better.

He grabbed the ceremonial knife and lifted it to the Xibalban's throat, but then paused. He needed to get home as fast as possible, which meant 'porting. A quick search through Iago's pockets came up with nada on the cell phone front, and he didn't need to look to know the bastard had 'ported in from wherever. Which meant they could be a hundred yards or a hundred miles from the nearest phone, seriously cramping his ability to phone home. But the bastard *had* 'ported in from wherever, and he was alone, which meant it was a real talent, not a borrowed one. And maybe Rabbit could borrow it in return.

He lurched to his feet, feeling the world tilt and spin around him, warning that he didn't have much magic left in him.

It was going to have to be enough.

Sticking the knife in his belt, he staggered out the door and down the pathway, trying not to imagine what Iago had done with Myrinne. "Please, gods," he muttered, slurring his words, his tongue gone numb from too much power drain. "Please let her be okay."

He was seeing double by the time he got to the cabin they'd been living in. He was afraid to call her name, afraid there wouldn't be an answer. He unlocked the door with a touch and pushed through. A step inside, though, he stopped dead, panic coming hard and hot when he didn't see Myrinne. Then motion blurred and he turned just in time to see her jump out from behind the door, screaming as she swung what looked like the leg from their sleeping cot.

The impact sent him sideways. He saw her mouth go slack in horror and remorse. Then the world blinked out in a natural fast-forward.

When he came to, he was sprawled in Myrinne's lap, which probably would've been nice if he hadn't been on the verge of puking. He forced the nausea down, though, and struggled up into a mostly sitting position. "How long was I out?"

"Only a couple of minutes," she said, voice quavering. "I'm sor—"

"Save it," he said shortly. "We've gotta move. Help me up, will you?"

His head hurt like hell. The spinning had stopped, but that was actually bad news, because it meant he'd gone to the next stage in the postmagic shutdown: i.e., the one right before unconsciousness. He didn't have time for the luxury of sleep, though. He had to get them out of there.

"Where are we going?" she asked when he'd sort of stagger-stepped them outside and partway down the beaten track in the snow.

"Back to Iago. Trust me." It hurt to talk, hurt to think. Hurt to put one foot in front of the other.

Myrinne's breath hissed out when she saw the mage and the woman sprawled on the floor, but she didn't ask, said only, "Tell me what to do."

"Stand back." Rabbit fell to his knees between Iago and the woman, and used Iago's knife to reblood his palm, then the Xibalban's. Taking the other man's hand in his and assuming the role of dominant power, he searched for the gray mist, found it, and climbed back inside the bastard's head. *Send us here,* he ordered, and pictured the gates outside Skywatch, outside the wards. Aloud, he said to Myrinne, "Take my other hand, and grab on to the woman."

"We're taking them with us?"

"Gonna try."

But the magic was sluggish, the power slow to come. The preteleport rattle cycled too slowly, cutting in and out like a bad engine no matter how hard he leaned on his connection to the barrier and Iago's faltering power.

They weren't going to make it. *Shit.*

"Let go of her," he ordered tersely. "Listen carefully. If I'm unconscious when we get where we're going, you're going to have to deal with . . . with my family, I guess you could say. Here's what I want you to do." He sketched out the best plan he could think of with his brain halfway inside Iago's. Then he fell silent, unable to spare the energy for more explanation. He dropped Iago's hand but kept the mind-link intact. *Gods help me,* he said inside his swirling skull. *Myrinne is important; I know she's important. Help me get her safe.*

This time when he leaned on Iago and forced the mage to initiate the 'port magic, the rattle cycled up faster, still not quite enough, but as good as it was going to get.

Hoping to hell he didn't send them into the side of a mountain or something, Rabbit closed his eyes and looked into Iago's mind, where he could finally see the glowing yellow teleport thread connecting him and Myrinne to their destination. *Take it,* he told Iago. *Send us there.*

The world lurched. Everything went gray-green.

And the Xibalban's dark magic sent Rabbit and his human home.

CHAPTER TWENTY-THREE

Nate was on the phone with Denjie, working out some of the kinks for the latest *EmoPunk* release and wondering what his second in command would do if he just said, "I don't fucking care; you deal with it," when the surveillance system monitoring the borders of Skywatch let rip with a two-toned alarm that warned they had drop-in company. The cottage wasn't linked to the security system, but Nate heard the siren coming from the mansion, and was on his feet before the first set of whoops had died down.

Denjie broke off midsentence. "What in the hell was that?"

"Doorbell. Gotta go."

"But what about—"

"Don't care. You deal with it." Nate slapped his phone shut and tossed it on the little table near the door on his way out. Then he hauled ass up to the mansion, through the building, and out the front door, which was where the commotion seemed to be coming from.

Someone—Jox, probably—had killed the alarm, but the entire population of the compound had mobilized to the front gate, which was wide-open.

Not good, Nate thought, but forced himself to slow down to a purposeful walk as he strode up to the crowd, aware that there were a couple of stragglers behind him still. "What's going on?" he asked nobody in particular.

Before he got an answer, the king bellowed, "Out of the way!" The crowd parted and Strike appeared, carrying . . . Holy shit, was that Rabbit?

The king's face was set and hard, with worry riding the edges, and it looked as if he were going to mow through anyone who got in his way, including Jox, who was tugging at his arm, trying to slow him down. Behind Strike strode Leah, looking as though she were in full-on cop mode as she half escorted, half dragged a young girl, a total stranger. Behind them was Alexis, looking borderline frantic as she talked fast, trying to convince Leah of something and not making headway.

When she saw Nate, Alexis locked onto him and mouthed, *Stop him!*

They might have their differences when it came to matters of state, but there was no arguing the fear in her face, so Nate put himself between Strike and the front door of Skywatch and said, *"Nochem."*

The word was meant to remind Strike that he couldn't think like a man when he was king. For a second Nate thought the other man was going to ignore him, blow right through him, but then it seemed to penetrate. Strike's head came up and he locked onto Nate, fury and annoyance hardening his cobalt blue eyes. "Get the fuck out of my way, Blackhawk."

"I will. In thirty seconds, once you've thought this through." Nate glanced at Rabbit, wincing at how thin the teen had gotten, how ragged. "Where are you taking him?"

"To his cottage," Strike said, his voice a low growl. "And if you don't stand aside, I'm going through you." The grief in his expression was that of a father or an older brother who'd almost lost family, or a *winikin* who had failed in his duty. Nate knew that Rabbit's disappearance had dragged on the king, tormented him. And because of that, he knew he had to be careful or Strike *would* go through him, losing caution to emotion.

"Think it through," Nate said, picking his words carefully. "Be rational."

The king bared his teeth. "Fuck rationality. I want him back where he belongs, where he should've been all along."

"Wait," said a soft voice, one that didn't belong to any of the compound's residents. The girl, who was in her late teens, dark-haired and pretty, and equally as rough-looking as Rabbit, if not more so, pushed ahead and put herself in front of the king. "When he knew he was going to pass out before you guys got to us, he gave me a message for you." She paused. "You're Strikeout, right?"

Pain flashed on the king's face, along with wary hope at her use of Rabbit's old, jeering nickname for him. "Yeah."

"He told me to give you this." She pulled a knife, but before anybody could take her down and protect their king, she flipped it in a practiced move and held it out to Strike, haft-first.

There was a ripple of surprise from the gathered crowd, one that mimicked the clutch in Nate's gut when he recognized the knife they'd lost to Iago back in Boston. Which meant Rabbit, at least, had been in contact with the Xibalban.

It also meant they had the Volatile's prophecy back in their hands.

"Thank you." Strike accepted the knife without comment or ceremony, and Nate had to force himself not to snatch it from him. As before, the knife called to him, made him want to touch it, to hold it.

The girl continued, "I'm also supposed to tell you to lock us both up and ward the shit out of the room, and that he'll explain the rest when he wakes up."

Which was so not good news, Nate knew, because it meant Rabbit believed the Nightkeepers had something to fear from him or the girl, or both. *Shit.*

Strike's expression went bleak, and he had to clear his throat before he said, "Was there anything else?"

She nodded. "I'm supposed to tell Jox not to burn the eggs."

Both the king and his *winikin* relaxed at that, letting Nate know that it was a safe word or something, a cue that the message was genuine and unforced. "Okay," Strike finally said. "Okay. We do what Myrinne says."

The girl looked startled. "How'd you know my name?"

"Lucky guess. Come on." The king led the way, with Jox at his side and Leah shepherding the girl. Myrinne. As he strode through the main door, the king called, "I want all magic users downstairs near the storerooms in five minutes to help me set the wards." Which was something of a relief, because it meant he was taking Rabbit's warning to heart and setting some serious magic.

Nate stayed back until Alexis joined him, and had a feeling his own expression mirrored the worry on her face. "What do you think?" he asked.

She glanced at the starscape overhead, which was dimmed some by the front lights of Skywatch. "I think it's going to be a long night. What do you think?"

"That we're going to run out of storerooms if this keeps up." They'd wound up locking Lucius back down in the room he'd occupied his first couple of days at Skywatch, on the theory that the single room was easier to ward, and the sturdy walls and the lack of windows made physical locks more practical and efficient.

She nodded. "Won't argue with you on that."

"That's a first."

"Not my fault you've got warped ideas of logic." But she held out a hand to him. "Come on, royal adviser. We've got some work to do."

Surprisingly, though, once they had the wards up and the royal council had convened in the kitchen over chips and salsa, the king didn't fight them on the idea of major security measures.

"Look," he finally said, "I'm not stupid. We've already had a taste of what happened when Iago got someone inside, and for crap's sake, I'm one of the few people here old enough to remember the massacre. It's not like I'm looking to throw the doors open and invite what-the-fuck inside."

But he was still reacting as much with emotion as logic, and history said that when the jaguar kings started thinking like men and fathers rather than kings, bad things happened. Nate might not buy into the whole cycle-of-time thing, but he believed in basic psychology, which said that Strike needed their help. The fact that Nate and Alexis were pretty united in their recommendations was a huge swing in their favor, forcing Strike to finally agree—albeit reluctantly—to having Jox set up additional surveillance in each of the storerooms. Granted, the motion detectors and infrareds couldn't detect 'port magic—and it wasn't yet clear whether Rabbit had added *that* to his arsenal too, though how'd he get home otherwise?—but the gadgets couldn't be influenced by a mind-bender, either.

After that, they waited to hear back from Leah, who had taken Myrinne to the kitchen for some food with a side of interrogation, or Anna, who'd taken the knife so she could translate the normal script as well as the starscript.

Leah arrived first. "Iago has had him for just over a week," she announced without preamble, then went on to sketch out a summary of the teens' imprisonment, and what little Myrinne knew about the Xibalban, which wasn't anything they hadn't already figured out.

While she was talking, Strike rose and started pacing the length of the royal suite's sitting area. By the time she was finished, he looked like he wanted to put his fist—or a fireball—through the wall. He held himself back, but Nate almost wished he'd let fly and burn off some of the emotion before it made him do something stupid.

"Gods damn it," the king finally said. "We should've fucking gone after Iago weeks ago."

"We couldn't find him," Leah pointed out, "just like we couldn't find Rabbit."

That brought Alexis's head up. "Can you lock onto Rabbit now?" she asked the king.

He stopped pacing for a second, then frowned and shook his head. "No. I can't. Which means we were right; Iago knows how to make people invisible to 'port magic. He must've blocked Rabbit's 'port lock right

there at the museum, then let him go—I don't know . . .
so he could watch him, maybe. Wait until he got into
enough trouble that he needed rescuing, and might be
desperate enough, lonely enough to join Iago's team."
His voice went ragged when he said, "Did you see the
kid's arm? He's wearing the goddamned hellmouth." He
stopped, facing a wall, but instead of putting his fist
through it, he leaned his forehead against the painted
plaster and said in a low, hollow voice, repeating what
Leah had just told them, "Iago was going to sacrifice
them, during the equinox. Another two days and he
would've been dead."

"He made it out," Alexis started to say, but Nate
waved her quiet, and she was surprised enough that she
actually shut up.

Knowing he'd have to apologize for—or pay for—that
one later, Nate rose and crossed to Strike. Pitching his
voice so the others couldn't hear, he said, "With all due
respect, *Nochem,* get a fucking grip."

Strike stiffened, pulled away from the wall, and turned
to glare. "Ex*cuse* me?"

Ignoring a sudden memory of being hung off the side
of a warehouse roof, Nate stared him down. "You want
to be upset, do it on your own time. Right now we need
you in the king zone." He paused. "Don't make me
quote the writs at you." The king's writ, which set out
the priorities of the ruling Nightkeeper, was unfortunately apt under the circumstances, a reminder that the
king looked to the gods and his people first, followed by
mankind and the end-time war. His own desires as a
husband, father, and friend were way down on the list.

Strike's lips twitched. "Bet that'd hurt you far more
than it'd hurt me." But he inhaled a long breath and
visibly centered himself. By the time he'd exhaled, he
nodded to Nate. "Okay. Sorry. And thanks."

"Don't mention it. Seriously."

They rejoined the others, and Nate tried not to see
Leah's quiet nod or Alexis's covert thumbs-up. He didn't
want to be good at this advisory crap, godsdamn it.

"You guys ready for me?" a quiet voice asked from

the doorway. Nate looked up to see Anna holding the Volatile's knife balanced in her palm, crossing her sacrificial scar.

A hush took hold of the room.

"What have you got for us?" Strike asked, waving her in.

She set the knife on the coffee table and took one of the empty armchairs, leaning forward at the edge of the chair so she could point to a line of text inscribed at the base of the handle portion of the carved knife, which had been formed from a single piece of obsidian and polished to a deep black shine. "See this here? It's a regular, nonstarscript inscription." Tracing the fluid beauty of the Mayan glyphs, she translated, " 'The Volatile challenges the sky.' "

"Well, that's not good news," Alexis said, frowning. "If he's going after the gods, then it's a pretty good bet that he's either one of the demons, or Xibalban. What confuses me is the apparent link with Ixchel and, by extension, with me."

Nate shot her a look. "We're not handing you over to Iago, if that's what you're afraid of."

"I'm not going to argue with you on that one." But she'd paled, nonetheless.

He leaned close and said under his breath, "The prophecies aren't immutable. Strike and Leah proved that." But he knew she was having trouble with the hypocrisy of believing they needed to follow the gods and prophecies, but choosing to disbelieve the one that specifically related to her.

He, on the other hand, had no such issue. If the Volatile—whoever or whatever it was—wanted Alexis, it would have to go through him to get to her.

"What about the starscript?" Strike asked.

Anna shook her head. "That's the strange thing. There wasn't any."

Silence followed that pronouncement, formed of a combination of surprise and consternation. "That's it?" Alexis said, looking shattered. "Nothing else? Nothing about Ixchel? The inscription on the statuette said Camazotz would succeed unless the Volatile is found. Does that mean we have to find and destroy the Volatile before the equinox? I hope not, because I don't see it happening."

Nate cursed inwardly. "Maybe Rabbit will know something."

"He's out cold," Jox said, "and not likely to be coherent enough to answer questions until sometime tomorrow. Whatever happened to the poor kid, he's used up."

Strike nodded. "Then that's a wrap. We'll reconvene tomorrow morning, unless anyone gets any brilliant ideas between now and then."

The members of the council disbanded and went their separate ways, Jox and Anna to their adjacent quarters in the royal wing, Nate and Alexis in the direction of the residences.

When they got to the door that was the most direct route to the cottages, she paused. Normally—at least every night over the past week—they would've headed out to his cottage by tacit consent. Tonight she hung back.

Because he'd been getting a slightly off vibe from her ever since the Volatile's prophecy was read, Nate said, "No pressure, but you look like you could use the company." *Keep it light,* he told himself. *Don't make it weird if the answer is no.*

But his gut went sour when he saw the answer in her eyes a few seconds before she shook her head and looked away. "I'm pretty tired."

They hadn't taken a night off from each other since they'd started sleeping together again, and it was part of their unspoken agreement that they . . . well, didn't speak about it. It seemed like the best way to have a more or less casual thing, given that they both lived in the compound and would continue to do so regardless of how things ended up between them. They were together when they wanted to be, apart when they wanted to be, and if it'd wound up that they wanted to be together more than they'd wanted to be apart, then that was another thing they were leaving unspoken. At least, they had up to that point.

Tonight, though, Nate found he didn't want to let it

go and keep it casual. The confirmation that the Volatile was an enemy of the gods had shaken him as much as it'd affected her. He was churned up, pissed off with the situation, and with the gods-awful obscurity of it all. Why couldn't the gods just tell them what the hell they were supposed to be doing? Yeah, fine, he knew all the rhetoric about the difference between the long, tenuous skyroad and the wide-open hellmouth. But it seemed like the gods had had ample time to get their messages through, and instead kept letting the supposed saviors of mankind get their asses kicked over and over again, setting them up for an impossible battle when the end-time came.

But being pissed off at the gods wasn't what Alexis needed from him right then; he could see it in her eyes, in the way she'd turned toward him, and how her face had gone a little wistful as she looked at him.

Catching her hand when she would've headed toward the residential wing to spend the night alone, he said, "Then let me rephrase. *I* could use the company. And it doesn't have to be anything more than that." Though he'd like it to be; he wanted to hold her, to feel her curled up next to him and know that for tonight, at least, she was safe.

She went still for a moment before she turned back to him, her eyes guarded. "Really. I don't think it's such a good idea." She rubbed her hands up and down her arms, as though she were cold, or getting goose bumps. "I think I'll just call it a night."

Because she looked like she needed it, he moved into her, wrapped his arms around her, and rested his cheek on hers. "Lexie, talk to me. I'll listen."

She leaned into him for a moment and drew a deep, shuddering breath. Then she pushed away from him and took a big step back. "Fine. You want the truth? Don't say I didn't try to avoid it. And it's not a magic thing or an equinox thing. It's a totally, depressingly human thing. A girlie-girl emotional thing. You sure you're up for it?" She paused, waiting for him to beg off.

He squared himself opposite her instead, as though they were getting ready to spar. Which was about what it felt like. His rational self was yelling for him to back off, to let things stay the way they were. But another side of him, the side that didn't want to sleep alone—that side had him saying, "Lay it on me. I can take it." He twitched a grin. "Hell, I'm dealing with being a royal adviser, which was one of the last possible things I ever wanted to be. If I can handle that, I can handle whatever's bothering you. Maybe I can even help you fix it."

"Doubtful. At least, not the way you're thinking." She took a steadying breath. "I'm in love with you."

CHAPTER TWENTY-FOUR

Of all the things Nate had expected her to say, that wouldn't have even made the list.

I'm in love with you. The words rocketed around in his brain, bouncing off one another without making any real sense. Not just because he hadn't expected to hear them from her, though he hadn't, and not because he'd never realized she'd been headed in that direction, even though that was true too . . . but because he hadn't heard those words strung together with that meaning and tossed in his direction before.

Not ever.

He had every reason now to believe that his parents had loved him, and no doubt they'd told his infant self so repeatedly. But he had no memory of those times, didn't remember even a hint of his parents. His earliest memories were of foster homes stuffed with too many kids, run by adults who'd spent the foster stipends on themselves and left the kids to fend. Sure, there had been one or two good families, ones he would've stayed with if given the choice. But he'd been moved along instead, and the opportunities for "I love you" had dwindled with the years. It wasn't the sort of thing he'd heard in juvie, wasn't the sort of thing he'd *wanted* to hear in prison, where he'd learned more than he'd ever wanted to know about sex as a commodity. Since then he'd had a string of relationships, again growing fewer and farther between as the years went on and he'd poured himself into the business . . . and his obsession with his fantasy woman, Hera, who was nothing more than a two-dimensional, watered-down version of Alexis herself, whose face fell progressively as he just stood there, staring, vapor-locked by her declaration.

Then she smiled, only it was one of acceptance rather than hope. "Yeah. That's about what I figured. You can't say I didn't warn you."

She turned and started walking, and he was so jammed up in his own head that she was most of the way to the residential wing before he unglued his feet from the damn floor and went after her. He caught her arm. "Alexis, wait."

She turned back and fisted her hands on her hips, and though there was hurt and resignation in her eyes, he didn't see any tears, which made him feel both better and worse at the same time: better because he didn't think he could've handled it if she cried; worse because it meant she'd expected exactly the reaction he'd given her.

"It's okay, Nate. My feelings, my problem." There were tears in her voice, though, which made him feel like crap.

"They're not a problem," he said, because that was the gods' honest truth. "I just . . . I need time to process. I've never . . ." He fumbled the delivery, not sure he wanted her to know that the whole love thing was something he understood in theory, but not in practice or reality.

"Like I said, it's okay. But if you don't mind, I'd like to hit my rooms and unwind. It's been a hell of a day."

"Understatement of the year," he said faintly, still not sure what he was supposed to do or say. He knew he'd blown the moment, but didn't know how badly; knew he wanted to do better, but wasn't sure how. "I just . . . I wasn't thinking about love or forever. Once we took the gods and destiny and prophecy and all that shit out of the equation, there didn't seem to be any reason for it, you know? We're here for another four years, and either the world's going to go on after that or it's not.

Either we're going to have a future or we're not, you know?"

She swallowed, then nodded. "Yeah, I do know. Thing is, I've spent too long living in limbo, waiting to figure out who I am and what I'm supposed to be doing."

"And you've got that figured out now?" He wasn't asking to be funny, either.

That got a crooked smile out of her. "Some of it, anyway. And loving you is one of the things I've figured out. I didn't mean for it to happen, didn't want it to. But I woke up next to you this morning and realized I was exactly where I wanted to be, despite everything. I want to be with you, live with you, combine my life with yours. I want to rip out that gods-awful carpet in the cottage and lay down polished oak, and sneak some smoke motifs in among the hawks. I want to wear your *jun tan* on my arm, and I want you to wear mine. I want us to fight over what Strike and Leah should and shouldn't do, and leave all that shit at the door, so it's just the two of us when we're at home, no gods, no destiny, no prophecy, just a man and a woman in love." She paused, looking at him, her grin going even more crooked. "And the thought of that scares the living shit out of you."

"Yeah," he said, because it did—not just because of what she'd said, but because he could picture a whole bunch of it, and that brought nothing but panic. He didn't know how to love her, how to be her mate. He didn't even know if he wanted to do either of those things. He'd been so certain he was going to buck prophecy that he hadn't even gone there. "I wish I could give you what you want," he said finally, knowing that was about as lame as it got. "But I can't say the words when I don't know what I'm feeling."

"Well," she said after a moment, "it's like I said before: I might not like what you say some of the time—hell, lots of the time—but I know you only say what you're thinking. In this case, I'd rather hear the truth than have you knee-jerk an 'I love you' when what you really mean is, 'I want us to keep sleeping together.' So thanks for the honesty, at least."

"If . . ." He faltered, not sure what he wanted to say, but knowing it couldn't be good for them to part like this almost exactly forty-eight hours before the vernal equinox, when she and her magic were supposed to play a major role in their very survival. He finally said, "You know I'll do anything I can to protect you, right? And I mean anything."

Her smile went sad. "I know. But the thing is, you've already proved your point. The gods—or destiny, or whatever—might control some of what's going on around us, but they don't control us as people. They don't control our hearts. I fell for you because of the man you are, not the one you should've been. And if the very things that made you who you are mean that you can't love, or don't know how to love, or need more time, or just plain don't love *me*, then that's just my bad timing." She lifted a shoulder, though there were tears in her eyes now, and her voice broke a little when she said, "Another lifetime, maybe."

She reached up on her tiptoes and touched her lips to his in a kiss that tasted of farewell. And this time when she walked away, he didn't go after her. He stood there looking after her long after the door to her suite closed quietly behind her, leaving him alone.

And later, when he lay in bed, equally alone, he stared up at the picture of the sea and sky, and realized for the first time that none of his father's paintings had any people in them.

Alexis had meant to go straight to bed, but once she was inside her suite she found herself prowling the small space, unable to settle. She was tempted to go find Izzy and invite her for a drink, which used to be her normal routine when she was involved in a relationship implosion, whether as the dumper or dumpee. This was different, though. This was the first time she'd gone all the way to "I love you."

"Go find Izzy," she told herself. "She'll talk you out of it." But that was the problem, really, because she knew the *winikin* would try to do exactly that. Alexis, though, wasn't in the mood to be talked out of loving

Nate. She wanted to wallow in it, revel in it, and curse him for being an emotionally stunted asshat, who also happened to be gorgeous, intelligent, more or less rational, a strong counterweight to her opinions on the royal council, and an increasingly powerful mage of the sort she wanted at her back during a fight.

Oh, yeah, and he was great in bed. But still, an asshat.

So instead of calling Izzy, she hit the minifridge for the split of decent champagne she'd bummed from Jox and stuck there on the off chance Nate surprised her and they had something to celebrate. "Face it," she told herself as she tore the foil, undid the cage, and popped the cork, "you didn't think you'd be celebrating. This is 'drown your sorrows' bubbly."

Not only that, it wouldn't hurt to anesthetize her growing fear of what was going to happen at the equinox. Up until this point she'd managed to mostly push thoughts of Camazotz to the back of her mind. Now, though, with the clock ticking down and the two prophecies combining to warn her against the Volatile while at the same time urging her to find him, she was stumped . . . and scared.

Figuring that if she were going to drown her sorrows, she might as well do it right, she booted up her laptop and jacked it into some sort of easy listening station, heavy on the instrumentals, and drew a bath and added some bubbles. She swapped out her clothes for her good robe, pinned her hair up atop her head, and took the bottle with her into the bathroom.

Within a half an hour, the champagne and bubbles had eased the physical aches, if not the ones inside. She let her head fall back on the edge of the tub, thinking as she sometimes did of who might've lived in her suite before the massacre, and whether she—or he—had ever done what she was doing at that moment: soaking away a shitty day and wishing the future could be something other than what was written.

Thinking that, she drifted off to sleep . . . and dreamed of a dark-haired warrior with a hawk's medallion and the power to make her heart and mind soar.

                    *   *   *

Anna was up early the day before the vernal equinox. Okay, in reality she hadn't slept more than a few minutes at a time the night before, so the concept of being "up" was pretty relative. The equinox was still more than twenty-four hours away, but as she lay in her bedroom at Skywatch beneath a sheet and light blanket, she could feel the power buzzing beneath her skin, feel the visions trying to break through. Yet more than anything she wanted to pull the covers over her head and wait until it was all over. Or better yet, go home and pretend that she was nothing more than human, that the marks on her arm were just tattoos, the yellow quartz pendant just a piece of costume jewelry. She missed her bed, missed her home and her husband. She didn't want to be where she was, didn't want to be *who* she was.

Groaning aloud at the self-pity, she tossed the covers off her face and said sternly, "Get up. Stop being such a girl."

In her mind, the exhortation echoed in Red-Boar's voice. The older Nightkeeper had wanted her to be as strong as Strike, if not stronger, wanted her to care as much as her brother did, wanted her to turn away from the modern things she craved and focus on tradition and duty. *Don't be such a girl,* he would snarl. *Do it again.* And though they'd been only pretending to work the spells because the barrier had been offline and there was no knowing whether it would ever come back to life, she'd done as he'd said, and had tried harder and harder to be a good Nightkeeper . . . until the day she'd left for college and hadn't looked back. Only now she *was* back, and it wasn't clear that she was being all that helpful. She'd endangered Skywatch and the Nightkeepers by insisting on keeping Lucius alive even though he was a clear threat. Hell, she'd barely even managed to help during the meeting with Iago, getting a single useful detail out of him when there had been so much more to gather, if only she'd known how. But that was a job for a mind-bender like Red-Boar. Or his son.

It was the thought of Rabbit that finally drove her out of bed. He, like the rest of them, hadn't asked to be born into this mess. What was more, he'd started off at a serious disadvantage, child to a single parent who'd denied him a true Nightkeeper name and refused to accept him into the bloodline until almost too late. Strike and Jox had done their best with the kid, but they'd walked a fine line, trying to help without alienating Red-Boar, who had been antisocial at his best, pathological at his worst.

Then there was Rabbit's magic, which both awed and scared Anna—a sentiment shared by most of the Nightkeepers and all of the *winikin*. It might not be fair, but there it was: his magic didn't play by the rules and neither did he. Was it any wonder most of them had tried not to get too close? *That doesn't make it right,* her conscience nudged; *he's just a kid.* He was the same age as most of the freshman undergrads in her intro lectures. And he needed help.

Moving slowly, feeling sore all over though there was no reason for it, she dragged on a pair of jeans and a long-sleeved pullover and headed for the kitchen.

Izzy met her in the main room, handed her a mug of coffee—cream, no sugar—and aimed her for the stairs that led to the lower level. "Jox says you're to go down right away."

"Great," Anna muttered into her coffee. "I've been dressed for, like, three minutes and I'm already late." But she headed downstairs. She hesitated outside Lucius's warded door, but then kept going to the adjoining rooms where they'd locked Rabbit and his friend— girlfriend?—the previous night.

Seeing the gold-red shimmer of wards across the doorway and not in the mood for magic, she raised her voice. "Knock, knock? Izzy said you were waiting for me."

A muffled voice called, "Just a sec." Magic hummed just behind her jawbone, the red-gold shimmer cut out, and Nate opened the door. "Come on in."

After what Izzy had said up in the kitchen, Anna was expecting to be the last one there. She hadn't, however, anticipated how much it would bother her to see Strike, Leah, Jox, Nate, and Alexis looming over Rabbit, who was sitting on the side of a camp cot, wearing track pants and a hoodie and staring at the floor, jaw set in the sort of mulish intransigence she'd always associated with his sire.

His hair had grown out from its skull trim to a military brush, and he was thinner than before, especially through his sharp-angled face, as though the last vestiges of the childhood he'd continually rejected had been burned out of him. His eyes flicked to her momentarily, and she felt him weighing her, trying to decide whose side she was on. Then he looked back down, and she didn't have a clue where he'd shelved her.

The sight of him was a forcible reminder that he wasn't a kid at all. Hell, he was light-years from the freshmen she'd just been comparing him to. He was, what, eighteen? Yet at the same time, he was a stronger mage than any of them, save, perhaps, for Iago. And that, she knew, was the problem. Humans and Nightkeepers alike feared that which they could not control.

Help him, whispered a familiar voice inside her skull, one that she knew was a construct of her own mind, a bit of wishful thinking. Even so, she shot back, *I'm going to try. It's not like he makes it easy, you know.*

Besides, she'd already endangered the Nightkeepers by bringing Lucius into the mix. Where did she draw the line?

"Okay," Strike said, breaking the tense silence. "We're all here. Let's get started." When Rabbit just kept staring at the floor, throat working, the king prompted, "Don't worry, kid; you're safe now. Just start at the beginning and walk us through everything that's happened since the museum bust." He took a risk and gripped Rabbit's shoulder, though the teen wasn't big on being touched.

Rabbit didn't shake him off, though, didn't even react. He just stared at the floor and whispered, "I killed the three-question *nahwal.*"

Which was so not what any of them had expected him to say. And it so incredibly not good news.

Shock rippled through the room. Strike's jaw went very tight, and Leah nodded as though she'd figured it'd been something like that; Jox muttered under his breath and cast his eyes upward to the gods. Anna's stomach knotted, and her breath whistled out as she tried to even conceive of such a thing. She'd nearly died in her one encounter with a *nahwal*; it was difficult to imagine killing one, impossible to work through the implications besides the most obvious: that there would be no more free answers for the Nightkeepers.

Nate and Alexis seemed to be the only ones who didn't have any outward response to the news, which seemed odd, given that they were the ones who'd nearly died trying to enact the three-question spell. More, Anna had assumed they'd been planning on enacting the spell again, during the equinox. It only stood to reason, given their need to find the Volatile.

As her own shock dimmed, Anna gave the two of them a long look, realizing that while they stood side by side, there was a distance that hadn't been there before, an awkwardness that didn't bode well for tomorrow's battle. Alexis might be able to call on the goddess alone, but a Nightkeeper was always stronger with a mate than without, which made it seriously bad timing if they were arguing, or worse, had broken up again. Just as Patience's and Brandt's magic had weakened the more they fought, so too would Nate's and Alexis's. And frankly, Alexis needed all the magic she could get.

Get a grip, people, Anna wanted to snap. *This is a war. Let's be practical.* But the current crop of Nightkeepers hadn't grown up steeped in the old ways, and didn't always buy into the expectations of their ancestors' times. That added a too-human element to what should've been a warrior's life and a soldier's strategy.

One problem at a time, she warned herself, but felt a skirr of worry at the realization that the members of the royal council weren't at their best going into the equinox. Strike was messed-up over Rabbit, as was Jox to a lesser extent, and Leah was trying to keep the two of them on an even keel. They were trusting their advisers to balance them out, perhaps not realizing that Nate and Alexis were having issues of their own. That left it up to Anna to oversee all five of them and bring some perspective, which was exactly what she didn't want to do. It was like she'd told Red-Boar the year before, when he'd pressured her to rule in her brother's place: She didn't want to lead the Nightkeepers. Hell, she didn't even want to *be* a Nightkeeper.

But, like all of them, she hadn't exactly been given much choice in the matter.

"Okay, people, let's take a breath," she said, aware that they'd all sort of frozen in the wake of Rabbit's announcement. "We knew something had happened to the *nahwal*; now we know what. Let's move on. I don't know about you guys, but I'm going to get comfortable."

Ignoring Rabbit's quick sidelong look and her brother's scowl, she dropped down to the floor and sat cross-legged.

Seeming to shake himself out of wherever he'd gone in his head, Jox said, "Wait. I'll get some folding chairs."

Because gods forbid the king sit on the floor, Anna thought with a kink of amusement at the thought of her little brother, who'd regularly eaten worms and bugs as a child, being unable to sit his ass on the floor.

Nate dropped the ward to let the *winikin* through, but when he went to reset the guard, Anna said, "Wait. Why isn't the girl in here? Myrinne?"

"Because it's not safe," Nate said immediately. "We don't know who or what she is."

"She's important," Rabbit said without looking up, the hoodie falling forward to shadow his face.

Anna said, "How so?"

One shoulder lifted. "Dunno. She just is."

She crouched down and got in the teen's face. "Your father saved my life twice last year, which means I owe him. Since he's not here to tell me to take my owesies and shove them, you're going to have to do it . . . or else you're going to have to let me help you."

He looked at her for a second, and she saw a flash of the boy she remembered from years past, one who'd wanted to be a good kid but had always seemed to get in trouble regardless. Then that flash was gone and there was only the pale blue of his eyes, which went hard and dangerous when he said, "I'll tell you everything, but you've got to promise me that she'll be okay. I don't care what she is, or what the witch or Iago did to her; she stays safe. She doesn't become anyone's bond-slave, she's not blood-bound, and she's not sacrificed. You let her go free and set her up however she wants, or I'm not talking."

"Out of the question," Strike said. "It's too dangerous."

Rabbit didn't even look at the king, kept looking at Anna. "You say you owed my old man? Then make it happen."

"*If* we agree to this," Anna said, emphasizing the "if," "then you have to swear to mind-wipe her before she leaves—and I mean wipe, not light blocks, not something that you think you're going to reverse when we're not paying attention."

The teen's face went white, then flushed brick-red. "You knew?" Now he did raise his head. He stared at her full-on. "You knew I could mind-bend and you didn't tell me?"

"We figured it out after you left," Anna said. When he kept on glaring, she firmed her voice. "Rabbit, we guessed. We didn't know for sure until just now." He'd confirmed it by his reaction, which was potentially good news for Lucius.

Rabbit looked up at Strike and Jox, and his voice shook when he said, "If you didn't know about the *nah-wal*, and you didn't know about the mind-bending, then why didn't you come looking for me more than that once back at the museum? Did I finally reach my last forgivable fuckup or something?"

Anna started to respond, but Strike cut her off with a sharp gesture and motioned her away from the teen. She backed off and Rabbit stood, letting his hood fall back as the king strode toward him, got in his space. The teen stuck out his chin as if he were looking for a punch.

Instead of throwing a fist or an accusation, though, Strike said, "I tried. Jesus, kid, I tried. We all did. Leah and I couldn't pick you up, not even a trace. You were off my radar—still are; Iago blocked your 'port lock back at the museum, then let you loose to see what would happen or something. Since I couldn't lock, we've had Carter turning over all the rocks he can think of. Leah's called in favors. Jox even went to New Orleans to search." His voice went rough when he said, "We've looked at John Does in half a dozen morgues, and thanked the gods each time the body wasn't yours. We've been killing ourselves trying to find you."

Rabbit hesitated, but his expression didn't change. "And now that I'm back?"

"We'll find a way to deal with whatever's been done to you, and whatever you've done." Strike paused. "You're a fuckup, but you're family. Nothing's ever going to change that. Got it?"

The teen swallowed hard and nodded. His voice was thick when he said, "Got it." After an awkward pause his lips twitched a little. "Please tell me we don't have to hug now."

"Sorry. That's nonnegotiable." Strike pulled Rabbit into a manly hug, with lots of backslapping and such.

Anna's throat lumped with relief, coupled with a kick of surprise when she realized that Rabbit wasn't that much shorter than Strike anymore. They'd always assumed the kid was small because he was a half-blood. Maybe he was just taking longer to grow into himself.

When they finally pulled apart, Rabbit said, "What about Myrinne?"

Strike grimaced. "As king, I can't accept her running around here, never mind being set free, without some sort of assurances." When Rabbit started to protest, he held up a hand. "As a man, though, I can't overlook the fact that I brought Leah here under very similar circumstances."

"With the exception that I wasn't raised by a witch or held prisoner by the enemy for any great length of time," Leah put in, laying it out flat. "Sorry, Rabbit, but we just can't have her here without some sort of oversight."

"I won't have her blood-bound," Rabbit said. "Not to me, and not to anyone else. If that's your answer, then we're out of here." He paused, expression darkening. "And if you think you can stop me, just try it."

Anna didn't like the way Strike got big at Rabbit's tone, didn't like the idea of picking a fight she wasn't entirely sure the Nightkeepers were going to win, so she stepped between them, turning her back on Rabbit and facing Strike squarely. She looked him in the eye and said, "I'll take responsibility for her."

Which was more than promising to babysit. Even without the blood-bond, if a Nightkeeper claimed a human, the mage was responsible for—and liable for—the human's actions, eye for eye, tooth for tooth, same as with a bond-servant.

If Myrinne betrayed the Nightkeepers, Anna would be punished as a traitor; if she killed one of them, Anna would be sacrificed in return. The same was true for Lucius, but the blood-bond allowed her a degree of control over him. Without the blood-bond she would have no magical leverage over Myrinne, no recourse if the girl attempted to escape, or worse. Which meant Anna was essentially hooking her safety to the behavior of a witch's brat she'd barely spoken to.

The world seemed to freeze for a second as her rational side screeched, *What in the flying hell are you doing?*

She was repaying her debt to Red-Boar by doing what was necessary to keep his son within Skywatch, within the reach of magi who could—hopefully—help him deal with whatever Iago had done to him. Whatever else that meant in terms of her own life and freedom, she'd deal. She was, whether she liked it or not, her father's daughter, heir to the jaguar bloodline, whose members were notorious for making decisions based on emotion. *Damn it.*

Strike's eyes searched hers. "Are you sure?"

She was aware of Rabbit holding his breath behind her, aware of a flash of hope coming from him. Within that flash, that emotion, a fragment of a vision broke through, showing her Rabbit and Myrinne hand in hand, running along a beaten snow trail. The vision was from the previous night, she knew, but the Rabbit she saw in the vision was no teen, no boy. Tall, strong, and purposeful, wielding his magic out of necessity rather than anger, he was a man, a Nightkeeper protecting the woman he'd chosen as his mate, even if he didn't fully recognize the connection yet, or believe in it.

"Yes," she said clearly. "I'm sure." If having Myrinne

to lean on, to protect, would help Rabbit find the man the Nightkeepers needed him to be, then it was worth the risk.

Or so she told herself.

Strike glanced at Jox, then at Nate and Alexis. "Arguments?"

"Numerous," Alexis said dryly. "But none on this particular matter. Fact is, the options are pretty much all equally risky, and this is the one that'll keep the Nightkeepers intact."

"Agreed," Nate said without looking at her.

Sitting on the other side of Strike, Jox nodded. "I'll do what I can to help," he said to Anna. Knowing the royal *winikin* as well as she did, she could tell he hated the added exposure she was piling onto herself, but knew it was the only and best option within a culture where both debt and responsibility were weighty matters.

"Then it's settled," she said, pushing the words past a sudden tightness in her throat. She sat back down and waited until Strike and Rabbit had done the same before she said to Rabbit, "Okay. Myrinne described her experiences to Leah pretty thoroughly, but I think it'd be good if you start from the beginning and walk us through what happened, what you learned from Iago."

"There's a second archive," Rabbit said quietly, looking at his knuckles, which had gone white with fisted tension. "A library. I found out that much."

Anna's breath froze in her lungs, and the world seemed to contract to just the two of them as she whispered, "Iago has it?"

"No. Not as of last night, anyway. He used my powers to . . . question a woman." Rabbit's tone and the disgusted twist to his lips made the word "question" into a curse. "He kept asking her where her father hid the stuff."

The connection sparked on a gasp, and Anna blurted, "Sasha!"

"Did she tell him where to find the library?" Nate asked quickly, his eyes going dark and intent.

Rabbit shook his head. "No. Her mind is superstrong." He paused. "It was, anyway."

Anna went still. "Why do you say that?"

"She was linked to Iago when I reversed his mind-bend and tried to fry his cortex."

Horror gathered in Anna's gut, alongside despair that they might've already lost their next-best chance at finding the library, and the woman Lucius had sought for reasons she didn't yet understand but wasn't willing to ignore. "Is she dead?"

"She was breathing when I left her. They both were." He looked to Strike. "I can take you back there."

The king nodded and stood. "Let's go." But they returned within twenty minutes, empty-handed. Sasha and Iago were gone.

Lucius didn't know where he was, didn't know how to get back to where he was supposed to be. At times he wasn't even sure he knew where he was supposed to be, only that it wasn't where he was, so he kept walking, even though he didn't seem to be getting anywhere.

His legs ached, but the road he traveled along never changed. The surface was smooth-packed dirt unmarked by tire tracks or hoofprints, though he occasionally saw the tracks of other pedestrians, always headed in the direction he was going, never the other way. On either side of the road, rocky, gray-brown plains stretched out to join somewhere in the distance with a gray-brown sky that held no clouds. There was only gray-brown everywhere, and the road that stretched out in front of him and behind him.

A part of him wondered if he'd died, if this was the journey the Maya spoke of, where the dead traveled through Xibalba to be sorted according to their actions in life. Those who died a violent death went straight to the sky, while everyone else had to meet a series of underworld challenges, and cross a river whose overlord needed to be paid with the jade pebbles buried over the eyes of the dead.

So far, though, Lucius hadn't been challenged by anything worse than boredom, nor did he remember dying, and he had to imagine that wasn't the sort of thing a guy forgot. Last thing he remembered was—

Oh, shit. Calling Anna for help as the green haze descended on him. Had he gone *makol*? Had the Night-keepers sacrificed him while he'd been caught up in the Day-Glo fugue?

Amidst a strange sort of calm that had him continuing onward instead of freaking out and running screaming into the distance—or just standing still and screaming—he found he didn't blame Anna and the others if that was what they'd decided. Risk was risk, and one grad student's life didn't matter much when balanced against the dozen Nightkeepers who needed to save the world. If he'd gone *makol* and put the Nightkeepers in danger, then they'd done what they'd needed to do.

If that was the case, he decided, he was okay with dying.

The moment he thought that, a shadow appeared in the distance, growing closer as he continued walking. Pretty soon he could make out a high stone arch stretching over the road, with huge, openmouthed serpents carved on either side.

Beyond it was a wide, sluggish river.

On instinct, Lucius reached into his pants pocket and found two hard, round objects in there. Pulling them out, he stared at the jade beads. *That's it, then,* he thought, sadness breaking through the fog. *Game over.*

"Turn around," a multitonal voice said, coming from nowhere and everywhere at once. "She needs you."

Lucius stopped dead, and the fog blinked out of existence. He could see details all of a sudden, could see that the rocky plains on either side of him were painted curtains writhing with reptilian movement from the other side, and the archway was cracked and broken and black, the water brackish and stinking.

A pit opened up in the center of his stomach, yawning, dark, and terrifying.

"Who said that?" he called, his voice falling flat in the echoless space.

There was no answer, but suddenly he had control over his limbs again and could turn around on the path. He took a step back in the direction he'd come. The moment his foot landed, a terrible scream arose from the waterway, then another.

Lucius didn't think, didn't look back. He just started running toward the light that appeared in front of him, at the other end of the road of the damned.

Back to the land of the living.

It took most of the day for the members of the royal council to debrief Rabbit and Myrinne, alternating between them when Jox announced it was time for one of the exhausted, malnourished kids to eat or sleep, or both. By the end of the day, as Alexis headed to her rooms to change, shower, and generally take a big breath, she wasn't convinced they knew much more than they had going in. Or rather, they knew more, but what they'd learned probably wouldn't go very far toward helping them the next day, when they would 'port to the intersection beneath Chichén Itzá and defend the barrier against Iago and Camazotz.

The plan was for the Nightkeepers to 'port to the safe house early in the morning and stake out the tunnel entrance. Problem was, they weren't even sure Iago would be working his magic through the intersection. Rabbit didn't know if the mage had found the actual hellmouth, the place where the Xibalbans had called the *Banol Kax* through to earth in A.D. 951. If Iago knew where the hellmouth was, then he had direct access to Xibalba, do not pass go, do not collect, no need for the Nightkeepers' intersection and its tortuous connections to the sky and underworld.

If Iago didn't show at the intersection—which Alexis strongly suspected would be the case—the Nightkeepers would do as they had done during the winter solstice and eclipse, uplinking and banding together to hold the barrier that separated Xibalba from the earth. Strike and Leah would call on the power of Kulkulkan, and Alexis would add Ixchel's strength to the mix. The barrier was a psi-entity that stretched everywhere and nowhere at once, which meant that if they managed to fortify it with enough power at Chichén Itzá, it should prove impenetrable at the hellmouth. In theory. In reality, they had no frigging clue. And that was the worry that had Alexis unable to settle in her rooms, and had her pacing from one to the next, touching a light fixture here, a book there, somehow needing the tactile reminders, the solidity of the earth plane.

She and Ixchel were supposed to counteract the first of the demon prophecies, but Alexis had no idea how. The others were acting as though the first prophecy were a moot point, given that Iago planned to bring through all seven of Camazotz's sons simultaneously. But she wasn't so sure. If there was no such thing as true coincidence, if everything that was happening was truly influenced by fate, or destiny, or the gods, then shouldn't the gods have foreseen Iago's threat? Assuming they had, then that meant Ixchel was supposed to serve a larger purpose, or else she and Alexis wouldn't have formed the Godkeeper bond.

Right?

"I don't know!" Alexis practically shouted. "I don't know why she picked me, or how I'm supposed to use her powers." Her stomach twisted on a gut-deep fear of failure, fear of death. Fear of losing the people she loved.

Frustrated and heartsore, she threw herself on the sofa, then bounced back up almost immediately when she couldn't stand not to be moving. It wasn't just the fears and worries that kept her going, either; the magic of the coming equinox rode her hard. She could close her eyes and tell where the stars were overhead just by feeling their pull and seeing the faint color shimmers they gave off in her soul. The barrier was thinning, and with it her self-control. She wanted to scream and throw things, wanted to drive off into the desert in one of the four-wheelers Jox kept in the garage, wanted to spin the tires and kick up sand and jump the vehicle from hill to hill, though she'd never actually driven one of the damn things.

Then she heard a knock on the door. She knew who it was without question, and in that instant all the crazy, jumbled needs inside her coalesced into a single emotion.

Desire.

She opened the door and saw Nate standing there, exactly as she'd expected, wearing jeans and a soft black pullover that did nothing to gentle the angles of his face and the edgy tension surrounding him. She arched a brow, but before she could work up a witty opener, he said simply, "I know you don't owe me a damned thing, and you might not want to be around me right now, but I had to come. I need you to know that if I could've figured out how to love anyone, I would've loved you."

The simplicity of that, the finality of it, drove the breath from her lungs and sent a spear of pain through her heart. It took her a second, but once her throat unlocked, she said, "Then why can't you?"

"Nature, maybe, or nurture. Maybe both. Probably both." He lifted a shoulder. "It took me a while to see it, but if you look at the pictures of my parents, my mother's always the one surrounded by other people, while my father is always apart just a bit. And the paintings . . . they're all of places seen from a distance. No people, no close-ups. If that's not detachment, I don't know what is. Add his DNA to my growing up in the system, and you've got a guy who likes people okay but does best alone." He exhaled long and hard. "Look, I've tried to feel the things other people feel, and it . . . it just doesn't work. It's just not in me to love someone." His eyes went very sad. "Not even you. I'm so sorry."

Alexis bowed her head as all the restless energy drained into a moment of pure, profound emotion. It wasn't heartache; that would come later, she knew. It wasn't failure, either, though she was due for a heaping pile of that too. No, this was a piercing regret that the things they'd already had together were the end of it, even if they survived the equinox. There would be no moving into Nate's cottage and waking up next to him each morning, no trying to cook for each other and sneaking food from the main mansion when the stuff didn't turn out, no hardwood floors and little smoke-motif knickknacks.

"Alexis, please say something," he pressed when she'd been silent for too long. His lips twitched in a small, sad smile. "Either that or rack me a good one and slam the door. Whichever works for you."

"Maybe it's better this way," she said slowly. "Maybe it's better to go into tomorrow without this between us."

Better to go into battle with nothing she was looking forward to except more fighting, more training. More war.

Maybe that was what this had been about all along. Maybe the goddess had been trying to teach her to let go.

He exhaled a long breath. "Good. Okay . . . good." He didn't look as though he thought it was good, but she understood that too. "So . . ."

"So . . ." Now she did smile at him, letting him know it was really okay. "See you tomorrow." She shut the door between them, not slamming it, but shutting it slowly and letting the latch engage with a final-sounding click.

Then, and only then, she finally collapsed onto the couch and put her face in her hands. Her hair, unbound and still moist from her shower, fell forward in long, ribbonlike strands.

And when she wept, her tears were rainbows.

CHAPTER TWENTY-FIVE

March 21

The Nightkeepers joined up well before dawn, and Strike 'ported them to the temple site—except for Rabbit, who remained at Skywatch along with Myrinne and Lucius. The three of them were locked in the warded storerooms with armed *winikin* standing guard, two at a time, in four-hour shifts. All but Hannah and Wood, who were still in hiding with the twins.

The Nightkeepers' numbers were dwindling rather than building, Nate realized with a shimmer of unease.

They waited in the deep darkness that held on to the rain forest in the final hour before daybreak while Michael checked the surveillance system in the small house near the temple. When his all-clear signal came through Strike said, "Okay, gang, it's more than twelve hours before the equinox and eleven or so before the tunnel inside the temple opens up. Let's start with just a couple of people on watch outside the temple, and rotate through every two hours. Volunteers?"

Nate raised his hand, figuring that if he had to stay cooped up in the little house with the rest of them for very long, he was going to go batshit crazy. From the number of hands showing, he wasn't the only one.

Strike snorted. "That's about what I thought. Okay,

it's me and Nate on first shift. The rest of you duke it out for the next one. We'll add one extra person per two-hour block, with everyone on station by midafternoon."

"Keep your eyes open," Leah said, pressing Strike's hand. She patted her hip, where she wore a medium-range walkie-talkie. "Call us if you see anything."

Each of them had one of the radios, tuned to lucky channel thirteen. The walkies wouldn't do much good down in the tunnels, but should be a simple, effective method for staying in contact during the aboveground portion of the stakeout.

Strike dropped a kiss on his mate's lips. "Count on it." They stood together for a moment, leaning into each other, and a faint golden glow sparkled, haloing them as their strong love reached out and touched Kulkulkan's power.

Unable to do otherwise, Nate glanced at Alexis, who stood beside him. She caught the look and her lips turned up, as though she were determined to keep it light between them after what'd happened the night before. "Special effects courtesy of the equinox," she whispered.

He should've said something smooth and equally light, but what came out was a soft, "You look tired."

"Gee, thanks. You too."

"Didn't sleep worth shit." As he'd lain awake in the cottage, staring at the ceiling, Nate had told himself it was better to spend that final night alone, that he'd be sharper and more rested without Alexis in his bed. It'd turned out he wasn't very good at lying, even to himself.

"Ditto," she said, and lifted a shoulder. "I probably shouldn't have said anything the other night about . . . you know. Sorry."

"No." He caught her hand, unable to leave it like that. "No, never. I'm . . ." He trailed off, unable to find the right word.

Her eyes narrowed. "If you say 'flattered,' I'll fireball you in the nuts."

Strike's voice interrupted. "Come on, Blackhawk. First shift's leaving."

"Lucky save," Alexis murmured. But then her anger drained and she said simply, "Take care of yourself, okay?"

"Yeah. You too." There wasn't anything more to say after that—at least nothing he could say truthfully, or that would come easily and feel real, so Nate followed his king out of the cottage and didn't look back.

Strike led the way, carrying a small flashlight that reminded Nate of the miners' lamps he and Alexis had used in the ATM caves. The beam was just as pitiful, their surroundings just as dark. As they entered the path to the temple, the rain forest closed in on either side of them, pitching the darkness even blacker. Nate tried to shrug off the feeling, which was pretty close to a certainty, that this was the last time he'd be traveling along the narrow path, the last time he'd be glancing back and seeing only the glimmer of light through the dense vegetation, though the safe house was only a few hundred yards away.

It's nerves, he told himself. *Nerves and the equinox.*

When they reached the temple, and the point where they would split up to stand watch, Strike lifted a hand. "Wait."

Nate looked up, surprised. *"Nochem?"*

"I want you to take this." The king held out his hand into the thin flashlight beam. On his palm rested something long, narrow, and flat, and glittering black. It was a knife, Nate saw, then realized that it wasn't just *a* knife; it was the knife of the Volatile prophecy. *His* knife.

Everything inside him went tight on a single, greedy word: *Mine!* It was the same way he felt about Alexis, the same way he'd always felt about her; it was just as simple as that, and as complex. He took the knife and balanced the weapon on his palm, staring down at the polished black stone and trying not to feel how well it fit in his hand, how natural it felt, in a way that no other ceremonial knife had done before. He knew the blade with a deep, thrumming possessiveness that seemed to originate from just above his breastbone. He wanted to keep it, to wear it, to blood himself with its blade.

He glanced at his king. "I swear that I'll die before I let the Volatile hurt her."

"I know."

They parted without another word. Taking up his position, Nate settled in to watch the small temple, and the surrounding rain forest. Periodic check-ins via walkie-talkie all brought the same message: *All's quiet.* Eventually the sky went from black to blue, then deepened through purple to a vicious red that filtered through the leafy canopy and turned everything to blood. The light pinked out quickly to day, but that violent red hue stayed with him, seeming prophetic even to a man who refused to live by prophecy.

His worries weren't superstition, though; they were logic. How were they supposed to hold the barrier with so few magi? *Not good odds,* his gamer's brain reported. *We need a new strategy.* Only they'd already explored all the options, hadn't they?

He withdrew the carved obsidian knife from his belt and flipped it through his fingers a few times, becoming familiar with the perfect balance of the blade and the feel of the worn carvings as he waited.

And waited.

There was no sign of Iago as the day warmed and the birds and monkeys started doing their thing overhead. The surveillance shifts changed, and changed again, and still nothing. In fact, exactly nothing happened all gods-damned day. By dusk, all of the Nightkeepers were hunched in the forest, watching a whole lot of nothing. Nate had positioned himself very near Alexis, as he had done all day whether she liked it or not, because the equinox magic was sparking in his veins, and his skin felt tight across his bones. Close to nightfall, when she glanced in his direction and their eyes met, he saw rainbows. Then she nodded to Strike and Leah, concealed in a cluster of ferns nearby, and he turned to find them deep in conversation, with the satellite phone forming a third party, no doubt bringing Jox in on the discussion.

When Nate's walkie crackled, calling the Nightkeepers in, he was moving before the king had finished speaking. He and Alexis converged on the royal couple's position, and Strike said without preamble, "We'll drop down into the tunnels now. We've got about an hour."

Nate nodded. "Yeah. It's time." He paused. "Anything from Skywatch?"

"Nothing," Leah reported. "It's totally quiet there, just like here."

"Iago's at the hellmouth," Nate said grimly, which meant it was going to come down to a battle of magic versus magic. And pretty much everything they knew about the Xibalbans—which wasn't nearly enough—suggested that the Nightkeepers were going to be seriously outmatched. Add in the seven death bats and the Volatile, and they were pretty close to fucked.

Rabbit knew when darkness fell, even though he was locked in the lower level of the mansion, stuck in a windowless storeroom. He could feel the stars moving into position, feel the barrier thinning and the magic calling out to him.

There was something else calling out to him, as well. Something that shouldn't have been able to get through the wards surrounding Skywatch, not to mention the additional shield around his room. But the whispers penetrated, tempting him at first, taunting him. Then, as the equinox drew near and the power sink opened up inside him, lighting him with magic, the whispered temptation gave way to a demand. An order.

Open your mind to me, Iago said, his mental tone vibrating with the power of a mind-bender, power he'd stolen from Rabbit in the first place. *Add your magic to mine.*

"Fuck you, asshole," Rabbit said aloud. "How did you get in here, anyway?"

He didn't expect an answer, and was surprised as shit when a chuckle vibrated along the connection. *You invited me.*

"Did not!" Rabbit shouted, indignant. But beneath the bluster lay the suspicion that maybe he had. He'd been lying there all day, alone, in a room he'd ordered the *winikin* to strip of as much of the flammables as possible. TV was boring, he wasn't in the mood for the game-loaded laptop Nate had hooked him up with, and his IM convo with Myrinne had lost steam a few hours earlier when she'd decided to nap, still recovering from her imprisonment.

So yeah, he'd been lying there, thinking of Iago, thinking about how he'd crawled inside the Xibalban's head. He'd mentally retraced what he'd done and how it'd felt to tell someone to die and almost have it work. And maybe, just maybe, while he'd been doing that, he'd inadvertently reached out and made contact.

Anger kindled within Rabbit. Fury, and a burning need to protect what was his—his family and home. Myrinne.

Well, guess what? he thought, burning with the magic. *Two can play this game.*

He lay back on his cot, closed his eyes, and fisted his hands, digging his fingernails into his palms until blood flowed. Rather than fighting off Iago's mental touch he sought it, grabbed on to it, followed it to its source. Whereas before it had been difficult to find his way into the Xibalban's mind, it was easy this time, as though he were following the same path he'd blazed before.

I've got you, you son of a bitch, he thought, keeping the flare of triumph to himself as he slid smoothly into Iago's brain. Then, suddenly, he was looking through Iago's eyes, seeing what Iago saw.

And damn it, the Xibalban wasn't anywhere near Chichén Itzá. The vegetation was wrong, the temperature and heavy cloud cover were wrong. And the temple Iago was facing looked like nothing Rabbit had ever seen before—all soaring stone arches cut directly into the side of a mountain, framing a godsdamned cave that was carved to look like a screaming skull.

It was the fucking hellmouth. The entrance to Xibalba.

Like what you see, Bunny-boy? Iago jeered, having yanked the nickname from Rabbit's brain somehow. *Good, because you're not going anywhere.*

Mental shackles clamped down on Rabbit, and the pathway he'd followed into the Xibalban's brain vanished in an instant. He turned to run, to flee, to fight, but couldn't. He was cut off from his body, cut off from

Skywatch and any ability to warn the others, cut off from Myrinne and any hope of escape.

He couldn't do a godsdamned thing except scream inside his own soul as Iago pressed his palms flat against the edge of the cave mouth and said a quiet spell, drawing on Rabbit's power and his own to open the ancient hellroad, which had been locked tight more than a thousand years earlier, when the ancestral Nightkeepers had driven the demons from earth in the wake of the slaughter that had leveled an empire. Those Nightkeepers had trusted their true descendants to hold the barrier, and they had, for more than a thousand years.

It'd taken a half-blood to fuck everything up.

Lucius's journey back from death seemed much quicker than the trek out to the archway; one minute he was on the roadway, putting one boot in front of the other. Then suddenly he was at a set of double doors. There was no wall or anything, just the doors, sitting in the middle of no-frigging-where.

Taking a deep breath, he grabbed one of the doorknobs, twisted, and opened the panel slowly, so he could stick his head through and take a look.

Without warning the door, the road, and the world around him vanished, and he was falling. There was blackness all around him, the sensation of gravity and air whipping past him, but no sound or smell. He opened his mouth and screamed but nothing came out; there was only silence. He couldn't even hear his own rapid heartbeat or his pulse.

Then he hit bottom, landing sprawled out on a giving, yielding surface. It was still dark but he could hear again. There was pain too. Monstrous, crushing pain that split his head and made him scream in pain, the howl coming out alien, like that of an animal, not a man.

He writhed, digging his fingers into his scalp, tearing at his hair, trying to make the agony stop, make it all stop. *Oh, sweet Jesus. If this is what living feels like, send me back to death!*

Slowly, though, the pain leveled. His skull felt overstuffed, but he could think now, could almost focus his eyes. He blinked, saw a fluorescent light overhead, and realized that it wasn't really dark after all; it had all been in his mind. A nightmare, maybe, or a warning. He was in a bare room, lying on a cot. And wonder of wonders, he was seeing normally, with no luminous green haze obscuring his vision.

He looked around, recognized his surroundings from his first night in New Mexico, and thought, *I'm still in Skywatch, back in the dungeon, or whatever they want to call it.* Which meant the Nightkeepers hadn't sacrificed him, after all. They'd locked him up until the green haze passed. That must be why the voice had sent him back; it'd known that he wasn't quite dead yet. Gratitude washed over him. He hadn't wanted to die; he wanted to live, wanted to help the Nightkeepers in the battle ahead.

His internal clock said it was nighttime, but he was pumped up, invigorated, ready to get rolling. Riding that energy, he stood and headed for the storeroom door, gave it a jaunty knock. "Yo! Anyone out there? Feeling human again, here."

There was a startled clatter from out in the hallway, then the sound of footsteps. A moment later the door opened a crack to reveal Jox's face, pale with shock. "Did you just knock?"

Lucius frowned and almost looked behind himself, to see if he'd missed there being someone else in the room. "Um, yeah?"

"You shouldn't have been able to reach the door. It's warded."

"Apparently not so much."

"No, the ward's working. Which means you're back to being fully human." Jox's face relaxed; his whole body easing as he let the door swing a little wider. "A *makol* couldn't have come through. A normal guy with a so-so academic record and a talent for getting his ass in trouble, though . . . he could get through just fine."

Lucius grinned, feeling as if he could run a few hundred laps and bench-press a Jeep. "Guilty on all counts, though I'll have to talk to Anna about maligning her servant."

"Meh. Student, servant, big diff." The *winikin* lifted a shoulder. "One of these days you and I can sit down and I'll let you in on a few of the high points of the whole servant thing." He flashed his forearm, which bore the *aj-winikin* "to serve" glyph, along with a pair of jaguars, one for Anna, one for Strike. "There are ways to work the bond magic, if you're interested."

"I'm interested. Seriously."

"Come on." Jox stepped back. "You've gotta be starving. You haven't eaten in several days. I'll catch you up on things while you eat."

"That sounds . . . Hang on, *how* long?" Lucius shook his head, unable to believe he felt so good after being in one place for days. Never mind wondering what the hell had gone on inside his head while he'd been walking along on that big-ass Xibalban treadmill. "Whoa. Hello, mind-fuck."

Jox snorted. "Come on, human." He turned away and headed for the staircase.

Lucius followed, but the moment he was clear of the door, something foul shoved him viciously aside, into a small corner of his own consciousness. His bones shifted and popped, his skin stretched tight, and the world went into slow motion. And everything got real green, real fast.

He stretched out arms grown longer than normal, reaching for the *winikin* with fingers now tipped with pointed nails.

Jox, run! Lucius screamed, but his lips didn't move; no sound came out; the scream stayed stuck inside his head as his body was taken over by the *makol* that had somehow hidden deep inside him, fooling even the Nightkeepers' ward magic.

The *winikin* didn't turn, didn't know to defend himself. He was halfway up the stairs when the creature that wasn't Lucius anymore grabbed him from behind, got an inhumanly strong grip on the back of his neck, and slammed him into the wall.

Jox went limp, and Lucius—or the thing that had been Lucius—let him fall. Going to one knee beside him, the creature searched him and came up with a flip-blade buck knife. Flicking the blade open, the *makol* grabbed the *winikin*'s gray-shot hair and used it to pull his head back, baring his throat.

The connection suddenly clicked in the small part of Lucius that still belonged to him. It was the goddamned equinox. A day for blood sacrifice.

The knife descended. Lucius flung himself out of the corner of his mind, mustered all the mental control he'd never had, and shouted, *"Hold!"*

The knife froze. Then, furious at the interruption, the *makol* turned its attention inward, grabbing what was left of Lucius's consciousness and clamping down, squeezing, pressing until everything went dark and life as he knew it ended.

In the final hour before the equinox, the air inside the Nightkeepers' small aboveground temple shimmered with gold and rainbows as the barrier greeted the Godkeepers. Alexis, Strike, and Leah joined together in the magic that would open the tunnel leading down to the intersection.

"Pasaj och," Alexis said in synchrony with the royal couple, and bowed her head in prayer as blood from her sliced hand dripped to the ground in sacrifice. She wore her mother's combat shirt beneath her Kevlar, and for the first time felt at home, felt as though she belonged in the warrior's garb, at the front of the pack. This was it, she knew; this was what her parents had wanted for her, what Izzy had trained her for. She had the power, the respect. But with it came a responsibility she wasn't sure she could fulfill.

Rainbows against demons. It seemed impossible, even more so knowing that the Volatile was out there somewhere, waiting for her.

"Steady," Leah murmured out of the corner of her mouth. "One step at a time."

"Easier said than done," Alexis replied.

"Amen to that, sister."

Then the magic stabilized, and the tunnel was fully open. "In we go." Strike led, with Leah and Alexis falling in behind him, Nate behind her, and then Anna, Patience, Brandt, Jade, and Sven. As usual, Michael shielded the rear.

They had debated closing the tunnel once they were inside, but that would've meant they could be trapped underground. Leaving it open, though, ran the risk of someone—or some*thing*—coming up behind them, which Alexis didn't like one bit. She was coming to realize, though, that her job as an adviser wasn't to steer the Nightkeepers' away from risk—that was impossible. All she and Nate could do was to manage the risk as best as they could, and then pray.

Or rather, she would pray, and he would keep stubbornly pretending that the gods and destiny didn't rule their lives, despite all evidence to the contrary.

As they passed into the tunnel, lighting their way with powerful hand lamps she'd bought to replace the lameass flashlights they'd been using in the tunnels up until now, she looked back and caught Nate staring at her. Granted, she was in front of him, so it wasn't likely he'd be looking elsewhere. But the intensity in his gaze, and the way his amber eyes locked on hers, let her know that he was looking at *her*, thinking about her.

What is it? she wanted to say. *Tell me.* But she didn't, because what would be the point? She'd said what she'd needed to say, and he'd done the same. They had, finally, reached the end of their personal debate. As he would say, "Game over." *And this so isn't what I should be focused on right now,* she thought as she faced forward and followed Strike and Leah into the tunnels that ran down to the subterranean river, and eventually to the altar room.

Yes, Nate was important to her—she was in love with him whether he liked it or not, godsdamn it—but the moment she'd learned how to call the goddess on her own, their relationship had become separate from the needs of the Nightkeepers. And right now the Nightkeepers and their magic had to be her primary concern. So she faced forward and followed the tunnel into the earth, and tried to keep her mind on the connection at the back of her brain, where the rainbows lived.

As she walked, she prayed for the strength to do what

needed to be done, and the smarts to recognize what that might be. There was no ripple in the barrier energy, no sense of the goddess beyond the low thrum of color. Alexis knew she was out there, waiting. But for what?

"Frigging obscure prophecies," she heard Nate growl from behind her, his low words amplified and thrown forward by the tunnel walls. "Couldn't just spell this shit out, could they?"

Alexis stifled a snort, and immediately felt better. Maybe it was blasphemy—okay, probably—but she couldn't say he was wrong. What good did it do for them to know they needed to defeat the Volatile if they didn't know how to find it?

No doubt Leah had been right when she'd speculated in council that the sheer length of the skyroad, running through the extra four layers of heaven that hell lacked, attenuated the ability of the gods to interact with the earthly plane and compromised their ability to connect with the Nightkeepers. Even Kulkulkan had "spoken" to Leah only a couple of times, during their initial binding. Alexis couldn't say for sure that Ixchel had ever talked to her in words; the few times she'd thought she'd caught a snippet of thought that didn't feel like her own could've just been wishful thinking. Besides, as Strike had pointed out, the gods created and the demons destroyed, and creation was a much harder energy to push through the barrier than was destruction. Entropy in action, and all that. All of which pretty much left the Nightkeepers floundering with visions and gut instincts, and prophecies left by their ancestors based on . . . well, visions and gut instinct.

Which just sucks beyond sucking, Alexis thought as she hiked in her queen's wake. And there she went with the blasphemy again, which probably wasn't a good thing to be coming from a Godkeeper on one of the cardinal days. But it had already been a long day of waiting, and the silence in the tunnel was getting to her, raising the hairs at her nape and puckering goose bumps on her arms. The empty quiet, broken only by the sound of their breathing and the scuff of boots on the stone, seemed to be waiting for something. Or someone.

Then Alexis saw Leah glance from one side of the tunnel to the other, and Strike scrub a hand down the back of his neck. Which meant Alexis wasn't the only one feeling it.

"Something's coming," she whispered as unease shivered through her and took up residence in her gut. "Something bad."

"I know," Nate said. He'd moved up close, so close that she could feel his body heat and his energy. She didn't reach back to him, but knowing he was there steadied her. Whether or not he was her lover or mate, he was a warrior she could count on. She only hoped he could count on her in return, hoped they all could.

The air remained tense as they worked their way deeper into the tunnel system. Soon Alexis could hear the drip of water up ahead, signaling that they were near the subterranean river that would lead them to the altar room. They took the narrow pathway beside the waterway, then turned away from the river to the sacred chamber. There was no sign of pursuit or ambush. The only thing menacing them was the heavy feeling in the air, a sense of something watching them, waiting. The grating edginess of it served only to exaggerate the hum of magic in Alexis's blood as the stars and planets aligned, inching into position in the final thirty-minute countdown to the equinox.

Then they turned the final corner and came to the arched doorway leading into the altar room. The tunnel widened, allowing Leah to move up and walk at Strike's side. Nate joined Alexis, and the others paired up behind them, with Michael forming the rear guard alone.

They went in with their autopistols drawn and fireball magic at the ready, but the chamber was empty. There was no sign of Iago, no sign of anything out of place. Only there *was* something, Alexis realized as Strike lit the ceremonial torches around the perimeter of the room and the Nightkeepers extinguished their hand lamps, letting the room fall to firelight.

In that firelight, she could see a shimmer walk all the way across the back wall behind the *chac-mool* altar.

Without thinking, she reached for Nate's hand and tugged him up beside her. "Do you see that?"

He frowned. "See what?"

"I'll take that as a no." Alexis turned to the others. "Does anyone else—"

Anna screamed suddenly, cutting her off midquestion. The king's sister dropped to her knees and grabbed her right forearm in pain. "Lucius, *no*! Don't do it! Don't—" Her eyes rolled back in her head, and she went limp and toppled over onto her side, convulsing.

"Anna!" Strike bolted to her side and dropped to his knees beside her as she writhed.

Bowing her body in an arc, she shrieked, "Nooo! Not Jox! Not the *winikin*! *Please!*"

Shock and horror rattled through the Nightkeepers as they realized that the *makol* must have fully overtaken Lucius and had somehow escaped its warded room and attacked the *winikin*.

Panic jolted Alexis, alongside magic and a howl of grief. She grabbed instinctively for Nate's hand. *"Izzy!"*

Strike lunged to his feet, snapping, "Join up!"

Nate pulled free of her hand and got in the king's face. "No! You know we can't go back."

And the hell of it was that he was right, Alexis knew. The goddaughter inside her screamed for them to return to Skywatch immediately, yet the warrior in her knew that whatever was going on back there, it wasn't their main battle. The more important fight was the one that reached for her even now, as the rippling curtain of light darkened and solidified along the back wall of the stone chamber, and she began to see movement behind it, the imprints of huge bodies pressing against what could only be the barrier.

Strike grated, "Stand aside, Blackhawk. You may not give a shit about anybody but yourself, but I'm not leaving them to die. Rabbit is my responsibility. Jox is mine. They all are."

Leah moved up to stand at Strike's side, her face pale and drawn. "We have to go," she said. "Skywatch can't fall a second time."

"The Nightkeepers are your priority, and mankind," Nate insisted, refusing to give way. "Not the *winikin* or

Rabbit. As much as it sucks to say it, the immediate future rests on us and what we do here today."

Of them all, Alexis thought she might be the only one to see what it cost Nate to say that, the only one to hear the pain in his voice, see the horror in his too-controlled expression. He glanced at her, a mute plea for some backup against the furious king, and Alexis stepped up to add her voice to his.

Only her feet didn't move at first. Then, when they did, they carried her away from the argument, toward the rippling barrier, where she saw colors and darkness battling one another for the upper hand, and achieving only a stalemate. *Come,* the colors seemed to say. *I need your help.*

"Alexis, what's wrong?" Nate's voice held sharp worry, but he sounded suddenly far distant, his tones wavery and indistinct.

The fabric of the universe dominated her vision, reaching out and drawing her inward. "Call your god," she said to Strike, only it wasn't her voice; it was the goddess speaking through her, expending enormous energy to push the message down the skyroad to earth. "The hellroad is open at the city of the clouds. The battle is there."

Alexis's mind was suddenly filled with an image of great, soaring mountains. Bare and snow-covered at their tops, lush and green at their foothills, they wore thick clouds of mist halfway down, where the cold mountain winds met moist tropical air and formed rainy, cool bands of precipitation. High conical mounds speared through the canopy, green-covered and with a hint of square-edged stone here and there. Lost pyramids rising up from the jungle floor.

Her voice shaking with the effort of the magical contact, which was draining her quickly, Alexis described the scene as best as she could. When she started to sway, she felt a strong arm loop around her waist and knew it was Nate.

"Strike needs a ground-level image to 'port," Nate said. "We can't zap in midair."

His voice didn't seem so far away now, as she leaned

into his strength, his warmth, and felt her own energy drain. She was aware of Strike and Leah leaning over Anna, who had gone silent and still, aware of the awful tension in the room as the Nightkeepers awaited the decision. Skywatch or the hellmouth? The battle for home or the battle for the world?

Strike's choice was, she realized, very like what his father must have faced in the moment the *Banol Kax* broke through the intersection and sent their lava creatures to kill the *winikin* and children back at the training compound. What had happened before was happening again.

Alexis concentrated, sending her need along the sky-road link, and was rewarded with a second, ground-level picture, one that grew dim and gray as her energy faded. Then there was a rasp and a hiss of pain, and Nate was clasping her hand in his bloodied grasp, boosting her power with his own. The image clarified, one of carved stone and a gaping skull mouth wreathed in gray-white vapor.

"It's high in the mountains," she said, "just below where the clouds begin. There's a river flowing in and down, and a dark, deep tunnel." She kept going with the description of the screaming skull and surrounding cloud forest, trying to give her king enough for the 'port link. When she ran down, when there was no more left that she could think to add, she sagged against Nate, feeling his energy as her own, his fatigue as her own.

With the message passed, the wall behind the altar returned to stone, and Alexis's Godkeeper connection returned to a baseline shimmer at the back of her skull. The room stopped spinning, and some of her energy returned—thanks, she suspected, to the blood link with Nate.

Knowing he would need his own strength, she pulled away and forced herself to stand on her own two feet, unswaying, as she faced Strike. "We have to go where the battle is."

Expression stony, the king glanced at Nate. "What do you think?"

"I agree with Alexis."

"Fuck." Strike gestured for the others to link up. "Let's go."

Alexis knew he never would've done it based on their say-so, knew that he recognized it as the right course too. But even so, she felt a sharp bite of responsibility, of worry. As the 'port magic revved up around them, she tried not to imagine what was going on back at Skywatch . . . and failed miserably. The stories of the prior massacre were too ingrained in her mind, her worry for Izzy and the others too sharp. So as the world slid sideways and went gray-green, she sent a prayer into the barrier: *Gods protect our* winikin. *They're the only family we have left.*

The Nightkeepers materialized in the place she'd described to Strike, the vapor-laden air snapping away from them with an audible pop. The atmosphere was thick with the smell of death and decay, but thin with altitude and cold. The clearing they had landed in was lit by torchlight, and Alexis clutched Nate's hand hard at the sight of the screaming skull mouth and the dark, brackish water leading into the cave system. For a second everything inside her rebelled at the thought of going inside. Then her eyes locked on a glitter of purple and gray, and rebellion went to horror.

Mistress Truth's headless body, still garbed in purple velour, was spiked to the wall of the cavern, pointing the way inward, a grisly sacrifice to a brutal pantheon.

Anna said quietly, "Call home. Please. I did what I could through the blood link, but it wasn't much." She was very pale, still rubbing her forearm where the *ajaw-lel* mark was clearly paining her, but she'd abided by the king's decision to follow the battle rather than their hearts.

"Already on it," Strike said. He had the satellite phone pressed to his ear, but shook his head and clicked it off with a curse. "Nothing."

"Oh, there's something, all right," Alexis said, her own voice feeling as if it were coming from far away. She wasn't sure if that was her talking now, or the goddess. The power conduit felt different somehow, as though it were vibrating on an entirely new frequency. "Listen. Feel."

There was a faint whistling noise, almost a high scream, barely audible to human ears. The earth beneath their feet shimmied slightly, the faintest of tremors. The cloud forest around them, dank and ancient and rotten, was silent. The air hummed with a waiting tension.

Nate said, "I think—"

A huge, grating crack rent the air, the ground gave a massive heave, nearly throwing Alexis off her feet, and the cave mouth shuddered and started to move. At first she thought it was collapsing. Horror coalesced and built when she saw that it wasn't collapsing at all; the upper jaw of the screaming skull was hingeing, the scream growing wider as the skull mouth stretched open.

Then, darkness spewed from the opening. Evil. A gout of foul purple-black smoke came first, followed by an unearthly howl that nearly sent her to her knees. She was barely aware that Nate held her up, that he shielded her with his body as a dark shape hurtled from the hellroad and took flight, flapping its great, leathery wings as it disappeared into the darkness beyond the torchlight. Then another. Another.

They were bats, she realized with sharp terror. Huge bats, each the size of a subcompact. Three of them, then a fourth, then two more, until all seven of the death bats had flown free of the cave. Camazotz's sons had been freed by Iago. The powerful altar stone must have overcome Iago's lack of the obsidian knife that Nate wore in his belt, Alexis thought. Or else they'd been wrong and the Volatile's knife had never been one of the prophecies; it was something else. But what?

The death bats screamed as they wheeled up and dived back down aiming for the Nightkeepers, then screamed again when Michael's shield spell sent them tumbling back.

"We're too late," Nate shouted over the thunder of wings. "Iago breached the barrier!"

"Not yet," Alexis shouted, not sure how she knew, but positive she was right. "He's torn a hole, but it's fixable. We can weave it shut."

It wasn't until she said the word that she understood its import. Weaving. Rainbows. It wasn't about fighting the demons with rainbows, never had been. Her job was to repair the barrier. It would be up to the others to fight the bats.

"Tell Leah to call Kulkulkan," she gasped, feeling the goddess reach into her and start pulling her into the magic. Or was Ixchel pulling the magic from her? She couldn't tell, wasn't sure, wasn't sure of anything beyond the fact that this was what she'd been born to do; this was her fate and destiny.

"They're already on it," Nate answered. He was bracing her, channeling the magic into her as the bats slammed into Michael's shield again and again, denting it and threatening to break through. "The others are linked up. Ready for the boost?"

She nodded, so full of magic already that she thought she might burst with it, so full that she couldn't talk, couldn't think, could only cling to him as the Nightkeepers formed the sacred circle, with Strike and Leah using their joined power to channel the golden clarion call that would bring the creator god to earth. Then Nate linked hands with Anna, and Michael reached for Alexis's free hand, completing the circle and linking their power to hers.

And for a few seconds, she *was* a god.

Power streamed through Alexis, into her, lit her up and sent her higher than she'd ever been. She reached up and touched the sky, stretched down and thrust her roots deep underground. Then the clouds parted overhead, the night went day-bright, and a rainbow speared down, slamming into the ground at her feet and making the earth shudder with its force. *This one's for you, Izzy*, Alexis thought, saying a prayer for the only mother she'd ever really known.

And, finally understanding what she had to do, she pulled away from Nate and stepped into the rainbow.

She heard him shout her name, but couldn't answer. Pain speared through her, followed by exhilaration and the sense of moving, accelerating, shooting up into the air. She had a moment of free fall in reverse as she traveled up the rainbow, up the column of light to a place in the sky where there was a huge, gaping split. Only it wasn't the sky that was split, she saw once she reached it. It was the barrier. She could look through the tear and see the other side, straight into hell. There she saw lava-orange *boluntiku* and the green-eyed shadows of *makol* without their human shells. Behind them were black, blank shapes of unimaginable evil, *Banol Kax*, surrounded by their lesser demons, the armies of hell, gathered together on a wide, gray-black plain that was somehow on the same level as the earth's atmosphere.

The creatures strained toward her, toward earth, held back only by the barrier, which was unraveling strand by strand as she watched.

And there, as she hung within the rainbow itself, Alexis heard Ixchel's voice, faint with distance. She couldn't make out the words, but she understood.

Taking hold of the rainbow, she pulled on a strand of blue, looping it and tossing it across the gap to snag one ragged edge of the sky. Magic sparked at the place where the blue strand touched the edge, and again when she looped red to the other side of the gap. Then she began to pull on the strands, tugging them together, trying to seam the sky itself.

Slowly, very slowly, the tear began to narrow.

A trumpet scream sounded behind her, and she glanced back to see a snakelike slide of motion, a glowing gold-and-crimson dragon with an elongated snout and whiplike tail. Kulkulkan.

The creator god rose up in the sky and spread his great feathered wings as he hovered above the rainbow, bugling a battle cry, becoming the serpent and the rainbow as they had been carved on the ceiling of the stone temple. Then Kulkulkan screamed again and pinwheeled in the air, locking onto the death bats, directed by the mental link he shared with Leah and Strike, who stood near the hellmouth with their warriors.

The king and queen had her back, Alexis thought, and was warmed by the knowledge, steadied by knowing she wasn't alone, even though she felt so lonely up there in the sky, sitting on a rainbow, sewing the world back together. But the rainbow strands held. The barrier was closing. Slowly, but it was closing.

For a second she actually thought she was going to pull it off. Then there was a massive heaving on the other side of the barrier, a concerted rush as the *Banol Kax* sent their forces toward the weak spot, a massive battering ram of evil seeking to force its way through to earth. The creatures hit the barrier at a spot below the tear, and the fabric of psi energy bowed under the pressure, straining at the torn spot.

Shouting, Alexis pulled on the threads with both hands and hung on to the rainbow with her legs, fighting to keep the gap from widening. Then a long, squidlike tendril of evil snaked through the opening, wrapped around her, and yanked her off the rainbow.

And pulled her through the gap to hell.

CHAPTER TWENTY-SIX

The moment Alexis broke contact with the sacred circle and physically stepped into the rainbow, Nate knew she was in serious trouble. When he saw her shimmer and start to fade, he didn't hesitate. He flung himself after her.

Instead of the rainbow, though, he found agony.

Flames lashed at him; lightning struck at him as he was transported someplace else, someplace between the earth and sky, another layer that wasn't the barrier, but was so much worse. He twisted in the lashing wind and rain, suspended in the midst of a terrible storm. "Alexis!" he cried, shouting so hard his voice cracked on the word. *"Lexie!"*

But she wasn't there. They'd been separated by the magic, because she belonged in the rainbow and he didn't, never had.

He thrashed, screaming, not with the pain, but because he needed to get to her, needed to protect her. "Gods-*damn* it!" he shouted into the storm. "She needs me! I won't let it end like this. I can't. For gods' sake, let me help her. She'll die without me!"

And, he realized in the extreme of his panic, he would die without her. A sudden parade of impressions flashed through his mind, kaleidoscoping images of the two of them together in the past, the good times and the bad. Then he saw himself in two different futures, one that continued for many years, one that cut short in 2012, both without her in them. Both unacceptable. Lightning slapped at him, arching him double in pain as he contemplated a future without Alexis and realized that all along his so-called honesty had been a front, a terrible lie. He'd been trying to be honest with her, and in the process had lied to himself. He might not have started out wanting a life with her, a future with her, but now that he was facing one without her, he realized it was the last thing he wanted. The one thing he wouldn't tolerate.

"Give her back!" he shouted to the storm, to the gods. "She's mine. I love her!"

The moment he said the words, the moment he truly accepted them for what they were and what they meant, his powers bolted wildly, careening to a new level he'd never experienced before. The magic whiplashed through him, fighting the storm, fighting captivity.

Feeding on the power, he tipped back his head into the storm and roared, "I. Love. Her!"

The universe seemed to pause, seemed to take a breath. In the sudden stillness a door unlocked in his mind, and he suddenly saw his own dreams. He'd dreamed of his mother and father as his infant self remembered them. He'd dreamed of being with Alexis in the temple cave, of losing himself in her as she'd pressed back against a twin column of stalagmites and cried his name at the back of her throat.

And all along he'd dreamed of flying. Of being free, not of love or duty, but free of gravity. Free of the earth.

A warm, magical glow kindled in his heart. Only it wasn't his heart. It was the hawk medallion.

Son of a bitch, he thought. *The fucking thing really is magic.*

Acting on instinct, on impulse, he palmed his knife from his belt. Only it wasn't his usual knife; it was the ceremonial blade Strike had given him. The weapon felt like an extension of his own arm, cool on his flesh as he nicked first his tongue, then each of his palms in sacrifice.

Cupping both bloodstained hands around the medallion, he lifted it and pressed a kiss to the etching, where the hawk became the man, and the man became the hawk.

"I love her," he said simply. "I'll do whatever it takes."
And, in accepting that deep down inside, he let himself
go fully to the magic, relinquished control, and gave himself to destiny. He tipped his head back as the storm
began anew, now rotating around him in a funnel cloud of
gray-black and lightning, and he roared, "Gods take me!"

And, keeping Alexis in his mind, his love for her at
the forefront, he dived headfirst into the funnel.

The winds whipped at him, ripping at his clothing, at
his flesh. His skin stretched tight and tore; his whole
body split apart. Pain slashed through him, beat at him,
and he screamed with the pain, with the power. His
clothes shredded and fell away. The wind screamed with
him, and then he heard another voice, an inhuman screech
that reached deep inside him and brought recognition,
longing, and a sense of the freedom he'd always sought,
the freedom he'd thought love was trying to take away.

He flailed his arms and legs against the whirling vortex,
screaming again and again, the creature's cries drowning
out his own. His skin burned, his bones ached, his flesh
and tendons sang with unfamiliar tension.

Gradually, though, his flailing gained purpose and
rhythm. He waved his arms and felt them bite into the
storm winds, arched his spine and felt the motion alter
his course. An unfamiliar slapping noise surrounded him,
filled him up, and he waved his arms harder, and started
to make progress.

Then he saw a flash of color and light up ahead; a place
where the storm had cleared, leaving a rainbow behind.
"Alexis," he shouted, and heard only the creature's scream,
but didn't care about that, cared only about getting to her.
He started swimming through the air, flapping arms that
had become fifteen-foot wings, spreading something that
felt like fingers but seemed to have sprouted out of his
ass, wide and flat and feathered—a tail? what the fuck?—
and letting his legs flatten out behind him, curling his talons, each the size of the forearm of his human self.

Understanding was both a shock and a relief, and a
sense of rightness like he'd never before experienced.

He was the sacred black hawk-eagle, and the hawk-
eagle was him.

The medallion banged against his breastbone as he flew. It was still hanging around his neck alongside the king's eccentric, both of the chains having somehow grown to accommodate his new size and shape. He carried the sacred knife with him too; it had changed when he did, becoming an obsidian band that hung around his ankle, marking him not just as a shifter, but as the Volatile.

He wasn't supposed to challenge the sky by fighting the gods.

He was supposed to fly.

Before, he'd rejected his destiny. Now he just freaking rolled with it, because he'd chosen the path, and the woman, and she was what mattered right now. She was everything.

He screamed again, this time not even trying for a human word, but going only for volume. He was a predator, a raptor calling his challenge against the enemy, a male trumpeting possession of his mate as he broke free of the funnel cloud and found himself on the earth plane, high in the sky. The air was thin, the world very small below him. With night-bright vision he saw the mountains and cloud line, the bumps of ancient pyramids, and realized with a shock that was more acceptance than surprise that he was seeing things now from the angle in his father's paintings.

This, then, was what had kept Two-Hawk apart, what had tainted the others' perceptions of the bloodline—the fear of shifters, and the secret he had carried for his son.

Well, shift this, Nate thought, then pressed his wings close to his body and dived. The wind whipped past and sang freedom in his ears as he plummeted from the heights where the funnel cloud had left him. He flew toward the bright spot near the cloud city, fear gathering in his chest as he saw the tear in the sky and the darkness beyond.

"Lexie!" he called. "Lexie!" The words came out as a raptor's scream, but, incredibly, he heard an answer.

Nate. It was a whisper in his mind, a faint connection through the love bond they'd shared, the one he'd tried to sever because he'd been too set in his old patterns to

see that things had changed around him, that *he'd*
changed.

He called her name again and she answered again,
and he tracked the response not to the rainbow or the
tear in the sky, but to the darkness beyond.

Gods. She was on the wrong side of the barrier. *And
oh, holy hell.* The split was getting bigger by the second.
The starry night sky strained on either side of the gash,
while red blackness oozed down, bleeding evil onto the
earth.

He could sense the creatures on the other side more
than he could see them, could sense the tentacled thing
that held Alexis, draining her energy from her and using
it to tear the barrier. Her strength was fading, her connection to the goddess almost lost, and all because of
him, he knew. He'd been almost too late figuring out
what she meant to him, almost too late accepting that
sometimes the gods got it right, destiny or not.

But almost doesn't matter worth a damn, he thought,
trumpeting the attack. *I'm here now, and watch out, because I'm coming for my woman!*

He dived through the gap with his curved beak gaping
wide and his razor-sharp talons extended in attack. In
an instant, blackness enveloped him, slowing his wings and
wrapping around him like a heavy, viscous oil, weighing
him down and driving him away from Alexis. He could
see her, a rainbow shimmer up above him, could hear
her cry his name as he fell.

No! He tumbled, losing the rhythm of flight as the
black goo flared to *boluntiku* orange, lava-hot and cloy-
ing. *NO!* He fought the creature's hold as it went solid
and slashed at him with a raking six-clawed hand.

Nate howled and reached for his power, calling up a
fireball, shaping and throwing the fire magic with his
mind because his hands had turned to wings. As he did
so, his medallion heated and flashed bright white, and it
was as if he'd just thrown a fucking atomic bomb. There
was a deep, thrumming thump, then a pause as the world
went still.

Then all hell broke loose.

The fireball's detonation roared, vaporizing the goo in

an instant and slamming Nate to the gray-black ground. The shock wave kept on going, radiating away from him, blowing the *boluntiku* and disembodied *makol* back, sending them tumbling end over end, their gods-awful screeching noises nearly lost beneath the thunder of the explosion. Then light flashed, pure, golden, and brilliant, and so bright Nate had to close his eyes and look away. When he looked again, the *Banol Kax* had been driven back to the horizon, and the creature that had been holding Alexis aloft was gone. She was safe from the explosion behind a rainbow barrier, but now she was falling, screaming, "Nate!"

And the gap in the barrier was even wider than before, hanging open, blown larger by the explosion. Worse—the *Banol Kax* had regrouped and were headed for the opening freight-train fast.

Fuck me. Nate didn't hesitate. He turned his back on the gap and the demons, kicked hard off the ground, and arrowed toward Alexis. The king's writ might say that Strike had to prioritize other things above his family, but Nate was bound by no such scripture. And he was damn well prioritizing Alexis, the way he should've been doing all along. He powered to her, got above her, and then dived, matching her free-falling speed as the rocky, gray-black surface rose up to meet them.

At practically the last second he got ahead of her and swooped up, scooping her from the air. She shrieked and grabbed on, but then started struggling, trying to bail off. He didn't get it for a second; then he realized she had no idea who—or what—he was. "It's me!" he shouted, only it came out as a hawk's cry.

But she stilled, lying flat on his back, hanging on to his feathers, pulling hard enough to hurt but not hard enough to keep her in place if things got tough. "Holy shit," she said, voice rattling with fear, with shock. "Nate?"

Which pretty much proved she could hear him through the screeching, maybe because she loved him. Or at least she had; that might be open to some debate in about thirty seconds or so, he realized with a deep clutch of dismay. She'd been raised by the most traditional *wini-*

kin of them all. What if she couldn't deal with what he was?

"Wh-what's going on?" Her voice shook; her whole body was trembling.

With fear of rejection lodged deep inside, knowing there was no time for fancy explanations, Nate put himself into a glide, his body somehow knowing just what to do even though his brain didn't. "It's a long story, obviously," he said, "but the short version seems to be that I'm an asshole and a shape-shifter, in whichever order you prefer. I'm the Volatile. And I love you."

She went very still, letting him know she'd translated from "hawk" to English just fine. Then, moving slowly and keeping a death grip on whatever piece of him she could get hold of, she sat up and straddled his shoulders, hooking her legs into the thickened chain holding the medallion, and using the eccentric's chain as a handhold. Then she leaned into him, getting out of the whip of the wind as she said, "Let's do our job, Nightkeeper. We've got a barrier to seal and some demons to kick back to hell. It's like we agreed before: The other stuff doesn't belong mixed-up with the gods."

It wasn't what Nate had hoped to hear, wasn't what he'd said, and the hollow opening up inside his gut warned that he might not get what he wanted. Not being what he was. But she was right that they had a job to do and not much time to do it, so even though her response cut deep inside his soul, he screeched a battle cry of agreement. "Hang on!"

Then they were arrowing up toward the tear in the barrier, toward where the creatures of the underworld had gathered, waiting for the rip to reach the surface of their world, setting them free on the next.

Trumpeting the attack, Nate gathered his fireball magic, felt Alexis lean on her rainbow magic, and then together, as one, they dived into the battle they'd been born for.

Alexis was Ixchel and the goddess was she. They were one, woven together, the ancient entity working through her, guiding her magic as they neared the tear in the fabric of the universe and the enemy attacked.

The *boluntiku* lunged, snapping with razor-sharp teeth and claws, their lava-hot bodies vapor one moment, solid the next. But their form didn't seem to matter to the magic; Alexis spread a loop of cool blue light and threw it at the one nearest the gap. The lasso whistled into the creature, impacted, and clung, burning cool against hot. The *boluntiku* arched and screamed in pain, clawing at the tether, alternating between vapor and solid as it thrashed. Steam rose, along with a hissing noise and a terrible smell as the light ate into the lava creature, cooling it to stone.

Within minutes there was a statue where the thing had been.

"Score!" Nate shouted. "Hang on; we'll get those others out in front!"

Though the words were an avian screech, she heard them in her skull, her head translating what her heart wasn't sure it could cope with. Even as she formed another loop, tightened her knees on her mount's warm, solid neck, and they banked to meet the next attack, part of her struggled to deal with the fact that her mount and Nate were one and the same. He was a shifter. He was also the Volatile, who was her protector, not her enemy. And he'd said he loved her.

A day ago, even a few hours ago, she would've given anything to hear him say that. Even now, the words thrummed through her heart like a melody of color. But there was a discord within that song, a splash of warning, of fear and knowing that Nate's being a shifter fit too well. It explained his fierce independence and dislike of following orders. It explained his need for freedom, for privacy, for his own space.

"Alexis, look out!" Nate's shout warned that she'd been thinking too much, fighting too little. She jolted to awareness just as a fanged creature rose up out of nowhere and grabbed at her, getting an edge of her shirt before falling free. Nate jammed a wing tip down and spun, so his belly faced the demon as it screamed and slashed. And scored.

Nate howled in pain and they tumbled for a second before he recovered and beat for the sky once again, gaining altitude, though obviously laboring.

Alexis leaned into him, calling, "That bomb thing. Can you do it again?"

I'll try. This time his response was purely mental, traveling along a bond she wasn't yet ready to fully acknowledge or accept. She wrapped herself around him, following the link and opening herself to him, offering up to him all of the goddess's power, and her own.

The fire magic spluttered to life around them, hissing and spitting and simultaneously gleaming with all colors and none. Holding on to the magic, he flew a wide arc around the five *boluntiku* closest to the barrier, and she tossed a loop of blue light that encompassed them all. Then, together, they threw his fire magic. White light flared, though softer than before, not a detonation so much as a firecracker. And when it cleared, the creatures had all turned to stone. The power drain, though, had been incredible.

Alexis's body had gone numb, and her brain felt sluggish. Beneath her, the rhythm of Nate's wings faltered and slowed, and his mental touch was weak. But though the lava creatures had been neutralized, the other demons weren't far behind, and the barrier was almost completely torn—it could be repaired, but just barely, and she had to get there fast.

Even as she thought that, the black, tentacled creature that had pulled her through the barrier in the first place rose from the ground and planted itself squarely in front of the rip. For a second she thought it was going to dive through to earth. Then she realized it was waiting for her, planning to fend her off while the others escaped through the barrier.

Nate sent, *What do you think?*

I'm guessing the phrase "we're screwed" isn't very helpful.

A ripple of amusement came down the shared link, and his energy strengthened just a little, or maybe hers did. *Not so much,* he agreed, then sobered. *You think your rainbow lasso trick will work? I'm tapped.* He'd used himself up getting to her, and saving her, and keeping them aloft.

It'll have to, she thought in return, but really, the answer was no. When she came down to it, Ixchel was a goddess of peace, not war. But failure simply wasn't an option. "Let's go!" she said aloud, and kicked her heels into his feathered sides. "Git-up!"

That got her a beady, backward glare. *I'm not a polo pony, princess.* But then he obeyed, flattening his wings to his body and diving for the attack, and she was screaming and hanging on as tightly as she could while they dove through hell, headed for the *Banol Kax.*

The word "kamikaze" came to mind, as did the phrase "what the fuck are we doing?" but really, there wasn't another option, wasn't anything to do but die trying. So she tightened her grip and called on the rainbow magic, bringing it not from blood sacrifice, but by thinking about Izzy, who'd raised her the very best she'd known how to; about her mother, who'd given her life for the former king; about her father, who'd done his part by loving his family, simply loving them . . . and about Nate, whom she both loved and feared now, in almost equal parts. Not because she thought he'd hurt her intentionally—he was too much his own man for that—but because she needed someone who needed her, who loved her willingly and took joy in the fact. Not someone who resented the emotion, and spent as much time away from her as with her. She'd tried to take love on many conditions before and it hadn't been enough. This time—the last time—it would be all . . . or it would be nothing.

Now wasn't the time for those thoughts, though. It was the time for love, the time to bring things together rather than ripping them to pieces. So she concentrated on the good times, on the strong times. She thought of the angle of Nate's jaw in the morning light and the feel of his skin against hers, remembered the taste of him, and comfort of waking up beside him and knowing she wasn't going to face the day alone. And as she thought those things, remembered those moments, the magic came.

Rainbow light flared around them, cocooning them in a protective barrier.

Nate screeched and flew faster, searching for a way around the Hydralike creature, which was a thick stalk of darkness with tentacles that whipped around it in a dark cloud, leaving no room for error. Alexis poured all that she had, all that she was, and all that they were together into the shield magic as they arrowed through a narrow gap between two flailing whips of evil.

One tentacle grabbed for them while another swiped deadly claws across her shield magic. Alexis cried out, feeling the deep furrows in the magic as though they'd been drawn across her own skin. Nate bellowed a challenge and dived, twisting, pinwheeling them away from the demon, and then they were free and arrowing up toward the gap.

The demon gave a great roar, leaped up, and snatched them from the sky.

Alexis screamed as the thing's grip collapsed her shield inward. Yanking her MAC from her weapons belt, she unloaded the clip into the demon and barely made a dent. The thing laughed, a booming, echoing sound, and a gaping mouth opened in its thick, stalklike trunk. The tentacle that held Nate and Alexis started moving toward the fanged maw.

Suddenly golden light bloomed all around them, and trumpets sounded, seeming to come from everywhere at once. The Hydralike demon roared denial as a sinuous crimson-and-gold serpent shape arrowed through the gap in the barrier and dived, all full of anger and righteous wrath and justice, the creator god Kulkulkan come to save his children, the king and queen of the Nightkeepers coming to free their advisers.

Gold light sparked and hissed as the feathered serpent beat its red-plumed wings and scraped a huge, furrowed gash in the demon's flesh. The creature howled in pain, losing its grip on Nate and Alexis, who fell free.

Go! they heard Strike call, his mental touch borne on the skyroad. *Close the gap! We'll buy you some time.* Kulkulkan dived, hissing and scratching as the demon reached to grab the god and other *Banol Kax* moved in, flanking the feathered serpent, surrounding him.

"Get to the gap!" Alexis shouted, not sure if Nate had heard Strike's instructions. "We've got to fix it!"

Even now she could feel the planets moving past the equinox, could feel the barrier starting to thicken and set in place. In a few more minutes there would be no hope of closing the tear. She had to work fast.

When they reached the gigantic rip, she was shaking with fatigue and nerves, and the sinking fear that she wasn't going to be strong enough, that she had already lost before she'd begun. Nate grabbed on to an edge of the barrier with his hooked talons, perching precariously in the gap itself. *Do your thing, babe.*

"I don't know if I can." Failure pressed at her, alongside the knowledge that she wasn't just disappointing the Nightkeepers; she could very well be dooming the world, and all because she'd used up her magic, because she wasn't strong enough, wasn't good enough. She was a pale shadow of what she should've been, what she would've been if she'd been raised as had been meant, if she'd known all that she was supposed to know.

She knew Nate sensed all those things from her, thought that he would try to reassure her. Instead, though, he said, very softly, *I love you, Lexie.* And then he opened to her, sending her all the love that was inside him, all his respect for her, his fascination with her, his awe at the person she was—imperfectly human, and perfect for the man he'd become while knowing her.

The emotions were colors, but to call them rainbows was too little, too weak a term. They were sparkles and illumination, loving blues and purples and greens so much deeper and more vibrant than anything that had ever come from cool white light, and sensual reds, oranges, and yellows that kindled fires in her nerve endings, reminding her of the slide of skin on skin, the explosion of orgasm. The strength of those feelings lit her up from within, leveling her, strengthening her, and bringing magic from love rather than sacrifice.

She raised her hands, and colors flowed from her fingertips, the strands of light taking flight and heading unerringly for the jagged edges of the barrier. She started at the top, high into the sky, and began to weave, folding the colors together and fighting the darkness onto one side of the barrier, light onto the other. When the anchors were set, she held her breath and tugged on the rainbows.

And watched the gap draw together at the top.

Way to go, babe! The hawk's screech was so full of manly pride it almost sounded human. Or maybe it *was* human; she hadn't fully dealt with that yet. All she knew was that she couldn't do this without him, that she needed his love, his strength. He was her anchor, her support, just as she had been his during the fight. They'd deal with the rest later, as people rather than warriors. She hoped.

She kept working, weaving the strands of light into the barrier and tying them off, forming a magical patch over the blockade built by her ancestors. It was easy at the top, but grew increasingly more difficult lower down, partly because tension was pulling the edges apart, partly because the equinox was fading, and partly because she was fading. Her head pounded in synchrony with her heart, and sweat beaded her brow and trickled down her spine. Her hands shook as she heard trumpeting behind and below, and knew the king and queen were fighting a rear-guard action, buying time.

Move it, she told herself. She had to hurry! The adviser in her couldn't believe she was letting Strike and Leah fight for her when it should've been the other way around. But the Godkeeper in her knew this was her battle, her destiny, and—

Focus, love. It was Nate's voice, cool and blue with calm, tinted red with love. He poured more energy into her, poured love into her, supporting her and steadying her. She let herself lean, let herself believe in him, in them, for the moment at least. She got past the midpoint of the patch job and the tension lessened, though the barrier was thickening as she worked, making it more difficult to draw the edges together, more difficult even to thread the tear with rainbow light. But the gap drew together; the opening narrowed.

When it was as small as she dared, she said, "Let's switch sides." Nate obligingly ducked through, so they were on the earth side of the barrier, where they belonged. She kept working, threading and pulling madly, bringing the torn edges together as she sent, *Nochem? Time for you guys to haul ass, or we're going to have to come in there after you.*

Coming! came Strike's reply. There was a trumpet fanfare that ended on what sounded suspiciously like a raspberry, and then a golden blur arrowed through the last narrow gap. When the flying serpent god was through, back in the thin air of the Andes mountains, high above the cloud forest, Alexis worked as fast as she could, as fast as she dared, threading and pulling like a madwoman.

She tied off the final suture just as the Hydralike demon hit the gap, slamming into the seam and straining the rainbow weft. The patch job parted and groaned, stretching slightly. But it didn't give.

"It's holding!" Alexis called, and was answered by Nate's screech of joy and Kulkulkan's clarion bugle. And as they watched, the hold grew stronger still, the barrier knitting together along the sewn line, healing along a seam of magic. Her heart kicked at the sight. "We did it!"

Congratulations! Strike sent. *Come back down, okay?* He and Leah were on the ground near the hellmouth, she knew; Kulkulkan was a separate entity, one they could call to earth and link with mentally on the cardinal days. When the equinox was past and his job was done, he would return back up the skyroad.

As if knowing that time was near, the flying serpent bugled a trumpet blast of joy and approval, and turned north, powering up for the race back to Chichén Itzá. Though the demons could come through Iago's hellmouth, the gods had to use the intersection. Alexis raised a hand in farewell as she flew through the sky astride a giant hawk.

And that was pretty messed-up, she realized as the fight drained and reality began to intrude. She was riding Nate, and Nate was a hawk. A shape-shifter. The Volatile.

Like her thoughts, the sky went dark, returning to the blackness of night with the passing of the magic.

When we get home I'm going to eat about a gallon of mac and cheese and crash for a week, he sent along their mental link. *How about you?* She knew he felt her unease, and was trying for something light, something that would avoid the strangeness that suddenly loomed between them.

"Chocolate and Tylenol," she said as her stomach growled in syncopation with her headache. "And a bubble bath."

I could get behind the bath idea, he said, projecting an image that made her blush and heated her blood to boiling.

But her response was tempered with unease. "Nate, listen. I—" She broke off, not because she didn't know what to say, but because she suddenly couldn't breathe. Her lungs were locked, not shut, but bloating, like they were full of water. Heart hammering, she grabbed for her throat, mouth working, trying to scream but unable to get out a sound.

What's wrong? Nate asked quickly.

The goddess, she sent along their mental link. *Something bad is happening!*

In the distance Kulkulkan's glowing golden form faltered, and they heard a trumpet of distress. The creator managed another few faltering wing beats, then began to lose altitude. Soon he disappeared from sight.

Alexis felt the world constricting around her, inside her. The rainbow magic sparked within her head, arcing wildly, loving magic gone wrong. *Help,* she cried as she slumped sideways and started to slide. *Help me!*

Hang on! Nate folded his wings and dived for the earth, for the Nightkeepers, but it was already too late. Alexis's vision went dim, then dark.

The last thing she heard was Rabbit's voice screaming, *Stop it; you're killing them!*

Iago shrugged off Rabbit's attack and shoved him into a mental corner, leaving him weak and impotent as the Xibalban renewed his attack on the intersection.

The mage stood in the altar room beneath Chichén Itzá. The torches belched purple-black smoke, and the air rattled with foul magic. Desiree's body lay sprawled on the now-cracked *chac-mool* altar, leaking blood. The crimson wetness filled the lines carved into the stone, highlighting the sacred patterns and pooling in a horrible parody of the good, pure magic the Nightkeepers had performed in that same chamber. On the floor lay what was left of the ancient artifacts bearing the demon prophecies, which had been broken to dust beneath Iago's boots as an added source of power.

Rabbit could feel the equinox, could feel a battle raging on the magic plane, light against dark, but he couldn't follow it. All he knew was the part he was being forced to play, his magic joined with Iago's as the Xibalban's plan came to fruition.

When the Nightkeepers had appeared at the hellmouth and joined battle against the death bats and the *Banol Kax*, Rabbit had expected Iago to throw his powers on the dark side of the battle, to swing the fight in his favor. But he hadn't. Instead, he'd smiled and 'ported directly into the altar room, and begun a set of spells Rabbit had never heard before. Hell, he'd never heard of them before, didn't know what they were intended to do. But though he wasn't able to follow the intricate spell casting in the old language, he'd readily pulled the intent from Iago's mind.

The bastard was dismantling the skyroad.

If he succeeded, Strike, Leah, and Alexis were all in jeopardy, as they were linked to their gods. Even worse—if there was anything worse than losing, like, a quarter of the Nightkeepers' fighting force, along with the royal couple—if the Xibalban succeeded in destroying the skyroad, there would be no more hope of the gods coming to earth. No more Godkeepers. Potentially no more visions, save for those sent by the ancestors, who were on a lower plane than the gods.

Rabbit knew he had to stop the Xibalban. Too bad he didn't have a fucking clue how he was supposed to do that. Iago controlled both of their minds, and his magic was so much stronger.

Think, Rabbit told himself. *Fucking think!* It was hard to focus as Iago repeated the short spell for the eighth time and the chamber started shaking itself apart, locked in an earth tremor that felt like it was going to take out most of Mexico, never mind just the tunnels.

The Xibalban stepped up to the broken altar and withdrew a sharp stone tool from his belt—not a knife, but an awl of sorts. Bracing his chin against the edge of the broken *chac-mool,* he stuck out his tongue and drove the awl directly through it.

Agony flared in Rabbit's mouth as though he'd made the sacrifice himself. He tasted blood and magic as Iago stood and felt in the pocket of his dark robe, then pulled out a long string that was knotted at regular intervals, with each knot holding a wickedly pointed thorn. The thorn rope was one of the oldest of the Maya's sacrificial tools, one that had been used to allow the kings to talk to the gods.

Now the Xibalban used it to close the lines of communication. He threaded the string through the hole he'd punched in his tongue and started pulling it through as he recited the spell one last time, nine repetitions for the nine layers of hell that would hold sway once the earth was cut off from the thirteen layers of heaven. As he did so, the tremors became a quake, not just on the physical plane, but on the magical one as well. Rabbit could feel the barrier itself shudder with the force of the attack, could feel the skyroad starting to come apart.

Don't be such a girl, he heard a familiar voice whisper at the back of his mind. *Do something!*

His old man wasn't there; he was long gone. But he was right too, Rabbit knew. So he gathered his magic and scraped his tired self together, preparing for one final attack. Iago wasn't paying attention to him except to drain his power and use his strange half-blood magic to fuel a spell that shouldn't have existed, shouldn't have worked. Rabbit knew he couldn't cut off the connection; he'd tried and failed already. He couldn't take over Iago's mind, either, because the bastard was watching for that. But what if he added to it? Could he use a power surge to kick the bastard offline, maybe fry his synapses?

Maybe, he thought. *Possibly.* It was worth a shot. And if he fried his own cortex in the process, that'd suck, but at least he would've been a hero once in his life. The thought of dying made him sad. But the idea of taking Iago with him almost made it okay. Almost.

Knowing there was no hope for it, no other option, Rabbit closed his eyes and thought of fire. Thought of telekinesis. Thought of mind-bending. Thought, quite simply, of magic in all its forms and glory. He felt the power grow within him, felt the madness and heat of it batter him, swirl around him, making him feel larger and smaller all at once. When it reached its apex, when he could call no more magic, contain no more power, he turned out of the small corner of Iago's mind that he'd been occupying and flung himself at the mage's consciousness.

He sensed Iago's focus shift in the last second before impact, felt the Xibalban bring his own magic to bear. Then they collided, and the world blew apart.

Magic was a firestorm, a power surge that overloaded Iago's mind and derailed his spell casting. Rabbit grabbed on to the mage's consciousness, hung on, refused to let go. The Xibalban tried to flee back along the connection to Rabbit's body, but there was no way Rabbit was letting the bastard wake up in Skywatch, so he dug in, feeding power into the spell, pumping it up. He sensed Strike, Leah, and Alexis caught in the dying skyroad. Instinctively knowing that he couldn't do anything to repair the road, that it was already too late, Rabbit turned his attention to his teammates, feeding them all the magic he could muster, trying to overload the connections and kick them free.

Iago roared and fought his hold, scoring at him with harsh, destructive magic that burned like cold fire, biting deep into Rabbit's mental self. But Rabbit just screamed and held on, and kept pushing power to his friends, trying to save them if he couldn't save himself.

As he reached the absolute end of his power, and his consciousness flickered and dimmed, he sensed the others starting to blink out of the skyroad: Strike first, then

Leah, then Alexis. After that, Rabbit's consciousness went blank.

Then there was nothing, only darkness.

Some time later he cut back in, just long enough to realize that he wasn't inside Iago anymore. He was back in his own body, only not. It was more like he was floating over it, waiting. Then, finally, he started floating away, up toward the sky, where warriors went directly after they died in battle.

As he did, he found himself wishing he'd kissed Myrinne when he'd had the chance.

Alexis woke slowly, fighting through the layers of sleep. Her head hurt and her stomach was an empty ache, but even more, her soul felt hollow and her skull felt too big, as though her brain had shrunk, or something else had been taken from the space.

"That's it," a voice said from somewhere above her. "Come on; you can do it."

It was Nate's voice, she realized, just as it was Nate's hand holding hers; she knew the good, solid feel of him like she knew herself. Only did she really? As the mists cleared, she remembered the hawk, and Nate's newly discovered talent, which left them . . . where? She didn't know. And as she opened her eyes and found herself lying on the ground outside of the torchlit hellmouth, she knew Nate saw her fear, because his expression blanked as he squeezed her hand once and let go.

"Nate," she said, just his name, then fell silent because everything was too much, too confusing. He was wearing someone's shirt tied around his waist like a loincloth, and another thrown over his shoulders but not buttoned. Apparently clothes didn't shift with the man.

That detail, that confirmation that what she remembered had really happened, was almost more than she could handle.

"I'm glad you're okay." He held out a hand. "You ready to sit up?"

The rest of the Nightkeepers were clustered behind him, including Strike and Leah, who looked as ragged as Alexis felt. "The gods are gone, aren't they?" she said dully. "The skyroad is gone."

"We're still here," Strike said. He lifted his satellite phone. "The *winikin* are okay. Jox thinks there was enough of Lucius left in the *makol* that he forced the creature to escape rather than killing anyone, though I guess it was a pretty close thing. And Rabbit . . . we'll have to see about him when we get back." He paused, exhaling. "At least the barrier is still intact, thanks to you."

"Me and Nate," she corrected.

"Yeah." The king nodded. "Blackhawk too." It didn't escape her notice that he'd gone back to Nate's bloodline name, though, or that the others were giving him a wide berth. The realization angered her, but shamed her too, because wasn't she doing the very same thing? He was no different from the man he'd been before. He'd simply discovered his talent.

It was a small effort to put her hand in Nate's, but well rewarded by the glint of thanks in his eyes as he pulled her to her feet. She kept hold of him when he would've let go, and together they linked up with Leah as they formed the sacred circle that would allow Strike to 'port them back to Skywatch.

The king initiated the 'port, and as the magic took hold, Alexis sent a prayer into the barrier, even though she suspected the gods couldn't hear them anymore: *Please let Rabbit be okay.* He'd saved her, she knew, somehow pushing her out of the Godkeeper link just as the skyroad collapsed.

She hoped to hell it hadn't been his final act on earth.

CHAPTER TWENTY-SEVEN

Anna sat by Rabbit's bedside long after the others had eaten and crashed to sleep off their postmagic hangovers. She dozed fitfully, ate whatever Jox brought her, and by the time the new day dawned, she was blatantly defying Rabbit's whole *I don't like being touched* thing by holding his hand. She didn't leak him any power, partly because she didn't have any to spare, and partly because she had a feeling it wasn't power that he needed; it was a reason to come back. She thought she could sense him waiting between the worlds, trying to make up his mind. Or maybe she was projecting and he was in a coma, plain and simple.

In case she was right about the hovering thing, though, she talked to him, reminding him that the Nightkeepers needed him, that they loved him. The words caught a little in her throat, though, because they felt like lies, or at least the sort of thing Rabbit would've snorted at and said, "Yeah, whatever."

In terms of numbers and absolute power, the Nightkeepers were stronger with him than without, but from a more realistic standpoint, the amount of chaos he dumped into their lives probably came close to outweighing the benefits. And while Strike and Jox loved the kid like he was an exasperating family member, and Anna herself felt strongly about him because he was his father's son, the feelings of the other Nightkeepers and *winikin* could probably be described as ambivalent at best.

Which, again, more or less applied in her case as well. At least it ought to. She'd brought Lucius into their midst and refused to sacrifice him. Somehow the *makol* had hidden behind Lucius's humanity long enough to get through the wards and lull Jox into believing the danger was past. Then, as Jox had described, the creature had gone full *makol* and attacked. Then at the last possible second, the creature had frozen and seemed to struggle within itself, then shrieked in rage and agony and bolted from the compound. Anna wanted to think that had been the spark of Lucius retained within the creature, wanted to believe that he would come back to himself once the equinox passed. Unfortunately, Strike hadn't been able to get a 'port lock on him, which meant he was dead or underground . . . or Iago had him.

Now, more than ever, they were going to have to find the Xibalbans' encampment. They needed to recover Lucius before Iago got at the knowledge inside his skull. Ditto for Sasha Ledbetter. Both recoveries were going to present new problems, but it wasn't as if they had a choice. Each cardinal day from there on out would bring another opportunity for the *Banol Kax* to assault the barrier, and now the Nightkeepers were going to be functioning without the help of the gods. It was unclear how much—if any—of their Godkeeper powers Leah and Alexis had retained, but they had to assume a massive power drop. Which brought her thoughts circling back to Rabbit.

They needed his power. Hell, in a way they needed his chaos too. He stirred things up, kept them thinking and guessing, which was going to be vital over the next few years as they got closer and closer to the drop-dead date.

"Which is why you need to come back to us, okay?" she said to the teen around lunchtime the day after the equinox, though time didn't have much meaning down in the storeroom cell block.

Rabbit lay too still. His pallor was gray, his breathing

slow and shallow. His profile was sharp and forbidding, his lips turned down in a sneer very like the one that formed his fallback expression when he was awake. The thought that she might never see that snotty 'tude again was a fist to Anna's heart.

Leaning close to Rabbit, she kissed his cheek. "We love you. You hear? You need to come back."

And, incredibly, his lips moved. A word emerged, breathy and faint, but still a word. A request. "Myrinne."

Anna was on her feet in seconds. She pulled down the wards with a thought and yanked open the door. Jox, who'd been keeping guard out in the hallway, shot to his feet.

"Get the girl out of her cell," Anna snapped. "I want her in here five minutes ago."

"I don't think that's such a good idea," the *winikin* said carefully.

I didn't ask for your opinion, she wanted to snarl, but knew it was just another sign of the larger trend, the one where Strike had been leaning more on Nate and Alexis than on her. The others viewed her as an outsider, a commuter who showed up for the ceremonies and then left again. But all that was what she'd wanted, wasn't it? She didn't get to complain now that she'd gotten the distance she craved.

"Fine," she said to Jox. "Do what you have to do. Ask Strike for permission. Whatever."

Strike agreed, of course, and less than five minutes later he and Leah brought Myrinne to Rabbit's room themselves, locking and warding the door behind them.

Anna tried not to twist her fingers together, tried not to think that this could be a huge mistake, that she was making yet another call that would prove to have disastrous consequences. They didn't really know anything about Myrinne's ancestry, or her connection to the witch's magic. For all they knew, they were about to throw gasoline on a smoldering fire.

But this was something tangible Anna could give him, something she could do. "He asked for you," she told the girl, who was pale but defiant, and wore a sneer not unlike Rabbit's own.

Myrinne looked like she was going to say something snotty in return, but then she got a look at Rabbit, and the sneer gave way to rage. "What did you do to him?" She crossed the room in quick, angry strides and checked his pulse with efficient movements that suggested training. Then she glared at Anna. "What did you give him?"

She shook her head. "It's not drugs; it's magic. He fought Iago."

Myrinne stared at her, eyes narrowing. "And?"

"And he didn't get out of Iago's mind fast enough. I think he's trapped somehow. I think he needs to be reminded that there are people here who care about him." Anna paused. "He saved our lives last night." Which was true. When all was said and done, he'd been a hero when they'd needed one.

Myrinne nodded, seeming satisfied. "That I believe." Implying that she could think the best of Rabbit, but would cheerfully think the worst of everyone around him.

Which, Anna realized, was exactly what he needed.

Turning her back on the others, Myrinne spun the chair Anna had been using, so she could sit sideways on it and lean over Rabbit's limp form. "Hey," she said very softly. "You did good. Now it's time to come back, okay? We'll figure out the rest of it together." She leaned in and touched her lips to his.

And damned if he didn't react, jolting like he'd been zapped with a Taser, then drawing a deep, shuddering breath very unlike the shallow rasps he'd been taking up to that point. A long shudder racked his body. Then, slowly, his arms came up to her shoulders, her face. His eyes opened as he traced her cheekbones, then her lips. And he smiled, probably the first pure smile Anna had seen from him since her return to Skywatch.

"Now, that was what I forgot to do," he said, his voice husky from disuse, and probably a few other things as well. "That was what I wanted to come back for."

Then, as Strike, Leah, and Anna looked on, Rabbit kissed Myrinne for real. And magic hummed in the air.

After sleeping off her postmagic hangover and eating way too many Oreos from the bag she'd brought back to her suite with her the night before, Alexis pulled herself together and went in search of Nate.

She'd just gotten out the door of her suite when Izzy turned the corner, headed in Alexis's direction. The *winikin*'s face softened to a smile. "You look better."

Before, Alexis might've checked what she was wearing, and maybe straightened her ponytail. Now she just nodded. "Thanks. I feel better." She'd been pretty ragged by the time they'd made it back. Sleep and food had fixed most of what ailed her. Now she needed to deal with the rest, which meant heading to the cottages out back. To Nate.

Izzy fell into step beside her, but stayed silent, as though unsure of what to say, or how. Which was a huge change in itself, because Alexis had never known her godmother to be at a loss for words.

When they reached the doorway leading out to the pool deck, Alexis stopped and turned to the woman who had raised and shaped her. "I owe you my life," she said simply. "If it hadn't been for you, I would've died during the massacre. If it hadn't been for you, I wouldn't have known who and what I am when the time came to find out, and I wouldn't have been able to deal nearly as well with the transition. I love you with all my heart, and much of who I am I owe to you."

Izzy raised an eyebrow. "Why do I hear a 'but' coming?"

"Because you're a smart woman, and you know me well." Alexis risked a small smile. "I love you. But I can't be what you want me to be."

"Sweetheart, you already are. You always have been."

It took a moment for the words to penetrate. Another for confusion to set in. "Huh?" Okay, that wasn't brilliant, but still.

The *winikin*'s smile went a little crooked. "Okay, maybe not always, but close enough." She caught Alexis's hands, squeezed them. "You're not your mother, and I never wanted you to be. You're what you were meant to be: a strong, independent woman, and a royal adviser. You helped save the world last night, and you're probably going to do it again before all this is over. Just because I don't agree with your taste in men, that doesn't make you a failure."

The look on her face when she said the last part brought a bubble of laughter to Alexis's throat. "You sure about that?" But then she sobered. "He's a shifter, Izzy."

"I know. Who are we to argue with the gods?" The *winikin* gave Alexis a little push. "Go on. Do what you have to do."

Alexis opened the door, but turned back to say, "Don't you want to know what I'm going to do?"

"Whatever your choice, I'll be proud of you. I always am. Now go."

Alexis went, and she went with a lift beneath her heart, a benediction she hadn't expected, hadn't needed, but one that mattered nonetheless. She wasn't sure if she'd changed or if Izzy had, but she had a feeling things were going to be different between them from now on.

The buoyancy brought by that revelation sustained her all the way to Nate's bungalow, then deserted her in an instant. In its place nerves flared as she raised a fist and knocked.

He opened the door immediately, as though he'd sensed her approach, or had been waiting for her. Maybe both. His big body filled the doorway; he was wearing khakis and a button-down shirt that was open at the throat, revealing the medallion and the eccentric. Business casual with a twist, she thought, and felt a lump gather in her throat. She saw his laptop open behind him, his cell phone beside it. "You working?" she asked, her nerve faltering a little. "I can come back later."

But he shook his head. "Just talking to Denjie about the new *VW* game. I guess between the writing delays and sagging sales on the other installments, the parent company that's been handling the games doesn't want *Hera's Mate*. They're ending the series instead."

She winced, thinking that as far as omens and signs went, that wasn't a good one. "I'm sorry."

He lifted a shoulder. "I'm actually relieved. It's time to move on." He hadn't leaned toward her, but it sure felt as though he had. His energy reached out to her, enveloped her, made her yearn.

"That's new," she said inanely, pointing to a carved black wrist piece that peeked out from beneath his left shirt cuff.

He shook it down and showed her the carvings. "I'm pretty sure it is—or was—the obsidian knife. Part of the whole Volatile thing, I guess."

She smiled a little. "Magic."

"Yeah." Now he did move, stepping out of the doorway and crowding her, looking down at her with everything she'd ever wanted or needed in his eyes. "You come out here to talk about my new man-bracelet?"

Nerves shimmered just beneath her skin, warming her and making her jittery. "No. I came to ask you to take me flying."

His eyes blanked, and he exhaled a long, slow breath. "Whoa. That was so not what I was expecting you to say."

Her lips curved. "Well, actually I came out here to take you to bed, and stay with you for good, if you'll have me. But I figured we should go flying first."

Now it was his turn to smile as the shock in his eyes gave way to heat and a slow build of joy. But he said, "You don't have to do this if it freaks you out."

"I have to do it *because* it freaks me out," she corrected. "At least, it does a little, and I need to get past that." She leaned up and touched her lips to his. "This is your talent. I'll love it because it's part of you, and I love you."

He leaned into her, leaned into the kiss, then murmured. "I love you too." And as though the words had been the trigger, he stepped outside and began to change, the lines of his body blurring and shifting; his clothes tearing and falling away to reveal feathers and wings as he became a raptor the size of an SUV.

When it was done he stood there opposite her, his clawed feet balancing oddly on the flat ground, his wings half spread, as though he were ready to take off at any second, or shield her from an attack. "Well?" he asked, the word a soft scree aloud, a translated thought inside her head.

"You're amazing," she said simply. "You're perfect. And you're mine."

He had nothing to say to that, but she didn't mind, because she was pretty speechless herself, and tears were starting to film her eyes and leak a little, because this was all so important.

"Yeah," he said, and she felt his mental touch as a kiss. Then his mood shifted, and he said, "Grab the knapsack just inside the door, okay? I packed clothes."

Grinning at the memory of him wearing a makeshift loincloth, she did as he'd asked. Once she'd grabbed the bag and was back outside, he dipped a shoulder and she climbed up, settling herself in the hollow between his sleek head and powerful shoulders, and twining her feet and hands in his chains as she had done before. Nerves kindled, sweeping her burst of excitement away.

"Hang on!" he warned, and then hunkered down and kicked off, then began beating the air with powerful strokes of his wings, a fast tempo at first as they skimmed the ground alongside the ball court, headed for the mansion, then slower as he gained altitude. She halfway thought he would head the other way, straight out the back of the compound to the emptiness beyond, keeping this between them, a private thing.

Instead, he buzzed the mansion.

He banked around the ceiba tree with a fierce cry of joy and sent them flashing past the residential wing, then the pool. She saw the windows and openmouthed faces, saw Sven holler with joy and backflip off the diving board as they skimmed directly over him.

Then they were away from the mansion and Nate was powering up, sending them arrowing toward the thermal currents high above.

On a whisper of love, Alexis cast a light shield spell around them. When he glanced back, she sent, *We're in radar range, and too close to Area 51 for comfort.*

Yikes. Good thinking. He paused, then sent a soft, *Well?*

Which was when she realized she'd forgotten to be weirded out, even a little. Maybe sleeping on it had helped adjust her perceptions, or maybe her psyche was ahead of her brain for a change, but his shifting talent was the last thing on her mind as they winged over the canyonscape, with the sun beating down on them from above, warming her skin.

It was the first full day of spring, she realized suddenly. A time for rebirth and growth, for starting over. A new dawn for the Nightkeepers.

"It's perfect," she said, speaking aloud, though she knew he'd catch the words from her head. He didn't seem to be able to 'path in human form—for which she was grateful, because a girl needed some privacy—but she liked the mind-link they formed while flying. She liked flying too, she realized as she watched the ground flash past and listened to the wind song rustle through his feathers. "You're perfect."

He started angling downward, spiraling through the layers of air, his wings outstretched in a glide that took them to a small cave, one he must've sighted from the air, or maybe scouted out earlier in the day, who knew?

When they touched down, Alexis had a moment of nerves at the sight of the dark cave mouth. Given her last couple of cave adventures, she wasn't exactly looking forward to going in there. But it wasn't a hellmouth, didn't have a river. It was soft and dry and welcoming, and when they moved inside she saw that the walls were marked with pteroglyphs, images painted by the men and women of another time, another culture than their own.

She dropped down from astride the hawk and looked in the knapsack, knowing he would've packed a blanket in addition to clothes. She turned her back on him as she spread the blanket on the dusty cave floor, giving him a moment of privacy, and by the time she turned around he was back to human form, stark naked and aroused. They lay together, loved together under the warm desert sun of springtime, and when the moment came they climaxed together, the orgasm punching through even stronger than before, because it was love now, not just sex. . . . In that moment she felt a sting on her forearm, and thought she saw a shimmer of rainbows reflected on the cave wall.

A few minutes later, as they lay cooling together, she raised her forearm and held it beside his. They each wore a new mark. A loving mark.

He leaned over and touched his lips to hers. *"Jun tan."*

Late that night, when the stars and the moon had turned the world outside his cottage windows to something mysterious, Nate lay awake, watching his mate sleep.

There was no panic in his soul, no regret. Nothing except an absolute and perfect rightness that might've made him suspect that he and Alexis had been destined for each other all along . . . if he believed in that sort of thing. Which he didn't. Just in case, though, he sent his thoughts skyward and whispered, "Thank you, gods."

Little was actually settled in real terms, of course. Rabbit was awake and talking, but there were major questions about his connection to Iago and what it would mean going forward. Myrinne was another consideration, as was the search they were going to have to man in order to find Iago's compound, and Sasha and Lucius. And the library.

The next few months—and years—were going to be complicated and dangerous, but he wouldn't be facing them alone, or unarmed. He had a talent, a purpose, and a role within the Nightkeepers. More important, he had Alexis. Tipping his head back so he could look at the painting hung above the bed, which glowed shadows-on-gray in the moonlight, he whispered, "I get it now, Father."

The paintings didn't symbolize detachment at all, he'd realized. There were two people in every one of them: the artist . . . and the woman who'd clung to his shoulders and laughed with joy as they flew the skies together, looking down on the canyon, the ruin, and the sea. The paintings were his mother and father. They were love. And, as Nate curled into Alexis and breathed her scent, he knew that one thing would remain constant in the months and years and battles to come: With her, he was finally free.

Read on for a sneak peek at the third book
in the Final Prophecy series from
Jessica Andersen,

SKYKEEPERS

Coming from Signet Eclipse in August 2009.

Sasha Ledbetter's boots felt strange on her feet, constricting after she'd spent so long going barefoot, with her sturdy lace-ups shoved under the cot in her cell. Her chest tightened, though that was from the nerves that flared when she finally—*finally!*—heard footsteps in the hallway. One set. Coming toward her room.

In all the time she'd been held prisoner by Iago and his freak-show disciples, this was the first time she'd looked forward to hearing the measured tread of boots in the hallway outside her cell. Before, it'd always meant interrogation. Terror. Endless questions without answers. Pain without end. This time, though, she wasn't the same dazed creature the masked, red-robed interrogators would be expecting. A little while ago she'd awakened with both her palms sore from shallow cuts that had already scabbed over, her thoughts clouded with a dream of a brown-haired man bending over her, his eyes flickering from hazel to luminous green and back again. But though that was weird enough, far stranger was the clarity of her mind and the strength that flowed through her body, which had been weak and wasted, and was now whole once more.

A small, panicked part of her thought that this was a dream, that her soul had once again retreated deep inside her as the red-robes dragged her to the small stone room that smelled of incense and blood. But no, she had to believe this was real. She could feel the pinch of her boots and smell her own fear as the footsteps came closer.

She didn't know why or how she was awake, whether they'd forgotten the drugs or withdrawn them for some purpose. She also didn't know how it could be possible that her bedsores had healed overnight, and her muscles had grown strong once again, her arms and legs lean and toned. She knew only that she'd somehow been given a slim chance, and she didn't intend to waste it.

Her heart hammered as she curled her fingers around the plastic spork she'd taken from her meal tray, leaving the oversalted microwave dinner uneaten. Letting the jagged round end poke between her fingers, she imagined shoving it into one of Iago's gloating green eyes. She hated him, hated what he'd done to her, and to her father, Ambrose. Hell, for all she knew, the bastard had killed her Aunt Pim, too, setting Ambrose on the downward spiral to his death.

It fit. It played. And it rankled deep inside Sasha, taking her from the rebellious but naive young chef she'd been prior to her capture and making her into something else, someone else. Someone who could—and would—do whatever it took to get away from Iago and his so-called Xibalbans, who were nothing more than a group of delusional psychopaths who worshipped gods nobody sane believed in anymore, preparing for an apocalyptic threat that existed only in their minds. In that, they were very like her father.

Damn him.

A ball of hot fury kindled in her chest, as the lock to her cell door rattled. Moments later the panel swung inward, sending the meal tray scraping aside with a screech of plastic across the floor.

Sasha didn't stop to think or look. She attacked in silence, springing from behind the door and slamming her makeshift weapon into the face of the big man who stood in the doorway. She nailed him in the left eye, the spork sinking in with a moment of resistance followed by liquid give.

Blood and fluid spurted and the man shouted, spun,

and staggered, clapping both hands to his ruined face and dropping to his knees just inside the door.

Sasha caught an impression of shaggy brown hair and massive shoulders, but it was the gray robes of a Xibalban acolyte that caught her attention, and the incongruous flash of black at his wrist. He wasn't a red-robe, wasn't tattooed with the blood-colored quatrefoil glyph that the others wore on their right inner forearms. Instead, he wore a small black glyph shaped like a jaguar's head, one that she recognized from her childhood.

Telling herself it didn't matter, that she didn't have time to stop, look, or think—or regret for even an instant—Sasha dodged around him and through the door, then spun to shut and lock the panel behind her.

She bolted down the corridor with her blood humming in her ears, then stopped at an intersecting corner and took a quick look around, trying to get her bearings. To try was the best she could do, though, because the hallway looked much like her cell—bare and functional, only with drywall painted plain gray rather than the impervious plastic-lined metal that lined the walls of her cell. But beyond that? Nada. No character, no windows, no nothing. Just blah and more blah. She might be in a repurposed guerrilla compound in Central America near the Maya ruin where Iago had captured her, baiting her with her own father's skull. Or she might be on the thirtieth floor of a high-rise somewhere in the States. There was no way to tell.

For the first time since she'd come out of her drugged fugue, Sasha faltered. Even if she got free, what would she find outside? How would she get home? For that matter, where the hell *was* home? Ambrose and Pim were dead, her apartment had undoubtedly been cleared and re-rented, and there were precious few who would've missed her, or even noticed she was gone. Tears threatened at the unbe-*freaking*-lievable suckfest of her situation, and she wondered whether, if she closed her eyes very tight and wished hard enough, she'd wake up in her bed back in Boston and find that the last eleven months had been a terrible dream.

But this wasn't a nightmare, she knew. This was reality, or at least a version of it created by some very disturbed minds.

Remembering that the red-robes had always dragged her to the left, she went right, running, her breath whistling in her lungs as she braced herself each second for a shout of discovery, the crack of one of the rifles the red-robed guards carried across their backs. She passed a row of solid metal doors, then turned another corner and faltered to a stop when the hall dead-ended at an ancient-looking wall, one with interlocking stone blocks that ran up and over in an arch pattern, making it look like a doorway, though there was no doorknob. There was a circular depression off to one side, carved in the shape of a stylized house symbol. Thanks to Ambrose, she recognized the Mayan *way* glyph, which could mean both "home" and "doorway."

The question was, did she want to pass through this particular doorway? The stones were too much like the ones in the interrogation chamber. What if she'd run in a circle?

There's no time to second-guess, she told herself, her pulse drumming so loud in her ears that she wasn't sure she'd be able to hear the sound of pursuit coming up behind her. Whispering a prayer to the gods, though she'd left Ambrose's religion behind a long time ago, she pressed the flat of her palm against the glyph, hoping against hope that it was a pressure pad.

For several agonizing seconds, nothing happened. Then a groaning noise came from the stone panel and it began to move, sliding sideways into the wall, rumbling on some hidden mechanism. Exhaling with relief and wiping away a spurt of tears, Sasha pushed through into the stone-lined corridor beyond, moving as quietly as she could, keeping her senses on high alert.

The air in the stone tunnel was cool, with the peculiar dampness she associated with stone churches and temple ruins; ambient light came from bare bulbs hanging off an electric line that was bolted to the low ceiling, a jarring anachronism. There was another doorway at the far end, this one wooden and cobbled together with what looked like iron straps and rosehead nails. What the hell was this place?

She didn't know, didn't really care except to wonder what was on the other side of the wooden door, and where she was going to find herself when she came out into the open air. *If* she came out into the open air.

No, don't think that way, she told herself. *Keep it positive.* She was going to get out, she was going to find some cops—or mercenaries, depending on where she was—and she was going to come back and kick . . . Iago's . . . ass.

She was going to do it for her father, and for the months she'd lost because a group of nutjobs had convinced themselves that the mythical Nightkeepers were real, that Ambrose had somehow stolen and hidden some imaginary library that held clues about an apocalypse that wasn't coming.

Gritting her teeth as anger surged, Sasha reached for the handle of the strapped wooden door. Before she could touch it, though, it swung open.

Iago stood there, with a half dozen red-robes at his back. The bastard's green eyes widened, then snapped narrow in anger as he roared and lunged, shouting, "Grab her!"

Sasha spun and ran for her life. Adrenaline raced through her bloodstream, urging her on as she skidded on the slick stones underfoot, headed for the sliding door and the prefab tunnels beyond. The stone doorway was still open, beckoning her onward. Gunfire chattered, and she screamed as she threw herself through the door. She scrabbled for the pressure panel, trying to get the door to shut again, still screaming as bullets flew through the door and slammed into the drywall opposite her, chewing through the thin walls in an instant and showing more stone behind the wallboard.

Sobbing with terror, she yanked at the door, trying to force it to shut, her thin veneer of toughness dissolving as reality set in, bringing the dull knowledge that she wasn't ever going to get out of here, that she was going to—

"Leave it, for fuck's sake!" Rough hands grabbed her and yanked her away from the door. "Come on!"

Those same hands dragged her down the corridor, hauled her into a stumbling run, but Sasha was barely aware of moving, didn't know where they were headed, whether into danger or away. Her entire attention was focused on the man who dragged her at his side.

He was a total stranger. He was freaking huge.

And holy shit, he was gorgeous.

His deep green eyes, more forest, where Iago's were piercing emerald, gleamed beneath elegant brows. His lean-bridged nose had a pronounced ridge in the middle, and that, along with a square, stubbled jaw and thick, wavy black hair took his looks into fiercely masculine territory, while a poet's mouth and the paleness of his skin saved him from looking thuggish. The whole effect was one of darkness and light, of contradictions and raw, potent sexuality.

His body lived up to the promise of his face; he was built, bulked, and entirely male. Heat came off him in waves, all but sparking red and gold in the air between them.

"Who are you?" She barely managed to get the question out as she stumbled at his side. "Where did you come from?"

"Explanations later. We've got to haul ass to the rendezvous point." He glanced at her with eyes that gave away nothing. "That'd go lots faster if you stopped staring and started running."

His rudeness wasn't enough to shake Sasha out of her where-have-you-been-all-my-life vaporlock. Catching a glimpse of his right forearm, though, was.

Her brain cataloged the data. He was bigger than average. He oozed charisma and sex appeal. And he wore two glyph tattoos on his right inner forearm, both done in black: the stone bloodline, and the warrior. The marks were straight out of the stories Ambrose had crammed into her brain throughout her childhood, usually following them with a rambling diatribe about her responsibilities to the world in the years leading up to the 2012 doomsday.

She screeched to a halt, pulling away from him with

the leverage of surprise. "You think you're a goddamn Nightkeeper!"

He stopped dead and turned to face her, growling, "No, sweetheart, I *am* a goddamn Nightkeeper. And right now, I'm the only thing standing between you and a one-way trip to visit your old man in the afterlife. So, what's it going to be? Are you going to shut up and move your ass, or am I going to have to carry you?"

"I—" she began, but didn't get any further than that.

He muttered a sharp expletive under his breath, scooped her up against his chest as though she weighed nothing, and took off running. He slapped a palm against a pressure pad as they ducked through another doorway that led to a stone tunnel, and a stone slab grated into place behind him. For a second Sasha thought they were going to make it. Then a hollow boom sounded and the hallway around them shuddered.

The universe seemed to take a breath. Then, with a terrible, howling roar, the tunnel collapsed around them.

JESSICA ANDERSEN

NIGHTKEEPERS:

A NOVEL OF
THE FINAL PROPHECY

*First in the brand new series that
combines Mayan astronomy and lore with
modern, sexy characters for a
gripping read.*

In the first century A.D., Mayan astronomers predicted
the world would end on December 21, 2012. In these
final years before the End Times, demon creatures of
the Mayan underworld—The Makols—have come to
earth to trigger the apocalypse. But the descendants of
the Mayan warrior-priests have decided to fight back.

**"Raw passion, dark romance, and seat-of-
your-pants suspense, all set in an
astounding paranormal world."**
—#1 *New York Times* bestselling author J. R. Ward

**Available wherever books are sold or at
penguin.com**